The Ultimate Hunt

An Alaska Wilderness Mystery Novel

Robin Barefield

Alaska Wilderness Mystery Author

PUBLICATION
CONSULTANTS
WE BELIEVE IN THE POWER OF AUTHORS

8370 Eleusis Drive, Anchorage, Alaska 99502-4630
books@publicationconsultants.com—www.publicationconsultants.com

ISBN Number: 978-1-63747-393-1
eBook ISBN Number: 978-1-63747-394-8

Library of Congress Number: 2024906860

Manufactured in the United States of America

CHAPTER 1

Saturday, October 11
7:00 p.m.

Troy Horner raised the hood of his raincoat as he exited Planet Fitness in the Midtown Mall in Anchorage. A light mist had filled the air when he'd parked his car and entered the gym. Since then, the mist had turned to heavy rain. *Typical October weather*, he thought as he hurried to his car. He was still grumpy about having to work on a Saturday. His boss had promised he'd only need him for two or three hours, but the audit had taken all day, and he hadn't left the office until nearly 5:00 p.m.

Through the hood of his raincoat, he heard the muffled sound of footsteps hitting the wet pavement behind him. Maybe he'd left something at the gym, and one of the Planet Fitness employees was running after him to return the forgotten item. He turned to see who was behind him and felt what he thought was a wasp sting him in the right arm. Large hands then grabbed him by both shoulders. Troy tried to fight his attacker, but the world faded to black a moment later.

CHAPTER 2

Monday, October 13

8:03 a.m.

I opened the large glass doors of the Kodiak Braxton Marine Biology and Fisheries Research Center and stepped into the lobby. I pushed the hood of my raincoat away from my face and cursed the weather. Relentless rain had pounded Kodiak for the past eight days, and according to the meteorologists, there was no end in sight. Low-pressure systems waited in line to pummel the Aleutian Islands and Kodiak. I needed to take a vacation to someplace warm and dry.

I heard a familiar voice call my name as I rounded the corner at the end of the hall and headed toward my office. I feared my mood was about to get even worse.

I stopped and turned toward my boss. "Good morning, Peter."

Peter Wayman wore a charcoal gray suit, a starched white shirt, and a maroon tie. He made me feel very underdressed in my jeans and sweatshirt. His short-cropped black hair sported touches of gray at the temples, but the gray hair didn't diminish his handsome face. Instead, the gray accented his cocoa complexion and intense brown eyes.

"Jane, I'm glad I caught you," Peter said. "I have good news." He paused for effect. "I think Tamron is about to donate more money to the marine center." He moved closer to me and lowered his voice. "And they're hinting at a very substantial grant."

"That's great, Peter," I said, dreading what he'd say next.

"I think Corban is very impressed with your work."

4

The Corban he referred to was Corban Pratt, an executive with Tamron Oil.

"Corban will be in town in a few days, and he's invited us to a dinner with a consortium that's promoting tourism in Kodiak. The dinner is Thursday evening at seven at the Baranof Inn. I assume you'll be able to attend?"

My mind spun, trying to devise any plausible excuse to skip the dinner, but then I heard myself say, "Sure. I'll be there."

"Thank you, Jane." Peter spun on his heels and headed down the hall toward his office.

I unlocked my office door, turned on the light, and hung my soggy raincoat on a hook. I set my computer bag on my desk and collapsed into my work chair.

After a few quiet moments to gather my thoughts, I pulled the computer out of the bag. I was about to place the bag on the floor when my phone chirped. I didn't recognize the number, but it had the Alaska prefix 907, so I answered.

"Jane, this is Linda Duncan, Steve's wife." Her voice was so soft I could barely hear it.

"Hi, Linda," I said. My stomach tightened. I barely knew Linda, but her husband, Steve, was a local charter plane business owner and pilot. Steve and I had bonded two years earlier when we'd found the remains of one of his planes that had blown up midflight.

"It's about Steve," Linda said.

"Yes?"

"He's been sick," she said.

I briefly recalled my friend Dana saying something about Steve having a strange illness. Had he died?

"He has Guillain–Barré syndrome. Do you know what that is?"

"I've heard of it, but I don't know much about it." I did know it wasn't good.

"It's rare," Linda said. "It's a poorly understood condition where your immune system goes into hyperdrive and attacks your nerves. In Steve's case, it's paralyzed his entire body, and the doctor had to put him on a ventilator so he could breathe." Linda's voice broke, and she paused for a moment. "Jane, Steve woke up one morning and felt fine, but by four o'clock that afternoon, a medevac plane was whisking him away to Anchorage. He couldn't walk or move his arms, and he was barely breathing."

"Linda," I said, "I'm so sorry."

"It's okay, really. He's getting better. The doctor said it might take a year or two, but he should fully recover. He's taking physical therapy here in Kodiak now. He can breathe fine but still can't walk, so he's in a wheelchair. That's why I'm calling."

"What can I do?" I asked.

"He's going stir crazy," she said. "He obviously can't fly. He goes to the office and does paperwork, but he gets tired by noon and has to come home and take a nap. He has me take him back to KFS after dinner, and he sits on the back deck and stares down at his floatplanes lined up at the dock."

"Is he depressed?" I asked.

"Very," she said, "but there's something else . . ."

"Yes?" I said when she paused.

Linda laughed softly. "He thinks he's uncovered something suspicious happening in Trident Basin."

"With the floatplanes?"

"He's watched a Beaver pull up three times to the dock, load a passenger or passengers, and then take off."

I didn't understand what was suspicious about passengers boarding a floatplane, so I waited for Linda to elaborate.

"This all takes place after dark."

"Isn't it illegal to fly after dark?" I asked.

"Yes," Linda said. "The floatplanes here fly by VFR, or visual flight rating. Technically, a pilot can fly VFR at night if they have three miles of visibility, but with all the mountains here, no one ever tries it."

"And Steve thinks the pilot of this Beaver is doing something suspicious?" I asked.

Linda sighed. "I think he's just bored, but he swears something fishy is going on. It's like that old Alfred Hitchcock movie where the guy has a broken leg and is bored, so he sits and stares out his window."

"*Rear Window*," I said. "The main character sees what he thinks is a murder in the apartment across from him."

"Exactly," Linda said. "I think Steve has *Rear Window* syndrome."

I laughed. "What can I do to help?"

"He wanted me to call you," Linda said. "He knows the police would think he was crazy if he reported what he's seen, and he thinks you're a good detective. He'd like you to see what's going on and tell him if you agree it's suspicious."

"Okay," I said hesitantly, "but does he know when the plane will be there again?"

"It's landed at Trident Basin on the past two Sundays, so he asked me if you could meet him at seven p.m. on Sunday at the KFS deck. He promised he'd have sub sandwiches and coffee."

"I'll be there," I said.

"Really?" Linda asked in surprise.

"Sure," I said. "I love nothing more than a good mystery, and I'm happy to do whatever I can to get you two through this difficult time."

"Thank you so much," Linda said.

I spent the next twenty minutes preparing for my 9:00 a.m. class. When the class was over, I returned to my office. I was unlocking my door when I heard my phone ring. I'd left it on my desk during my class. I hurried inside and answered it. "Marcus."

"Hi, Jane. Leslie Daniels."

"Hi, Leslie, what's up?" Dr. Leslie Daniels was the marine mammal biologist with the Marine Advisory Program for the University of Alaska. Over the last two years, she'd led a group of scientists investigating a large number of whale deaths near Kodiak. I was the plankton specialist in the group, and I believed a large percentage of the whale deaths were due to toxic algal blooms. Blooms of toxic algae were becoming more common as the North Pacific warmed, and baleen whales consumed tons of algae daily, making them likely victims of poisonous blooms. The food base was also changing as the oceans warmed, so the whales could be starving to death because of less nutritious plankton replacing the more desired species in their diet.

7

"We did a whale necropsy on a humpback washed up on Chirikof Island," Leslie said, "and I have some plankton from its stomach for you to analyze. Is it okay to drop it off at your lab in a few minutes?"

"Sure," I said. Whale necropsies were not my favorite activity, and I was happy to have someone else collect whale stomach contents for me to analyze.

"It's degraded," Leslie said. "The whale's been dead for a while, so I doubt you'll be able to determine much, but it's worth a try."

"I'll take a look at it," I said.

"I'll be there in twenty minutes."

I locked my office door and headed down the stairs to my basement lab. I made space for the incoming plankton sample and began preparing everything I'd need to analyze the plankton. Being out of my office and back in the lab felt good.

I planned to test for two groups of toxins from the whale's gastric samples: saxitoxins, the culprits linked to paralytic shellfish poisoning, and domoic acid, the neurotoxin responsible for amnesic shellfish poisoning in humans. While I knew that one or both groups of toxins would likely be present in the sample Leslie brought me, the question was, How much toxin had the whale consumed? Had it ingested a lethal level of toxic algae? Since scientists didn't know how much of either of these toxins it took to kill a whale, my analysis would be suggestive rather than definitive.

I typically used similar but different techniques to test for the two classes of toxins—an enzyme-linked immunosorbent assay and a receptor-binding assay—but first I'd need to centrifuge the samples before analyzing them.

Leslie dropped off the whale samples, and we chatted for a few minutes before she left. Then I set to work.

I was utterly absorbed in my assays when I heard a knock on the lab door, followed by someone pushing the door open. The tall, thin frame of Geoff Baker stepped into my lab.

"What's up, Doc?" he asked. "You don't usually shut your lab door."

I hadn't even realized the door was closed. Leslie must have shut it when she left the lab.

"I'm analyzing whale samples," I said.

"Ah," Geoff said, "from the whale that washed up on Chirikof?"

I shook my head. "How do you know these things?" I asked. "I'm a member of the whale necropsy group, and I didn't even know about the whale until Leslie called me this morning."

I looked into Geoff's blazing, blue eyes. A wide grin spread across his face. He sported his usual facial hair stubble and had pulled his long, red hair into a tight ponytail.

"How many times do I need to tell you, Doc? You have to listen to the radio to know what goes on around here." He looked around my small lab. "You don't even have a radio or Bluetooth speakers for your phone in here, do you?"

When I'd first taken a job at the marine center three years earlier, Geoff had been a graduate student and began calling me "Doc." Since then, Geoff had earned his own PhD and was a "Doc" in his own right. Still, he continued to refer to me as Doc, and the term of address always made me smile.

I poured myself a cup of coffee from my thermos and sat on a lab stool. "Okay," I said, "since you're so in tune with what's happening on this island, what do you know about a consortium hoping to increase tourism here?"

I'd never seen Geoff's face flush red so quickly. He sat on the edge of my desk. "Don't get me started," he said.

"Peter roped me into going to a meeting with the consortium members."

"Get out of it," Geoff said.

"He's our boss. I can't get out of it."

Geoff let out a long breath. "Why is Peter involved with them?"

"He's not," I said. I lowered my voice in case anyone was lurking in the hall outside my lab. "Corban Pratt is associated with the consortium, and Pratt invited us. Peter feels certain that Pratt and Tamron are on the verge of giving the marine center another grant, and he wants to keep the guy happy."

Geoff groaned. "I think this consortium is bad news. They claim they want to pump money into Kodiak and push tourism here. They want to bring more cruise ships to the island, which I think is a terrible idea. Then, they want to change the downtown and make it more 'cruise-ship friendly.' Do you know what that means?"

I shook my head. I'd never seen the laid-back Geoff so animated.

"This group of money-hungry developers wants to destroy the local merchants and create a facade of a quaint Alaska fishing village to show to the tourists. They'll run the locals out of business."

"Isn't tourism good?" I asked.

"I have no problem with tourism," Geoff said, "but people should come to Kodiak to see the real town. This island has a lot to offer visitors, and tourist dollars are good for the economy. This consortium doesn't want to help Kodiak. They want to line their own pockets."

"And cruise ships?" I asked.

Geoff shook his head. "Cruise ships aren't right for Kodiak. You can't see this island in five hours. This consortium wants to make the downtown area appear cozy and quaint so the cruise ship passengers can get off the ship, spend their money in stores owned by consortium members, and then climb back on the ship in time for dinner. How does any of that help this island?"

I shrugged. Geoff held strong opinions on many things, and I suspected he'd overstated the consortium's intentions. I wondered how I'd missed hearing about this controversy brewing in the town I called home. Maybe the consortium meeting would be more interesting than I'd thought.

I spent three more hours in the lab after Geoff left, but my assays yielded only muddled results. I called Leslie and gave her the bad news.

"One of these days we'll find a fresh whale carcass," she said, "and then we'll finally get some results."

* * *

After I arrived home, I ate a tasteless microwave meal and sipped a glass of wine. Then I called Dana. While Geoff had a good grasp on Kodiak gossip, Dana Baynes was the true pro. She was my go-to person when

I needed to know anything about anyone. Dana was the bear biologist with the Kodiak National Wildlife Refuge. She was short and petite and had an oversized personality.

"Jane, I haven't heard from you in a while. What do you want to know?"

"Hey!" I said. "I don't just call you when I need information."

"But you want to ask me something, don't you?"

"Well, yes, but first of all, how are you and Jack doing?"

"We're fine, but we haven't done anything exciting in a while."

We chatted for a few minutes, and then I asked my question. "What do you know about a consortium trying to infuse more business into town?"

Dana groaned. "I don't know who's in the group, if that's what you want to know. I think a few local people are involved—the division of tourism lady and the mayor—but I hear most of the so-called consortium is from out of town: Anchorage or the lower forty-eight."

"Geoff thinks the consortium is evil, and he believes the members plan to gut the local businesses and install their own tourism-type shops."

"That's many people's concern, but I think it's overblown paranoia. Still, I'm not sure this consortium is good for Kodiak. Bad things happen when a bunch of outsiders move into a town and start making changes."

"Would the mayor support the consortium if he believed it was bad for Kodiak?"

"I don't know," Dana admitted.

"Maybe I'll learn something," I said.

"What do you mean?"

"Peter strong-armed me into going to a meeting and dinner with the consortium members," I said. I went on to explain how Peter had confronted me in the marine center hallway that morning.

Dana apparently felt no sympathy for me. "Good," she said. "Call me when you get home. I want to hear all about it."

CHAPTER 3

Monday, October 13

4:00 p.m.

Troy Horner brushed at the raindrops falling on his face. He curled into a tighter ball and tried to go back to sleep, but he soon gave up. Slowly, his foggy mind began to clear. He sat up, looked around, and inhaled the overpoweringly earthy smell of moss and dirt and spruce needles.

Where am I?

The last thing Troy remembered was leaving the sports medicine clinic after spending his Saturday working on what his boss called an "emergency audit." Then, he recalled walking in the door at Planet Fitness in Anchorage. How had he ended up in the middle of a soggy rainforest? He looked down at the camo raincoat he was wearing. He'd never seen it before. His pants (also camo) must have been waterproof because although the ground felt cold, his legs weren't wet. He touched the warm sweater under his raincoat and looked down at the new pair of hiking boots on his feet. Nothing made sense.

Little light penetrated the tall spruce trees, which stretched as far as he could see in every direction. Was he on the Kenai Peninsula? Had he been in a car wreck and stumbled dazed into the forest? He patted himself down and didn't feel any injuries. Maybe he needed to find a road and flag down a passing motorist.

Troy shook his head and tried to remember what had happened to him. He again looked down at his raincoat and noted the bright-white patch on the jacket. The diamond-shaped patch meant no more to him than anything else.

After spending several moments trying to clear his head, Troy decided he couldn't stay where he was. He had little protection from the elements and no food. He took a drink of cool water from the bottle he'd found on the ground beside him and stuck the bottle in his jacket pocket.

He turned in a circle, wondering which way he should start hiking. Everything looked the same to him. He glanced at his watch for the time, but it was gone. He had no way to determine the time or even the day. Had he left it at the gym?

He eventually picked a direction and began hiking. After what seemed like an hour, just as he'd begun to think he was walking ever deeper into the woods, he caught a glimpse of a red light and two buildings in the distance. The light disappeared, and he began to think he'd imagined it. A few minutes later, he saw the red glow again and started running toward it.

"Hey, help!" he called as he ran. "Is anyone there? I need help!"

Troy looked in the direction where he'd seen the light instead of watching the ground for obstacles. He continued to yell and wave his arms. His foot connected with a large rock, and he somersaulted onto the forest floor. A moment later, something whizzed over his head, and he looked up in disbelief.

Someone had taken a shot at him. He'd be dead right now If he hadn't stumbled over that rock.

CHAPTER 4

Wednesday, October 15

5:00 p.m.

A wide smile spread across Janet Friland's freckled face as she walked down the dock in the St. Paul Boat Harbor in Kodiak. She inhaled a deep breath of sea air and savored the aromas of fish, seaweed, and beach. She'd come to love the smell and would miss it when she went home.

Janet felt she had morphed from a girl into a woman over the last summer and fall. Her body was in great shape, and she felt strong and capable. She loved physical labor and didn't know if she'd ever be happy working in an office, if she became a lawyer, or in a hospital, if she decided to become a doctor or nurse. She could imagine the look on her mother's face if she told her that she'd decided to make a career out of commercial fishing. The thought made her laugh out loud.

Janet had arrived in Kodiak the previous May from Washington, DC. One of her cousins, Eric, had spent a year between high school and college working as a commercial fisherman in Alaska, and he'd told her that it was the best year of his life. Janet also wanted a break from school. Her mother had suggested a few months abroad in France or Italy, but Janet wanted to test herself. She'd flown to Kodiak and had walked up and down the docks, asking boat captains if they needed a crew member for the upcoming salmon season. Most captains were uninterested in hiring a young woman with no experience, but Gerald Lyman, the captain of the *Ella Lynn*, had taken pity on her and said he'd hire her for one salmon "opening," as he'd called it. If she didn't pull her weight, she was off the boat. If she did okay, he'd offer her a job for the summer.

The rest of the crew of the *Ella Lynn* teased her mercilessly for the stupid mistakes she made during those first few weeks, but Janet learned quickly, and she never got seasick, no matter how rolly the sea conditions got. At the end of the salmon season, the captain chose her and one other crew member to help him catch his halibut quota. This meant swapping out the salmon seining gear for halibut longline gear. Then, Janet had had to learn how to do a different type of fishing altogether. She'd loved every minute of it.

Gerald was now preparing to shut down the boat for the winter, and in a few days, Janet would pack her gear and fly home to live with her mother in DC. Her mom was a five-term senator from Ohio, and Washington was the only home Janet had ever known. Her parents had recently divorced, and she planned to live with her mom while she attended Georgetown University. She felt ready for college now. She'd spent five months toning her body, and now it was time to expand her mind. She was also looking forward to seeing her mother and little brother. She hated to admit it, but she felt homesick.

Janet bounded up the ramp to the street level and headed toward the rusty blue Ford pickup owned by her captain. She had a list in her back pocket and was going to the hardware store, the marine supply store, and the grocery store to pick up supplies for the boat. The marine supply store would close in a few minutes, so she'd go there first.

She couldn't get used to how quiet the harbor was. It seemed as if overnight, it had gone from shouting voices and rumbling boat engines to silence. She hadn't seen or heard a single person since she left the *Ella Lynn*. After the Alaska Department of Fish and Game shut down the Tanner crab season for the year, most of the fishermen packed up and left.

Janet had just opened the pickup door when a muscular, middle-aged man approached her. She hadn't even noticed him until he was a few feet away from her.

"Excuse me, ma'am," he said. "How do you get to the other boat harbor?"

Janet had begun to give the man directions to St. Herman's Boat Harbor when she felt a pinch on the back of her arm. She was swiveling her head to look at her arm when a set of huge hands grasped her from behind, and her knees buckled.

CHAPTER 5

Thursday, October 16

7:00 p.m.

I parked my new RAV4 in the lot adjacent to the Baranof Inn and hurried into the hotel. I took a sharp right and walked down the short hall to the conference room. The room was packed. Most of the people held a drink while they stood and mingled. At first, I didn't recognize anyone I knew, but Peter stood up from a round table near the window and motioned to me.

I made my way across the room to Peter. He and his lovely wife, Danine, sat alone at a table for eight. I immediately felt underdressed. Danine wore a formal gown, and Peter wore one of his tailored suits and ties. I smoothed my simple wrap dress and quickly sat next to Danine.

We were just starting to chat when a hand gently touched me on the shoulder.

I looked up into the handsome face of Corban Pratt, his light-brown eyes focused on me, a slight smile turning up the corners of his lips.

"There you are," he said. He motioned to the empty chair next to me. "Mind if I sit here?"

"No," I said. "How are you?"

Corban sat. "I'm great." He lowered his voice. "Sorry to make you come to this boring thing. I think I just wanted to make my evening more enjoyable by inviting you."

I felt my face grow hot. I hated the position I was in. I liked Corban Pratt. He was nice and gorgeous, but I didn't want our relationship to move past the acquaintance or maybe the friend stage. I wasn't sure what Corban wanted, but I knew Peter expected me to be nice to him. Peter expected him to authorize another large grant from the Tamron Oil Company to the marine center, and he didn't want me to do anything to jeopardize the funding.

"Are you part of this so-called consortium?" I quickly asked to change the subject.

"No, no," Corban said. "I know several of the people from Anchorage who are involved in this, though, and they'd love to have the backing of Tamron."

As we talked, people began to take their seats, and four other people sat at our table. Within minutes, servers were rolling large carts of prime rib into the room and delivering plates filled with mashed potatoes, grilled asparagus, and large dinner rolls. The staff members with the meat served each person a thick slice of prime rib.

"This is quite a spread," Peter said.

After the main course, the servers brought out dessert. I couldn't remember when I'd eaten so much.

I was nibbling at a few bites of chocolate cake when a tall man with short black hair and blue eyes approached our table. "Pratt," he said, clapping Corban on the shoulder.

"Jerry Burns," Corban said and then stood to shake hands with the man. "I wondered where you were."

Jerry made a dismissive gesture with his right hand. "I'm always late to these things. I had a call I couldn't avoid at the last minute." He looked down at me. "Who's your lovely friend?" he asked.

Corban introduced Peter, Danine, and me to Jerry Burns.

"Ah, the marine center," he said. "That's one place I haven't been yet."

Jerry's accent was upper-crust British, and I wondered what he had to do with this consortium. When Jerry continued toward the front of the room, I asked Corban about him.

"He's a banker in Anchorage," Corban said, "and he's one of the leaders of this consortium." He dropped his voice to a whisper, and I had to lean toward him to hear what he said. "I find Burns charming, but I don't trust the guy. He always seems to have an agenda."

At the front of the room, a middle-aged woman with long, dark hair tapped on the microphone and began speaking.

"Welcome, everyone. I hope you enjoyed your dinner."

This comment was greeted with an enthusiastic round of applause.

"We don't want to keep you here all night, so let's get this party started." She paused and looked around. "My name is Madeline Turner, and for those who aren't yet acquainted with our group and our goals, we're trying to bring more businesses and money to Kodiak."

This statement generated a smattering of applause, and as I looked around the room, I saw several people sitting with their arms crossed in front of them. I carefully studied the crowd and recognized the city mayor, Jim Small, seated at the same table as Sandy Greenfeld, the tourism director at Discover Kodiak. They both had smiles on their faces as they listened to Madeline speak. I also saw the man who owned the marine store as well as Beth Craft, the owner of my favorite coffee shop. They both sat quietly as she spoke. Jennifer Brite, the bookstore owner, scowled at Madeline, the hostility apparent on her face.

"I'm a tourism developer for Empress Cruises," Madeline continued, "and we have plans to bring more ships to Kodiak. Before we can do that, though, we need to have more things available here for our passengers to see and do. As I'm sure you locals can understand, we often reach port on a cloudy, rainy day, when it's impossible for our passengers to take a flight-seeing trip to see bears. Sometimes, the seas are too rough for passengers to book fishing trips, and they have nothing to do except walk the streets. If we make port on a Sunday, most stores in town are closed, and our passengers have nothing to do and nowhere to spend their money while they're here." She paused and looked around the room. "We'd like to help local merchants develop an atmosphere that's friendly to tourism. When the shops and museums remain open, our passengers have something to do, no matter the day or the weather."

I felt my muscles tighten as I listened to this woman. Who did she think she was? She believed Kodiak should change its way of doing business to keep her cruise ship passengers happy. I wondered how much money the passengers spent while their ships were in port.

I heard a restless energy in the room as many members of the audience shifted in their chairs. "Maybe Kodiak doesn't want your cruise ships here," a man called from the back of the room. Several in the audience applauded this outburst.

Madeline emitted a nervous laugh. "I'm sure you want to make more money," she said. "We're trying to help you help yourselves."

After Madeline's last statement, a dozen people left the room. I glanced toward the front of the room and saw the mayor crane his head toward the door to watch the exodus. He turned toward Sandy Greenfeld and said something.

Corban's banker friend Jerry stood and walked to the podium. He briefly conversed with Madeline, who then returned to her seat.

Jerry held up his hands, palms out, in a calming gesture. "Ladies and gentlemen," he said, "please sit down and hear us out. Madeline is sometimes a little too direct." He smiled at the tourism developer, who sat near the front of the room. "We're not trying to tell you how to run your city or when the merchants should open or close their doors. We want to invest in the Kodiak tourism industry and bring more money to your town. We have experts like Madeline in our group who can offer merchants advice on best business practices to help them collect more of those tourist dollars, but what Madeline offers is only advice. You can listen to her or ignore her. It's up to you."

I knew Jerry thought he was calming the room, but his condescending manner and haughty British accent did nothing to appease the merchants gathered there. I wanted to get up and leave, but I knew Peter wouldn't be pleased if I departed before the end of the meeting.

Five other members stood and talked. Their comments ranged from boring to insulting. Finally, the ordeal ended, and I shot from my chair. I told Peter and Danine good night and turned to tell Corban I was leaving but found him standing near a neighboring table, talking to a beautiful brunette in a red evening dress. I decided he wouldn't notice if I slipped out, so I hurried out of the hotel and raced to my car.

When I got home, I called Dana and reported on my experience. I was a newcomer to Kodiak, and the consortium's tactics irritated me. I could only imagine how much they must have angered longtime residents.

CHAPTER 6

Sunday, October 19

7:00 p.m.

I pulled up my hood and climbed the stairs to the deck behind the Kodiak Flight Services office. The steady rain seemed to be increasing in intensity, and I was happy the deck had a roof over it. Steve sat in a chair, a blanket over his lap. He looked no different to me, but I knew he couldn't walk. When he spoke, his voice sounded weak.

"Jane," he said. "Thank you for coming. I have a thermos of coffee here, but my hands don't work very well, so I'll let you pour it."

I sat in the chair next to Steve. I picked up the thermos and empty cup and poured myself a cup of coffee. The rainy night air felt chilly, and I wished I'd worn a heavier coat.

"How are you doing?" I asked Steve.

He shook his head. "Better, I think, but it's a slow, frustrating recovery. I'd never heard of Guillain–Barré syndrome before, but it's completely taken over my life."

"I am so sorry," I said. "But Linda says you should fully recover?"

"So they tell me, but it's hard to believe at this point. I know I'm a burden to Linda, but she doesn't complain. I started coming here at night to get out of the house and give her a break. The fresh air does me good."

I didn't know what to say. Steve stumbled over some of his words and spoke more slowly than usual. I feared his recovery would take a long time.

"I think I'm wasting your time here tonight," he said.

"Why?"

"I don't think the plane will come in this weather. The visibility is bad, and it's supposed to get very windy."

A gust of wind rattled the deck as if to emphasize Steve's point. I looked down at the floatplane ramp, partially illuminated by two lights on tall poles. I admired the five teal and white KFS planes lined up next to each other in their stalls at the dock. "Tell me about what you've been seeing," I said.

"Three times in the past two and a half weeks, I've watched a black Beaver land at the dock after dark. The first time I saw it was on a Wednesday; the last two times, it showed up on Sunday nights. I thought it would return this Sunday if the weather was good." Steve paused a moment and seemed to be catching his breath. "Each time, it arrived on a bright night, so I'm sure the pilot could see where he was going with the aid of his GPS, but he was flying under minimums. He arrived from the east, so he didn't pass over the airport. I turned on the radio the last time and didn't hear him call the tower. He just snuck into town and landed."

"Did he stay overnight?" I asked.

Steve slowly shook his head. I could barely see him as the night grew darker. "As soon as he landed, he began filling his tank from jugs he had in the plane. While he fueled the plane, two big guys came down to the dock. Once, they led a young woman down to the plane. She could barely walk, and the men finally carried her to the plane. At the time, I thought she was drunk. They pushed her into the back of the plane and shut the door. The next time, the two guys carried something down to the plane that looked like a carpet roll. I wondered how they'd get it into the plane, and they spent quite a while pushing it into the back cargo area, but they managed. Then, last Sunday, they brought two young people, a man and a woman, down to the plane, and they both looked drugged. The pilot barely spoke to the men, and as soon as he'd finished refueling, he taxied and took off to the east."

I studied Steve carefully. Was his bored mind inventing something out of nothing? Was he concocting nefarious actions where none existed? Was his mind intact, or had the Guillain–Barré affected it as well as his legs and arms?

Steve must have read my mind. "I know this sounds crazy," he said, "and that's why I wanted you to see it with your own eyes. Unfortunately, I don't think the plane will come in this weather. The pilot would have zero visibility."

"Do you think he'll come on the next clear night?" I asked.

"I'd bet on it."

"Then call me next time you hear the plane approaching," I said. "I'll drop what I'm doing and rush over here."

"Thank you, Jane. I wouldn't bother you if I didn't believe something bad was happening. You're good at solving crimes, so I appreciate your help. The police would laugh at me if I told them I thought the plane was doing something illegal."

"Do you think the pilot's transporting these people against their will?"

"I think it's very possible."

"You sound tired, Steve. Would you like me to give you a ride home?"

"No, I've wasted enough of your time. I'll sit here and watch the storm until Linda comes to pick me up. She'll be here before long."

I made my way home, mulling over what Steve had told me about the mysterious goings-on at the floatplane basin.

CHAPTER 7

Monday, October 20

10:30 a.m.

A knock on my open office door broke my concentration on the tests I was grading. I looked up at Peter's smiling face.

"Jane," he said. "I haven't had a chance to speak to you about the dinner the other night. Did you enjoy yourself? You left suddenly after dinner, and Corban asked where you'd gone."

I felt a flash of anger, but I pushed it away and reminded myself that Peter was my boss. I took a deep breath and forced a smile. "The food was good," I said.

"It was," Peter said, "but I got the feeling you didn't like the rest."

"Did you?" I asked. "I thought those people seemed rude and condescending—especially Madeline Turner. Who does she think she is, telling the Kodiak residents and merchants how we need to change our town to make it more enjoyable for her cruise ship passengers?"

Peter chuckled. "Jane," he said, "sometimes you have to listen to a lot of nonsense to reach your goals. Especially when you have your hand out asking for money."

I wanted to remind Peter that asking for money was his job, not mine, but instead, I said, "I'm happy to meet with Corban for dinner, but I don't want anything else to do with the consortium people."

Peter looked as if I'd slapped him. "I understand," he said, then turned briskly and left my office.

I felt pressure building behind my eyes, but I didn't regret what I'd said. Peter had no right to ask me to do these things.

As if Corban Pratt had overheard my conversation with Peter, he called a few minutes later.

"Hi," he said. "Sorry to bother you at work, but I wanted to check on you. You disappeared the other night."

"Sorry. You were locked in conversation with some of the other guests, and I didn't want to interrupt you to tell you I was leaving."

"What did you think of that ordeal?"

I paused. I'd already upset Peter, and I didn't want to insult Corban and his friends with the consortium. "It was a great meal, but I disagreed with what some of the speakers said. I don't think the Kodiak merchants should necessarily have to cater to cruise ship passengers. If the merchants thought the ship passengers would spend money in their stores, I imagine they'd open their doors, even on a Sunday."

"I agree," Corban said. "Madeline Turner was especially rude. I talked to Jerry when the event ended, and he was furious with her for alienating the Kodiak people in the crowd."

Corban's response surprised me, and I liked the man a little better than I previously had. "The meal was good, anyway," I said.

"Speaking of meals . . . ," he said. "I'm up in Anchorage, but I'll be back in Kodiak on Wednesday for a meeting with your boss. Can I interest you in dinner Wednesday night?"

I cringed, but I said, "Sure. When and where?"

"How does seven o'clock at the Baranof sound?"

"I'll be there."

I stayed in my office until nearly six, grading tests and working on my assignment plan for the next few weeks. I liked the research part of my job but was less fond of the teaching. This semester, I was teaching an advanced genetics class to a group of eight graduate students, but I'd also been tasked with teaching introductory college biology to fifteen high school students. The biology class was part of an outreach program with the University of Alaska. The biology instructor at the community college couldn't or wouldn't teach this course, so the university had contacted me, and I'd naturally said yes. The high school students were good kids and eager to learn, but the class took much of my time and energy. It had been years since I'd studied entry-level biology, and I'd had to relearn things I'd long forgotten.

I finally decided I'd had enough, and I escaped my office. I stopped and grabbed a sub for dinner and then headed home. I parked in my driveway and battled the pounding rain until I unlocked my door and stepped inside. When I pushed back my raincoat hood, I heard my phone ringing in my computer bag. I set the bag on the couch to the right of the door and answered without looking at the display.

"Jane," a deep voice said.

I took a seat on the couch next to my computer bag. "Nick?"

"How are you?" he asked.

"I'm fine. It's nice to hear from you. Where are you?"

Nick Morgan was an FBI agent I'd met two years earlier when he'd come to Kodiak to help investigate a floatplane explosion that had killed a US senator. He had returned to Kodiak the following year to aid in the investigation of a string of murders of young women. I was attracted to Nick from the start, and our relationship had morphed from acquaintances to friends to something else. Unfortunately, I wasn't sure what the "something else" was, since Nick rarely called.

"I'm in Seattle right now, but I'm heading to Kodiak tomorrow."

My pulse quickened. "Why?"

"Business, I'm afraid. The daughter of a US senator is missing. She was working on a fishing boat, and the boat was in port. She left it one afternoon to run errands for the captain and never returned." He paused a moment. "I don't know what I can do, but when I heard she went missing in Kodiak, I volunteered for the assignment. I was already in Seattle, so I'm nearby."

I laughed. "Nearby by Alaska standards," I said.

"I know I've been terrible about staying in touch, but I'd love to see you while I'm in town."

"Where are you staying?"

He chuckled. "I'll leave that up to you."

My face grew hot. "I have plenty of room."

"I'll have to meet with the Kodiak police when I arrive, so I probably won't be there until eight or so. I'll call you when I make it to town."

After we hung up, I sat back on the couch and exhaled a long, slow breath. I'd nearly given up on ever having a long-term relationship with him. I reminded myself that just because he was coming to town and wanted to stay with me, I might be no more than a port in a storm. I'd long wondered if Nick had a woman in every city where he spent time. As a behavioral analyst with the FBI, Nick traveled around the country, often spending months in a city while he assisted the police in finding a killer or a kidnapper. His marriage had been an on-again, off-again affair, but he and his wife were now divorced. Perhaps Nick was one of those men who couldn't manage without a woman in his life, and maybe I was just one of many. I knew I couldn't judge men, and my track record was not good. I needed to proceed with caution with Special Agent Nick Morgan.

I was so lost in thought about Nick that when the phone I still held in my hand rang, I jumped. This time, I looked at the display. It was Dana.

"What do you want to know?" I asked.

Dana laughed. "Just because you know more about the consortium than I do doesn't mean you know anything else about this town."

"I'm enjoying my moment in the sun," I said. "I might know something else you don't." Nick hadn't sworn me to secrecy about the senator's missing daughter, so I decided it was okay to tell Dana.

"A US senator's daughter disappeared from the boat harbor," Dana said.

"Darn, how did you know?"

"I never give up my sources. I also hear that the FBI is coming to town. Will your handsome agent be here?"

"Yes," I said. "I don't know how you hear these things. Nick will be here tomorrow evening."

"Good," Dana said. "If he's not too busy, you can bring him to my party."

"Party?"

"We have a new assistant Refuge manager, so Jack and I are throwing him a 'welcome to Kodiak' party."

"Do you like him?" I asked.

"I think I do," Dana said. "So far, so good, anyway. The party is on Saturday at eight at our place. Bring your gorgeous FBI agent with you."

CHAPTER 8

Monday, October 20

8:00 p.m.

Troy waited until dark and then crawled out of his hiding spot. The days and nights were beginning to run together, but he thought he'd been hiding in the woods for nine days—or was it ten? The night before, he'd discovered a hollow underneath a spruce tree. He'd curled up in it and then raked moss, spruce cones, and dirt over his body. He'd bent his body into the fetal position and remained still all day. As he stood up and tried to walk, his legs didn't want to work correctly. Every muscle in his body ached. He felt tired, hungry, and thirsty.

On his first day in the woods, Troy had found a headlamp in his coat pocket, but he didn't dare turn it on and give away his position to those shooting at him. He kept himself hydrated by filling his water bottle from the silty streams he crossed, but he was growing weaker by the hour from hunger.

After three days of hiding day and night, Troy realized that the sporadic shooting stopped after dark. He didn't know what would happen if he used his headlamp, but he had to do something. He needed to find food if he'd have any chance of surviving this ordeal.

Troy had switched on his headlamp and now held it in his hand, pointing it at the ground so he wouldn't trip on a root or a rock. Even though tripping had saved his life earlier, he didn't want to repeat the experience. He didn't know where to go, but he walked carefully through the woods.

After an hour of hiking, he saw a red light in front of him, and he moved cautiously toward it. When he drew near, he saw that the light illuminated a small metal crate. He hurried to it and lifted the lid. The crate held several paper bags and bottles of water. He snatched one of the bags and a water bottle and ran behind a tree. He slowly opened the bag and looked at its contents suspiciously. It held a ham sandwich wrapped in plastic and an apple. Putting aside his reservations, he pulled off the plastic, devoured the sandwich in three bites, and then attacked the apple. He took a long drink of water and stuffed the bag and the water bottle in his pocket. He wondered for the hundredth time what was happening in the bizarre world he'd been thrown into.

Ever since the night when he'd first discovered what he thought of as the "food trough," he'd looked for food each night and then moved far away from the trough before finding another hiding spot. He soon realized there were several troughs scattered throughout the forest and wondered if there were other "prey animals" like him out there. There must've been. Why else would the troughs hold so many paper bags?

One day, while hiding behind a tree, he saw a man dressed in camouflage carrying a large rifle. The man was clearly a hunter searching for prey. Troy knew that if he showed himself, the hunter would shoot and kill him. Troy understood the man was hunting him.

On another day, as he curled up in the hollow beneath the spruce tree, Troy heard a series of shots ring out and then heard a woman scream. He knew then that he was not the only prey animal in the forest, and he felt certain that the woman who'd screamed was now dead. How long would it be until a hunter shot him? He couldn't live in the woods forever. Eventually, he'd lose this crazy game.

Troy remembered watching the Hunger Games movies. Instead of deer, elk, or bears, the hunters in these woods hunted humans. He wondered if a successful hunter mounted the heads of his human prey on the wall in his trophy room.

CHAPTER 9

Tuesday, October 21

3:47 p.m.

The Alaska Airlines jet touched down on the wet runway and taxied to a spot in front of the small terminal. Nick pulled his bag from the compartment over his seat, waited his turn to descend the steps, and hurried through the rain to the terminal. As soon as he walked through the door, the smiling face of Alaska State Trooper Dan Patterson greeted him. Nick had worked with Patterson the previous year on a serial killer case, and the two had quickly formed a friendship.

The two shook hands. "How is Jeanne doing?" Nick asked. He knew Jeanne had miscarried a year earlier, and Patterson had confided in him that she'd become so depressed she'd nearly committed suicide. Jeanne was pregnant again, and Patterson had said he was very worried about her.

Patterson shrugged. "She's doing okay so far."

Nick smiled and nodded, and the two men pushed through the crowd into the parking lot. Nick placed his bag in the back seat of the trooper SUV and swung into the passenger seat.

"Congratulations on closing your big case."

Patterson shook his head and looked at Nick. "Thanks," he said, "but I hope I never see anything like that again. It was a massacre."

As they cruised out of the lot toward Rezanof Drive, Nick said, "What can you tell me about the senator's daughter?"

"Not much," Patterson said. "We're meeting with Detective Horner and Chief Feeney in a few minutes."

"Is this Maureen's case?" Nick had worked with Detective Maureen Horner and Chief Feeney on a previous visit to Kodiak.

"Yes," Patterson said. "The disappearance happened in the boat harbor, so this is KPD's case."

Nick nodded. "Maureen's good. I'm glad she's on the case. I wish I could say the same about Feeney."

Patterson sighed. "I'm sure Feeney thinks this case could be big, so he'll want to insert himself into the middle to get as much publicity as possible."

Nick watched out the window as Patterson drove into town on Rezanof and followed it to Mill Bay Road. The rain pelted the windows, and the wipers worked furiously to clear it. Nick smiled. He'd seen Kodiak in the beautiful light of a long summer day and the brutal cold and wind of an icy winter night. He felt he was beginning to understand the island's many moods. He liked Kodiak. The place was never boring, and the people he'd met seemed tough and capable.

Patterson pulled into the KPD parking lot, and the two men entered the building. Detective Maureen Horner was waiting for them and shook hands with Nick.

"While it's nice to see you, Agent Morgan, I'm sorry we need you again so soon." Horner smiled, and her blue eyes flashed.

"Maureen, please call me Nick. After all, we've been boating together," he said, referring to the last time the pair had worked together. After a high-speed chase, he and Detective Horner had struggled with a serial killer on his boat. The killer shot Horner and nearly killed her during the ordeal.

"How are you doing?" Nick asked.

Horner held up her hands and spun in a circle. "All better," she said. Her black slacks and gray blouse accentuated her tall, athletic frame.

Horner led them down the hall and into the conference room. A carafe of coffee sat in the middle of the table. Horner grabbed a stack of Styrofoam cups from a cabinet at the side of the room and set them beside the carafe.

"Drink at your own risk," she said. "We should make you sign a disclaimer before you drink it."

"I'll take my chances," Nick said. "It's been a long few weeks."

"Are you helping with the serial murder case in Seattle?"

Nick nodded.

"Are you making any headway?" she asked as she took a seat across the table from Nick.

Nick shook his head. "Not much," he said. "The killer is smart and likes to play games. He'll eventually make a mistake, but I'm worried about how many women will die before that happens."

Patterson sat beside Nick, and the three chatted until Chief Feeney arrived.

"Agent Morgan," Feeney said.

Nick stood and shook hands with Feeney. The chief pointedly did not say hello to Patterson.

"Apparently, the FBI thinks we here at the Kodiak Police Department can't solve our own cases."

Nick sighed. Feeney was one of those cops who felt threatened by outside help. Nick dealt with this all the time all over the country, and he was growing tired of trying to walk on eggshells.

"I'm here because the daughter of a US senator disappeared. I go where they send me, and I hope I can help."

Feeney sat at the head of the table, his dark eyes glowering at Nick and then Patterson. "I don't know why you're here." He nodded at Patterson. "This is a KPD matter. Why are the troopers involved?"

"I asked him to come to the meeting," Horner said. "Janet Friland disappeared from the St. Paul Boat Harbor. She could be anywhere on the island by now if she was abducted."

Feeney barked out a laugh. "I think she decided she wasn't ready to go home to Mommy, so she took a cab to the airport and flew to Fiji."

"Sir," Horner said evenly, "we checked airline passenger manifests, and she was not on any planes leaving the island."

Feeney shrugged and sat back in his chair.

Nick thought Feeney looked terrible. He'd added a few pounds to his already-flabby stomach. Red veins streaked over his nose and cheeks, and his bloodshot eyes made him look like a man who liked his whiskey a little too much.

"Maureen, why don't you tell us the details of the case," Nick said.

Horner opened her laptop, but she barely looked at it as she shared what information she had. "Nineteen-year-old Janet Friland was working on the fishing vessel *Ella Lynn*, captained by Gerald Lyman. Janet was taking a year's break from school and wanted to do something different. Her mother said her cousin had worked on a fishing boat in Alaska and loved it, so Janet wanted to do the same thing."

Feeney blew out a sharp breath. "Only rich, privileged kids get to take a break from school to"—he made air quotes with his fingers—"'find themselves.'"

Horner ignored the interruption and continued. "Lyman hired Janet in late May. He said she was a fast learner and a hard worker. Once the salmon season ended, he kept Janet and another crew member to help him fish his halibut IFQs." She nodded at Nick and clarified, "Individual fishing quotas. Anyway, Janet stayed on to help Lyman put away gear and get the boat ready to be lifted out of the water and stored in the boatyard for the winter. On the day Janet disappeared, Lyman had sent her to buy some groceries and other supplies. We know she never left the harbor because Lyman's truck was still parked where he'd left it."

"Nobody saw anything?" Nick asked.

"No one we've talked to," Horner said. "The harbor is quiet right now. Without a Tanner crab season this year, most fishermen have left."

"Had Janet unlocked the door of the truck?" Nick asked.

Horner shook her head. "It's an old truck, and Lyman doesn't lock it. The door was closed, and Janet and her backpack were nowhere to be found."

"Did you talk to the other crew member?" Patterson asked. "The one who helped fish for halibut."

"He left the boat several days earlier and wasn't even on the island," she said.

"Did you dust the truck handle and door for prints?" Nick asked.

"We did, but we didn't find anything useful. We got some smudged prints, but not enough to work with."

"Detective Horner is very thorough," Feeney said.

Nick looked at Feeney and nodded. "I know she is, but I'm just brainstorming with her." He turned back to Horner. "There's not much to go on here, is there?"

"No," she said. "Janet Friland left the *Ella Lynn* and vanished into thin air."

"Was she dating anyone?" Patterson asked.

"Lyman said that, to the best of his knowledge, she wasn't seeing anyone. I asked around at the bars in town. She occasionally walked up the hill to the Baranof for a beer and a burger. The bartender knew her and said she was young and pretty, so the guys at the bar noticed her, but she never saw her leave with anyone."

"I spoke to her mother," Nick said. "She claims that Janet was planning to fly home on the eighteenth, and she said Janet was excited to get home and see her family and friends. Her mother doesn't believe Janet would disappear on purpose."

Feeney snorted. "Mothers don't know everything."

Patterson let out a sigh. "What do you plan to do next?" he asked Horner.

She shrugged. "I think I've hit a dead end."

"With your permission, I'd like to recanvass the dock and talk to everyone I can find there," Nick said.

"Detective Horner will accompany you," Feeney said.

Nick smiled at Horner. "Fine with me."

"I can start tomorrow morning," she said.

Nick asked Patterson if he had time to drive him back to the airport to rent a car. He'd need his own transportation to get around town, and he didn't want Patterson to know he was staying at Jane's place. He wanted to keep that information to himself for now.

CHAPTER 10

Tuesday, October 21

6:50 p.m.

I turned off the stove and dished up a plate of spaghetti and sauce. I guessed Nick would eat before he got to my place, but I'd cooked enough for him in case he was hungry. I took my plate and a glass of wine into the living room and set them on the coffee table. I pulled the curtains shut over the large picture windows looking out onto Lily Lake and picked up the remote to turn on the television. I was surprised to see a shot of Kodiak on the national news.

"Friland disappeared without a trace from the boat harbor in this sleepy little Alaska town," the news commentator said.

Sleepy?

"Today on the Senate floor, Florida Senator Martin Cale comforted Friland's mother, Ohio Senator Laura Ames. The two Senate Republicans fought bitterly over the recent spending bill, but Ames seemed to appreciate the quiet words Cale spoke to her this afternoon."

The screen showed a thin middle-aged woman with short-cropped dark hair looking up into the face of an overweight, balding man with a fat face. She nodded her head while he spoke.

Next, the news anchor appeared on the screen. "Beth," he said. "I understand the FBI is now on the case of the senator's missing daughter?"

The screen showed the raven-haired reporter. "That's right, Paul. The FBI announced this afternoon that they have an agent on the ground in Kodiak."

35

"Let's hope they can find her," the anchorman said. "We'll be right back."

I finished my plate of spaghetti and walked to the sink to wash it. The knock on my door surprised me. I wasn't expecting Nick so early. I ran my hand through my hair, opened the door, and ushered him into my home. His hug and kiss sent shivers through me.

Nick held me by the shoulders and took a step back. I felt myself sink into his clear, dusty blue eyes and fought to regain my composure. His black hair had a few more gray streaks than I remembered, and it was about an inch longer than I'd ever seen it. Under his down jacket, I could see he wore a fleece pullover and blue jeans over his slim, muscular frame. He looked nothing like an FBI agent.

"You've lost weight," I said.

He shrugged and smiled. "When I get busy, I forget to eat."

"Have you eaten tonight?"

He laughed. "I was planning to grab a burger or something before I came here, but I forgot. I was anxious to see you."

"Lucky for you, I saved you some spaghetti, and I happen to have Chivas. Would you like a scotch and water?"

He took off his coat and laid it on the couch. "You are an angel."

While I watched him eat, we caught each other up on our lives. He'd spent the last two months helping Seattle police chase the unknown killer who'd murdered at least eight women. Nick said they were getting nowhere with the case. The killer left no apparent DNA on the victims. Crime scene analysts had recovered touch DNA on two of the victims—one sample from a belt and the other from a shoe—but the two samples didn't match each other, and they didn't match any of the profiles in CODIS, the criminal DNA database. The authorities had no reason to believe the DNA had come from their killer, so the samples weren't helpful for now.

"He'll screw up eventually," Nick said. "How about you?" he asked. "Are you all healed?"

I lifted my left arm in the air for show and tell. "I'm almost completely healed," I said. A few months earlier, a killer had shot me in the shoulder. The rehab had been difficult, and I wasn't sure I'd ever be pain-free again, but I'd decided not to think about the injury and to move forward.

"You scared me," Nick said. "When Patterson called me and told me what had happened, I wanted to drop everything and fly to Kodiak."

I believed Nick would have come if I'd asked him, but he'd been in the middle of a case at the time, and I didn't want to pull him away. He'd called several times in the month after I left the hospital, but then he called less frequently. I hadn't heard from him in over a month before he'd phoned to tell me he was coming to Kodiak to help find the senator's daughter. I'd tried calling him twice, but both times, he was too busy to talk for more than a few minutes. I had no claim on Nick and refused to ask why he didn't call more often.

"Tell me about the senator's daughter," I said.

Nick shrugged. "There's not much to tell. She worked and stayed on a fishing boat in the St. Paul Boat Harbor. The boat's captain sent her to get supplies, and she never returned. She never even made it to his truck to run the errand. She just disappeared into thin air."

"What about the boat captain? Could he have done something to her and then made up the story about her disappearing when she went to pick up supplies?"

"Detective Horner with the KPD doesn't seem to think the captain was involved in her disappearance, but I plan to find him and talk to him tomorrow. I also want to see if he'll allow us to search his boat." Nick took a sip of his drink. "Then, I plan to talk to everyone I can find in that boat harbor. Someone must have seen something. She disappeared near the harbormaster's office in the middle of the day."

CHAPTER 11

Wednesday, October 22

5:20 p.m.

The next evening, I zipped my jacket as I left the marine center. Sometime during the day, the clouds had disappeared, and the evening felt crisp and cool. In truth, it was cold, and it was time to start wearing my heavy winter coat.

I dreaded my evening. Instead of sitting in a restaurant making small talk with Corban Pratt, I'd much rather spend the evening with Nick Morgan. I smiled as I remembered the previous night and wondered what spending the rest of my life with Nick would be like. I breathed out a long sigh. Until he retired, he'd remain married to his job. I was nothing more than a diversion for him.

I arrived at the restaurant in the Baranof a few minutes before seven. Corban was waiting at the front and smiled when I approached. He nodded to the hostess, who led us to a table by the window overlooking the boat harbor.

I ordered a glass of merlot, and Corban asked for a glass of pale ale made at the local Kodiak brewery. After we'd ordered our dinner, Corban told me about a project he was working on for Tamron Oil. Corban wasn't involved in the oil business, but he handled charitable donations and other PR work for the company.

My mind wandered as he talked, but I tried to pay attention and smile at the appropriate times. I liked Corban, but I found him a bit boring and pompous. I was not physically attracted to him, even though he was very good looking.

Corban pushed a strand of his wavy, dark-blond hair out of his face as he grew animated about a project he was working on in Talkeetna. His brown eyes appeared to grow darker when he got excited.

When he finally wound up his story, I asked him what he did for fun. At first, the question seemed to confuse him, and I realized he loved his job and thought it was fun.

"I mean outside of work," I said.

Corban smiled. "I do some hunting and fishing, and I like to travel. I went to Tanzania last year."

The waitress interrupted Corban with our plates of food. We had both ordered baked halibut, and it looked delicious.

I began eating as Corban continued. "I went on a sheep hunt on the Wood River a few weeks ago."

When Corban finished talking, he dug into his plate of food. I was about halfway done with my meal when my phone buzzed. I glanced at the display, planning to ignore the call, but when I saw Steve Duncan's name, I excused myself and walked toward the front of the restaurant.

"The plane is landing," Steve said.

"I'm on my way," I replied.

I felt terrible about running out in the middle of dinner, but this was my opportunity to see if Steve was right to be suspicious about the plane or if he was inventing a mystery where none existed.

I returned to the table. "I'm sorry," I said to Corban. "A friend has an emergency, and I have to leave."

"Now?" Corban's fork, loaded with halibut, froze in midair.

"I'm really sorry," I said. "When you're in Kodiak next time, call me, and I'll take you out to dinner to apologize. How about Kodiak Hana?" I grabbed my coat off the back of the chair, put it on, and picked up my purse.

Corban stood. "You don't need to apologize," he said. "We all have emergencies from time to time. I hope it works out okay."

I turned and rushed from the restaurant. Corban was a decent guy, and I hated leaving him in the middle of dinner.

I started the car, pulled out of the parking lot, and rushed over the bridge to Trident Basin and the KFS office. I parked in front of the building next to one of the KFS vans and hurried around the side and up the stairs to the back deck. Steve sat huddled in a chair in the dark, a blanket over his lap.

"I called you as soon as I heard the plane circling," he whispered. "It pulled up to the dock about five minutes ago. The pilot is refueling it right now, but nothing else has happened yet."

I sat in the chair beside Steve and stared at the dock. The full moon and stars shone brightly in the sky, and I could clearly see a man pouring jugs of fuel into a black Beaver. Steve and I sat silently while we watched the pilot. I felt confident no one on the dock could see us sitting on the darkened deck.

Nothing happened for several minutes, and then, three people appeared at the top of the ramp leading down to the dock. As they descended the ramp, I saw that two of them were large men, and they were assisting a woman with long, dark hair. She walked between the men, and they held her arms. Her legs appeared wobbly, and she tripped once and nearly fell. The men held her upright, practically carrying her, as they rushed her down the dock to the plane.

I looked at Steve, and he nodded. I didn't want to get sucked into Steve's drama, but I had to agree with him. Something wasn't right here. Was the young woman sick? Perhaps the pilot planned to fly her to Anchorage for specialized medical care. No, Steve had watched other scenarios similar to this. A chill ran through me. I felt certain the men had kidnapped and drugged the woman and were now flying her someplace, but where and why?

The two large men pushed the woman into the back of the plane and shut the door. They exchanged a few words with the pilot, who was now done refueling. By the time the men reached the top of the ramp, the pilot had untied the plane from the dock and had started the engine.

Steve and I remained silent until the plane began taxiing for takeoff. "What do you think?" Steve asked.

"I think those men just kidnapped a woman."

Steve nodded. "I don't think there's any doubt."

"We have to call the police," I said.

Steve shook his head. "The plane is gone now. They'd think we're crazy."

"We have to do something!"

"If we could get the plane's tail number, we could make a report, but I can't see the number from here."

"We need to get closer," I said.

"I think something's covering the number. I looked at the plane through my binoculars and couldn't see anything."

"Steve, this is bizarre. It's brazen for someone to kidnap people from the end of the dock in Trident Basin."

"They must've realized that no one's at the dock after dark. I wouldn't be here if I weren't sick and bored."

"Where do you think the pilot's taking that woman?"

"I have no idea."

I sat with Steve for another half hour while we tried to figure out what we'd witnessed. Finally, I told him I was leaving and asked him if he needed a ride.

"Linda will be here to get me any minute," he said.

"When do you think the plane will be back?"

"In a few days," he said. "Do you want me to call you?"

"Yes indeed! I want to find some way to look at the tail number so we can report the pilot."

* * *

Nick was seated at my small dining room table when I got home. Papers littered the table, and his laptop sat in front of him. He stood and embraced me.

"How was your date?" he teased.

"If it was a date, I'm a terrible date. I left in the middle of dinner."

Nick looked concerned. "Why? Did the guy upset you?"

"No," I said. "A friend called me, and I had to leave."

Nick knew Steve from an earlier case, so I explained about his sickness and how he spent his evenings sitting on the back deck of KFS. I told Nick what Steve had witnessed and said that he'd asked me to join him on the deck the next time the plane arrived so he could get my opinion. I described what we'd seen and said I thought we'd witnessed a kidnapping.

Nick's eyebrows raised. "Are you sure?" he asked. "There are other logical explanations for what you saw."

I shrugged. "Why was the plane flying at night? Why couldn't the woman walk unassisted to the plane? Why did the two men shove her into the back of the Beaver? I don't even think they helped her put on a seat belt."

"I want to see this with my own eyes," Nick said, "and you need to get the tail number. If nothing else, you should report the pilot to the FAA. Even with a bright moon, I'm sure the guy is flying below minimums."

"Steve is afraid that if we report the pilot to the FAA, he'll simply move his operation elsewhere."

"This sounds like an Alfred Hitchcock movie."

"Whatever's happening at Trident Basin could explain what happened to your missing young woman," I said.

Nick nodded. "I'll talk to Steve tomorrow. I don't know what you saw tonight, but it does sound suspicious."

"Steve doesn't think he has enough information yet to report the plane to the police."

"I'll talk to him off the record for now," he said. "I'll tell him I'm just collecting background information."

"Did you get anywhere on your case today?"

Nick shook his head. "No one saw anything. Janet Friland vanished as soon as she left the fishing boat."

CHAPTER 12

Thursday, October 23

9:10 a.m.

Nick called Kodiak Flight Services to see if Steve was there and had a few minutes to talk to him. Steve said he'd be in his office for another hour or two and told Nick to stop by anytime.

Nick headed to Trident Basin and parked in front of the KFS building. Camouflage filled the front office as hunters awaited their flights into the Kodiak wilderness. Nick stepped around the camping gear, boxes of food, and cases of beer and knocked on the door to Steve's office. Steve called for him to enter, and Nick stepped through the doorway and closed the door to shut out the noise from the outer office.

He approached Steve's desk and held out his hand to Steve. Steve's handshake was weak, and when Nick released his hand, it dropped to the desk.

"Jane told me you have Guillain–Barré syndrome," Nick said.

"Yes. It's been an adventure."

Nick noted that Steve's speech seemed slower than he remembered, and he wondered how much the disease had affected his mind.

"She said you should completely recover."

"So the doctors tell me, but I've done plenty of research, and I know that not everyone recovers." Steve quickly changed the subject. "Jane says you're in town to investigate the disappearance of a senator's daughter."

43

Nick nodded. "Senator Laura Ames's daughter, Janet Friland, disappeared from the St. Paul Boat Harbor, and as far as I can tell, no one saw anything."

"I have an idea about what happened to her," Steve said.

"Tell me about the strange plane," Nick said as he sat beside Steve's desk.

"Would you like a cup of coffee?" Steve asked.

"I'm good."

"I don't know anything for certain," Steve said, "and I'm not ready to call the police."

Nick nodded. "I know. Jane told me the same thing. I'm just gathering information at this point."

Steve sat back in his chair and grasped its arms. With a neurological condition, Nick imagined his hands were either tingling or painful.

"Four times in the past three weeks, I've watched a black Beaver with no discernable markings land at the floatplane dock at Trident Basin after dark. Each time, the plane approached from the east, so the pilot didn't fly over the tower at the airport, and I doubt the air traffic controller even realized he'd landed. He stayed low, close to the water each time. Three nights were bright with moonlight, but there was no moon one night, so only the stars and the few lights at the dock illuminated the plane. Each time, I watched the pilot pull fuel jugs from the plane's cargo area and begin refueling it. While he was refueling, two big guys escorted someone down to the plane and helped them into the seat behind the pilot."

"Jane said the people had trouble walking on their own?"

"The first time I saw them, they led a young woman or a girl to the plane. It was similar to what Jane and I saw last night, but the first time, they carried the girl to the plane because her knees kept buckling. She was small, so one of the guys picked her up and carried her. The next time, the two guys carried something that looked like a rolled-up carpet. I couldn't tell what it was, but it looked heavy, and they had trouble stuffing it into the plane. Then, the time before last, the two men escorted two people down to the plane. That night, there was no moon, and I couldn't see much."

"Then, once the pilot refueled, he left?" Nick asked.

Steve nodded. "He never says much to the two men. They just do their jobs and leave."

"Let me get this straight," Nick said. "You believe these people were drugged and forced into the black plane?"

"Yes," Steve said.

"And you saw no markings on the plane?"

"No, I looked at it with binoculars, but I didn't see anything. I think the pilot covered the tail number with something. During the day, a pilot could never get away with flying a plane without a tail number, so he must cover the number with something he can remove when flying legally during the day."

"Do you have night-vision binoculars?" Nick asked.

Steve shook his head. "No, but I could borrow some from a friend. I doubt they'd help on the bright nights, but they'd be good for the darker nights."

Nick nodded. "Any thoughts on where the plane might be headed after it leaves Kodiak?"

Steve shook his head. "The pilot always departs to the east, away from the tower, and then I think he turns north, but he could circle and fly in any direction. I can't figure out what he's doing."

"It's clear again tonight," Nick said. "Do you think the plane will come tonight?"

"Maybe, but I doubt it'll come again so soon."

Nick handed Steve a card. "Call me if you hear the plane approaching, and I'll get over here as fast as I can."

Nick went out to his car and thought about Steve's story. If Steve had approached him with this tale himself, he would have passed it off as a bored, sick guy making something out of nothing. The fact that Jane agreed with Steve lent more validity to the situation. Still, he'd have to see this with his own eyes before he believed that someone was kidnapping people from the floatplane base. He thought about the senator's daughter. Did these men kidnap her and push her into the back of a floatplane? Possibly, but he'd need more information before he went down that rabbit hole.

CHAPTER 13

Thursday, October 23

7:15 p.m.

Troy had heard several gunshots during the day, and once, he'd heard a woman scream. The sun had set, and the forest appeared dark as he peeked through the spruce needles and moss covering him. This time, he'd dug his hiding spot with his bare hands, and his fingers still ached. His fingertips had bled, and he hoped to find a natural depression for tomorrow's hiding spot. Each night, he tried to hike farther away from the buildings he'd spotted the first night. He believed the people trying to kill him were staying in those buildings, so it made sense to move away from them. Even with his headlamp, however, he found it challenging to discern directions in the darkness. He needed a compass or a GPS.

Troy also didn't want to travel far away from the food troughs. He'd found four of them, but he didn't know if he could get back to any one of them. He wished he'd chosen a career as a backcountry guide, because his accounting skills weren't much use here.

Once Troy was sure it was dark, he brushed off the spruce needles and stood. He felt stiff and sore after remaining curled up in the fetal position all day. He stretched and then stood motionless for a few minutes. Once he thought it was safe, he turned on his headlamp but didn't put it on his head. He held the light low to the ground to make himself less visible. After a few more minutes, he headed into the surrounding woods.

Troy hiked for an hour before he saw the red light dimly illuminating the metal box. He walked toward it but then stopped and took several steps back. Someone was standing in front of the metal box. Troy's heart hammered as he tried to decide whether to run or stand still and hope the person hadn't seen him.

"I won't hurt you," a female voice said. "I'm a prey animal, too. Come get your food. We have ham and cheese sandwiches and an apple tonight—surprise, surprise! You'd think they could give us something else for a change."

Troy slowly approached the food box and the woman. When he drew near, he could see her slim outline, but her face and hair were covered with the hood of her coat.

"How long have you been here?" he asked.

The woman shrugged. "Several weeks? I've lost count."

"Do you know what's going on?"

"These maniacs are trying to kill us. Before they dropped me in the wilderness, they told me I was a prey animal."

Troy couldn't remember it, but maybe someone had told him the same thing, and that was why he thought of himself as prey and the humans with their guns as the predators.

"We have to do something to get out of here," he said. "There has to be a road somewhere."

The young woman shook her head. "We're on an island," she said, "and it's just us and them. Our only escape is when they hit us with one of their bullets."

"Are you sure this is an island?"

"Pretty sure," she said. "I've been on the rocky beach a few times in my travels."

"What should we do?" Troy didn't think it was possible, but his panic was ratcheting up a notch.

"We aren't doing anything," she said. "We'll both get killed if we try to hang together. Grab your sandwich and get out of here."

"But . . ."

"I mean it," the woman said. "Get out of here."

CHAPTER 14

Friday, October 24

10:20 a.m.

I unlocked my office door and dropped the stack of biology quizzes on my desk. The high school kids I taught were allowed to leave the campus on Monday, Wednesday, and Friday mornings at nine o'clock to attend their college biology class. They were good kids, and I enjoyed them. I didn't enjoy the time and effort it took to relearn basic biology so I could teach the class. I told myself it was good to refresh my basic knowledge, but it felt like a slog most of the time.

A few moments after I'd closed my office door, someone knocked on it, and from the sound of the knock, I knew my visitor was my boss. I inhaled a deep breath. "Come in."

Peter opened the door and stepped into my office; a broad smile creased his face. "How are you this morning, Jane?"

This didn't bode well. Peter never made small talk unless he wanted something from me. Come to think of it, Peter never spoke to me at all unless he wanted something.

"I'm great, Peter. How are you?"

He ignored the question and jumped straight to the reason for his visit to my office. "I had dinner with Corban Pratt last night."

Here it comes.

"He mentioned that you had to leave in the middle of your dinner with him the other night. Is everything okay?"

"It's fine," I said. I wanted to tell Peter it was none of his business, but I thought better of it. "A friend had an emergency, but it's okay now. I spoke to Corban last night, and we rescheduled dinner for tonight." I knew the sooner I told Peter what he wanted to hear, the sooner he'd leave.

"Great," he said. "It looks as though Tamron is planning to increase the funding on our grant."

* * *

After Peter left my office, the rest of the morning passed quietly. At noon, another knock on my door awoke me. I'd fallen asleep on the stack of quizzes I was grading.

Geoff Baker didn't wait for me to invite him into my office. He opened the door, and his tall, lanky form slid through and plopped down on the chair by my desk. "What's new?" he asked. "Did you just wake up?" He squinted his dark-blue eyes at me, and the corners of his mouth curled up into a slight smile.

"Maybe," I said.

"Grading exams?"

"Biology quizzes," I groaned.

"You shouldn't have to teach a beginning biology class," he said. "Why don't you complain?"

"No one forced me to teach it, and I thought it would be easy. I didn't realize how much I'd forgotten about basic biology. The kids are good, though. Maybe I'd enjoy it if I knew what I was doing." I laughed and sat back in my chair. "What are you up to?"

"Not much," he said. "Hey, I was thinking that maybe you should stay in touch with these consortium people so we know what they're up to."

"I'd rather eat dirt," I said. "What can we possibly do to change their plans?"

"You go to their meetings and then tell me what they said, and I'll rat 'em out on the radio. People are upset about these strangers coming onto our island and making big changes without our consent, but no one really knows what they're doing."

"Ask the mayor," I said. "He was at the meeting."

Geoff snorted. "Of course he was. He was probably busy handing out keys to the city."

"I'm not going to their meetings," I said, "but if I hear something, I'll let you know."

Geoff swiftly changed course. "What's going on with the senator's daughter?"

I shrugged. "She disappeared," I said. "I don't think the police have any leads. No one seems to know what happened to her."

"She's probably sitting on a beach in Bali."

I smiled. "Maybe I'll join her."

I didn't dare tell Geoff about the mysterious airplane and what Steve and I had witnessed. He'd call the afternoon radio show with the news. I'd learned to be careful about what I told him and Dana.

I spent the afternoon analyzing plankton samples in my lab and then snuck out of the building at 4:45 p.m. I needed to run to the grocery store and then prepare for another dinner with Corban Pratt.

A few minutes before seven, I pulled into a space in the Kodiak Hana parking lot. Corban waited for me inside the door. The popular restaurant was crowded on a Friday night, but Corban had secured us a table next to the window. I looked down at the channel that led to the boat harbor. Two sea otters bobbed in the calm water, and an eagle swooped down and landed in a spruce tree on Near Island across the channel from the restaurant.

Corban was dressed in a camel-colored corduroy shirt that accented his brown eyes. He wore blue jeans and hiking boots. "Thanks for having dinner with me again so soon," he said.

"I want to apologize again for running out on you the other night."

"No need to apologize. We all have emergencies!"

The server took our drink orders, and we also ordered dinner. I was preparing to ask Corban what he thought about the consortium when I saw the long, muscular figure of Jerry Burns approaching our table. Corban didn't notice him until the British banker tapped him on the shoulder.

"Jerry." Corban stood and shook Jerry's hand. "I didn't know you were in town."

"Since yesterday," the banker said.

"Are you at the Baranof?" Corban asked.

"I am. I'm surprised I haven't run into you."

Jerry turned and looked at me. "It's nice to see you again. Your name is Jane, right?"

"Jane Marcus," I said.

"Have you bought Kodiak yet?" Corban asked and then laughed.

Jerry visibly cringed and looked around the restaurant to see if anyone was listening to their conversation. Just then, the server arrived with our drinks.

After she'd left, Jerry said, "We don't say things like that, Corban." He raked a hand through his short black hair. "We're here to inject money into this beautiful town."

"Sure." Corban smiled and winked at him.

"Call me later if you want to get a drink," Jerry said to Corban. He smiled at me. "It's nice to see you again, Jane."

After he'd left our table, I asked Corban what he thought of the consortium.

"I like Jerry, and we sometimes hunt together. We went on a guided sheep hunt on the Wood River in late August. However, I disapprove of a group of people who want to walk in and swallow up a town for their own financial gain."

"They say they'll bring in new customers for the merchants. Do you believe them?"

Corban took a long drink from his beer bottle. He spoke in a low voice. "These people know how to bring in tourists by the thousands, and sure, the merchants they don't buy out will make a little more money, but the residents will no longer recognize the city or the island. They aren't here to make anyone rich but themselves."

I sat back in the booth. Geoff had been spot-on with his analysis of the consortium.

"Kodiak has enormous tourism potential," Corban continued. "The largest brown bears in the world live here, and visitors can take a flight-seeing trip to see them in the wild." He waved his hand toward the window. "The fishing fleet here also holds tremendous appeal for tourists who've been watching *The Deadliest Catch* and similar shows for years. Kodiak is beautiful, quaint, and a bit mysterious." He shrugged, and I noticed the gold flecks in his wide, brown eyes. "It's a marketer's dream, but do you want thousands of people roaming the streets buying trinkets?"

I nodded. "I get it. 'Call someplace paradise, kiss it goodbye.'"

"Exactly," Corban said. "Appreciate your unpredictable weather here. If anything will keep this consortium out of your city, it's the weather."

I suddenly liked Corban Pratt better than I ever had, and I had to admit to myself that I'd resisted letting him into my world because Peter had demanded I spend time with him.

CHAPTER 15

Saturday, October 25

8:15 a.m.

I returned from my morning jog to find Nick pacing the living room while he talked on the phone. I gave him a wave and headed for the shower. When I emerged from the bathroom thirty minutes later, he was still talking on the phone. I knew Nick planned to return to the boat harbor, hoping to find new people to interview about the disappearance of Janet Friland. My exciting plans for the day included doing laundry, cleaning the house, and making an appetizer for Dana's party.

As I was gathering my dirty clothes, Nick entered the bedroom. I dropped the clothes basket and accepted a warm embrace and a long, slow kiss from Agent Morgan.

"I wish I could stay here today, but I'd better get back out there and do my job." He shook his head. "If only Kodiak had more surveillance cameras."

"Aren't there any cameras at the boat harbor?" I asked.

"Yes," Nick said, "but none pointed toward the spot where the truck was parked. We have a shot of Janet walking down the dock and up the ramp, but then we lose her as she nears the truck. I think her abductors knew where the cameras were located, because we couldn't find a shot of them or their vehicle at the time we know Janet disappeared."

"And no one at the harbormaster's office saw anything?" I asked.

Nick shook his head. "There are no windows on that side of the harbormaster's building. Nobody saw anything."

I thought about the black Beaver and the men Steve and I had watched lead a drugged or drunk woman to the plane. I wasn't sure Nick believed that Steve and I had witnessed anything suspicious. I wasn't certain, either, but I thought the mysterious plane and the unstable passenger might have had something to do with the missing Janet Friland.

Nick looked at his watch. "I'd better get going. I'm scheduled to meet Detective Horner at the harbormaster's office in a few minutes. We're going to start from square one and see if we missed anything."

* * *

Nick returned to my house a little after 3:00 p.m. and told me he'd learned nothing new at the boat harbor.

"I have a flight to Seattle booked for tomorrow," he said. "The investigation there seems to be breaking wide open, and they need me. I've been talking to Seattle homicide detectives all day."

"What about Janet Friland?" I asked.

"I've hit a dead end for now, but I plan to return. Maureen Horner is a good detective, and she'll let me know if someone comes forward or she finds any new evidence in the case." He paused for a moment, reached out, and squeezed my shoulder. "You let me know what happens at Trident Basin with the Beaver." His blue eyes bored into mine. "Be careful, Jane. Don't do anything reckless." His hand trailed down my arm until he was holding my hand. "You have a way of finding trouble."

I knew Nick wasn't leaving for personal reasons. He was needed for a serial killer case in Seattle. Still, I felt rejected by him again, and I couldn't help but wonder if he'd called his girlfriend in Seattle to tell her he'd be there soon.

It was too dark to see much on our drive to Bells Flats, where Dana lived. Once Nick and I had left the city limits, I concentrated on the dark, twisting highway in front of me. I drove out Rezanof Drive around Dead Man's Curve. After we passed the turnoff to the airport and then the coast guard base on our left, the road hugged the coast. I turned right onto Russian River Road and followed it to Dana's driveway. A handful of cars were parked along the road in front of Dana's house, and I parked behind a green truck. I saw no sign of Dana's golden retriever, Sergeant, and I guessed Dana had restrained the enthusiastic dog so he wouldn't maul her guests as they arrived.

Dana opened the door with a bright smile, her green eyes sparkling. She'd met Nick once before and greeted him. "Agent Morgan, I'm so glad you could come to our party."

Nick looked down at my petite friend. "Please, call me Nick."

"Come in," Dana said and then whispered in my ear, "What a hunk."

Dana told us to throw our coats on the bed in the guest bedroom, and I deposited my smoked salmon appetizer on the table with the other food. Dana's boyfriend, Jack Parker, brought me a glass of merlot and asked Nick what he wanted to drink. Eight guests were at Dana's when we got there, and before long, another twelve were crowded into her small living and dining room, some spilling into the kitchen.

A few minutes after we arrived, Dana led a man with an athletic build, thinning black hair, and round glasses through the crowd to meet me. "This is the guest of honor tonight," she said. "Jane, meet Carter Brown, our new assistant Refuge manager."

I held out my hand and shook Carter Brown's sweaty palm. I thought I recognized him and felt certain I'd seen him somewhere before.

"Jane is a biologist at the marine center," Dana said.

Carter smiled and nodded, but I wondered if he knew what the marine center was. As Dana led him away to meet someone else, I looked around for Nick and found him deep in conversation with Dana's boyfriend. Jack was a former air force officer and currently worked as a meteorologist for the National Oceanic and Atmospheric Administration. I liked Jack, and he seemed to ground Dana. The two of them made a good couple.

I recognized most of the guests but didn't know many of them well. Most worked for the Kodiak National Wildlife Refuge with Dana. One of my good friends, Liz Kelley, sidled up beside me, a beer bottle in her right hand.

"I didn't see you. When did you get here?" I asked.

"A few minutes ago," Liz said. "Dana was introducing you to Carter, so you were distracted."

Like Dana, Liz was petite with dark hair, but that's where the similarities ended. Dana's hair was short and curly, while Liz had long hair, usually plaited in a braid. Dana had an open, friendly personality, while Liz was buttoned-up and sometimes hard to read. Liz carried a gun for her job as a park ranger, and she wasn't afraid to hand out tickets to campers twice her size when she found them doing something illegal in the park. It had taken me a while to warm up to Liz, but I now liked and respected her.

"Do you already know Carter?" I asked.

"I met him the other day," Liz said. "He seems nice, but he sure looks uncomfortable tonight."

I nodded. "Poor guy. Dana won't rest until she introduces him to everyone at this party."

Liz laughed. "And then she'll be sure to toast him a time or two in front of the entire group."

On cue, Dana said, "Let's hear it for our new assistant Refuge manager!"

Carter Brown stared at his beer while everyone clapped for him.

"Leave the poor guy alone," Liz said in a low voice.

"I think I've seen Carter somewhere before, but I don't know where," I said.

Liz shrugged. "He's just one of those guys who looks like someone you know."

I knew what she meant. He looked like many guys his age, with a receding hairline and glasses. Maybe that was why I thought I'd seen him before.

"Is Dave here?" I asked. Liz's husband was a floatplane pilot.

She nodded. "He's around here somewhere. "I saw your FBI agent." She smiled at me.

"He's not my FBI agent," I said.

"But this is the first time I've ever seen the two of you together at a social occasion."

"He's heading back to Seattle tomorrow."

"What about the senator's daughter?" Liz asked.

Before I could answer her, a middle-aged man I didn't recognize raised his voice above the din of the crowd. "Does anyone know anything about Shuyak Island?"

Liz groaned. "Here we go."

"The state government sold it to someone," Dana said, crossing her arms over her chest.

"How do you sell a state park?" the man asked, wiping his wispy, dark hair out of his eyes.

"Don't ask me," Dana said. "The whole thing stinks."

"I heard that the guy who bought it's a friend of the governor," a tall woman with short, blonde hair said. "They're building some sort of private hunting club there." I recognized this woman as a secretary at the Refuge office but didn't know her name.

The woman turned her head toward Liz. "Ask Liz," she said. "Liz works in the state park system."

Liz held up her hands, palms out. "I do not get involved in the politics of the state government, and I know nothing about Shuyak."

"I heard the *Retriever* made four trips to Shangin Bay about eight months ago, loaded with building supplies," the wispy-haired man said.

"If the new owners want a lodge, why not use the old Port William Cannery on the south end of the island?" a short man with dark hair asked.

The wispy-haired man laughed. "Have you seen that cannery lately? It's falling apart."

"Besides," Dana said, "that place has some bad juju. First, one caretaker killed the other caretaker, and then they had a big oil spill there. The place is probably haunted."

"What's going on with Shuyak?" I asked Liz once the conversation in the room had returned to normal. "Is it no longer a park?"

Liz shrugged. "Apparently not," she said. "The state government quietly set it aside and let someone buy or lease it."

"Is that legal?" I asked.

Liz shook her head. "I wouldn't think so, but it's no longer part of the state park system."

"What about the animals?" I asked.

"A private individual might have bought the island, but the state manages the animals. I'm sure the troopers are watching things closely there." She dropped her voice to a whisper. "This is just a rumor, but I hear it's already operating as a hunting lodge."

I felt a tap on my shoulder and smiled as Nick stepped beside me. He and Liz greeted each other. The two had worked on the same task force on the serial killer case. We mingled for another hour, and then I told Dana we were leaving.

Once we were in my vehicle, I asked Nick what he thought of the evening.

"A nice group of people," he said. "I especially enjoyed talking to Jack."

"He's a smart guy."

"Did I understand someone bought an island that was recently a state park?"

"I guess," I said. "I hadn't heard about it until tonight."

"Where is Shuyak?" he asked.

"It's about fifty miles north of here. It was designated a park after the *Exxon Valdez* oil spill in 1989. A Sitka spruce forest covers it, but I don't know much about it. I went up there once to help with a whale necropsy. It's beautiful, but it gets some nasty weather."

Nick laughed. "If it's anywhere near Kodiak, I'm sure it gets some nasty weather."

CHAPTER 16

Monday, October 27

11:18 a.m.

After I was finished with my morning class, I returned to my office to grab my computer and phone. I planned to spend the rest of the morning and the bulk of the afternoon in my lab and wanted my devices with me. I listened to soft music on my phone while I examined and cataloged plankton samples brought to me from a recent set of trawls in the water near Kodiak. My phone buzzed a little after 11:15 a.m.

"Dana," I said. "Great party the other night. I meant to call and thank you for inviting us."

"Have you talked to Mandy?" Dana's voice sounded strained.

"Mandy Carlson?" I asked. "No. Why, what's up?"

"Her assistant at the museum disappeared yesterday?"

"Disappeared?"

"Yes. Mandy and her assistant were working late, and Mandy asked her to run out and buy some dinner for them. When she didn't come back, Mandy called her but got no answer. She went outside and found the assistant's car still parked in front of the museum. She apparently vanished between the lab where they were working and her car."

"Just like the senator's daughter," I said.

"Exactly," Dana said. "Do you want to go over to Mandy's house with me after you get off work today? She sounded pretty upset."

"Of course," I said.

I immediately called Nick's number, but the call went to voicemail. I knew Nick was probably busy with the investigation there, so I left a message for him to call me as soon as he could.

After staring through a microscope at tiny bugs and plants for two hours, I stood and stretched. I ventured out of my lab and down the hall to Geoff's lab. I heard the music before I reached his open door. He sat at his desk, engrossed in his work, as he scribbled in a notebook. He looked up when he heard me enter the lab.

"Doc," he said. "How's it going?"

"You look hard at work."

He smiled and scooted the chair away from his desk. He stretched and straightened his legs in front of him. "I always work hard," he said. "What's up?"

"Too much, but I wanted to give you my consortium report."

He sat straight. "I'm all ears."

"Unfortunately," I said, "your instincts were right on track. Corban Pratt, the guy with Tamron whom Peter insists I wine and dine for the good of the marine center, is friends with one of the leaders of the consortium, so I asked him what he thought about the group."

"What did he say?"

"These aren't his words exactly, but he implied the consortium plans to buy out as many business owners as possible and then turn Kodiak into a picture-perfect quaint little Alaska fishing village."

Geoff nodded. "I know that's their plan, but how do we stop them?"

"Why don't you write an editorial for the newspaper?" I suggested. "Maybe you can inspire business owners and other citizens to write their own editorials, and we can let the mayor know his constituents don't think this consortium is such a great idea."

Geoff crossed his arms over his chest and stared at the floor for a few moments. Then he raised his gaze to my face. "I'll do it," he said.

I locked my lab door at 5:00 p.m. and returned to my office to grab my coat. I managed to avoid Peter as I skirted by the main office. I zipped my coat and pulled up my hood when I walked out into the chilly mist. Just as I was climbing into my vehicle, my phone rang.

"I'm in town," Dana said. "Do you want to meet at your place? We can drive over to Mandy's in my car."

Dana was already waiting when I pulled into my driveway. I grabbed my computer bag and got into her car.

"No news on Mandy's helper?" I asked.

Dana shook her head. "I called Mandy this afternoon, and she hadn't heard anything."

Mandy lived alone in a small house near mine. For the past two years, she'd been the curator of the Alutiiq Museum, a beautiful museum dedicated to preserving the heritage of the Alutiiq people from the Kodiak Archipelago. Mandy, an Alutiiq woman, graduated with a master's degree in anthropology from Brown University before returning to Kodiak to take over the reins of the museum. Mandy's flare for creating exhibits and planning events was a great asset to the museum, and she seemed to love her job.

Dana knocked on Mandy's door, and she greeted us. We both hugged her while she sobbed. Once we were seated in her cozy living room with big mugs of tea, Mandy told us what had happened.

"Charlotte and I were working on a new display of Refuge Rock. We'd been working on it all week and decided to get together yesterday and put in a marathon session to finish it." Mandy took a long sip of tea and seemed to fight back tears.

I knew the story of Refuge Rock. In April 1784, Grigory Shelikhov, a Russian ship captain, explorer, and fur trader, decided to establish a settlement on Kodiak Island. He chose the spot for his outpost at Three Saints Bay, near the present-day village of Old Harbor. The Alutiiq people in the area resisted Captain Shelikhov and his men and fled to a small island attached to the mainland of Kodiak at low tide by a land bridge. The Russians responded by attacking the island with guns and cannons. They slaughtered at least two to three hundred men, women, and children during the unrelenting massacre. After the attack was over, the Russians captured over one thousand people and detained four hundred, including children, as slaves. As visitors to the museum learned, the history of the attack at Refuge Rock serves as a reminder of the brutal treatment of the Native people of south coastal Alaska by the Russians and, later, the Americans.

Mandy set down her teacup and continued. "We still had quite a bit to do, and it was getting late. At six thirty, I sent Charlotte to Subway to get us something to eat. I got engrossed in my work and lost track of time. When I looked at my watch, it was nearly eight, and Charlotte still hadn't returned. I called her cell, but the call went to voicemail." Mandy shook her head, and tears rolled down her cheeks. "I started worrying about her. I knew her mom wasn't well, so I thought maybe she'd had a family emergency. Charlotte is so conscientious, though, and I couldn't imagine her not calling me if something had happened and she wasn't coming back to the museum."

Mandy paused again and wiped the tears from her face. "I went outside, planning to drive to Subway to look for her, but her car was still parked at the museum. I called her father, but he hadn't seen her, so I called the police. Charlotte's uncle is a policeman, so they began searching for her right away."

"Did they find anything?" I asked.

Mandy shook her head. "Nothing."

"Did it look like she'd gotten in her car before she disappeared?" Dana asked.

"No," Mandy said. "Her car was still locked. I don't think she ever made it to her car before someone grabbed her."

"Have you heard about the senator's daughter?" I asked.

Mandy nodded. "Same thing happened to her at the boat harbor."

A chill ran through me as I again thought about the mysterious plane at Trident Basin.

Dana and I tried to lift Mandy's spirits, but it was hard to think of anything positive to say, so we finally hugged her again and told her to let us know if the police learned anything new.

"Wow," Dana said as she shifted the car into drive and pulled away from Mandy's house. "What's going on in this crazy town?"

"I don't know," I said. I considered telling Dana about the events surrounding the plane that Steve and I had watched, but I thought better of it. If I told Dana, everyone would know, and Steve and I needed to gather more evidence before we reported the situation to the authorities.

"Is your Agent Morgan investigating Charlotte's disappearance?" Dana asked. "She might not be a senator's daughter, but it looks as though she's been kidnapped. Doesn't the FBI handle kidnappings?"

"Nick flew back to Seattle yesterday," I said. "I called him today and told him about Charlotte. He's planning to fly back here later this week."

"By then, Charlotte's trail will be cold," Dana said as she pulled into my driveway.

"Nick said the lead KPD detective on the case is very good, and he's in contact with her." I shrugged. "They found nothing to help them in the disappearance of Janet Friland, and she disappeared from the center of town in the middle of the day. Charlotte vanished at night from an isolated parking lot. I doubt they'll find much."

"You're assuming the two disappearances are related."

"You're right," I said, "but I doubt we have two kidnappers in Kodiak, so I think it's likely that the two events are connected."

Just as I was beginning to get out of Dana's car, she said, "Did you notice how quiet Carter was the other night at my party?"

"He did seem quiet," I said.

"He's nothing like that at work. I don't know what was wrong with him."

I sat back down on the passenger seat and smiled at Dana, who was brightly illuminated by the dome light. "I think he hated being the center of attention. Especially when he didn't know some of the people. I think it's possible he felt self-conscious."

Dana nodded slowly. "Maybe," she said.

CHAPTER 17

Monday, October 27

9:00 p.m.

When Troy awoke and brushed the spruce needles and moss from his face, he was surprised to see it was dark. Was it night or morning? He pulled his headlamp from his pocket and illuminated his left wrist. He kept forgetting that they'd taken his watch from him. For the first several days, he'd maintained a good feel for the time, but his mind had become sluggish, his brain full of cotton wool.

He slowly stood and brushed the moss from his jacket. Maybe he'd head to the nearest food trough and pick up a water bottle and a food sack. He'd forgotten to get a full water bottle the previous night and ran out early in the morning. He followed the trail illuminated by his headlamp and shuffled slowly toward the food box.

Troy studied the ground as he stepped over tree roots and avoided large rocks. Suddenly, he heard a loud noise to his right, and a few seconds later, a large bear burst out of the woods and stood on the trail directly in front of him. Troy froze as the bear glared at him. He had no idea what to do. Should he turn off his headlamp, or would the sudden darkness cause the bear to pounce on him before he could escape?

The bear let out a huff and popped its teeth. It made a sharp jump forward with its front feet, and Troy prepared to die. For the last several days, Troy had feared a bullet ripping through him and taking his life. At least a bullet would be a fast death, though. How long would it take him to die if a bear jumped on him and began eating him?

The bear watched Troy for several more seconds, then emitted another huff and slowly turned and ambled down the trail. Troy remained frozen in place until the bear had disappeared into the woods. Then, his knees buckled, and he fell to the spongy moss covering the ground. He crawled to the nearest spruce tree and leaned against the trunk. He silently wept and hoped he'd soon awaken from this nightmare.

Two hours passed before Troy continued his trek to the food trough. He imagined sounds coming from every direction and swung his headlamp in an arc, checking the woods on either side of him. As he neared the trough, he saw a young man lift the metal box's lid and remove a sack and a bottle of water. Troy watched the man for a few seconds and then warily approached.

The man stood next to the food box, illuminated by the beam of the red light mounted over the trough. He must have been hungry because he tore into his sandwich and devoured it. He'd just taken a bite of an apple when Troy approached him.

The man looked up, the apple clutched in his right hand. When he saw Troy, he threw the fruit and sprinted into the woods.

Troy called to the man and told him he wouldn't hurt him, but he didn't return, and Troy could hear him thrashing through the spruce trees.

He retrieved a sack and a bottle of water and retraced his steps to his hiding place. At first, he'd changed hiding places every day, but he'd discovered a large hollow under a spruce tree where he could more comfortably curl up during the day and camouflage himself with spruce branches and moss. He knew he should hike and explore new territory. The woman he'd met at the food trough had told him they were on an island. Maybe if he got to the shore, he could flag down a passing boat. There had to be some way to get out of this forest and away from the maniacs hunting him.

Troy again wondered how many people like him were hiding in these woods and how many had died from a bullet shot by a high-powered rifle. Would he be the next prey animal to be shot by a hunter?

CHAPTER 18

Tuesday, October 28

12:10 p.m.

Brooke Hamilton swiped a strand of black hair from her face and smiled as she left the Homer Bookstore. She couldn't wait until work was over for the day and she could dig into one of the three romance thrillers she'd bought. The next best thing to a love life of her own was reading about fictional characters falling in love.

Brooke turned right on the sidewalk and headed toward the small law office where she worked as a receptionist. A black sedan pulled beside her as she walked, and a man lowered the passenger window. Brooke tried to ignore the car and kept walking.

"Excuse me, miss," a deep male voice called. "Can you give us some directions?"

Brooke slowly turned and looked at the man in the passenger seat. She caught her breath. This guy could have stepped out of the pages of one of her books. He was dreamy. He had wide-set gray eyes, a neatly trimmed beard and mustache, and curly black hair. His face looked tanned, as if he'd just returned from the tropics. When he talked, his perfectly aligned white teeth gleamed.

"We're visitors in town. Can you point us toward a good restaurant for lunch?"

The man's voice was so low she could barely hear him, so she approached the vehicle. In addition to the driver and passenger, a third man sat in the back seat. They all had smiles on their faces. "Where are you from?" Brooke asked. The man's eyes could hypnotize her.

"Chicago," the man said. "Have you ever been there?"

Brooke shook her head. She'd never been anywhere—except through the books she read.

"Where should we eat lunch?" the man asked again.

Brooke was so mesmerized by the gray-eyed man that she paid no attention to the man in the back seat when he opened his door and exited the vehicle. "I like La Baleine Café," she said. "It's near Ramp 1 on the Spit."

"La Baleine Café?" the man asked.

Before Brooke could answer, she felt a pinch on her shoulder. She turned to check out the source of the pain, but the world faded to black.

CHAPTER 19

Tuesday, October 28

8:30 p.m.

I'd just settled on the couch in front of the TV and was about to search for a movie to stream when my phone buzzed. I retrieved it from the kitchen counter and looked at the display. "Hi, Steve, what's up?"

"The plane just landed," he whispered.

"I'm on my way," I said. I disconnected and hurried to my bedroom to pull on a heavy sweater and my hiking boots. I was surprised to hear the plane was there. When I left work, it was raining. I hurried out my front door and looked up at the starry sky. The clouds were gone, but I didn't see a moon. I wondered how the pilot could see where he was going under such dark conditions.

When I arrived at KFS, I parked by the office and hurried up the back stairs leading to the deck.

"It's already gone," Steve said by way of greeting me.

I looked down toward the dark, quiet dock. "That must have been a quick turnaround," I said.

"The pilot threw a few gallons of gas into the tank, and two men carried a rolled bundle down the dock and stuffed it in the back of the plane. I don't think they said a word to the pilot. By the time the men were up the ramp, the pilot had untied the plane and was leaving the dock."

"Could you tell what was in the bundle?"

"It looked like a carpet wrapped in black plastic."

"Do you think there was a person inside?"

"I couldn't say for sure," Steve said, "but I'd put money on it."

Steve sat only a few feet away from me, but I could barely see him. "How could the pilot fly on such a dark night?" I asked.

"He must have relied heavily on his GPS. I wouldn't want to be out there flying tonight. Another low-pressure system is supposed to move over Kodiak sometime this evening, so I'm sure that's why the pilot was in such a hurry. Since it's so dark tonight, I looked at the plane through a pair of night-vision binoculars I borrowed from a friend."

"What did you see?"

"Not much. The tail number is covered with something. I'm sure of it. I think something is also covered on the side of the plane. If it's a commercial plane, the name of the flight service would probably be on the side of the fuselage."

"I wonder where he was headed."

"I don't know," Steve said, "but the pilot never adds much fuel, so I don't think he's flying far."

* * *

As soon as I got home, I called Nick.

"Morgan," he answered, but he sounded distracted, and I knew he must not have checked the display on his phone to see who was calling.

"Is this a bad time?" I asked.

"Jane," he said. "I'm sorry. I was expecting a call from a crime scene technician. I'm at a scene where a body was just found, and I want to get a Bureau crime scene tech here to take a look at the evidence."

"I'll call you later, then," I said and was about to disconnect.

"No, no," Nick said. "Talk—please. I could use a happy diversion."

"I just wanted to let you know that Steve saw the mysterious plane again. He called me, but by the time I got to KFS, the Beaver was already gone."

"What happened?"

"Two guys carried a large roll down to the plane and shoved it in the back. He said it looked like a carpet, but there could have been someone inside the roll. He also said that the pilot seemed to be in a hurry, and he thought perhaps he was trying to beat the bad weather forecasted for tonight."

"Could he make out the tail number?"

"He borrowed some night-vision binoculars, but he didn't see any markings. He thinks the pilot covered the number with something."

Nick let out a long breath. "To be honest, I think Steve is imagining nefarious plots where there are none. I suspect the plane belongs to a private pilot, and the guy is making trips back and forth to his lodge on the island."

"How do you explain the disabled passengers?"

"Jane, Steve doesn't know if these men are carrying a human concealed in a roll of carpet," Nick said. "I know you saw the men escorting a young woman who looked drugged, but there's no reason to believe they were forcing her into an airplane against her will. She didn't try to get away from them. She didn't scream. The idea that these guys are taking people against their will seems far-fetched to me. Besides, if they were kidnapping people, wouldn't they try to do it somewhere less public? Mind you, I think the guy is flying under minimums, and he should receive a citation, but I doubt he's doing anything else illegal."

"It's very dark tonight. Steve said he must be relying on his GPS to fly."

"He won't be long for this world if he continues to do that," Nick said. "I contacted the FAA to see if anyone had filed a flight plan from Anchorage or Homer to Kodiak for the night you last saw the plane, but they had no record of it."

"The pilot could have flown down from Anchorage without filing a flight plan, couldn't he?"

"Sure," Nick said. "It's possible."

"What about Janet Friland and Mandy's assistant, Charlotte?" I asked. "They both vanished. Couldn't someone have whisked them away on a plane?"

"Maybe," Nick said, "but why? It seems crazy to me."

I heard yelling, and Nick stopped talking. I waited for more than a minute before Nick said, "I have to go. They found another body. Be careful, Jane."

CHAPTER 20

Thursday, October 30

7:58 a.m.

I ran from my car to the front door of the marine center in the wind and driving rain. The storm had arrived on time and hadn't relented for the last day and a half. I passed Peter in the hall, and he nodded to me. He seemed distracted, and I felt relieved that he didn't want to chat with me and pressure me into doing something I didn't want to do.

I unlocked my office door and shut it behind me. I was already prepared for my afternoon genetics class and didn't feel like peering through a microscope in my lab. Looking out my window at the gray day, I watched the tree limbs whip in the wind. I had plenty of work to do but didn't want to do any of it.

I grabbed my phone from my computer bag and called Mandy Carlson. Her phone rang five times, and I was just about to disconnect when she finally answered.

"Hi," I said. "Is this a bad time for you to talk?"

"No. I'm at the museum, but I don't feel like working," she said. "It's nice to hear a friendly voice."

"How are you doing?"

"Okay, but I miss Charlotte."

"Have the police told you anything? Do they have any leads?"

"They haven't told me anything," Mandy said. "I don't think they have any suspects. I keep worrying that someone will find her body."

"I know this must be tough for you. Have you heard about any other missing people in town?"

"Just the senator's daughter," Mandy said.

After we'd said goodbye and I told her to take care of herself, I sat back in my chair. *Should I call the Kodiak police or the troopers and tell them about the mysterious plane?* I could call Sergeant Patterson with the Alaska State Troopers. I'd met him several months earlier, and he seemed bright and capable.

I was frustrated with Nick. Why wasn't he taking the strange occurrences at Trident Basin more seriously? Two young women had vanished, and investigators didn't know what had happened to them. The only way off the island was by boat or plane. It seemed possible that someone was whisking them away somewhere, but where? And why?

I only knew of two missing people, but Steve had watched possibly six people being escorted or carried to the plane. Had others disappeared in Kodiak? Nick hadn't mentioned any other missing people, but maybe no one knew they were missing. Many young men and women came to Kodiak in search of employment as part of the crew of a fishing boat. A few stayed through the winter and might not immediately be missed if they disappeared.

I wondered if anyone had vanished from other nearby towns. As I knew well, "nearby" was a relative term in Alaska, with Homer 159 miles away from Kodiak, and Anchorage 250 miles to the northeast.

I hadn't looked at a map in a while, but I fired up my computer and confirmed that Seward, Soldotna, and Kenai were all located between Anchorage and Homer. Then I searched for news reports of missing persons in the various towns. I started with Anchorage, but crime reports overwhelmed the news from Alaska's largest city. I worked my way down the Kenai Peninsula but found nothing of interest for Seward, Soldotna, and Kenai. I hit paydirt in the *Homer News* online newsletter. On October 28, Brooke Hamilton, a receptionist at a law office, vanished after leaving the Homer Bookstore during her lunch hour. Friends said Hamilton had mentioned nothing about leaving town on a trip, and those at the lawyer's office where she worked claimed she never missed work unless she was sick. They reported that she was in a good mood on the morning she disappeared.

I swiveled my chair, facing the window, and stared out at the storm. Was Brooke Hamilton's disappearance related to the disappearances of Janet Friland and Charlotte? I picked up my phone and speed-dialed a friend.

"Jane!" Sid answered on the second ring. "How are you? I haven't heard from you in a while."

I smiled at the sound of Sid's deep, calm voice. From the moment I'd met him a few months earlier, I'd had a crush on this man. I reminded myself that he had thirty years on me, and at this point in his life, he wasn't looking for another relationship.

"How have you been?" I asked.

"Just returned from a hunting trip to Uganik Bay, and I have a freezer full of deer meat. Do you want any?"

"Not at the moment, but thank you." I knew better than to admit to anyone in Kodiak that I wasn't fond of wild game meat. Such an admission would make me "less Alaskan" in their eyes.

"It's here if you want it," Sid said.

"Did you take your boat to Uganik?" I asked. Sid lived aboard his forty-six-foot sailboat in Dog Bay.

"No," he said. "I wanted to concentrate on hunting and not worry about my boat dragging. What are you up to? Are you staying out of trouble?" Sid had helped save my life after a killer shot me a few months earlier.

"Of course I'm not staying out of trouble—this time I got recruited, though. Can I run the situation by you?"

"Shoot," Sid said.

Sid was a retired sergeant with the Alaska State Troopers, and he was friends with Sergeant Patterson, the current lead trooper on Kodiak. Still, I knew Sid wouldn't tell Patterson about the strange plane if I asked him to keep quiet. He might urge me to report the matter, but he wouldn't call Patterson unless I asked.

I told Sid about Steve Duncan's condition and the nights he'd spent sitting on the back deck at KFS. He didn't interrupt as I told him about the strange plane flying after dark and the two large men helping disabled-looking passengers into the back of the aircraft. I said Steve had called me, and I'd watched the plane arrive and leave once.

"Have you heard about the missing young women in Kodiak?" I asked.

"I heard about the senator's daughter," he said.

"Charlotte Porter, an assistant at the Alutiiq Museum, also disappeared. Her boss, Mandy, is my friend."

"Let me make sure I'm connecting the dots here," Sid said. "You think a kidnapping ring is abducting young women and spiriting them away in a plane after dark?"

I had to admit the words sounded far-fetched when they came out of Sid's mouth.

"Something like that."

Sid chuckled, low and smooth. "If anyone else told me this story, I'd say they were crazy, but I trust you. You might be an amateur, but you're a sharp detective. What does your friend Agent Morgan think about it?"

I felt my face grow hot. I didn't think Sid knew about Nick. Did he know Nick and I were in a relationship? I shook my head. What did it matter if he knew? Sid and I were nothing more than friends.

"He thinks Steve has '*Rear Window* syndrome' and has sucked me into his drama."

"Did he tell you that?"

"No," I said, "but I can read between the lines."

"This plane arrives on clear nights, but it's obviously flying under minimums," Sid said. "Steve should report the pilot to the FAA."

"I know, but he's afraid the pilot will move his operation someplace else if he does. He wants to figure out what's going on before he reports the pilot."

"I'd like to see this for myself," Sid said. "Do you think Steve would mind if I join you two on the next clear night?"

"I don't think he'll mind. I'll call him and ask."

"I think we should go to KFS on the next clear night. If we wait for Steve to call us, the plane might be gone by the time we arrive."

I disconnected with Sid. I felt a weight lifting off my shoulders. Sid had more faith in my judgment than Nick did. I trusted Sid, and it would be good to get his opinion on the plane.

I called Steve and asked him if it would be okay to bring Sid with me to KFS on the next clear night. He hesitated at first, but I assured him that Sid would keep his mouth shut unless we asked him to involve Sergeant Patterson or the Kodiak police. Steve finally agreed and told me the forecast was terrible for the next two days, but Sunday was supposed to be clear.

CHAPTER 21

Thursday, October 30

5:40 p.m.

I shrugged out of my raincoat when I stepped into my house. I hung the wet coat on a peg and removed my boots. I didn't have the energy to cook something for supper, so I made a ham sandwich accompanied by a glass of water.

I settled at my small table and opened my computer. My afternoon genetics class had proved lively, and my brilliant graduate students asked me tough questions. I knew I needed to work harder to stay on my game with this group.

I worked for an hour until my buzzing phone interrupted me. I looked at the display and sighed.

"Good evening, Corban," I said.

"Hi, Jane. I hear it's raining down there."

"Yes, it is—I'm sure you're surprised."

"I'm planning to fly back down there tomorrow. I hope it's flyable."

"There wasn't much visibility when I left work," I said.

"Well, if I make it, do you want to attend a consortium meeting with me tomorrow night?"

I paused. I could think of no worse way to spend a Friday night.

"The meeting is at the Baranof and open to the public. This would be a good way for us to keep an eye on what this group is planning."

I could hear Geoff and Dana in my head yelling for me to go to the meeting and then report to them. I could also imagine Peter urging me not to reject any offer from Corban Pratt.

"What time?" I asked.

"Seven o'clock tomorrow evening," Corban said. "I'll call you when I get to Kodiak."

I was not a community activist, but I didn't like the idea of a group of strangers remaking Kodiak into a tourist destination so they could get rich. I'd accompany Corban, and I'd sit quietly and listen. Then, I'd repeat what I'd heard to Geoff and Dana and let *them* spread the word.

CHAPTER 22

Friday, October 31

6:55 p.m.

Seven people sat around the table in the conference room at the Baranof when Corban and I entered the room.

"Corban," Jerry said from his seat at the head of the table. "I'm glad you made it with the bad weather." He nodded to me. "It's nice to see you again, Jane."

"I barely made it," Corban said. "We circled for ten minutes before the pilot managed to sneak through the fog and land."

While Corban and Jerry chatted, I studied the people sitting at the table. I recognized Madeline Turner, the cruise ship woman who'd antagonized the local merchants at the consortium dinner. I also knew another person at the table, and his presence puzzled me. Carter Brown, the new assistant Refuge manager, smiled at me and nodded as he adjusted the glasses perched on his nose.

I fought the urge to call Dana and ask her why Brown was at a consortium meeting. Was the consortium urging the Refuge managers to make Refuge lands more accessible to tourists? I certainly hoped not. A road into the Kodiak wilderness would ruin critical habitat for the wildlife, including bears, that lived here. As I often reminded my students, the Kodiak National Wildlife Refuge spanned two million acres and covered two-thirds of Kodiak Island. I felt it was critical to keep the land intact and free from roads and most other human-made structures. Access to the Refuge was limited to hiking, boats, and small planes.

78

Corban and I sat behind the table in the chairs lining the wall. No one else arrived, and Jerry brought the meeting to order.

"Why aren't more Kodiak citizens here?" I whispered to Corban.

"I think I know the answer," he said. "I'll tell you later."

The first forty minutes of the meeting turned out to be less than stimulating as the group members discussed finances and properties available for sale in Kodiak. I was so bored that I was afraid I'd fall asleep and tumble off my chair. Once Madeline began to speak, things got a bit more exciting.

"I don't find the Kodiak merchants easy to work with," she said. "They aren't friendly and won't embrace the idea of change even if it brings them more money."

Several moments of silence followed her statement, and then Jerry said, "Madeline, no offense, but you have an abrasive manner, and I wish you'd stay away from the Kodiak merchants. You make them angry, and they won't be conducive to our plans if they're angry."

"I don't know what you mean," Madeline said, her face growing red.

"You're a great asset to our group, but you're not a people person. Please let someone else approach the merchants." Jerry spoke in a soft but firm voice and then quickly changed the subject to the individual roles and responsibilities of the group members.

The members discussed their roles and plans, and the meeting finally adjourned. I couldn't wait to get off the hard chair and start walking.

"Do you want to go to Henry's for a drink?" Corban asked once we left the hotel. "If we go to the hotel bar, we'll run into all of these people again. It's better to get away from here."

I agreed, and we drove the short distance to Henry's.

We chose a small table by the window, and I ordered a glass of merlot. Corban ordered a beer, and we made small talk until our drinks arrived.

"I hope trick-or-treaters aren't tearing my house apart right now," I said.

Corban nodded. "I forgot. This is Halloween."

"I bought two bags of candy to hand out to little goblins and witches. Now I'll have to eat the candy myself." After a sip of merlot,

I asked Corban, "So, why weren't more members of the public at the meeting tonight?"

"I don't think they knew about it," he said. "The consortium members want to appear transparent. They claim that all their Kodiak meetings are open to the public, but they don't bother to publicize most of them, so no one knows when they're having a meeting."

"I get it," I said. "When the public complains about the consortium shutting them out from voicing their opinions on important matters affecting the town, the consortium members can point to all the public meetings they've had here."

"Right," Corban said. "It would make more sense for the group to meet in Anchorage, where most of them live, but meeting anywhere other than Kodiak would destroy their mirage of openness."

"They're a scary group," I said, "especially Madeline Turner."

"Jerry told me he can't stand her, but the cruise industry has supplied the consortium with a great deal of money."

"I can't figure out why the assistant Refuge manager was at the meeting," I said.

"Was he the guy with the round glasses?"

I nodded.

"He wasn't wearing a Refuge uniform," Corban said.

"I noticed that. I guess he wasn't there as a Refuge representative, but why else come to the meeting? He only recently moved to Kodiak, and I doubt he cares what happens to the town or the merchants."

"Interesting," Corban said, staring through the window at the stormy Kodiak night.

It was nearly ten when I got home, but I knew Dana was a night owl, so I called her.

"Sorry it's so late," I said, "but my curiosity wouldn't wait until morning."

"What's up?" she asked. "Are you engaged to be married?"

I laughed. "Hardly. I attended a consortium meeting tonight, and Carter Brown was at the meeting."

"Carter? I wonder what he was doing there."

"I was hoping you would know. He wasn't wearing a Refuge shirt, and he didn't say anything."

"I'll ask around at work," Dana said, "but I can't imagine why he'd go to a consortium meeting."

"I thought maybe the consortium was trying to pressure the Refuge managers into something to make Refuge lands more accessible to tourists."

"That would be a decision they'd make in Washington, DC," Dana said. "I haven't heard any rumors floating around the office, but I'll keep my ears open. Why were you at the meeting, and what happened at it? I didn't even know they were having a meeting tonight."

I filled Dana in on the meeting and Corban's thoughts on why more members of the public hadn't attended.

"That consortium is up to no good," Dana said, "but I don't know what anyone can do about them."

CHAPTER 23

Saturday, November 1

8:20 a.m.

Dan Patterson laid his phone on the counter and sighed. He rubbed the back of his neck to ease the persistent headache he'd had for the last two days. His wife, Jeanne, walked up behind him, told him to sit on the kitchen stool, and began massaging the back of his head and neck.

"I need to drive to Chiniak," he said.

"What's wrong?" Jeanne asked.

"Brie just called to tell me that a young woman reported her boyfriend missing."

"Can't you send someone else to Chiniak?" Jeanne asked. "You need a day off."

"This is the fourth person on the island to go missing in the past few weeks," Patterson said. "I don't know if they're all related, but we've got a big problem here if they are. I'll call Maureen to see if she wants to ride with me. The other three cases were all hers, since they happened in town, but she consulted me on them. We managed to keep the last one, a missing crewman living on a boat, out of the news."

"You'll never get rid of that headache at this rate," Jeanne said.

He reached up to his shoulders and caressed her hands. "I'll be fine," he said. "How are you doing?"

Jeanne was nearly four months pregnant, and she'd said she felt great so far. After her disastrous miscarriage, Patterson couldn't help but worry about her and this pregnancy.

"I feel wonderful," Jeanne said. "Please don't worry about me."

They said their goodbyes, and Jeanne packed him off with a sack of leftover Halloween candy. She told him, "Make sure Maureen takes of some of it—don't eat it all yourself!"

* * *

Patterson picked up Detective Maureen Horner at her home. The winds had calmed, and the pounding rain had muted to a drizzle. The dark morning felt cold and dreary.

The detective ran out her front door and climbed into the passenger seat of the sergeant's trooper SUV.

"Good morning," he said.

Horner buckled her seat belt and turned toward him. "I appreciate you including me in this."

"I don't know what's going on here, but it's beginning to look as if we've had a string of kidnappings on this island," he said. "It makes sense for us to pool our resources and information."

Horner nodded. "I agree."

"Do you think you can get your boss to play nice?"

She chuckled. "I think that's too much to hope for, but I'll try."

"You've recently handled three missing persons cases, correct?" he asked as he left the city limits and began to increase his speed, heading southwest on Rezanof Drive.

"Actually . . ." She paused. "I might have four missing people."

"Four?"

"Yes, a young man called KPD yesterday afternoon and said his friend might be missing."

"'Might be missing'?" he asked.

"This is the sort of thing I'd normally put on the back burner, and I wouldn't consider it a pressing matter until I had more information. However, in light of the other recent disappearances, I am concerned."

"Tell me about it."

"This young man—Fred is his name—said he hadn't seen his friend, Thomas Stroud, in three or four days. He thought Thomas had flown to

Anchorage because he'd been talking about going up there to find work. He'd worked all summer as a crewman on a seiner, but he's currently unemployed. Fred said he only became worried after he tried to call Thomas several times, and his calls went to voicemail."

"Thomas lost his phone," he said.

"Exactly." Horner pulled a strand of her shoulder-length brown hair from her face and secured it behind her left ear. She looked at Patterson as he drove. "I usually wouldn't consider Thomas Stroud a missing person until I'd received more information, and he'll probably show up in a day or two. Considering the other disappearances, though, this caught my attention."

Patterson piloted the car around the curves along the scenic Kodiak coast. He barely noticed the breathtaking vistas. In the misty morning, everything appeared the same shade of gray. "Did Thomas pack up his apartment?"

"Fred had a key to the apartment, so I met him there, and we entered the premises," Horner said. "I have to admit that it did seem strange. A half-eaten pizza was on the coffee table, and dirty dishes were piled in the sink. His bedroom was messy, with clothes scattered everywhere, and we found a large duffel bag in the closet. Fred said he didn't think Thomas had any other luggage." She shook her head. "It looked like Thomas disappeared while sitting on his couch eating a pizza."

Patterson drove silently for several minutes while he thought about the various disappearances. They cruised past the Rendezvous Bar and Grill, his favorite restaurant on the island, and soon, Rezanof Drive turned into the Chiniak Highway.

"What about the third case? That was also a young man, right?" he eventually asked.

Horner nodded next to him. "Yes," she said, "and it's also a bit iffy."

"How so?"

"Leonard Jacks, who's thirty years old, disappeared from a boat in the harbor where he was living."

"Which harbor?"

"St. Paul Harbor."

"The same place Janet Friland disappeared."

She shrugged. "Maybe. From what little information I could dig up on him, he spent a great deal of time at the Breakers Bar."

"Who reported him missing?" Patterson asked.

"The skipper of the boat where he was living. He had no idea when Leonard disappeared. The skipper had been off the island for two weeks and had just returned. He went to his boat to check on things, and Leonard wasn't there. His sleeping bag and other gear were on the boat, but no Leonard. The skipper tried to find him but couldn't. He called us when Leonard failed to answer his phone and didn't show up anywhere after two days."

"Did the skipper have any idea where Leonard could have gone?" he asked.

She shook her head. "He said Leonard was a wanderer, but he couldn't imagine him going anywhere without his sleeping bag. He'd need it if he got a job on another boat."

"So, we have Janet Friland, Charlotte Porter, Leonard Jacks, and Thomas Stroud."

"Possibly," Horner said. "Tell me about the missing Chiniak man."

"I don't know much about him," Patterson said. "His name is John Shriver, and his girlfriend, Vera, is the one who called us about him. The dispatcher took the call. I hope I can find the cabin the couple share. I have directions to turn onto King Crab Way and then turn right on Spruce Way."

Patterson and Horner drove in silence for several minutes. Patterson thought about the missing people. Two women and two men, all young. Had someone murdered them and disposed of their bodies where they couldn't be found? How were they abducted? Charlotte, Thomas, and Leonard could have been taken at night; Charlotte was snatched in front of the museum after dark, when no one likely would have seen the abduction. But Janet disappeared in the middle of the day and in the center of town.

They drove past Middle Bay and Kalsin Bay and then took a left where the highway split. The fork to the right led to Pasagshak and Narrow Cape and Kodiak's space launch site. They turned left toward Chiniak.

The small log cabin Vera Austin shared with her boyfriend was easy to locate. It had a wide front porch and appeared charming and homey. Patterson pulled into a muddy driveway and turned off the engine. Two large black Labs barked as they ran toward the SUV.

"Here's where we get muddy," Horner said.

"I hope they're not mean," Patterson said, his hand on the door handle as he hesitated to get out of the vehicle.

"Nah," she said. "They're Labs. They'll be friendly but will probably jump all over us with their muddy paws."

She was right. As Patterson stepped from the vehicle, one of the Labs ran to him, muddy paws molesting his legs and stomach.

The front door of the cabin opened. "Panther, Pete, down. Leave them alone!" a young woman with shoulder-length, flaming-red hair shouted. Her command had little effect on Panther and Pete, who continued welcoming the strangers.

Patterson wiped at his muddy pants as he stepped into the cabin. He glanced at his companion and noticed her dirty jeans. She looked at him and shrugged.

"I'm sorry about them," the young woman said. "I should have put them in their kennels before you arrived." Tears flowed from her green eyes. "I just can't think straight today."

"You must be Vera," he said.

The young woman nodded as she wiped tears from her cheeks.

"I'm Sergeant Patterson, and this is Detective Horner."

"Come in," Vera said, and Patterson and Horner followed her into the cabin.

The inside of the cabin felt warm and cozy. Vera led them to a small sitting room, where two other young women sat around a wood-burning stove.

"This is Janelle and Tara," Vera said. "They're keeping me company."

The two officers sat on the empty love seat, and Vera sat across from them in a wooden rocking chair.

"When did you first notice that John was missing?" Patterson asked.

"When he didn't come home yesterday evening, I started to worry," Vera said. "He didn't answer his phone when I called him, and none of his friends had seen him in hours. Then I called his boss at the Port of Kodiak, and he never made it to work yesterday morning. John never misses work, so I knew something was wrong. Tara and I drove along the road to see if his truck had gone into the ditch." She nodded at her friend, who smiled sadly at her. "You know, the highway is dangerous, and John drives too fast."

"But you didn't see anything?" Horner asked.

"His truck was parked at the port," Vera said. "He must have parked and started to head to work, and then he vanished." Vera sobbed, and Janelle handed her a tissue.

"No one at work saw him?" Patterson asked.

Vera shook her head. "He starts work at six a.m., before it gets light out this time of year. None of his coworkers saw anything."

Patterson knew he needed to check with John's boss and coworkers to confirm what Vera had just told them. "Has John ever disappeared like this before?"

"What?" Vera looked confused. "No, of course not. He's very dependable."

"Vera," he said, trying to make his voice as soothing as possible, "I have to ask these questions, so please don't take them personally."

"Okay," she said, her voice squeaking.

"Were you and John getting along? Have you had any recent fights?"

"No," Vera said and then began to cry. "Well, we had a fight the other night. It was about a week ago. I wanted to go out, but John wanted to stay home and watch a movie. We don't go out very often, so I was mad."

Patterson waited for Vera to say more, but when she didn't, he said, "But you made up?"

"Yes," Vera said through her sobs.

If this was Vera and John's only recent fight, then Patterson didn't think their relationship had anything to do with his disappearance. Still, John's view of things might be different from Vera's. He'd learned long ago to never guess at what went on between two people involved in a relationship.

Horner asked Vera if John had called or texted her after he'd left home to go to work on the morning he disappeared, but Vera shook her head.

Patterson promised to keep Vera informed if they had any news about her boyfriend, and he made her promise to let him know if she heard from John.

"What do you think?" Patterson asked Horner when they were back on the highway and pointed toward Kodiak.

"I think we have another abduction to add to our list," she said.

Patterson nodded. "And absolutely no leads."

CHAPTER 24

Saturday, November 1

11:00 p.m.

Austin Green walked out of the bar and stood in the cool night air while he waited for the Uber to arrive. He knew he'd had too many beers to drive, so he'd have to retrieve his car in the morning. He was mad at himself for drinking too much and knew he'd hate himself in the morning. His buddies had kept buying rounds, though, and he didn't seem to be able to say no.

Austin had lived in Anchorage for two years. He flew up to his oil job on the North Slope, where he stayed and worked for two weeks, and then he returned to Anchorage for two weeks. He didn't love his job, but he did love Alaska. Anchorage was just a city, but he could be fishing on a stream or in the middle of the wilderness hunting for moose within minutes. His job paid well, so Austin could afford to charter a small plane and pilot to fly him to the middle of nowhere, and he could stay there for a week or two if he wanted. He dated, but he didn't have a steady girlfriend. He didn't want a girlfriend. He was too young to settle down and wasn't sure he ever would. He loved his freedom.

Austin usually didn't drink much, but sometimes, when he got together with his working buddies from the Slope, his willpower crumbled—tonight had been one of those nights.

A car pulled to the curb, and Austin thought it was his Uber. He walked toward the vehicle, and a man got out of the back seat and slammed the door. Another man rolled down the passenger window and smiled at Austin.

"Do you need a ride?" the stranger asked.

"I'm waiting for an Uber," Austin said. He sensed danger and began to back away from the car.

Austin felt the stab through his coat in his left shoulder, but before he could do anything about it, someone was pushing him toward the rear of the car. The back door opened, and strong hands shoved him onto the seat.

CHAPTER 25

Sunday, November 2

10:15 a.m.

When I turned off the vacuum cleaner, I heard my phone buzzing. I grabbed it and looked at the screen. "Hi, Steve. It's a nice day."

"Not a cloud in the sky," he said. "I think you and your friend should plan to come over to KFS at seven tonight. Linda is baking cookies, so I'll have coffee and cookies on the back deck while we wait."

"We'll be there," I said.

As soon as I ended my call with Steve, I phoned Sid, who said he'd pick me up at 6:45. Although I felt terrible for thinking it, I hoped the plane would come tonight because I wanted to get Sid's take on the situation. I didn't know what to think. One moment, I suspected the pilot and the other two men were kidnapping people, but then I felt certain I'd let Steve suck me into his drama. Nick was probably right, and there was a logical explanation for everything. And it did seem odd that they'd risk kidnapping people from a public floatplane basin. Still, something had been wrong with the young woman the men had escorted to the plane. She looked drunk or drugged. Who was she, and where did the pilot take her?

My phone buzzed again, and the display read *Unknown Caller*. My curiosity got the better of me. "Hello?"

"Jane, this is Jerry Burns." His voice sounded deeper and smoother over the phone. Why was he calling me?

"Hi, Jerry. What can I do for you?"

"I hate to sound forward, but I was wondering—are you and Corban dating?"

His question startled me. "No, we're just friends," I said.

"Could I be so bold as to ask you out to dinner, then?"

What is with this guy? I wasn't going anywhere with him. I didn't care how much intel I might learn about the consortium.

"Thanks, Jerry, but I'm in a relationship," I said.

"I'm not suggesting anything other than a friendly dinner," he said. "I'd just like to talk to you."

"I don't think so," I said, "but thank you."

"Okay, then." He paused. "Sorry to bother you."

After I'd disconnected, I sat on a dining room chair. What nerve the guy had. If he even thought his friend Corban was interested in me, why would he ask me out to dinner? How had he gotten my number, anyway? He'd called me on my cell phone. I never gave him my number. I'd barely said two words to him before today.

The phone call from Jerry Burns nagged at me, but I tried to shake it off. I turned on the TV and watched football while I folded my clothes. Maybe Corban had given Jerry my phone number, but why? What purpose would Corban have for giving Jerry my number? I decided to ask Corban about it the next time I saw him.

* * *

Sid drove up in front of my house at 6:45 p.m., and I grabbed the sandwiches I'd made for the evening, walked out, and climbed in his pickup. "I appreciate you joining Steve and me tonight," I said.

Sid smiled. "You piqued my curiosity," he said. "Besides, what else do I have to do tonight?"

We chatted and caught up on our drive over the Near Island Bridge. He told me about his hunt and the two bucks he'd shot.

"What did you do with all that meat?" I asked.

"I gave some of it away, but I had the rest made into sausage, ground meat, steaks, jerky, wild game sticks, you name it. None of it goes to waste." He looked over at me and smiled. "Are you sure you don't want some?"

"Maybe I'll try some of your jerky," I said.

"I'll have you over for spaghetti one of these nights. I know you'll like the Italian sausage."

We parked in front of the KFS office and walked around the building and up the stairs to the deck. Steve sat with a blanket over his lap.

I introduced Sid to Steve, but I got the feeling that they already knew each other. In a town the size of Kodiak, everyone knows everyone else, and before his retirement, Sid had been a state trooper here for years.

"I brought sandwiches," I said, setting the plastic plate on the table next to the chocolate chip cookies I assumed Linda had baked.

Sid said, "I brought my night-vision binoculars."

Steve nodded. "I borrowed a pair of those from a friend, but the lights on the dock interfere with them."

Sid looked down at the dock. "I didn't think about the lights," he said. "I wonder if we can get a different angle from the ramp end of the dock to avoid the glare of the lights."

"I'm not mobile," Steve said, "but you might be able to go over by the ramp, where the lights are at your back."

Sid grabbed his binoculars. "Let me check it out." He descended the stairs from the deck and hurried over toward the dock. He returned a few minutes later. "There's a little less glare over there. When we hear the plane approaching, I'll head over there and hide."

"Be careful," I said. "The men who load the passengers or cargo might be standing at the top of the ramp waiting for the plane to land."

We waited and whispered to each other until a few minutes after nine. I was beginning to think nothing would happen when Steve said, "Do you hear it?"

I strained to listen and finally heard the faint noise of an engine. Sid hurried down the stairs and headed toward the ramp to find a hiding spot. Steve handed me a pair of regular binoculars while he clutched the night-vision binoculars in his hand.

We sat quietly while the plane landed and glided to the dock. When it neared the end of the dock, the pilot jumped out and tied it to two of the cleats at the end of the wood planking. He then began to pull fuel jugs from the plane's rear and to pour the fuel into the tank on the fuselage.

I could see pretty well through the regular binoculars. I scanned the plane's side and tail for any numbers or other markings, but I saw nothing. I pulled the binoculars from my eyes and watched the two large men walk slowly down the dock with a roll of something covered with a tarp. Were they carrying a large rug or some other item under the tarp, or was a person concealed in the roll?

If I hadn't previously watched these guys leading a young woman to the plane, I wouldn't have had any reason to think the roll was anything other than a rug. I wondered what Sid would think. Whatever the men were carrying must have been heavy. They stopped twice to get a better grip on it and then struggled for several minutes to get it into the plane.

After the pilot had finished refueling, he helped the men push the roll into the aircraft. The men shut the door, then turned and retreated along the dock and up the ramp to the parking lot. The pilot started the engine and departed the same way he'd arrived.

Sid returned to the dock a few minutes after the plane had left.

"What do you think?" I asked him.

Sid shook his head. "Something isn't right. The pilot is flying under visual minimums, and I couldn't see any tail numbers on the plane. We should report him to the FAA."

"I know," Steve said, "but I'm afraid they'll just move whatever they're doing to someplace else, and we'll never have any evidence to stop them."

"I didn't see anything to make me think there was a human in the bundle they pushed into the plane," Sid said. "Do you think they had a person concealed in there?" He looked at Steve and then at me.

I shrugged and shook my head. "I don't know," I said. "The first time I watched with Steve, I felt certain the young woman they put on the plane was drugged, but I don't know what was in the roll they put on the plane tonight."

"I think it was a person," Steve said. "I assume he or she was unconscious, so the men had to carry whoever it was."

Sid stared at Steve for several seconds, then said, "If you believe these guys are transporting people against their will, then you should report it to KPD."

Steve didn't answer but instead changed the subject. "What do you think about the tail number?"

"I think it's covered with a plate of some sort," Sid said. "Where the number should be, I noticed a long rectangular area slightly lighter in color than the rest of the plane."

Steve nodded. "I thought so."

"It'd be good to see the number," Sid said. "Then we could find out who owns this plane."

"I've never seen it before around Kodiak," Steve said.

"Maybe the pilot flies down from Anchorage or Homer," Sid said.

We told Steve good night, and he promised to call me the next time he heard the plane approaching.

Once Sid and I were back in his vehicle, he said, "I don't know, Jane, maybe someone was rolled up in that tarp, but it looked more like a large rug or a carpet to me. I think what those men are doing is possibly illegal, but kidnapping is a stretch, and what would they be doing with all these people they're kidnapping?"

I shook my head. "I don't know, but it all seems strange to me. We know two young women are missing from Kodiak. Where did they go?"

Sid said nothing for a few moments. He pulled into my driveway and put the vehicle in park. "I think I'll give Dan Patterson a call. The two women disappeared from town, so they'd fall under the jurisdiction of the KPD. I bet Patterson knows something about the cases, though. I'll see if I can get anything out of him. Don't worry. I won't tell him about the plane yet."

CHAPTER 26

Sunday, November 2

9:00 p.m.

Troy saw two people standing near the lighted food bin as he approached it. One was a young man, and the other a young woman. Troy thought they both must be in their early twenties. He hid behind a tree and watched the pair for a while. They were dressed like he was and were conversing in whispers. The woman kept looking behind her and to the sides into the woods.

Troy slowly approached the pair. When they saw him, they both looked ready to bolt.

"I won't hurt you," he said. "I'm prey just like you."

When Troy reached the food bin, he opened it and grabbed a paper sack and a water bottle. He placed his empty water bottle in the trough.

The pair watched him silently, and Troy noticed the woman's hands were shaking.

"My name is Troy," he said. "Did you guys just get to this island?" He thought they must be newcomers because they both looked scared. He remembered how terrified he was for the first few days after waking up in this nightmare. Now he only felt tired and hopeless.

"I'm Brooke," the young woman said. "I've only been here two nights. We're on an island?"

"That's what someone told me," Troy said.

The young man held out his hand to Troy. "I'm Derek Tanner," he said. "I think I've been here about a week."

"I've lost track of time," Troy said, "but I've been here a while."

96

"Do you know what's happening here?" Brooke's voice shook as she asked the question.

"They're hunting us like wild game animals," Troy said. "Find a good hiding spot during the day, and stay there. It's safe to come out at night and get some food."

Brooke nodded, tears running down her cheeks.

Troy heard footsteps behind him and quickly turned to see who was approaching. It was hard to tell if the newcomer was male or female until the hooded figure neared them and pulled back her hood to reveal light-brown shoulder-length hair, brown eyes, and a sprinkling of freckles across her nose.

"I'm so happy to see others here." The newcomer paused momentarily. "But of course, I wish you didn't have to go through this nightmare."

Troy reached out his hand to the young woman, who looked like a teenager. "I'm Troy," he said, "and this is Brooke and Derek."

"I'm Janet," the newcomer said, a slight smile curving her lips.

Suddenly, another figure emerged from the forest, and Troy quickly recognized her as the woman he'd met a few nights earlier. She was the one who'd told him they were on an island.

"Hi," Brooke said. "What's your name?"

"Never mind," the woman said. "It's dangerous to get to know each other."

"Maybe if we worked together, we could find a way out of this place," Troy said.

The woman shook her head. "We'd just all get killed."

Derek took a step toward her. "How do you know?" he asked, his tone demanding.

"I know because I've already tried," the woman, whom Troy now thought of as "Icy," said. "After I got here, I joined two other women. We decided we'd either figure out how to get out of this forest or find the hunters, steal a gun, and kill them all while they slept." She paused and looked at the ground for a moment. "Once we figured out we were on an island, we decided to go with our second option. We hiked toward the hunters' compound. I didn't know where it was, but one of the other women had seen it. When we got within sight of the cabins, someone opened fire on us. I guess it was a guard protecting the hunters while they slept." She swiped at her right cheek as if wiping away an invisible tear.

"Bullets tore through my two companions," Icy said. "They were mowed down. I dived into the trees and don't think the shooter saw me. I barely got away with my life."

"Your friends died?" Brooke asked, her green eyes open wide.

"Yes," Icy said, "and that's why I don't want to get to know any of you." She pointed at Brooke. "Tomorrow, they could kill you, or you," she said, pointing at Derek, "or me. I don't want to lose another friend." Then she gestured to Janet. "Especially you," she said. "You are special prey. One hunter or a group of hunters specifically ordered you so that they could stalk and kill you."

"What do you mean?" Janet asked. "How do you know I'm—what did you call it—'special prey'?"

"You have a purple diamond," Icy said. "The rest of us have white diamonds on our coats. Anyone can hunt us, but you're off-limits to everyone except the one hunter or group of hunters who requested you as prey. I'm sure they paid extra to have you kidnapped and brought to this island."

Janet stared down at the purple diamond on her coat and then looked at the white triangles the others wore. Troy, Brooke, and Derek also looked at their jackets and then at the others.

"I wondered what the white diamond signified," Troy said.

"How do you know this?" Janet asked Icy.

"I heard it from someone else. She had a red diamond, and the woman who'd sent her into the woods told her what the diamond meant."

"What happened to her?" Janet asked.

Icy shook her head and looked at the ground.

"Who wants to shoot you?" Brooke asked Janet.

Janet touched her purple patch. "I have no idea," she said. A sob escaped her mouth.

Icy pointed at her again. "You stay away from me. I mean it. You're not taking me down with you."

Icy reached into the trough and grabbed a food sack and a water bottle. She began to back into the woods. "By the way," she said, "there are several food bins scattered throughout the forest. Don't use the same one every night. They know how many sandwich bags they put in each trough and where the prey is concentrated by the number of bags that disappear from each bin."

"I've been wondering," Troy said, "have you seen any game trail cameras?"

"I haven't seen any," Icy said, "but they could be well concealed."

Icy began to walk away but then turned toward the others. "You guys should all go your separate ways. You'll die if you try to stick together."

"Wait!" Troy called after her. "How many buildings did you see in the hunters' compound?"

Icy turned. "One long building, four small cabins, and a large warehouse, but there might be more. I didn't have much time to scope out the compound."

Troy watched Icy walk into the forest and disappear. Then he looked at the others. "Good luck," he said and then began to walk away.

He heard someone running after him after he'd hiked about twenty feet. He turned and saw Brooke, tears streaming from her beautiful green eyes.

"Can I come with you?" she asked. "I'm scared."

Troy stood still, not knowing how to answer her. Icy was right. Two people made a larger target than one person.

"I'll do whatever you tell me," Brooke said. "I'll be quiet."

Troy didn't want to be responsible for another person. He didn't want Brooke's life in his hands. "Okay," he finally said, "but you have to do what I tell you, and you have to remain quiet and still all day. It's not easy to do, especially if you have a cramp or need to go to the bathroom."

Brooke ran to him and threw her arms around him. "Thank you so much," she said, tears dripping onto his shoulder.

Troy was embarrassed and didn't know what to say, so he just accepted her embrace and awkwardly patted her on the back. "I don't know if I'll be much help, but it would be good to have some company," he finally said.

CHAPTER 27

Monday, November 3

7:43 a.m.

Driving wind and pelting rain assaulted me as I left my home. I ran to my vehicle and jumped in the front seat. Kodiak had many moods, and most of them were bad. When she was in a good mood, though, there was no place in the world more beautiful than this island. But this was not shaping up to be one of her better days. I squinted through the pounding rain as I drove across the Near Island Bridge to the marine center. I parked in the lot and waited for the rain to subside. Once I realized the rain had no plans to accommodate my comfort, I sprinted for the front doors of the building.

I stood inside the entryway for a moment and caught my breath. Behind me, the door burst open when Geoff entered the building. "Now that's weather," he said, a broad smile on his face.

I smiled and shook my head at him. I brushed the rain off my coat over the indoor mat and headed for my office.

My day zipped by at a smooth pace. For once, none of my beginning biology students asked me a question I couldn't answer, and they all seemed engaged and eager to learn. At 2:20 p.m., Leslie Daniels called to tell me she'd just finished another whale necropsy and had samples for me.

"This whale was fresher than the other ones I've done," she said. "You might get something from the stomach samples."

"I'll head down to my lab and start getting things ready," I said.

"I'll be there in a few minutes."

Not long after, Leslie dropped off the samples, and I went to work. At 3:40 p.m., a sharp knock on my door broke my concentration.

"Jane?" Peter slowly opened the door and looked into my lab. "I have some people with me who want to see what you're working on."

I frowned at Peter. He never showed up unannounced with guests. He liked me to have everything in order for a formal presentation.

Peter stepped into the lab, followed by two people. I inhaled a sharp breath when I saw who was accompanying him. Jerry Burns and Madeline Turner smiled at me when they entered what I considered my safe space. Peter had no right to bring them to my lab without consulting me, or at least giving me some warning. From the weak smile on his face, I could tell he knew I wasn't happy with him.

"Do you remember Jerry and Madeline from the consortium meeting?" he asked.

"Yes." I tried to smile at my visitors, but I knew it looked more like a grimace.

"Jane, it's good to see you again," Jerry said. "I don't think you've met Madeline Turner."

"No," I said. "Not officially. Jane Marcus." I held out my hand, and she barely brushed my palm with her fingers as she looked around my lab.

"Dr. Marcus is part of a team of scientists studying the recent mass mortality event regarding numerous whale deaths in the North Pacific," Peter said. "Dr. Marcus can explain in more detail."

A sigh escaped my lips, and I reminded myself to remain calm. "Sure," I said. "I happen to be working on some whale stomach content analysis right now."

"Yuck," Madeline said.

I ignored the comment. "Several theories prevail among scientists about why so many whales have recently died in the North Pacific," I said. "Perhaps the whales have surpassed their natural carrying capacity. In other words, the food hasn't changed, but the whale populations have simply outgrown their natural food supply." I took a drink from my water bottle. "This first theory seems unlikely, since we know their food has changed—both in quantity and quality. Gray whales, in particular, have a very specialized diet. They're normally bottom feeders and dig benthic gammarid amphipods out of the sediment. They filter the sediment through their baleen and retain the amphipods. Unfortunately, increasing seawater temperatures in the Bering Sea have reduced winter ice cover in the region where the whales feed, and an ecosystem of midwater fish has replaced the previously ice-dominated shallow ecosystem, favoring large communities of benthic amphipods. Gray whales have responded by migrating farther north to the Chukchi Sea, costing them time and energy."

Jerry sat on one of my lab stools and seemed to be listening carefully. Madeline looked around the lab and shifted from one foot to the other. Peter watched me, probably making sure I didn't embarrass him or represent the center poorly.

"This leads to theory number two," I said. "Whales are dying because their food supply is diminishing. Theory number three is that underwater noise pollution is somehow affecting the whales. The theory I'm researching involves toxic plankton. We know there've been several large blooms of toxic algae in the North Pacific in recent years." I shrugged. "Are the whales ingesting enough toxic phytoplankton to kill them?" I paused a moment. "Or, perhaps it's a combination of theories. Maybe the whales are already weakened by too little food, and the toxic plankton is finishing them off."

Jerry nodded to the lab table in front of me. "You're testing plankton from a whale's stomach to determine if it's toxic?"

I nodded. "By the time a whale carcass washes up on a beach where a necropsy team can get to it, the whale is usually too decayed to determine the cause of death, and I find inconclusive results from the plankton analysis. This whale"—I pointed at the stomach samples—"might provide something useful. The carcass was still fairly fresh when the marine biologist found it and conducted her necropsy."

"What kind of whale was it?" Jerry asked.

"A fin whale," I said.

"Okay, thank you." Madeline began walking toward the door. "We'll let you get back to your work."

Jerry smiled at me and shook his head. "Thank you, Jane, for allowing us to barge in on you like this."

I wanted to say that I didn't have much choice, but I graciously said, "No problem." I avoided eye contact with Peter, who followed Jerry and Madeline out of the room.

Less than a minute after they'd left, Geoff stuck his head in my lab. "Who was that?" he asked.

"Some of your favorite people," I said. "Our new friends with a key to the city."

"You're kidding me. Peter brought consortium people into the marine center?"

"Peter didn't even bother to tell me that he was conducting a tour of my lab."

"Man, that sucks."

"He's out of control when he finds a potential donor."

"And the consortium members have a lot of money. Maybe they're thinking of turning the center into a hotel."

I laughed and shook my head. "I hope not."

"What did you think of them?" he asked.

"The two who just came to my lab?"

Geoff nodded.

"The guy, Jerry Burns, is nice but a little too slick. The woman is miserable. I suspect she has the big bucks of the cruise industry behind her, so the other members put up with her. She talked at the consortium dinner I attended with Peter and was very transparent about her desire to turn Kodiak into a cruise ship destination, complete with trinket shops."

Geoff groaned. "We need to talk to Peter about letting these people support the center."

"I certainly plan to talk to Peter," I said, "but you know how he is. All he sees is green."

CHAPTER 28

Monday, November 3

8:00 p.m.

Cindy Gardner struggled to hold on to her grocery bags as she exited Safeway and headed across the parking lot to her car. The rain had subsided to an icy drizzle, and she ducked her head as she hurried across the wet pavement. When she reached her vehicle, she had to set some of the bags on the ground while she fumbled in her purse for her keys. Once she popped the trunk, she began lifting her bags into it. If she came to the store more often, she wouldn't have to buy so much heavy stuff at once, but she hated grocery shopping and put it off as long as she could.

Cindy had picked up the last bag from the pavement and was lowering it into her trunk when she realized someone was standing behind her. She whirled to confront the person and saw the hypodermic needle the stranger held in his hand. *Who is this guy, and what is he doing?*

She raised her hands to push him away, but the much stronger man overpowered her. The needle plunged into her arm, and her legs gave out moments later. She dimly saw a dark car pull up beside her, and then everything faded to black.

Tuesday, November 4

9:20 a.m.

After talking to John Shriver's boss for the second time, Patterson climbed into his SUV and sighed. He knew nothing more than he did after John's girlfriend, Vera, had reported him missing. He hadn't left the island on a commercial flight or ferry. His truck was found parked at his work site, and it yielded no information. John or someone else had locked the vehicle and left it where he usually parked. His boss said John never missed work unless he was sick. No one saw him arrive at work on the day he disappeared, and no one saw where he went after he parked his truck. Like Janet Friland, Charlotte Porter, and the other missing people, John Shriver had vanished into thin air.

Patterson's phone rang, and he pulled it from his pocket. "Maureen," he said, "have you learned anything?"

"No," the detective said, "and we have another one."

"Another missing person?" he asked.

"A twenty-nine-year-old named Cindy Gardner was abducted from the Safeway parking lot around eight thirty last night. The cashier who checked her out remembered Cindy as the first customer she handled after returning from her break at eight fifteen p.m."

"Did Cindy put the groceries in her car?"

"We found four bags of groceries in her trunk. The trunk was closed, but the car was unlocked," she said. "I'm standing beside the car now. There's not much to see here, but you're welcome to come out and look at it."

"I'm on my way," he said.

Horner was correct. There wasn't much to see once he got there. Cindy Gardner's blue Nissan Altima sat in a parking space near the front of the store. Four bags of groceries filled the trunk, but the interior of the car held very little besides a pair of sunglasses and a half-full bottle of water in the front seat console.

"Whoever took her was bold to abduct her so near the front of the store."

Horner nodded. "It's well lit here at night, but it was raining, and the checkout lady told me the store was nearly empty."

"Who reported her missing?"

"Her boss," Horner said. "She works in the financial department at the hospital."

Patterson wondered if his wife knew her. Jeanne was a radiology technician at the hospital. "Does she have any family here?" he asked.

"No," Horner said. "Her boss told me that Cindy moved here from Portland, Oregon, a few months ago, after her mother died. She went through a nasty divorce at about the same time and decided to start over somewhere else. She applied for the hospital job through an online job site. Her boss said she's quiet but nice. She didn't think she'd made many friends in Kodiak."

"What's going on here?" Patterson asked.

Horner shook her head. "I have no idea. People are disappearing without a trace. I have no leads on any of my cases." She ran her fingers through her hair. "I'll be honest: I don't know where to turn next."

"Young people," Patterson said. "Males and females, but they're all young."

Patterson returned to trooper headquarters and studied the thin file on the missing people. He added Cindy Gardner's name to the list and wrote down what little he knew about her. Six people had disappeared from Kodiak Island, and the police had no leads. Some had vanished at night, but others had disappeared in the middle of the day. How were they taken? Assuming it was a man, did the abductor drug his victims? Were they forced into his vehicle at gunpoint? Did he use a ruse to convince the men and women to climb into his car? In the case of John Shriver, he doubted this last scenario. Shriver was on his way to his job, and by all accounts, he was a faithful employee. What could someone possibly say to him to make him abandon his workday and climb into their vehicle?

When a serial killer had stalked the island a few months earlier, Patterson had been in this same situation. He'd felt lost and in over his head then, but at least he'd had people to question and leads to follow. He had so little information on these abductions that he had no reason to put a task force together.

He snapped up his phone when it rang. "Patterson."

"Dan, it's Maureen. I just spoke with Detective Brenner with the Homer PD. They have one and possibly two missing people there. He knew about the senator's daughter and thought we should compare notes."

"Were they young people in their twenties or early thirties?" he asked.

"Yes," she said. "The same profile as ours."

"I think we need to update Morgan. I'll give him a call."

Patterson phoned the agent, but after five rings, the call went to voicemail. Patterson left a message asking Nick to call him back.

An hour later, Patterson's cell phone rang. "Dan, it's Nick Morgan. What's happening up there?"

Patterson filled him in on the missing people and waited for the agent to reply.

After several moments of silence, he said, "I'd like to fly up there today, but I'm in a tense situation here, and things finally seem to be happening. We're certain we know who this killer is, but we don't have enough to arrest him. I think we'll wrap things up in a few days, and then I can head back to Kodiak." He paused again. "Do you want me to request another agent to help you immediately?"

Patterson scratched his head. He didn't know what the FBI could do that he and Detective Horner weren't already doing. "No," he said. "If you think you can make it back up here in a few days, we'll wait for you. In the meantime, I'll call FBI headquarters in Anchorage and fill them in on the situation."

"Please keep me up to date," the agent said. "You could have another serial killer on your hands."

"I hope not," Patterson said.

CHAPTER 30

Wednesday, November 5

6:15 p.m.

I stayed late to run more tests on the latest whale stomach samples Leslie had brought me. I'd been surprised by the levels of saxitoxins in the first samples, but I wanted to see if I could somehow quantify the amount of toxin. I liked working at night because the center was quiet, and I could work without distractions.

By 7:30 p.m., I admitted defeat. I'd done all I could do with the samples, and I decided I'd call a researcher at the University of Washington who was on the cutting edge of developing new techniques for plankton analysis. I packed up my stuff and headed for my car. I needed to run to the grocery store before driving home.

As I was putting the last bag of groceries in my vehicle, my phone buzzed. I looked at the display. "Steve, what's up?"

"I hear the plane circling," he said.

"I'm on my way." Luckily, I hadn't bought any frozen food. I closed the back door and jumped in the driver's seat. I made it over the bridge to Trident Basin in record time. I pulled in and parked next to the KFS office beside three other cars, probably left there by hunters who'd flown out into the wilderness to hunt deer for a few days. I hoped my SUV would appear inconspicuous parked next to the other vehicles. When I got out and thoughtlessly slammed the door, I immediately noticed the black SUV parked by the ramp leading down to the float-plane dock. The two men standing by the vehicle turned to stare at me, and I froze. One of the men seemed to be helping a young woman from the rear seat of the SUV, but he quickly pushed her back inside and shut the door.

I didn't know what to do. The last thing I wanted was to lead these men to Steve. I did the only thing I could think of. I walked up to the front door of the KFS office and turned the handle on the doorknob. Of course, the office was locked, and any reasonable person would know the charter service wouldn't be open after dark. I hurried back to my RAV4, pulled out of the parking lot, and sped across the bridge.

Once I was sure the men in the black SUV weren't following me, I pulled over to the side of the road and texted Steve. I told him what had occurred and said I didn't think it was safe for me to go back to KFS tonight. I asked him to call me and tell me what happened with the plane.

* * *

Twenty minutes later, I'd just settled on my couch when my phone rang.

"Did they see you?" Steve asked.

"Yes," I said, "but I pretended I was going to the office and didn't realize it was locked."

"Did you get their license number?"

"No," I said. "The only way I could have seen the back of the vehicle would have been to drive past it. Since it's a dead end in that direction, it would've been obvious I was checking them out. What happened with the plane?"

"Nothing," Steve said. "One of the guys walked down the dock, talked to the pilot briefly, and the pilot jumped in the plane and left. Either you spooked him, or they didn't have anything or anyone for the pilot tonight."

"They had someone," I said. "When I first saw them, the smaller of the two guys was helping a young woman out of the back of the SUV. When he saw me, he pushed her back onto the seat and shut the door."

Steve didn't reply, but I could hear him breathing through the phone.

"Steve," I said, "we need to call the police and report this. There's something illegal going on here. I think these guys are abducting people. Where is the pilot taking them?"

"I know," Steve said, "but I don't think the cops will believe us, and if they come down here in force, they'll scare off the pilot and the men from the SUV. If that happens, we might never get to the bottom of what's going on here. I know how the cops operate: they'll either keep things quiet but take forever to act, or they'll make a big ruckus and ruin the element of surprise. We need to get the plane's tail number somehow, and then the police can trace the plane and its pilot."

After I disconnected, I wrestled with my conscience. *Should I call Nick or Sid and ask for their advice?* I knew they'd both tell me to call the police and let them handle the situation. Steve was right, though. If the police showed up at Trident Basin, they'd scare away the pilot and the men who loaded the plane. The pilot would then probably choose another spot to land and load his "freight."

We have to get the plane's tail number, I thought. *Maybe I can sneak down to the plane while the pilot's refueling.* I decided I'd somehow get the tail number the next time the plane landed at Trident Basin.

I was still holding my phone when it buzzed again. The sound startled me back to the present, and I looked at the screen.

"Hi, Dana, how's it going?"

"I'm fine. I was wondering if you've heard any more about the consortium."

"Not really, but Peter brought two of the members to my lab on a tour of the center."

"Peter had better be careful. They're probably considering what to do with the center after they kick all of you out." She paused. "I haven't heard anything good about them."

I wasn't in the mood to talk about the consortium, but Dana continued. "I asked Parsons about why Carter Brown would go to a consortium meeting, and he had no idea." I knew who she was referring to: Charles Parsons, the Refuge manager. "He said he wouldn't have gone as a representative of the Refuge because the consortium hadn't invited a member of the Refuge to attend. He confessed that the consortium makes him nervous because its members are wealthy and well connected. He'd like to know more about their plans, but so far, they haven't reached out to him."

"Does he think they have enough political clout to pressure the Department of the Interior to make changes to the Refuge?" I asked.

"He wasn't specific," Dana said, "but I can imagine he fears the consortium might press for something like a road across the island, and that would be catastrophic to the integrity of the Refuge."

"I hope they don't have that many connections in DC."

"Something else," Dana said, "and I was shocked Parsons told me this. I think it was because I asked him about Brown. He confided in me that he wasn't very happy with Brown. He told me that he'd somehow convinced the state troopers to allow him to ride with them to Shuyak Island to check out the private hunting lodge there."

"What jurisdiction does the Refuge have on Shuyak? Isn't it state land?" I asked.

"It was state land, but now it's private. Somehow, some group managed to buy or lease it from the state. We're still not sure how it happened, and we're not happy about it. Still, the troopers can go there to check hunting licenses and make sure the lodge owners have their paperwork in order. They can also check to make sure a hunter didn't shoot something out of season or exceed bag limits."

"Why did the assistant Refuge manager want to accompany them?"

"I don't know," Dana said, "and Parsons was furious about it. Brown got off on the wrong foot with him."

"Did Brown say what they found on Shuyak?"

"He told Parsons that everything looked fine, and the lodge manager had all of his paperwork filled out and filed. He said it looked like a legitimate operation."

"Did he tell Parsons why he wanted to go there?"

"He said it was an opportunity for him to see more of the archipelago," Dana said.

"Did Parsons believe him?"

"No," Dana said, "and now Parsons doesn't trust him, so things are a bit tense in the office."

"How do you get along with Carter?" I asked.

"Fine. I think he's great to work with, but there's something a little off with him."

"Dana," I said, thinking. "Do you think the consortium bought Shuyak?"

"Ah," she said. "That's what I wanted to ask you. See if you can learn anything from your consortium buddies."

"I'll do my best," I said.

CHAPTER 31

Thursday, November 6

5:10 a.m.

I awoke to the sound of the wind rattling my windows. I knew storm-force winds of 60 mph were forecasted for the day, and I lay there worrying about damage to my roof. When one heavy gust slammed into the wall behind my bed, I feared the window might crash down onto me. I finally gave up on falling back to sleep and got ready for work. Maybe I'd get there early and plan my call to the professor at the University of Washington. I wanted to be organized and sound like I knew what I was doing.

Wind bent the trees sideways, and rain pelted the pavement when I left home a little after 6:30. I could barely see through my windshield, even with the wipers going full blast. I breathed a sigh of relief when I finally made it to the marine center lot. I looked at the nearby spruce trees and hoped none would fall on my SUV while I was at work. I cinched the hood of my raincoat and held my computer bag under my arm as I sprinted for the center's front door. Since I'd arrived early, I thought I'd have to use my key to open the door, but to my surprise, it was already unlocked.

As I walked down the hall to my office, I noticed that the light was on in the main office. I stepped inside and saw Peter sitting at his desk in his private office. I decided to confront him before I lost my nerve.

Peter looked up from his computer screen as I approached. "Good morning, Jane. You're here early."

"The wind woke me up," I said. "You're early, too."

"No," Peter said. "I usually get here at this time. I like to get some work done while the center is still quiet."

"I'm sorry to interrupt you, but I want to talk to you about the people from the consortium. I don't have a good feeling about them."

Peter leaned back in his chair. "I'm sorry we barged in on you the other day. I wasn't expecting them to ask to see you and your work. I should have refused to take them to your lab until I'd had a chance to talk to you."

I nodded and was about to say something when Peter held up his hand to stop me.

"I can't pick our investors, Jane," he said. "I wish I could, but I'm barely keeping this place afloat as it is. I'd take money from the devil if he offered it, and I'd think you'd appreciate that your job depends on me collecting money. If you start bringing in some big grant money, then maybe you'll be in a position to tell me how to do my job." Peter abruptly sat forward and returned his gaze to his computer.

Ouch! I quietly backed out of his office and walked to my private cubbyhole down the hall. Between the wind and Peter's angry words, my day was not off to a good start.

A little after 8:00 a.m., I called Prof. Anderson at the University of Washington, and we discussed my plankton for twenty minutes. He gave me some good ideas on ways to roughly quantify the amount of toxin in the plankton, but the results would still only amount to an educated guess. His advice did give me confidence that I was doing everything possible, though.

After the phone call, I spent the next two hours preparing for my afternoon genetics class. Once the course was over, I could spend the rest of the afternoon testing the plankton and writing up my results. A little after 11:00 a.m., my phone buzzed.

"Jane, good morning," Corban Pratt said. "Am I interrupting anything? Are you with students right now?"

"No," I said. "I silence my phone when I meet with students and leave it in my office when I have a class."

"Okay, good. I'm in Anchorage now, but I'll be back in Kodiak on Saturday. Could I take you out to dinner?"

"I'm sorry, Corban. I have plans with friends on Saturday." The lie slid out so easily that it startled me.

"Well, maybe next time, then."

"Sure," I said. "Hey, I have a question for you. Did you give Jerry Burns my phone number?"

"What? No, I'd never give out your phone number."

"He called my cell phone, and I can't figure out how he got my number."

Corban laughed. "Jerry could easily find your number online," he said. "The guy is a genius and has lots of resources. Besides, I'm sure I could find your number on the internet, and I'm certainly not as brilliant or well connected as Jerry Burns is."

"It's a little creepy to call someone who hasn't given you her number."

"Jerry can be creepy. I don't know what happened with his ex-wife, but she took out a restraining order against him."

"I'll keep my distance from him." I paused a moment. "Do you know if the consortium bought Shuyak Island?" I asked.

"Shuyak? It's north of Kodiak, right?"

"Yes, it's at the north end of the archipelago."

"Isn't it a state park?"

"It was, but someone recently bought or leased most of the island."

After a long pause, Corban said, "I don't know, but I'll ask Jerry the next time I see him. Did he say anything to you about it?"

"No, but I heard a rumor."

"I'll call you if I learn anything," Corban said.

* * *

My new tests on the plankton didn't yield any further results, so I sat in my lab until 5:30 p.m., writing up my report for Leslie Daniels. When I left the center, I was happy to find that the rain had stopped. Unfortunately, the wind continued to whip the tree branches back and forth. When I pulled into my driveway, I saw several downed branches and wished I had a garage to protect my vehicle. I headed indoors, popped a frozen dinner in the microwave, and poured myself a tall glass of wine. I wondered what Nick Morgan was doing and when I'd see him again. Then, I thought about Sid and realized I hadn't called him to tell him about the previous evening at KFS. I punched his number and listened to his phone ring.

He answered after four rings, sounding breathless. "Hi, Jane."

"Did I catch you at a bad time? You sound out of breath."

"The wind did some damage to my antennas. I was on top of the boat fixing them when I heard the phone ring."

We discussed the wind and the damage to his boat for a few minutes, and then I told him about running into the two men in the KFS parking lot.

"They saw you?" he asked.

"Yes, they definitely saw me, but I was a good distance from them."

"When you drove out of the parking lot, I'm sure they got your license plate number."

"I hadn't thought of that," I said.

"Be careful, Jane. These could be dangerous men. They might come after you if they think you're snooping into their possibly illegal business."

"Did you have a chance to call Sergeant Patterson?"

"No, but I will," Sid said. "We have to figure out what's going on here."

CHAPTER 32

Thursday, November 6

3:35 p.m.

Troy's nerves were frayed, and Brooke couldn't stop shaking and crying. The rain had started in the early-morning hours, and the wind began to blow soon afterward. The rain was miserable, but the fierce wind scared Troy more than he'd ever admit to Brooke. The giant spruce trees swayed violently as the gusts bent them nearly in half. Branches creaked and snapped, and a few slammed to the ground near where Troy and Brooke curled, buried by twigs and moss at the base of one of the tall trees. Troy was afraid one of the branches would fall on them and leave one or both of them maimed or worse.

The wind continuously blew off their camouflage that concealed them from the hunters, and Troy had to quickly rake more debris over them before someone spotted them. The only good thing about the rain was that it helped hold their cover in place. Troy felt as if the pelting droplets penetrated his skin, pushing spears of cold all the way to his bones. He feared he'd soon begin to suffer the effects of hypothermia.

He wrapped his arms tightly around Brooke to help keep her warm and try to calm her. Brooke whimpered softly every time he had to move to rake more moss and limbs over them, and she never seemed to stop crying.

Despite the weather, the hunting continued throughout the day. Troy had heard four gunshots, and one was not far from their hiding spot. Brooke jolted at the sound of each of the high-powered rifle shots, and he put his hand over her mouth when one shot sounded as if it was right on top of them. He feared she'd scream and give away their position.

At 3:30 p.m., Brooke began to squirm.

"What's wrong?" Troy whispered.

"I have to go to the bathroom," she said.

"You can't leave our hiding spot," he said. "It's too dangerous."

Troy feared that Brooke was not thinking clearly. The wind, rain, and rifle shots had completely unnerved her. He didn't know if she desperately needed to go to the bathroom or if she could no longer deny her impulse to flee. He held her tightly, but she suddenly kicked him and pushed hard against his chest. Troy loosened his grip, and Brooke jumped from their hiding spot and fled.

Troy raked more wet moss and branches over his body and curled into a tight ball. A few moments later, a shot rang out. He didn't hear Brooke scream, but from the proximity of the blast, he feared the hunter had been shooting at her. In her panic to flee, Troy didn't believe she'd last long. He felt tears bubble from his eyes and tried not to think about Brooke.

* * *

Somehow, Troy managed to fall asleep. When he awoke, the rain had stopped, but the wind continued. He didn't feel hungry, but he knew he needed to eat and exercise to provide his body with fuel to keep him from slipping into hypothermia. As it was, he couldn't stop shivering. He stood slowly, fighting against the pain from his aching muscles.

Troy stood still for several moments and then began to walk. He feared he'd find Brooke's lifeless body as he headed for the nearest food bin. He didn't have the energy to walk to another trough tonight, and he was afraid he'd get hit in the head by a falling branch if he stayed exposed too long.

When he reached the trough, he pulled a paper bag and a water bottle from it and dropped his empty water bottle into the bin. On the previous nights, he'd ripped into his sandwich and eaten it in two or three bites, but tonight, the sight of the ham and cheese sandwich made his stomach turn. He decided he'd hang on to it until later and was about to leave the illuminated circle near the trough when Icy suddenly appeared near the perimeter of the glow.

"The kid we talked to the other night was shot and killed today. I watched it happen," Icy said as she approached.

"What kid?" Troy asked.

"The guy," Icy said.

"Derek?" he asked.

She nodded.

"You saw him get shot?" The paper sack rattled as Troy's hands began to shake.

Icy nodded again. "Where's the girl who was following you?"

Troy shook his head. "I think she might be dead, too." He angrily wiped tears from his cheeks.

"You can't be so nice," Icy said. "If you try to take care of someone else, you'll both get killed. Stay by yourself and keep your senses sharp." She looked down at the paper sack. "Make yourself eat and drink. You need to keep your brain working, or you'll die."

Icy grabbed a food bag and a water bottle and disappeared into the forest. Troy had never felt so alone in his life. Maybe he'd stand out in the open tomorrow and get it over with. He was tired of avoiding the hunters. The sooner he died, the sooner he'd stop feeling terror and grief.

He headed back toward the hiding spot he'd shared with Brooke. When he was about halfway there, he heard something or someone. His immediate reaction was fear, but then he recognized the sound as a human whimpering. He headed toward the noise, the wet ground muffling his footsteps. As he approached, he shined his light at the form sitting with her back against the trunk of a spruce tree. Her legs were pulled up to her chest.

"Brooke?" He thought he must have been hallucinating because he was certain he'd heard a hunter shoot Brooke.

The young woman didn't speak or look at him.

"Are you hurt?" Troy asked. "Did you get shot?" He knelt on the ground beside her and checked her out with his headlamp. He didn't see blood, but he couldn't see her back. He slowly scooted next to her and sat beside her. After a few minutes, he put his arm around her shoulders.

"I'm sorry," Brooke said. She spoke so softly he could barely hear her. She nuzzled her face into his chest, and he stroked her hair.

They sat together for an hour, and then Troy encouraged Brooke to eat his sandwich and drink some water. He led her back to their hiding spot and found some newly fallen branches to cover them. He knew Icy was right. Brooke would probably panic again, and they might both get shot next time. He couldn't turn her away, though. He'd sacrifice his life to save Brooke if it came to it.

CHAPTER 33

Friday, November, 7

11:00 a.m.

Patterson sat in his chair, leaned his elbows on his desk, and rubbed his temples. He and Detective Horner had just spent the last two hours reviewing their missing persons cases. Instead of making progress on the cases they knew they already had, they'd found two more possible cases to add to the list. Horner took one, and Patterson took the other.

Her case was a young camper who'd disappeared from Abercrombie State Park in early September. The park ranger had found his tent and gear abandoned, but she didn't know the guy's name, so there wasn't much to go on. The ranger didn't believe he'd disappeared from the park and said she thought he'd spent most of his time in town at the bars. This information made it unclear whether the case fell under the jurisdiction of the Alaska State Troopers or the Kodiak PD. Still, for the present, Horner added it to her stack of files.

The disappearance Patterson was investigating was similar to Horner's case. Harry Nordyke was a 22-year-old who'd worked on a salmon seiner the previous summer. Harry drifted after the season ended, often sleeping in a tent at various locations around the island. He didn't have any close friends, but he did have a loose group of acquaintances. In March, a man who knew Harry fairly well had found Harry's tent and possessions at Pasagshak, a recreation area and sport-fishing destination about a thirty-minute drive from Chiniak at the end of the road system on Kodiak. The man checked the tent periodically for the next week, but Harry never returned. As with some of their other missing people, Harry might have walked away from his stuff one day and taken a plane or the ferry to the mainland.

At the time of Harry's disappearance, Patterson remembered asking a trooper to check the airline and ferry manifests to see if he'd left Kodiak sometime in March or April. They hadn't been able to find a record of Harry's departure from the island, so they'd searched the area around Pasagshak and found nothing. The trooper contacted Harry's brother, who said he hadn't spoken to Harry in over a year and didn't even know he was in Alaska. When more pressing matters arose, Patterson had put the case of Harry Nordyke in the filing cabinet and promptly forgot about it. Now, he berated himself for his sloppiness. Harry Nordyke had disappeared months before any of their other cases. Maybe if he'd investigated more thoroughly, he could have arrested the kidnapper or kidnappers and prevented the more recent abductions. However, like the last few cases, Harry had disappeared without a trace, leaving no clues to investigate.

Patterson checked his watch. No matter what happened today, he planned to take Jeanne to her doctor's appointment. She'd experienced cramping all night and was nauseous when he left for work. They were both terrified this pregnancy would end in a miscarriage, as her previous one had. He didn't think Jeanne would survive another failed pregnancy. She'd almost committed suicide after she'd lost her first baby. What would she do if she lost another one?

Patterson's private cell phone buzzed, lifting him out of his dark thoughts. He checked the display. "Sid," he said, "how's retirement?"

"I highly recommend it."

"I'll be there before I know it," Patterson said.

"You're about to have a baby to support," Sid said. "You're just starting out."

Patterson, who already had a grown son from a previous marriage, laughed. "Hardly," he said. "I'll just be an old dad this time around."

"How is Jeanne doing?" Sid asked.

"Day by day," Patterson said. He had no desire to voice his fears.

"I'm sorry to bother you at work," Sid said, "but I was curious. Did you ever find any clues to what happened to the senator's daughter?"

"No," Patterson said. "She walked down the dock and vanished." He paused. "This isn't public knowledge, but she's not our only missing person."

"I heard about the young woman from the Alutiiq Museum."

"They're only the tip of the iceberg. We have several, and no leads on any of them."

When Sid didn't respond, Patterson said, "Sid, do you know something?" Sid was an ex-sergeant with the troopers, and Patterson knew he had excellent deductive reasoning skills.

"I might have something," Sid said. "Let me get back to you."

"This can't wait. If you have something—anything—you need to tell me."

"I'm not sure it's anything, but if I think it could be related to your case, I'll call you immediately."

Patterson disconnected and stared at his phone. Did Sid have some information that could help his case? He was desperate for any leads. If Sid didn't call him back soon, he'd run him down and talk to him.

Patterson spent the next hour searching for relatives of Harry Nordyke. He didn't have many. He phoned his brother and asked him if he'd heard from Harry in the intervening months since the troopers had last spoken with him. The brother said he hadn't talked to Harry in a couple of years, but he said Harry rarely contacted him. He told Patterson that Harry was a wanderer and liked to do his own thing. Patterson asked about other relatives, but Harry's brother said their parents were gone, and they had no other siblings. He gave Patterson the name and number of an aunt, but when Patterson called her, she said she hadn't heard from Harry in five years. Neither the brother nor the aunt could think of any close friends who might know of Harry's whereabouts.

At 2:30 p.m., Patterson left trooper headquarters and drove to his house to pick up Jeanne. He felt cold fear as they sat in the doctor's office waiting to be called. He'd been in some life-and-death situations as a cop but couldn't remember ever being as frightened as he was at that moment. He didn't dare look at Jeanne because he knew she'd see the fear on his face.

"Jeanne Patterson," the nurse called, and he stood and followed his wife to the examining room.

CHAPTER 34

Friday, November 7

7:10 p.m.

The last clouds dissipated in the afternoon, and the temperature plummeted. According to the readout in my SUV, it was now twenty-eight degrees, and it was expected to drop into the single digits during the night. Conditions were perfect for a night flight by our mysterious pilot, and I decided not to wait for Steve to call to tell me the plane was circling. I called him at 5:00 p.m. and told him I planned to come over between 7:00 and 7:30.

"Park in the upper lot," Steve said. "Your car won't be as obvious up there."

I arrived a few minutes after seven. I parked in the upper lot and carefully walked down the road to the KFS building. I didn't see the black SUV in the main lot, so I sped across the opening and around the side of the building. I climbed the stairs and caught my breath. I could make out Steve's form in the moonlit night.

"Good evening," he said. "Have a seat."

I sat in the chair next to him and poured myself some coffee. "Help yourself to the cookies," he said. "I have something to show you. Stand in front of me."

I put my coffee mug on the table between us and stood. I watched in alarm as Steve struggled to push himself out of the deck chair. I walked over in front of him. "What are you doing?" I asked.

"It's okay," Steve said. He pushed himself halfway out of the chair and nearly fell back into it.

I didn't know what to do. I offered Steve a hand, but he told me to stand there and wait a moment. Finally, he stood erect. The moon illuminated the big smile on his face.

"You can stand," I said.

"I can stand, and I'll be walking soon."

I smiled. "Congratulations."

He dropped back into his chair. "This is a crazy disease. My muscles suddenly stopped working."

"But you should recover, right?"

"I'll recover," he said.

Steve was the first to hear the approaching plane. He turned on his headlamp and checked his watch. "It's almost eight," he said. "Showtime."

We watched the plane glide to a graceful landing in Trident Basin and then taxi to the end of the dock. The pilot jumped out of the plane and tied it to the dock. Then, instead of grabbing a gas jug from the rear of the aircraft, as I'd seen him do on previous occasions, he headed up the dock.

I didn't think; I reacted. I raced down the stairs from the deck, and with my back against the side of the building, I edged along it until I reached the front. I watched the pilot hurry across the parking lot to the porta potties at the back of the lot. I didn't see the SUV and the two big guys, so I decided this was my chance.

I hurried around the building to the ramp leading down to the dock. I jogged down the ramp and ran along the dock until I reached the black Beaver. As I neared the plane, I saw two large pieces of—something—on the side of the aircraft. The larger piece covered the plane's midsection, and I wondered if it concealed the name of a charter company. The smaller piece covered what I knew must be the tail number, toward the rear of the plane. Would I be able to remove the cover to see the number?

I hopped onto the float to see more closely how the metal pieces were attached to the plane. I pulled at the edges of the smaller piece. It wasn't metal. It was heavy vinyl. How could vinyl stick to a plane when the plane was airborne? I got my answer when I pulled hard at the edge of it. It didn't budge. I pulled harder and then a little harder. Finally, the vinyl gave, and I nearly fell off the pontoon.

I looked at the numbers and letters I'd uncovered: N6395T. I memorized the tail number and carefully replaced the vinyl. I rubbed my hand over the material to make it stick and hoped it wouldn't fall off the minute I walked away. It seemed to stick, so I hopped back onto the dock and looked toward the ramp. The ramp was the only way off the dock. Could I make it up the ramp to the parking lot before the pilot returned?

I sprinted across the dock as fast as possible and then hurried up the ramp. When I crested the top, I nearly slammed into the pilot. I screeched to a halt and looked at him. He appeared as startled as I felt. Behind him, the two big men held the arms of a young woman. The woman looked confused and groggy.

I fought to slow my breathing. I looked closer at the pilot, who had black, beady eyes and a pinched nose. His lips tightened into a slash across his face.

"Good evening," I said. I walked past the two large men and then hurried across the lot and up the hill to the upper parking lot. I unlocked my car and slid into the driver's seat. I placed my right hand on the top of the steering wheel and dropped my forehead onto my arm. I pushed down my panic, but my hands wouldn't stop shaking. *Do the pilot and the two other men know what I've been doing? Do they have my license plate number from our encounter a few nights ago? Will they come after me?*

Instead of going home, I drove to the marine center and parked in the lot. I texted Steve the tail number of the Beaver and told him to stay quietly hidden until the plane left. I explained that the pilot and the two big men had seen me.

When I reached my house, my phone was vibrating nonstop in my purse. As soon as I entered the house, I poured myself a glass of water and slumped at the dining room table. My hands continued to shake as I lifted the glass to my mouth. I used both hands to hold it while swallowing a long, cool drink.

I dug my phone out of my purse. I'd missed two recent calls from Steve and one from Sid. Sid had also tried to call three times that afternoon, but I'd ignored his calls because I knew he'd insist Steve and I call the police. I returned Steve's call.

"Are you okay?" he asked.

"I think so," I said, "but they saw my face."

"That's not good, Jane." He paused for several seconds. "What about the girl they had with them? She looked very unstable to me."

"The big men were holding her arms, but she wasn't resisting them. They seemed to be helping rather than forcing her. She didn't look at me, though. I could tell there was something wrong with her. I think she was drugged, but I couldn't say for sure."

"Maybe you shouldn't come back here for a while."

"It's time to bring in the police. I'll call Sid and tell him what I found and what we saw. He can call Sergeant Patterson."

"I guess so," Steve said. "We finally have something concrete to give the police."

I disconnected and called Sid.

"I've been worried about you," Sid said. "You weren't returning my calls."

"I'm sorry, but I have something to tell you."

I relayed the events at Trident Basin and said I had the tail number.

"They saw your face?" he asked. I could hear the concern in his voice.

"Just for a moment," I said.

"You have to be more careful."

"I had to take the chance to get the tail number."

"I need to take this to Patterson and the Kodiak police," Sid said. "We can't wait any longer. I talked to Sergeant Patterson today. He asked me not to tell anyone, but I think you and Steve should know."

"What is it?"

"The senator's daughter and the young woman from the museum are just two of several people who have disappeared from Kodiak recently."

"More missing people?" My throat felt dry, and I gulped water.

"I don't know how many," Sid said, "but we have to tell Patterson and the Kodiak police what we know."

"And the FBI." It came out as a whisper. "We should have told them earlier," I said.

"Sergeant Patterson and Detective Horner with KPD might have listened to you, but they wouldn't have taken you seriously until they realized how many missing people they had. I think they've only understood what they were looking at over the last few days. This all happened very recently."

"Will you call Patterson?" I asked.

"I'll phone him as soon as we hang up. Either you or he can call your friend with the FBI."

I disconnected with Sid and stared at my phone. Could Steve and I have stopped the recent abductions if we'd called the authorities sooner and told them about the strange plane and its passengers? Where had the pilot taken these people, and what happened to them after they left Trident Basin? Were they still alive? I refused to let my mind go there. I couldn't bring myself to believe I might have contributed to the death of someone.

I speed-dialed Nick Morgan and was surprised when he answered on the second ring.

"It's nice to hear from you," he said before I even had a chance to say hello. "How are you?"

"Not great," I said. "Do you have time to talk?"

"Sure, I'm at my hotel. It's pouring rain here, so we called a halt to our investigation for the night."

"Are you making progress?"

He laughed. "I don't know. We take one step forward and two steps back. I thought we had him the other day, but he outsmarted us."

"Do you think you know who the killer is?"

"I'm positive I know who he is, but we haven't found enough solid evidence against him to arrest him. It's very frustrating." He paused a moment. "What's happening with you?"

I was embarrassed when a sob escaped my mouth. I told Nick about everything Steve and I had seen at Trident Basin over the last few days. "I was afraid we were making something out of nothing," I said. "We should've gone to the police sooner."

Nick said nothing for several moments, and then, "I'm an idiot," he said. "I've been so wrapped up in this case that I wasn't thinking clearly about the Kodiak situation. I'm the one law enforcement person who knew what was happening with Patterson's cases and what you and Steve were watching at Trident Basin. I should have taken you and Steve more seriously." He let out a long sigh. "I'm sorry, Jane. This is not your fault. It's mine."

"How many people have been kidnapped?"

"I'm not sure, and I don't even think the Kodiak police and the troopers are certain. They have several missing people, but some may have left the island voluntarily and neglected to tell anyone they were leaving."

"Steve saw them escort one man to the plane, but are the rest women?"

"No," Nick said. "Patterson told me they have missing men and women. The one thing they have in common is that they're all young. Several of the missing are young people living on the fringes. One was an out-of-work crewman who was sleeping in a tent at Pasagshak. Another was a young man who was considering a job in Anchorage. His friend wasn't even sure he was missing. He thought that perhaps he'd flown to Anchorage for an interview and decided to stay there. He only became concerned after his phone calls to his friend went unanswered."

"But then there was the senator's daughter and Charlotte," I said. "They were reported missing immediately after they disappeared."

"Yes. I can't make sense of those abductions."

"Are you planning to come back up here to help investigate the disappearances?" I asked.

"I'm booking a flight for tomorrow," he said. "The investigators here will have to do without me for a while. I need to help the Kodiak police and the Alaska State Troopers get to the bottom of this mess. And Jane," he added, "I'm worried about you. These men have seen your face and probably know who you are from your license plate number. Promise me you'll be careful and not take any more crazy chances. You have a knack for getting yourself in trouble."

CHAPTER 35

Friday, November 7

8:35 p.m.

Troy awoke with a start, and for a moment, he forgot where he was. He looked through the tangled pile of moss and branches on top of him and squinted at the bright light directly above him. It took a minute before he realized he was staring up at the moon. Most days, he couldn't wait for it to get dark so he could escape his cave, stretch, pee, and get something to eat, but today, he'd somehow slept into the night.

Troy suddenly remembered Brooke. Was she gone again? He reached beside him and touched her warm body. She was curled up in a ball facing away from him and didn't stir at his touch.

"Brooke," Troy said softly.

Nothing.

"Brooke, are you okay?" he said louder.

This time, he got a moan in reply.

Troy began sweeping the moss, spruce needles, and small branches off them. The night was clear and cold. He turned on his headlight and noted how dim it was. He'd seen fresh batteries in the food bin and would grab a package tonight. He looked down at Brooke, who was more illuminated by the moon than by his light. She remained in a tight ball.

"Come on, Brooke. We need to get something to eat."

"I don't want to wake up," Brooke said in a small voice. "Just leave me here."

"Don't be difficult, Brooke. I said you could stay with me, but you had to do what I said." Troy tried to sound gruff but knew he didn't come across that way. He stared down at Brooke. He wanted to hold her and tell her everything would be okay, but he knew he'd be lying to her. For her own good, she needed to toughen up.

Slowly, Brooke uncurled her legs and sat. She looked up at Troy with a tangle of spruce needles in her long, black hair. Tears flowed from her large, green eyes. "I don't know how much longer I can do this," she said.

Troy reached a hand down to her to help her stand. "You have to stay strong," he said. "We'll get off this island somehow. We just need to survive until we get our chance." Troy wished he believed what he was saying and knew his words must sound hollow to Brooke.

He pulled her to her feet. "We'll just go to the closest food trough," he said. "I don't know how late it is, so I don't want to hike too far."

When they reached the food bin, no one was there, but after a minute, Janet, the young woman with the purple patch on her jacket, emerged from the woods. "I hoped someone else would show up," she said. "I feel so alone."

Troy felt bad for Janet, but he was not about to suggest she join Brooke and him. He had his hands full with Brooke and couldn't take on another responsibility.

"Do you know how late it is?" Brooke asked Janet.

Janet shook her head. "I think it's been dark for two or three hours, but I'm only guessing. They took my watch and phone."

"Have you seen any of the others?" Troy asked.

Janet emitted a sob and wrapped her arms tightly around her chest. "I heard someone get shot not far from my hiding place," she said. "It was horrible. I heard him scream, and then nothing. Then, a few minutes later, I heard these two men talking. The one was congratulating the other one for a good, clean kill." She shook her head rapidly back and forth. "I thought I was going to puke. They actually stood around for a long time, snapping photos and talking and laughing. It was horrible."

"What did they do with the body?" Troy asked.

"After a while, an ATV arrived, and I heard someone say, 'Let's load him onto the cart.' I guess they drove him away. What do you think they do with the bodies?" she asked. "You can't exactly put a human's head on the wall in your trophy room."

"I'd think even photos would be risky," Troy said.

"Did you know the guy who got shot?" Brooke's voice wavered as she talked.

Janet shook her head. "I don't think so," she said. "The only guys I've met are Troy and Derek."

Troy looked down at the ground. "Icy said Derek was killed."

"What!" Brooke and Janet said in unison.

Troy had kept the news from Brooke until now, but he knew she needed to know the truth. "Icy claims she saw him fall," he said.

"Who's Icy?" Janet asked.

"That's the name I made up for the woman who doesn't want to get close to any of us," Troy said.

"I like it," Janet said. "It fits her. If she won't tell us her name, we'll make one up for her."

The three stood in silence for several minutes, and then Janet asked, "Do you believe everything Icy says?"

Troy shrugged. "She *has* been here quite a while. I believe the facts she's told me, but I don't agree with her assessment of things."

"What do you mean?" Brooke asked.

"Icy thinks our only chance is to try to stay alive until someone arrives to save us," he said. "I don't think we can count on anyone saving us. We need to make a plan to attack the main camp."

"How?" Janet asked.

Troy let out a long sigh. "I don't know," he said. "I want to get closer and take a better look at the camp. Maybe I'll see if there's a way we can breach their security."

"No," Brooke said. "It's too dangerous."

Troy gently touched her shoulder. "We have to do something," he said.

CHAPTER 36

Saturday, November 8

8:12 a.m.

Patterson took a seat at the rectangular table in the KPD conference room. He faced Detective Horner across the table and a gruff Chief Feeney at the head of the table. Feeney held an enormous doughnut in his hand as he motioned to Patterson.

"We're taking the lead on this because most of the cases are ours," Feeney said to Patterson, his fat fingers sinking into the glaze on the doughnut.

Patterson sighed and rubbed the back of his neck. "I don't care who takes the lead," he said. "I just want to find these people and stop the abductions. Besides"—a slight smile curved the edges of his lips as he watched Feeney attack the doughnut—"this will soon be the FBI's case."

Feeney pulled the doughnut from his mouth. "Not if I have anything to say about it." His face turned red, and Patterson tried not to look at the sugar glaze lining the police chief's mouth.

Patterson noticed Maureen Horner bite her lip and quickly busy herself with the file folder on the table in front of her.

"How many do we have?" Feeney asked.

"Possibly eight," Horner said, "with at least two more in Homer."

"Let's worry about our cases," Feeney said. "We'll let the Homer PD take care of theirs."

Horner glanced at Patterson, and he knew what she was thinking. Feeney was a lousy detective and had no business being involved in an investigation of this magnitude. Patterson stated what should have been evident to any detective. "If the Homer cases are similar to ours," he said, "then we have to pool our resources and share information to get to the bottom of this."

Feeney's face reddened even further. He looked at Horner. "You can compare notes with Homer, but we have the lead on this."

Patterson knew that Feeney wanted the credit for solving a big case, but unless they could keep him out of the investigation, he was likelier to get credit for badly bungling things.

"I'll talk to Homer," Horner said.

Someone knocked on the conference room door, and a young woman cracked the door open a few inches. She nodded at Feeney and said, "Sir, you have a call."

Feeney stood and looked at Horner. "Keep me posted," he said, abruptly leaving the room without closing the door behind him.

Patterson stood and closed the door. "I don't know how you work for that man," he said to Horner.

"I ignore him," she said, "but he has driven away some good detectives."

"I think we need to get Sid Beatty, Steve Duncan, and Jane Marcus in a room and find out what they know," Patterson said. "I'm irritated that they didn't bring this to us sooner, but they apparently thought they needed the plane's tail number before we'd take them seriously."

"Were you able to trace the number?" Horner asked.

"Yes, it's owned by a charter company in Anchorage called Alaska Wilderness Adventures."

"Have you talked to anyone with the company?"

"No," Patterson said. "I spoke with Agent Morgan, and he volunteered to stop in Anchorage and pay the company a surprise visit this afternoon."

Horner nodded. "I'm glad Morgan is getting involved in the case again. When will he be here?"

"He hopes to make the evening jet, but it all depends on what happens at AWA."

"Should we wait for Morgan before we interview Beatty, Duncan, and Marcus?"

"No. I think we need to move on this as quickly as possible."

"I'm ready," Horner said. She paused a moment. "Maybe you should ask them to come over to trooper headquarters."

Patterson nodded. He knew Horner feared Chief Feeney would barge into the meeting if they held it at KPD. "I'll call them as soon as I return to my office. How does eleven a.m. work for you?"

"Fine," Horner said. "I'll be there."

Patterson returned to his office and called Sid Beatty, Steve Duncan, and Jane Marcus. All three agreed to meet him at trooper headquarters at 11:00 a.m. He popped two Excedrin to help dull the pain in his neck and the back of his head. He knew it was a well-deserved tension headache, and he needed to try to relax.

At least the news about Jeanne's pregnancy had been better than he'd feared. The baby seemed fine, but the doctor had ordered Jeanne to stay home and do as little as possible for the next two weeks. Jeanne had readily agreed. She wanted this baby more than anything and would do everything she could to ensure a healthy pregnancy.

Patterson knew he should also be encouraged by the turn in this investigation. If the pilot of the black Beaver was the one responsible for the recent abductions, then they now had a lead on him. Perhaps Nick Morgan would find the plane and the pilot in the next few hours, and they could wrap up their investigation.

But the pain in the back of his head warned him that the investigation wouldn't end so quickly or easily.

CHAPTER 37

Saturday, November 8

9:12 a.m.

I wasn't surprised when Sergeant Patterson called and said he'd like to interview me at trooper headquarters at eleven. I knew he'd probably also interview Steve and possibly Sid. From Patterson's tone on the phone, I knew he was not happy with me, and I braced myself to be scolded for not going to the police sooner with my suspicions about the black Beaver and the men I'd watched load passengers onto it. Would Patterson do more than simply scold me? Would he arrest and charge me for withholding material information in a police investigation?

I decided to call Nick and ask him what he thought I should do. I wondered if I should take an attorney with me to the interview. I reminded myself that I didn't have an attorney, and I was unlikely to find one on a Saturday. I speed-dialed Nick, but the call went to voicemail, and I remembered that he was probably on a plane heading to Kodiak.

I called Sid and told him I'd been invited to trooper headquarters for an interview.

"Me too," he said. "I think Patterson wants to talk to Steve, you, and me at the same time. He wants to learn as much as he can about the plane."

"Should I be worried? Will Patterson charge me with impeding a police investigation?"

"No," Sid said. "He has much bigger problems on his mind right now. He just wants to know what we know."

"Do you have any idea what this is all about? If the pilot and the two men we saw are involved in a kidnapping ring, what are they doing with the people after they put them on the plane?"

"I have no idea," Sid said. "I've been trying to figure that out, but I've gotten nowhere. The plane is a huge lead, though. I'm sure Patterson's already tracked it down."

At 10:15, Steve called me and asked if I'd also been summoned to trooper headquarters. I told him that Patterson had called both Sid and me.

"Linda's going to drive me over there in about twenty minutes. It takes a while for her to load me into the wheelchair."

"Sid said not to worry. Patterson only wants to know what we saw."

At 10:45, I grabbed my purse and headed out the door. I was nearly to my car when a familiar voice called my name. I looked up. "Hi," I said. "What are you doing here?"

He said nothing but continued to approach. Suddenly, I heard footsteps behind me. I turned to see who was there, and I froze when I recognized one of the two muscular men from Trident Basin, one of the two who'd led drugged people down the dock and helped them board the black Beaver. Was he here to silence me before I could talk to Sergeant Patterson?

When the man was a few feet from me, I turned to run, but he reached out and grabbed my arm. He roughly pulled me to him. I tried to scream when I saw the hypodermic needle in his hand, but from behind, another hand wrapped around my right shoulder and slapped over my mouth.

One of the reasons I'd purchased my little house was that I loved its seclusion in the middle of the spruce forest. I had a small lake in front of my home and spruce trees lining the sides. I had no neighbors across the street who could pry into my business, and I also had no one who could dial 911 and summon help for me.

I felt the needle plunge into my arm, and my fear slowly evaporated as the world faded to black.

CHAPTER 38

Saturday, November 8

10:50 a.m.

Patterson hung up his office phone. He'd spent the last two hours talking to the police and troopers from the towns on the Kenai Peninsula as well as Palmer, Wasilla, Big Lake, and Eagle River. He finished by calling the Anchorage Police Department. None of the smaller cities he'd called had reports of any missing persons whose disappearance fit the description of the abductions on Kodiak. Then, he called Anchorage and talked to a detective who told them they'd investigated three mysterious disappearances in recent weeks. They included two young men and one young woman who'd vanished into thin air.

Patterson felt he could include these three people in his list of disappearances. Their cases were nearly identical to those on Kodiak. The three had vanished, and no one had seen anything. They now had eight abductions in Kodiak, two in Homer, and three in Anchorage, for a total of thirteen missing persons. He reminded himself that they knew about thirteen abductions, but there were likely more. Spring was the time young people arrived in Alaska, and fall was when they left the state to find work elsewhere. Unless the young people had close friends in Alaska, they could easily disappear without anyone noticing. The idea sent a shiver through him. How many disappearances really occurred?

Patterson checked his watch. It was nearly time for Detective Horner and him to meet with Steve Duncan, Sid Beatty, and Jane Marcus. He shook his head. Jane had somehow managed to wind up in the middle of another police investigation. The woman had a nose for trouble, but he had to admit that she also had excellent detective skills.

He stood and stretched, then left his office and headed for the conference room. He heard a noise behind him and saw Steve Duncan wheeling himself down the hall. His chair was old-school. There was nothing electric about it. Patterson waited for Steve, reached down and shook his hand, and then moved behind him to push him the rest of the way to the conference room.

"How are you doing?" Patterson asked.

"Better," Steve said. "I can take a few steps on my own. It's hard work, but I can see slow, steady improvement."

"Good news," Patterson said. "You'll be back flying before you know it."

"I hope so. I can't take much more office work."

They were the first two to arrive in the conference room. Patterson turned on the light and then headed down the hall to grab a pot of coffee and some water bottles. He was returning to the room with his load of coffee and water when he dropped two of the water bottles.

"I've got it," Detective Horner said from behind him as she swooped in and picked up the two bottles from the floor. "Am I the last one here?" she asked.

"No," Patterson said. "We're still waiting on Sid Beatty and Jane Marcus."

Horner checked her watch. "It's not quite eleven yet. I'm sure they'll be here soon."

Patterson, Horner, and Steve Duncan sat around the table, and Patterson poured them each a cup of coffee. "Be careful," he said. "It's strong."

"Just the way I like it," Sid Beatty said as he entered the room and sat on the far side of the table next to Detective Horner.

Patterson slid a cup of coffee down the table to him.

"Jane's not here yet?" Sid asked.

"No," Patterson said. He stared into his coffee cup and wondered what type of relationship Sid and Jane Marcus had. Sid seemed more than just fond of her. He knew that she and Nick Morgan were involved in a romantic relationship. Maybe the woman had a thing for police types. He'd better watch himself. He snorted a laugh before he could catch himself.

"What's so funny?" Horner asked.

Patterson felt his face grow hot. "Nothing," he said. "I was just thinking of something. This investigation certainly isn't funny, though. We have a mess on our hands."

"Did you learn anything interesting from your calls?" Horner asked.

"Yes," Patterson said. "If you can stay for a few minutes after this meeting, I'll fill you in." Patterson didn't wish to discuss the details of the case in front of Steve, Sid, and Jane. He looked at his watch. "Let's get started," he said. "Dr. Marcus must be running a little late."

Patterson opened his notebook and looked at Steve. "Why don't you start from the top, Steve? Tell us everything you saw, along with dates and times, if you have them."

Steve placed a small notepad on the table, and Patterson noticed the effort it took for him to use his arms. He wondered if he would ever fully recover. How did he manage to operate his wheelchair with his weak arms?

Steve talked for the next ten minutes. He'd recorded the details of each time he'd watched the Beaver pull up to the floatplane dock. Patterson knew that without his knowledge of the missing people, he'd probably dismiss Steve's mysterious plane as the vivid imagination of a bored man. In light of all the young people who'd disappeared, however, Steve's story was both believable and plausible.

Once Steve had finished talking, Patterson asked if he could keep his notes with the times and dates when the plane had landed in Kodiak. Maybe he could match the dates up with the disappearances around the island. He fought back the urge to scold Steve for not coming forward sooner. Steve obviously didn't think the police would believe him, and Patterson admitted to himself that neither he nor Horner probably would have believed Steve at first. Still, once the disappearances had begun to stack up, they'd have come back to Steve, and maybe they'd be further along than they were now.

Patterson glanced at his watch again. It was nearly 11:20 a.m. "I wonder where Dr. Marcus is?" he said.

"I'm worried about her," Sid said. "The Beaver pilot and the other two men saw her at the top of the floatplane ramp. There's a light right there, isn't there, Steve?"

Steve nodded. "And the light was working last night."

"They also saw her car a few nights earlier, and if they recorded her license plate number, they'd have no trouble finding where she lives."

Patterson pulled his phone from his pocket and called Jane. The phone rang several times and then went to voicemail. Patterson looked at his phone as if it would tell him where she was. "Maybe she's driving and doesn't want to answer the phone." He looked at Sid. "When did you last speak to her?"

"Around ten a.m.," Sid said.

"I talked to her at ten fifteen," Steve said. "She was planning to be here at the meeting."

"Something must have held her up," Horner said. "I think it's too soon to worry."

"Jane is very conscientious," Sid said. "I think she'd call if she got delayed."

Patterson nodded at Sid. "We'll head over to her place if she doesn't arrive soon, but in the meantime, Sid, why don't you tell us about this plane and its occupants? You have excellent detective skills. What was your insight?"

"I'll be honest," Sid said. "At first, I thought Steve's imagination was getting the better of him. I wish I'd taken it seriously sooner, and I apologize for not coming to you when I knew about the plane." Sid shrugged. "I agreed with Steve at the time. You couldn't do much without a tail number, and we couldn't see the number."

Patterson looked at his notebook for a minute and then pushed it away from him on the table. He shook his head and looked at Sid. "I can't understand what's happening here. If kidnappers are abducting young people and flying them off the island, then where are they taking them? We suspect at least three people are involved in this. We have the pilot and the two men who are helping him. What's going on?"

"And I doubt any of those three men is in charge of this kidnapping ring," Horner said. "They're the hired helpers."

"A Beaver can fly 450 miles before it needs to refuel," Patterson said. "I assume we're looking for a destination within 450 miles of Kodiak."

"I think it's less than that," Steve said. "I've watched the pilot refuel, and he only adds a few jugs to his tank. Of course, I don't know how much is still in the tank, but he'd allow himself plenty of fuel in case he ran into bad weather. I calculated that he must be flying 250 to 300 miles at the most."

Patterson nodded. "So, he could be flying back to the mainland."

Steve shrugged. "But why would these people be flying down from Anchorage, abducting people on Kodiak, and then flying them back to Anchorage?"

"Agent Morgan plans to pay Alaska Wilderness Adventures in Anchorage a surprise visit this afternoon and find out who was flying their Beaver to Kodiak after dark," Patterson said.

"Is he taking backup?" Sid asked.

Patterson shook his head. "He doesn't want to do anything to tip them off. He hopes to take them by surprise, and with any luck, the plane will be at Lake Hood."

"They may already be on their guard," Sid said. "The pilot and the two other men saw Jane, and they had to know she was watching them."

At the mention of Jane, Patterson and Horner both looked at their watches. "Why don't we wrap this up for now." He looked at Horner. "Maureen, if you have a few minutes, will you join me? We'll drive over to Jane's house and see if we can find her. We can talk on the way."

Horner nodded, and everyone except Steve stood. "Do you have a ride home?" Sid asked him.

"I can call my wife," Steve said.

"Nonsense," Sid said. "I'll give you a ride."

Patterson and Horner stood back while Sid wheeled Steve out of the conference room and down the hall.

"I'm sure Sid won't be far behind us looking for Jane Marcus," Patterson said.

"Are the two of them friends?" Horner asked.

"Something like that," Patterson said. "He's very fond of her."

Horner followed Patterson to his office. "Let me look up Jane's address," Patterson said. "I know I have it here somewhere from the last time she inserted herself in the middle of an investigation."

"The murdered pilot," Horner said. "She nearly got herself killed, didn't she?"

Patterson nodded. "She's smart, but she takes too many chances."

"This time, she might have gone too far," Horner said.

* * *

As the SUV pulled out of the parking lot of trooper headquarters, Patterson said, "Three more abductions from Anchorage fit our profile."

"I found two more in Homer," Horner said. "Once I alerted them to what was happening here, they looked at their police reports more carefully and discovered they had two more potentially mysterious disappearances. They were like some of the ones we had here. Two young fishermen who might have decided to leave on their own, but their friends couldn't reach them, so they reported them as missing to the police. The Homer police didn't take the disappearances too seriously, because they thought both young men would show up eventually. When I told them what was happening here, they looked at the cases again, and they're both still missing."

"When did they disappear?" Patterson asked.

"One in mid-September and the other just a couple of weeks ago."

Patterson sighed. "I bet this is just the tip of the iceberg. These kidnappers seem to take twentysomethings who are loners and won't necessarily be missed. I asked the towns I called to look hard at any recent reports of missing people, no matter how sketchy they seemed."

"These guys screwed up when they kidnapped the senator's daughter," Horner said.

"They either screwed up or targeted her for some reason."

Horner stared out the window for several seconds and then looked at Patterson. "Interesting thought," she said. "Janet Friland's mother, Senator Ames, has her share of enemies in the Senate."

Patterson nodded. "Perhaps Janet Friland is the key to this case."

He pulled into Jane Marcus's driveway behind a dark-red RAV4. He didn't know if this was Jane's vehicle or if someone else had parked in her driveway. He and Horner walked to the front door and rang the doorbell. After several seconds, Patterson knocked on the door. When there was no reply, he knocked again. Finally, he jiggled the doorknob, but it was locked.

He looked at Horner and shrugged. "Let's look in the windows to see if anything's amiss."

The two officers walked around the house and peered through each window, but everything looked in order. They had a good view of the front room and the kitchen through the large picture windows facing the lake, but they saw no sign of Jane and nothing out of order.

Patterson took two steps back and blew out a breath. He knew he shouldn't jump to the worst conclusion, but based on recent events, this didn't look good. Dr. Marcus was slightly older than the other kidnapping victims, but perhaps she'd seen too much, and the kidnappers had taken her to keep her quiet.

As Patterson and Horner walked around the house to the driveway, a green pickup pulled up in front, and Sid Beatty climbed from the front seat and slammed the door. He must have quickly read the situation as he glanced from Jane's vehicle in the driveway to the two officers. Patterson felt defeated, and he knew he was displaying his feelings from the slump of his shoulders to his slow, deliberate gait. He should have done something to protect Jane as soon as he'd known that the potential kidnappers had seen her and probably knew her license plate number.

"She's gone, isn't she?" Sid asked as he approached Patterson and Horner.

"We don't know that yet," Horner said.

"But it doesn't look good," Patterson admitted.

Sid ran his fingers through his collar-length gray hair. "I should have kept an eye on her," he said.

"I don't mean to pry into your personal life," Patterson said, "but do you have a key to Jane's door?"

"What?" Sid cocked his head to the side. "No, no," he said. "We're just friends. I don't have a key."

"We need to check her house better," Patterson said.

"I know some of her friends," Sid said. "Let me make a few calls."

Fifteen minutes later, Dana Baynes arrived at Jane's house. "What happened?" she asked, scrutinizing the faces of Sid Beatty, Sergeant Patterson, and Detective Horner.

"Jane is missing," Sid said. "We need to get into her house to ensure she isn't sick or injured and unable to get to the door."

"Missing like Charlotte and the senator's daughter?" Dana's green eyes flashed at Sid, and her dark curls vibrated as her body trembled. "She's gone?" Her last two words were barely audible.

"We don't know where she is," Patterson said. "That's why we need to look in her house."

Dana pulled a key from her pocket and hurried to the front door. Her hands shook as she inserted the key into the lock. She pushed the door open and was starting to enter the house when Horner stepped in front of her.

"Please wait out here with Sid while Detective Horner and I check the house," Patterson said.

Jane's house was small and neat. It took less than a minute to walk through the rooms. Nothing seemed amiss, and the officers saw no sign of Jane. When Patterson emerged from the front door, he looked at Sid's and Dana's tense faces and shook his head. "She's not in there," he said.

Dana took a step back. "Not Jane," she said.

Patterson cleared his throat. He couldn't think of anything encouraging to say. "It doesn't look good," he admitted.

"I'll get a forensic team over here," Horner said. "I don't expect to find much," she added with a shrug, "but you never know."

"What can we do?" Sid asked. "There must be some evidence here."

"Not if it's like the other abductions," Patterson said, "but we'll take a hard look in case the kidnappers got sloppy this time." He nodded at Sid. "You know as well as I do that you and Dana need to leave now and let us investigate this."

CHAPTER 39

Saturday, November 8

2:22 p.m.

An Anchorage-based FBI agent met Nick Morgan when he departed security at Ted Stevens Anchorage International Airport. The young woman introduced herself as Agent Jennifer Adams. She wore her long, dark hair in a ponytail, and Nick thought she looked like a teenager. He tried to remember what it was like to be her age.

Nick threw his bag in the back of the black SUV sitting at the curb outside the airport. "It's cold," he said.

"Yes, sir," Agent Adams said. "It got down into the single digits overnight. It's only fifteen degrees now."

Nick buckled his seat belt. "Do you know where we're headed?"

"Yes, sir," Adams said. "Alaska Wilderness Adventures." She eased the SUV away from the curb. "You said no backup, right, sir?"

"Just you, Adams," Nick said and smiled at her. "I'm not expecting trouble, and I want to take them by surprise. This is a legitimate charter company. I want to hear how they explain why a pilot has been flying one of their planes to Kodiak after dark with the tail numbers obscured."

"I can't imagine a good explanation for that."

"Neither can I."

Agent Adams turned onto International Airport Road, and within five minutes, she was pulling up in front of the small charter office for AWA. She parked the SUV and followed Nick into the office.

A young woman sat behind a high counter, staring at a computer screen. It took her several seconds to acknowledge the agents as they stood at the counter. Finally, she looked up and pushed her large, round glasses up on her nose. "Yes?"

Nick showed the woman his badge, and her posture straightened. "Does your company have a plane with the tail number N6395T?" he asked.

"Yes," the woman said. "Why?"

"May we talk to your boss?" Nick asked.

"He isn't here," the dispatcher said.

Nick looked at his notebook. "His name is Butch Parker, correct?"

"Well, yes, I guess so, but Mr. Parker doesn't really run the business much anymore."

"Then who does?"

"His son, Blake, oversees the day-to-day operation."

"And is he here?"

The dispatcher shook her head. "He's out on a flight right now. He won't be back for an hour or so."

"Is he currently flying N6395T?"

"Yes." The dispatcher pushed her large glasses higher up on her nose.

"Can you tell me if you've had any recent charters to Kodiak?"

The dispatcher slowly shook her head. "I don't think so, but let me check."

Nick waited while the dispatcher punched keys on her computer and stared at her screen.

"No, sir," she said when she looked up from the computer. "No flights to Kodiak in at least the last three months."

Nick tapped the counter with his fingers. "We'll wait here for Blake to return."

The dispatcher shrugged.

Nick's phone vibrated, and he looked at the display. "I'll be back in a few minutes," he told Agent Adams and then walked out the front door.

"Dan," Nick said. "I'm at Alaska Wilderness Adventures now, but the manager and plane are out on a flight. I'll sit here and wait for him to return."

"We have a problem, Nick." Patterson's voice sounded tight. "Jane has disappeared."

"What do you mean?"

"I asked her to attend a meeting this morning," Patterson said, "and when she didn't show, Detective Horner and I drove over to her house. Her car is there, but there's no sign of Jane."

"Did you look in her house?" Nick wiped his sweaty hand on his pants.

"A friend let us in, and everything looked fine. We saw no sign of a struggle." Patterson added, "Horner has a KPD team there now, but I don't think they'll find anything useful."

"I'm on my way," Nick said and then disconnected. He called Alaska Airlines and booked a seat on the 3:50 flight to Kodiak.

He threw open the door to the AWA charter office. He motioned to Agent Adams. "Jennifer, I need a ride back to the airport."

"Yes, sir," Adams said, pulling her car keys from her pocket as she rushed out the door to the SUV.

Nick appreciated Adams for not asking questions. She simply followed orders from a senior agent. "I have an emergency down in Kodiak," Nick said. "After you drop me off, I want you to return to AWA and wait for Blake Parker and Beaver N6395T to return."

"Sir?"

"You need to convince him to accompany you to FBI headquarters," Nick said. "Can you do that?"

"Yes, sir, but what reason should I give him?"

"Tell him his assistance is needed for an ongoing investigation," Nick said. "I'll call your bosses in Anchorage and tell them what's happening. This is a major kidnapping case, at the least."

"The senator's daughter?" Adams asked.

"Her and several others."

Adams pulled up in front of the airport and looked at Nick, her eyes wide. "Yes, sir. I'll get the pilot downtown to headquarters."

Nick grabbed his bags and hurried into the airport. He looked at his watch. It was already 3:30 p.m., and if the flight was on time, the gate agents would be boarding it. Luckily, there was only a short line through security, but the gate for the flight to Kodiak was at the end of the concourse. Nick dialed the Anchorage FBI office as he hurried to the gate. He knew the lead agent at the Anchorage office very well, and he explained to him as quickly as possible about the abductions and the breaking evidence in the investigation.

"Sergeant Patterson contacted us a few days ago," Agent Keeson said, "but I wasn't aware they had new evidence in the case. I assume that's why you asked for an agent to meet you at the airport."

"Yes," Nick said. "We just got the evidence last night. We think the pilot of the Alaska Wilderness Adventures Beaver with the tail number N6395T is transporting people against their will to some unknown destination."

"I'll send another agent to the charter company to help Agent Adams," Keeson said. "I'll let you know when we have him."

Nick hurried down the ramp and onto the plane just before the attendants shut the door.

* * *

An hour later, the plane touched down on the runway in Kodiak. The tarmac was wet, but the sky was only partly cloudy and looked as if it was clearing. Nick knew that a clear sky meant a plummeting temperature. *Where is Jane? Is she cold, and did the kidnappers drug her? Do they plan to kill her?*

Nick hurried through the tiny, crowded airport and out the door. Patterson's SUV sat in front of the airport, and Nick opened the passenger door and climbed into the vehicle. He shook hands with Patterson.

"I'm sorry, Nick," Patterson said. "I should have had someone watching Jane and her house. I knew she saw the men at the basin, and I should have realized how much danger she was in."

Nick had been thinking the same thing, but he said, "You couldn't have known they'd abduct her. They must've taken her this morning, when it was light. That's a high-risk abduction."

Patterson nodded as he pulled out of the airport and headed toward town. "They took her this morning in front of her house. I think she was on her way to trooper headquarters for our meeting."

"Jane is smart," Nick said. "She'd never stand there and let one of the men she'd seen at Trident Basin walk up to her."

"They must have taken her by surprise, or perhaps they had a gun," Patterson said.

"Or, she knew her abductor and didn't sense the danger until it was too late," Nick said.

"You have agents meeting the Beaver when it returns to Alaska Wilderness Adventures?" Patterson asked.

Nick nodded. "The pilot of the Beaver, at least today, anyway, is the son of the owner of AWA. The son's name is Blake Parker, and I'd bet he's the one who flew the plane to Kodiak in the dark. According to the dispatcher, Blake runs the company, so no one would likely question him if he left Lake Hood in the evening."

"The manager is probably the only one who could get away with putting so many hours on the plane," Patterson said.

Nick nodded. "Let me call the agent to see if the plane has returned yet."

He dialed Agent Adams's number. "What's going on up there?" Nick asked as soon as she answered her phone.

"Nothing," she said, her voice a whisper. She remained quiet for a few moments and then must have left the charter service office because Nick could hear the buzz of airplanes in the background. "Sir," she said. "The plane should be back by now. I think the dispatcher tipped him off while I was taking you to the airport."

Nick cursed. He should have stayed at the office to keep an eye on the dispatcher. If she liked her boss, then of course she'd find a way to tip him off. On the other hand, she'd probably texted him on a phone or inReach, and she could have done that even if he'd been sitting in the office. No matter what happened in Anchorage, Nick didn't regret his decision to fly down to Kodiak. He was determined to find Jane before something happened to her.

"Call me as soon as you have something," Nick said and then disconnected.

He exhaled a long, steadying breath and told Patterson what Adams had said.

The two men remained quiet for several seconds, and then Nick said, "Let's look at Jane's phone records to see if anyone called her before she disappeared. If she knew her kidnapper, perhaps he called Jane to set up a quick meeting."

Patterson nodded. "I'll start on it as soon as I return to the office."

"Can I borrow one of your vehicles?" Nick asked. "I want to talk to Steve Duncan again."

"I'll do one better. I'll get you an SUV and a driver."

"Thanks, Dan," Nick said. "We've got to find her."

"I have a meeting set up right now with Detective Horner at KPD," Patterson said. "Jane's case is hers, and she can bring us up to speed on what they're doing. I'll ask her about the phone records. If she doesn't already have them, I'll see if she minds me getting them."

Nick couldn't remember ever feeling so helpless. He needed to act, do something—anything—to get Jane back, but what could he do? What would the kidnappers do with her? He doubted they'd whisk her away from Trident Basin. They had to know the authorities would be watching the floatplane dock. Would they put her on a boat to get her off the island? The police couldn't watch every vessel leaving the two boat harbors. They needed more information so they could narrow down the possibilities.

Detective Horner met Patterson and Nick at the front door of the police station and motioned for them to follow her to the conference room. Nick was relieved not to see Chief Feeney sitting in the room when they arrived. Perhaps Horner hadn't informed him of this meeting.

Nick appreciated that Detective Horner didn't pause for small talk. "The crime scene techs are still at Jane's house," she said. "I talked to them a few minutes ago, and they haven't found anything useful yet. I doubt they will, but I told them to keep trying." Her blue eyes pierced into Nick's. "This is like the others," she said, shaking her head. "We have nothing. What's happening with the plane?"

As if on cue, Nick's phone rang. "Agent Adams, what do you have?" he asked.

"Sir," Adams said. "Agent Peters and I decided to pressure the dispatcher. We felt she wasn't telling us everything about Blake Parker and the Beaver."

"Did you get anything out of her?" Nick asked.

"It didn't take long," Adams said. "She said Blake texted her, told her he had an emergency, and asked her to take him and the Beaver off the schedule for the next three weeks."

"Did she say how long she'd known about Blake and his emergency?" Nick asked.

"Not at first," Adams said, "but she finally admitted that she'd texted him to let him know we were looking for him."

"Did she know what Blake was up to? Did she know he was making night flights to Kodiak?"

"She says she didn't, but we're taking her downtown to question her further."

"Good job, Agent Adams," Nick said. "Keep me informed."

Nick put his phone back in his jacket pocket. He looked at Horner and Patterson and shook his head. "The dispatcher alerted Blake Parker, and he disappeared."

Patterson snapped his phone out of his shirt pocket. "I'll put out a BOLO to all state airports and law enforcement officers. He has to land and refuel somewhere."

Patterson left the conference room to make calls, and Horner sat back in her chair. "It's a floatplane," she said. "He could land anywhere to refuel."

"So far, he hasn't made many mistakes," Nick said, "but maybe someone will see the plane."

When Patterson returned to the room, they went over everything they knew about the case. For Patterson and Horner, this was a review, but Nick didn't know some of the information.

"How could so many people disappear, and nobody sees a thing?" Nick asked.

"Many of the people were abducted at night or in the early-morning hours, and some were taken in bad weather." Patterson shrugged. "However, the senator's daughter and the young woman in Homer disappeared in reasonably good weather, in the middle of the day. One was snatched in the boat harbor, and the other disappeared soon after leaving a bookstore in the middle of town."

"They must be fast and experienced," Nick said.

"Where are the kidnappers taking these people, and what are they doing with them?" Horner asked.

"Nothing good," Patterson said.

"I wondered if it might be one of those 'scared straight' things where wealthy parents pay someone to take their addicted kid to a tough rehab camp," Nick said. "But there's no indication that most of these young people have drug problems."

"Just the opposite," Patterson said. "The ones we've been able to piece together a background for are upstanding citizens preparing for their future."

"Jane is older. She doesn't fit the profile," Nick said.

"No," Horner agreed, "but they took her because she can identify them."

Nick nodded. "That's what worries me. If the kidnappers kept the others alive for some purpose and Jane doesn't fit the narrow parameters for their ideal victim, they might kill her to minimize the threat." Nick's hand began to shake, and he quickly dropped it to his leg and hid it under the table.

"We need to get ahold of that pilot," Patterson said. "He's the only lead we have."

"I want to speak to Steve again," Nick said.

"You should also talk to Sid Beatty," Patterson said.

"Who is he?" Nick asked.

Patterson's face turned red. "Sid is Jane's friend, and he watched the plane come and go one night. Sid is an ex-sergeant with the troopers, and he has good instincts. He lives on his boat in the harbor. I'll let him know you're coming."

* * *

Twenty minutes later, Nick sat in the passenger seat of a trooper SUV. His driver was a young trooper named Broghan Vena. Nick was relieved to find that Vena was not a talker.

Vena drove Nick to Steve Duncan's house and told Nick he'd wait for him. Nick rang the front doorbell of the small house. A few seconds later, an attractive woman in her thirties with layered light-brown hair and soft brown eyes opened the door.

Nick tried to smile and introduced himself.

"Sergeant Patterson just called and said you were on your way." She opened the door and ushered Nick into the house. "I'm Steve's wife, Linda. Steve is just waking up from a nap. I'll have him out here in a minute, but in the meantime, please take a seat in the living room."

Nick walked into the small, tidy room and sat on a comfortable pale-green couch. As soon as he was seated, a cat with long, white fur and piercing blue eyes jumped up beside him. Nick had nothing against cats, but he knew if the creature crawled onto his lap, he'd be wearing the white fur for the rest of the day. He tried his best to ignore the cat as the animal studied him.

"Jerry, get down," Linda said when she returned to the room, pushing Steve.

The cat jumped to the floor and disappeared under the couch.

"Jerry?" Nick couldn't help himself.

Steve smiled and held out his hand to Nick. "It's a long story," he said.

"I assume that you've heard about Jane?" Nick asked.

Tears trailed down Steve's cheeks. "It's my fault," Steve said. "I never should have involved her in this."

"Steve," Nick said, "don't blame yourself. I know Jane well, and she loves getting in the middle of dangerous situations. She's smart and capable, though."

Steve nodded. "I know. I didn't want her to run down to the plane and look at the tail number, but we wouldn't know what we do now if she hadn't. Did you find the pilot and the plane?"

"He found out we were looking for him and disappeared with the plane. I'm afraid we're back at square one."

Steve shook his head and wiped his eyes. "Poor Jane," he said.

Linda offered the two men coffee or water, but they both declined.

"I know you've been through this several times," Nick said, "but would you tell me everything again, including your thoughts on where this pilot could be flying his victims?"

Steve told Nick in as much detail as he could recall about each time he'd watched the Beaver land at Trident Basin. He also told Nick how the men saw Jane and her vehicle one night when she pulled into the parking lot at KFS. "Jane thought the men had drugged their victims, and she suspected they were taking them against their will."

"But none of the people the men helped down the dock to the Beaver ever tried to escape?" Nick asked.

"These are big, muscular men. I don't think the victims could have escaped if they'd tried."

"Still," Nick said. "No one screamed for help or did anything to indicate the men were taking them against their will?"

Steve shook his head. "It was strange," he said, "but I think the victims were either drugged or scared—probably both. I think the rolls of carpet or tarp held the victims the men thought might be a problem. I suspect they drugged those people until they were unconscious and then carried them to the plane."

Nick nodded. "It makes sense," he said. "Where do you think the pilot took his victims?"

Steve shrugged. "I've spent a lot of time thinking about where the pilot goes after he leaves here. I doubt he has enough fuel to fly back to Anchorage, so he must go somewhere to refuel and then heads back to Lake Hood." He shook his head. "It's a big radius. He could fly anywhere on the island or in the archipelago. He probably could also make it to the mainland—maybe to Geographic or Hallo Bay."

"Which direction does he go when he leaves here?" Nick asked.

"He's always taken off to the east and then turned north, no matter what the wind is doing," Steve replied. "I think he flies in that direction to avoid being detected by the tower. He stays very low, but I still find it hard to believe the tower's never picked up the plane on radar. I think you should check with the tower."

"Could you tell if he continues to fly north after he gains altitude?" Nick asked.

"I haven't been able to see him, of course, but I've listened carefully and never heard him circle and fly in a different direction. I don't think he's flying to the south end of the island, but I can't rule it out." Steve sat back in his wheelchair. "It's just a guess," he said. "I don't know anything for sure."

"You're an expert on this island," Nick said. "You've helped me more than you could know. Are you planning to sit on the KFS deck this evening?"

"Yes," Steve said. "I doubt the Beaver pilot will return there now, but I plan to watch in case he takes the chance."

"Please call me immediately if you see the plane. Do you still have my card?"

Steve looked at Nick and nodded. "Wouldn't it be nice if we could catch them trying to put Jane on the plane?"

* * *

Nick next asked Vena to drive him to the boat harbor in search of retired sergeant Sid Beatty from the Alaska State Troopers. He'd never heard Jane talk about Sid, but Nick knew there was a lot about Jane he didn't know. He planned to remedy that situation as soon as he found her.

Nick saw the mast long before he saw Sid's boat. As he walked down the long dock with boats tied in stalls on either side, he followed the tall mast of the sailboat as a guidepost for where he was headed. Finally, the gleaming white boat with green trim came into view. When he stopped beside the boat, he wished he'd called ahead. He didn't feel comfortable boarding a boat without the owner's permission. It was a good way to get shot.

The boat hatch swung open in answer to his dilemma, and an older man with gray, collar-length hair stepped on deck. "May I help you?" he asked. "You look lost."

157

Nick knew he must look foolish, but he quickly regained his bearing. "Are you Sid Beatty?"

"Yes," the man said. "And what's your name?"

"I'm Special Agent Nick Morgan with the FBI. Would you like to see my credentials?"

Sid shook his head. "I believe you. Sergeant Patterson told me to expect a visit from you. You have questions about Jane."

Sid threw the dish towel he'd been holding over his shoulder and motioned for Nick to follow him down to the galley of his boat.

"This is a nice boat," Nick said as he accepted a cup of coffee from Sid.

"Please sit," Sid said, pointing to the built-in bench on the far side of the small table. Sid sat across from him.

"As you mentioned, Sergeant Patterson suggested I speak to you," Nick said. "He said you watched the Beaver come and go with Steve and Jane."

"Once," Sid said. "I only joined them once. Jane wanted to get my opinion on the operation. She wasn't sure what to think, but she knew Steve believed the pilot and the other two men were drugging people and flying them someplace against their will."

"What impression did you get? Did you see the two men put someone on the plane?"

"I saw them put a roll of what I thought looked like carpet on the plane. Steve thought there was a human inside the carpet roll." Sid shrugged. "I thought his imagination was getting the best of him, but now, I wish I'd paid more attention to him. I knew about the senator's daughter and the other young woman who vanished in front of the Alutiiq Museum, but I had no idea how many people had recently gone missing on this island. If I had, the plane operation would have set off alarm bells."

Nick nodded. "I didn't put much stock in the mysterious plane, either. I thought the pilot should be arrested for flying under minimums, but I had too many bigger problems to deal with at the time." He paused. "You were a trooper on this island for a long time. Someone is apparently abducting young people and transporting them somewhere. What's going on? Where are they taking them? Where is Jane?"

"I wish I knew," Sid said. He stood, walked across the galley, and retrieved a large roll of paper. He returned to the table and spread out a map of the Kodiak Archipelago. "The plane flew north, but it could have made a big U-turn away from the island, where no one could see or hear it. Wherever it was headed, I don't think it was far. The pilot was flying after dark, a very dangerous thing to do around these mountains. I'd guess he only had to make a short hop to his final destination. I think it's safe to assume that when he left Trident Basin, he headed for someplace in the Kodiak Archipelago. To narrow down the possibilities, let's say the pilot continued on a northerly path." Sid pointed at the dot marking the town of Kodiak on the map. Then, he moved his finger north and pointed at Afognak Island. "I think we need to take a close look here."

Nick studied the map. "Do you have any idea where we should start?"

Sid shrugged. "There's a logging camp on Afognak and a couple of lodges but not much else. There's a state park on the eastern side and a chunk of the Kodiak National Wildlife Refuge on the northern portion."

"Have you talked to Sergeant Patterson about this?"

"Not yet," Sid said. "I was waiting until you'd had a chance to interview the pilot. Can you tell me how that went?"

Nick shook his head. "The pilot and the plane disappeared."

Sid slapped the table and cussed. "I blame myself for this. I should have listened to Jane and kept an eye on her after I knew the pilot and the other two men saw her walking up the ramp from the dock."

Nick sat back and studied Sid. *What type of relationship do he and Jane have?* He'd assumed they were acquaintances or maybe friends, but the tears trailing down Sid's cheeks suggested their relationship could be more serious. Sid was old enough to be Jane's father, but what did age matter?

"I blame myself for Jane's disappearance," Nick said. "I also should have listened to her and taken the situation on the island more seriously. As always, I was trying to spread myself too thin. She deserves better from me."

CHAPTER 40

Saturday, November 8

7:35 p.m.

Icy was at the food trough when Troy and Brooke arrived. She looked up at the pair and shook her head. "I see you didn't listen to me," she said. "You're still together. You're going to get yourselves killed."

"We're being careful," Brooke said.

Icy snorted. "Yeah, right." She threw her empty food sack in the trough, turned, and left.

"I don't like her," Brooke said. "She's mean."

"She's trying to help us," Troy said, "and she's right. Two people make a bigger target than one person."

Brooke looked up at Troy, tears filling her big, beautiful eyes. She stood on her toes and kissed Troy on the mouth. He took a step back. He'd been fighting his feelings for Brooke.

"I'm sorry," Brooke said. "Should I not have kissed you?"

"I'm not complaining," Troy said, "but for now, we have to focus on staying alive."

Brooke nodded and looked at the ground.

A young man with shoulder-length blond hair slowly approached the food bin. "Are you going to shoot me?" he hesitantly asked Troy.

"No, man, we're prey animals like you."

"Isn't this the craziest f-ing place you've ever been?"

Troy nodded. "It's surreal."

"I'm Brooke, and this is Troy," Brooke volunteered.

The tall, thin man held out his hand to Brooke. "Tom Stroud," he said. He shook Brooke's hand and then Troy's. "How do we get out of this place?" Tom asked.

"I don't know," Troy said, "but I've been thinking about it. I think we'll have to attack the main camp."

"Attack with what?" Tom asked.

"I'm working on it."

The three stood silently for a few moments, and then Tom said, "I have no idea how I got here. I think I left my apartment to go to the store, and the next thing I knew, I was in the woods, and people were shooting at me."

"I think they drugged us," Troy said. "I don't remember much, either."

"I remember a woman telling me to get dressed," Brooke said, "and then I woke up leaning against a tree."

"I'm ready to get a gun and shoot back," Tom said.

Janet wandered up to the group, and Brooke introduced her to Tom.

"I saw a young woman get shot and die right in front of me a couple of days ago," Tom said. "I wanted to see if I could help her, but I knew they'd shoot me, too."

"It's best to stay hidden during the day," Brooke said.

"I've figured that out," Tom said. "The day I saw the woman get shot, I was sitting in a spruce tree. It's not a bad hiding place because the hunters never look up. They look forward and to the sides and sometimes backward, but they never look up at the trees. But it's difficult to sleep when you're sitting in a tree, and if you go to sleep, you'll likely fall out of it."

"We sleep in a depression under a spruce tree with limbs and moss piled over us," Brooke said.

Tom nodded. "That's probably best," he said. "If you're buried instead of out in the open, you don't have to watch people get shot and die."

"I ran into a hunter today when I crawled out of my hiding place for a few minutes to go to the bathroom." Janet shook her head. "I thought I was dead."

"What happened?" Brooke asked.

"The guy looked at my jacket and kept walking."

Troy nodded. "The purple patch."

"What purple patch?" Tom asked.

Troy told Tom what Icy had said: only a particular hunter or group of hunters could shoot prey with a colored patch.

"You mean someone special-ordered you?"

"I guess," Janet said. "It's a good thing. I'd be dead right now if I had a white patch."

The group lingered around the food trough, talking for another hour, and then they reluctantly parted ways and headed back to their hiding spots.

Once Troy and Brooke had situated themselves in their little hollow and pulled the spruce branches and moss over them, Brooke said, "I think I love you, Troy."

Troy felt a flush of heat rush through him. He put his arms around her and scooted closer to her. "I have feelings for you, too, Brooke, but I think we should try to ignore how we feel until we're out of here and safe. When we're not depending on each other to survive, we might not feel the same way."

"I will," Brooke said. "I don't think we'll get out of here. I think they'll kill us." Her voice was so low when she said these last few words that Troy could barely hear them.

Troy kept his arms around Brooke until she began breathing evenly, and then he slid away from her and waited several more minutes. Once he knew she was sound asleep, he quietly climbed out of their little pit. He turned on his headlamp and ensured Brooke was adequately covered with branches and moss. Then he tiptoed away from their hiding spot and headed toward the hunting compound.

Troy hiked for what felt like an hour or more, and he began to worry he'd gone in the wrong direction. He kept a watchful eye on the sky. He had no idea what time it was and didn't want to get caught out in the open when it got light. Would he have time to get back to Brooke? Could he even find their hiding spot? In the dark, everything looked the same in the spruce forest. If Brooke woke up and found him missing, he worried she'd panic and try to find him.

Troy climbed up a hill to get a better view and saw a dim light a few hundred yards in front of him. The light revealed the shape of a small building, and he guessed it was a guardhouse. From what Icy had said, he knew there must be cameras or sensors of some sort protecting the camp's perimeter. If he got too close to the compound, the guards would know he was there and come after him. He wondered how many people had been killed just trying to approach the buildings.

He descended the hill and walked closer to the compound. He had to find some weakness in the defenses that he and his fellow prey could exploit. He approached the camp from the left and got within about three hundred feet of the nearest buildings. Running from tree to tree, he skirted the front of the camp to the right side. He saw one large building and four smaller cabins, but it looked like there were other buildings behind the ones he could see. A large warehouse sat on the right side of the compound. Perhaps if he and his comrades entered from the right side, they could breach the camp without alerting the guards. It would be risky, though.

Troy felt better now that he had a more complete idea of the camp's layout. Maybe with this knowledge, he could concoct a plan to get inside the compound.

He looked at the sky and was alarmed to see it brightening. He turned back to where he thought his hiding spot was and ran through the forest. He tripped over a tree root and sprawled on the ground. He stood, brushed himself off, and slowed his pace. His heart raced as dawn came and went, and he realized he was lost.

Suddenly, he heard the crack of a rifle shot, and the bark on a spruce tree less than ten yards in front of him splintered. He threw himself behind a tree and didn't move. He didn't hear anything except the pounding of his heart, but he knew he couldn't stay where he was because the hunter had seen him and would pursue him.

Troy crouched, waited a minute to still his mind, and then bolted. No other shots came. Perhaps the hunter was hiking toward his last position and didn't see him run. He didn't stop to find out if the maniac was behind him; he kept running as fast as possible. A piercing scream then froze him in his tracks. His body trembled as he tried to make sense of the sound. Then he heard it again and realized it was the call of a bald eagle perched somewhere above him in a spruce tree.

Troy blew out a slow breath to calm himself, and then he resumed running through the woods. He hurdled a fallen spruce tree and then saw a deep depression between two trees. He jumped into the hole, crawled back to the far end of it, and pulled moss, spruce needles, and dirt over himself. Once concealed, he pulled his legs up to his chest, making his body as small as possible, and waited for a man with a gun to walk up to his makeshift grave and blast him.

Troy felt sweat dripping down his back as he lay there helpless. He thought about his family and friends and his plans for the future. He liked his accounting job, but he didn't love it. He'd always wanted to teach at the high school level, but his parents had dissuaded him because they said he couldn't make a decent living as a teacher. He promised himself that if he survived this nightmare, he'd return to school and earn his teaching certificate. Life was too short to work at a job you didn't love.

He thought about Brooke and wondered if she was sleeping. He hoped so because he knew she'd panic if she awoke and found him gone, and he feared she'd leave her hiding spot and try to find him. He'd never forgive himself if something happened to her because he'd made the impetuous decision to try to find the compound.

He allowed himself to wander into "what if" territory for just a moment. What if he and Brooke made it out of this place? Would they have a future together? He imagined them living in a cozy house with two children and a golden retriever. Brooke was too beautiful for him, though, and he knew that once they got off this island, she'd return to her life, and he'd return to his. His presence in her life would only remind her of this nightmare.

Troy's muscles slowly relaxed, and he fell into a deep sleep.

CHAPTER 41

Saturday, November 8

8:30 p.m.

Blake Parker eased the Beaver into the dock at Anton Larsen Bay. Anton Larsen was accessible by a winding road from Kodiak. Although not a long drive from the town of Kodiak, the protected bay saved mariners heading for the town from having to go through unprotected waters around Spruce Cape. Anton Larsen was also where floatplane pilots could land if Kodiak was foggy. Fog often plagued Kodiak and the nearby mountain passes in the summer months, but Anton Larsen sometimes had better weather than town.

Blake initially considered Anton Larsen a better spot than Trident Basin to load passengers, but his customer had vetoed the idea. He believed Trident Basin would be easier to work from and thought the plane could land unnoticed after dark there, and it had for a while. Now, Blake didn't like being anywhere near this island. He'd received excellent pay for this extracurricular job, but no amount of money was worth spending the rest of his life in prison. This would be his last trip for his demanding client, and then what? He guessed he'd have to head for Mexico or South America. His wife and kids wouldn't miss him as long as he sent them money.

He had to wait fifteen minutes for the SUV to arrive from Kodiak. He was beginning to panic and had started to get ready to leave without his cargo when he finally saw the headlights bouncing down the road. He watched nervously to see if it would be his contacts or the Alaska State Troopers coming to arrest him.

"Sorry, man," Burt, the largest of the two big men, said as he got out of the driver's seat. "That road is in bad shape. The drive took longer than I thought it would."

"Get her in the plane," Blake said. "I want to get out of here."

The second guy, Kevin, pulled the woman out of the back seat. She was barely conscious and couldn't walk on her own. Blake looked at her and spit on the ground. This nosy woman had pulled the covering off his tail number and reported it to the police. Had she reported him for flying below minimums, or did she know or suspect he was transporting kidnapping victims? He hoped it was the former, but he wasn't willing to take the chance. If they could get rid of her, then no one would be left to testify against him.

Burt grabbed under her arms, and Kevin took her legs. The two men carried the woman to the plane and pushed her into the rear seat.

"Did you bring the jugs of fuel? I didn't have a chance to bring any with me."

"We have them," Burt said.

Blake emptied the four fuel jugs into his tank as fast as possible. Burt and Kevin stored the empty jugs in the back of the SUV and then headed up the road while Blake taxied for takeoff.

* * *

Bright lights illuminated the protected cove in front of the hunting lodge. Blake circled and landed. Four men met the plane as it idled up to the beach.

"Do you have her?" one of the men asked.

"I have her," Blake said as he jumped into the shallow water from the pontoon.

One of the men onshore hitched up his hip boots and helped Blake pull the plane into the beach. Then, two men climbed onto the pontoons, opened the rear door, and pulled the limp woman off the seat and brought her to the edge of the plane.

"She's completely out of it," one of the men said. "We need some help here."

The man standing on the beach motioned toward the lodge. "Get Damon and Floyd," he said.

One of the men ran back to the lodge, while the other stayed with the unconscious woman.

"I've been compromised," Blake said. "I can't go back to Anchorage or Kodiak."

"I know," the man standing on the beach said. "The police have your tail number, but we have a place to hide your plane. We cleared out our warehouse and made a makeshift trailer. We'll pull the Beaver up into the warehouse on the high tide tonight. You can stay here until things cool down, and then we'll get you someplace safe."

Blake nodded, feeling the knot in his stomach loosen a fraction. "That might work."

"Did you make up a cover story for your family and colleagues in Anchorage, or will they be looking for you?"

"No," Blake said. "No one should miss me for three weeks. I told my family I had a charter to fly a rich guy to Florida. I said it would take me three weeks. I told the dispatcher to take me off the books for three weeks, and she'll cover for me."

The man, Blake's client, said, "We'll take care of the plane. Why don't you head up to the lodge and get some rest? You can stay in cabin three."

Blake nodded and climbed up the hill from the beach. *And so, my new life begins.*

CHAPTER 42

Sunday, November 9

8:10 a.m.

Dan Patterson and Nick Morgan sat at the table in the small conference room at trooper headquarters; each had a cup of coffee, and a plate of cinnamon rolls sat in front of them.

Nick felt his stomach churn when he looked at the rolls. He had no appetite. He usually felt helpless in the middle of an investigation, but he'd never felt as desperate as he did right now. He had to find Jane and bring her home. He couldn't stand to think what the kidnappers were doing to her. He'd seen too much evil during his career as an FBI profiler and knew the unspeakable things humans could do to other humans. What horrors had Jane endured, or was she even still alive? He knew that if this were any other investigation, he'd rate Jane's chances of survival after twenty-four hours as minuscule. *She was kidnapped because she knew too much. What reason would the kidnappers have for keeping her alive?* He pushed the thought to the back of his mind. He needed to concentrate on what he could do, not what might happen.

"Blake Parker had to land the Beaver somewhere," Patterson said. "It would run out of fuel at some point."

Nick tapped the table with his right hand. "I think he refueled before we figured out he wasn't returning to his home base in Anchorage. Then he flew someplace safe and hid the plane."

Patterson blew out a breath. "Where does that leave Jane? Is she still on the island, or did they get her off another way?"

"They could have taken her by boat," Nick said. "Or, is there another good place for floatplanes to land near the road system?"

"Anton Larsen Bay," Patterson said. "Why didn't I think of it before now? The Beaver could land there to pick her up. I'll send a couple of troopers out there this evening to keep a lookout."

"One way or the other, I bet they got Jane off the island last night," Nick said. "They must think we're breathing down their necks, and they don't want to leave any loose ends."

"I wish we were breathing down their necks," Patterson said. "Without the pilot and the plane, we have nothing."

"Have you had a chance to talk to the air traffic controllers at the Kodiak tower?" Nick asked. "Did they detect Parker's Beaver on any of his night trips to Kodiak?"

Patterson shook his head. "They had no record of those flights and said they didn't pick up the plane on radar. According to Steve, he flew in very low whenever he landed at the basin. I think he avoided the radar."

"Were you able to get Jane's phone records?" Nick asked.

Patterson nodded. "The only people she called yesterday were you and Sid. She had incoming calls from Steve and me."

Nick nodded. "I missed a call from her. She called while I was on the plane flying up here. What about earlier calls? Have you had a chance to check out callers from the previous few days?"

Patterson shook his head. "Not yet," he said, "but nothing strange jumped out at me."

The two stared at each other for a full minute.

"Sid thinks the pilot could be flying the victims to Afognak Island. What do you think?" Nick finally asked.

Patterson stared at the table for several seconds and then stood. "Let me grab a map."

He returned less than a minute later with a topo map of the Kodiak Archipelago. He smoothed the map out on the table, and he and Nick stood and stared down at it.

"If the pilot flew north from Kodiak, then Afognak is a good choice, but why?" Patterson asked as he returned to his seat and swallowed a gulp of coffee. "What does the pilot or the people he's working for do with their victims?"

"Maybe they're forcing them into labor. Do you know of any big construction projects on Afognak?" Nick asked.

Patterson slowly shook his head. "No, and what would they do with the people after the project was done? Kill them?"

Nick returned to his seat and nodded. "It happens, but the forced laborers are usually migrants who aren't missed for a long time. Taking college-aged kids off the streets in the US is a bit riskier."

"Still," Patterson said. "Detective Horner and I noted how most of the missing people weren't missed for a while, and we can't be certain some didn't take off on their own. Maybe the kidnappers were looking for drifters or free spirits and screwed up when they chose the senator's daughter or a few of the others."

Nick motioned to the map. "I don't know where to start here. Do you have any suggestions?"

Patterson rubbed his chin for several seconds. "How do you feel about a plane ride?"

"Over Afognak?"

Patterson nodded. "It's a long shot, but maybe we'll see something."

"Sounds great to me," Nick said. "I can't stand sitting here doing nothing."

"Except for the areas of the island that have been logged, Afognak is heavily timbered, so it's difficult to see much on the ground. If someone has cleared an area to build something, though, it should be obvious."

"What about building permits?" Nick asked. "Should we check to see if any have been filed?"

Patterson grinned. "This is rural Alaska," he said. "No one gets a building permit here."

The two men stood and left the conference room. Patterson added, "Let me call Horner to see if she wants to join us. It's a nice morning for a plane ride."

The air smelled crisp, and the heavy frost hinted at the quickly approaching winter. While Patterson fueled the trooper Beaver, Nick chatted with Detective Horner once she arrived. She'd spent the last two hours checking in with airport managers around the state to see if any had news of Blake Parker and his black Beaver. It would have been much easier to locate a wheel plane than a floatplane. A floatplane could land on any unregulated lake or in any cove. It didn't need to land at an airport, but Parker would have to refuel the plane at some point, so Horner had asked the airport managers to track their fuel sales and watch for any unusual requests for fuel. She knew it was a long shot, but what else could they do at this point?

"No one's seen the plane," she said, shaking her head.

"I think it's gone to ground," Nick said. "It's in a hangar somewhere."

Horner nodded. "The plane was our only lead. I don't know where to go next."

"Let's hope we can see something from the air."

The floatplane trip was gorgeous on a rare cloudless, calm morning. They were over Afognak Island only a few minutes after departing Trident Basin. The island looked much like the north end of Kodiak, except there were fewer man-made structures. Patterson explained that Afognak stretched forty-three miles from east to west and measured twenty-three miles from north to south. It was a large island. Nick strained to see through the heavy layer of trees, but he saw little of the ground beneath them. A quick pass over the logging areas revealed scars in the forest, but Patterson didn't spend much time flying over those areas since the logging camp was a legitimate operation.

"I see an elk," Horner said from the rear seat.

Nick strained but never saw the animal. As they passed over an established lodge, Patterson pointed it out. He also noted the few remote dwellings they saw. After an hour and a half, Patterson said, "I don't see anything suspicious here."

"I can't see much of anything," Nick admitted. He felt defeated and helpless. *I promise I'll find you, Jane.*

CHAPTER 43

Sunday, November 9

3:20 p.m.

The light hurt my eyes, so I pulled the blanket over my aching head. The hand on my arm continued to shake me, and I groaned. "Go away," I tried to say, but my words sounded garbled. *Where am I?* I attempted to remember what had happened to me, but my head hurt too much to think. I just wanted to sleep.

"Jane," a kind, accented female voice said. "It's time to wake up now."

"No." I held the blanket over my head, but the woman was relentless.

"I have a nice, hot breakfast here for you," she said. "Why don't you sit up and have something to eat and drink."

I had to admit the food smelled good, and I wondered how long it had been since I'd eaten. I pulled the blanket from my head and looked into the pleasant face of a middle-aged woman who looked like she may have been Filipina.

"My name is Millie," the woman said. "Eat your breakfast, and I'll be back." She helped me sit and put the tray on my lap.

I had a dull headache and felt jittery, as if coming down from a high. *Where am I?* I thought again. I looked around the small room but saw nothing familiar. The walls were wood-planked, and the hardwood floor gleamed under a coat of polish. I'd been in hospital rooms before, and this didn't look like one. In addition to the bed, the room held two hard-back chairs and a small chest of drawers. I noted a built-in closet to my left. There were no windows in the room.

I cleaned every morsel from my plate. The food was good, and as my stomach filled, my headache receded. I looked down at my chest and ran my hand over the cotton gown I was wearing. It looked and felt like a hospital gown. It was certainly nothing I owned. *Who changed my clothes, and how long have I been here?*

I sat with the tray on my lap, sipping coffee until Millie returned. "Where am I?" I asked as soon as she entered the room.

"I'm not allowed to tell you," she said. "I'm sorry. Do you need to go to the bathroom?"

"Yes," I said. I fought against the fog in my brain. *Why can't she tell me where I am?*

Millie led me out of my small room down a short hall and opened the door to the bathroom for me. Three other rooms led off the hallway, but the doors were closed, so I couldn't tell what was in them. I saw no one else in the hall.

After I'd used the bathroom, Millie escorted me back to my room.

"What day is it?" I asked after I sat on the bed.

"Sunday, November ninth," Millie said. She opened a large drawer in the chest and began removing clothes.

I tried to think. What was the last thing I could remember? *I think I went to work on Friday, or was it Thursday?*

I looked at my wrist. "Where's my watch?"

Millie shook her head. "You aren't allowed to have a watch here."

"Why not? Who said?" My heart began to beat faster. *Am I being held captive?* Nothing made sense.

Millie didn't answer my questions, instead handing me a pile of camouflage-designed clothes. "Put these on," she said. "Put on all the layers. It's cold out there." She pointed to the windowless wall. "I'll be back." She turned and exited the room. I heard her lock the door once she was outside the room.

My mind reeled. Where was I? I couldn't remember anything from my recent past. What had I done to put myself in prison? I looked down at the pile of clothes on my bed. They'd provided everything from underwear (including long underwear) to insulated waterproof pants, a heavy sweater, gloves, and a hat. I recognized the brand and knew this was good-quality gear, but where were my clothes, and why did I have to wear these?

I tried to make sense of recent events while I pulled on the clothes. The heavy sweater and waterproof pants fit me perfectly, and I wondered how they knew my size. I pulled on the wool socks and laced up the stiff hiking boots. I sat on the bed with the gloves and hat beside me.

Fifteen minutes later, Millie returned. She stepped into the room and shut the door behind her. "Good," she said. "Everything fits."

"How did you know my size?" I asked.

Millie apparently took my question as a compliment. She smiled and nodded. "I'm very good at this."

"Where am I going dressed in heavy camouflaged waterproof clothes?" I asked.

"Into the forest," Millie said. "I'm sorry." She opened the closet and pulled out a hanger holding a camouflage coat. She handed it to me. "Put it on. It's warm, and it's waterproof."

I zipped up the coat and noted the orange triangle on the right breast. I pointed at it. "What's this?"

Millie rapidly shook her head from side to side. "Never mind," she said. "Put on your hat and gloves."

I did as instructed. "Millie, you have to help me out here. Where are you sending me?"

"Into the forest," she said. "Listen carefully to me." She lowered her voice. "It's very dangerous out there. As soon as you get into the trees, run and hide until dark. After dark, it's safe to come out of hiding and find a food station to get food and water." She handed me a bottle of water and a headlamp. "Put these in your pocket. You can trade the water bottle in tonight at the food station for a full one. You'll also find extra batteries for your headlamp at the food station."

"Why is it dangerous?"

Millie put a finger to her lip. "Very dangerous," she said again. "Now, no more talking. Follow me."

Sweat trickled down my back, and I wasn't sure if it was because I was overheated or terrified of an unknown danger.

I followed Millie down the hall until we reached an outside door. She opened the door and said, "Run fast."

I looked at her.

"Now," she said. "Run!" She slapped me on the back.

I didn't feel I had an option, so I ran. I'd only taken a few steps when I heard the crack of a rifle blast. The shot was in the distance, but my adrenaline surged, and I doubled my pace. I focused on the ground, trying to avoid rocks, downed limbs, protruding roots, and fallen trees. Millie had told me to hide, but hide where?

Another blast sounded. This one was closer to me. I jumped behind a tree and stood with my back to the trunk as I tried to catch my breath. I'd been in a few dicey situations in my life, but each time I'd understood the danger. Right now, I was not only confused by the random gunshots but also couldn't determine where the shots were coming from. Which direction should I run? I tried to overcome my panic, but I felt I could die at any moment.

I ran a few more steps but froze when another shot rang out. I saw a small depression in the ground at the base of a huge Sitka spruce. I collected a few fallen spruce limbs, crawled into the depression, and pulled the limbs over me. I lay on my back and brushed dirt, moss, and spruce cones over me until I could see nothing above me. I curled into a ball and fought the urge to scream. I'd never been claustrophobic, but I felt as if I'd been buried alive, and if the shooter or shooters noticed the strange pile of limbs and debris and shot into it, I'd die instantly.

I needed to think. I remembered sitting with Steve at Trident Basin. The pilot and his two thugs had seen me. *Did they kidnap and drug me like they did the others? Is this where the pilot flew the other victims? Where am I?* I had no memory of an airplane flight, so I assumed I must have been drugged. *What's going on here? Why are people shooting in the woods?* Perhaps they were deer hunters, but why had Millie given me hunting clothes and told me to run?

An unsettling thought occurred to me. Maybe the hunters were hunting me. Bile rose in my throat. *Have the people who were kidnapped been brought here—wherever here is—and hunted like wild animals? No way. No one is depraved enough to do something so abhorrent.*

175

I tried to piece together the last hours and minutes I could remember before I'd ended up here. I remembered Sergeant Patterson calling and asking me to come to trooper headquarters for a meeting at 11:00 a.m. *Did I attend the meeting?* I had no memory of a meeting, so someone must have kidnapped me sometime Saturday morning. As hard as I tried, I couldn't remember anything about the event or my abductors.

Once the adrenaline in my system had finally dissipated, I fell asleep. The occasional cracks of a rifle snapped me awake, but the shots slowed and eventually stopped by evening.

When I awoke, I carefully parted the branches and pushed the dirt away from my face. The forest was dark. I stood and brushed away the spruce needles and moss. I pulled my headlamp from my pocket and turned it on. I quickly placed my hand over the light to dim its glow. A few feet from me, I heard something move in the woods and froze. I let out a shaky breath when a buck walked out of the trees and looked at me. I didn't know which of us was the most terrified, but the deer knew how a prey animal should act. He looked at me and fled.

I was not hungry and had no desire to wander through the woods in the dark to find a food station. I still had two-thirds of a bottle of water. I'd have to find food and water tomorrow, but tonight, I just wanted to go to the bathroom and find a better place to hide.

CHAPTER 44

Sunday, November 9

6:10 p.m.

Patterson's cell phone rang the moment he stepped into his house. He pulled the phone from his pocket and sighed. It had been a long, frustrating day, and he was ready to have a drink of scotch and talk to his wife.

"Sid," Patterson said. "What can I do for you?"

"I've been thinking," Sid said. "Maybe we should be looking at Shuyak Island."

Sid's words hit Patterson like a slap across the face. With all the recent strange happenings on the island, Shuyak made perfect sense as a place of interest. Why hadn't he thought of it sooner?

"I'm listening," Patterson said. He stood inside his front door, not wanting to walk across the carpet until he'd removed his boots.

Jeanne poked her head out of the kitchen and looked at him. When she saw he was on the phone, she retreated.

"How much do you know about the sale of Shuyak?" Sid asked. "All I've heard are rumors."

"I have little more than that," Patterson said. "I was informed that the state park had been transferred into private hands. When I asked my superiors questions, they told me the move came from the governor's office, and they told me not to ask questions."

"Why isn't the press all over this?" Sid asked. "How can the governor get away with selling a state park?"

Patterson paused a moment. "I don't think anyone bought the land," he said. "My understanding is that the land designation changed from a park to a lease. I'm sure the governor would justify the move by pointing out how much money he'd save by transferring a remote park in the Kodiak Archipelago to a land lease. Instead of spending money on maintaining buildings and trails and hiring park rangers and assistants, the state can now make money from the land from lease fees. Folks in Anchorage and Fairbanks would likely consider it a smart move."

"But who's leasing it?" Sid asked.

"I asked," Patterson said. "An offshore corporation has the lease, but my superiors never gave me the name of an actual human."

"Do you know what they're doing with the land?"

"Yes," Patterson said. "They have a hunting and fishing lodge there. I think they mainly take fishermen and deer hunters."

"Shuyak is a good place for both," Sid said.

"I sent troopers there in September to check licenses, and everything seemed in order. I don't have to tell you about budget issues. We can't afford to fly up there very often to keep an eye on things."

"I'm sure the new residents realize your constraints," Sid said.

"Yes, well," Patterson said, "I think it's time to pay the hunting camp another visit. I remember how to check a hunting license. I'll fly two of my wildlife troopers over there, and we'll attempt to take a closer look at the operation."

"If I can help in any way, let me know."

* * *

After he'd eaten dinner, Patterson called Nick. The FBI agent sounded exhausted and depressed. "I talked to Sid about an hour ago," Patterson said, "and he suggested we check out Shuyak Island."

"The name sounds familiar," Nick said. "I heard something about it not long ago."

"Shuyak's at the northern end of the Kodiak Archipelago, south of the Barren Islands," Patterson said. "It's beautiful and wild. It's only twelve miles by eleven miles but has more sheltered interior waterways than anywhere else in the archipelago. It's a paradise for camping, bird watching, fishing, and hunting. When the state had money after the 1989 *Exxon Valdez* oil spill, most of Shuyak was designated a state park."

"Now I remember," Nick said. "Somehow, someone recently bought the park, and now, it's private land."

"Technically, the land designation was changed from a park to a lease," Patterson said.

"What is the lessee doing with the property?"

"It's a hunting and fishing camp," Patterson said. "I don't know much about it, but I plan to take two of my wildlife troopers over there tomorrow and check licenses. I'd like to take you with me, but I'm afraid an FBI agent might spook them."

"Good point. It can't hurt for you all to check out the place," Nick said. "We don't have any other leads, and I'm out of ideas."

"We'll head over there first thing in the morning. I'll let you know what we find."

CHAPTER 45

Monday, November 10

8:10 a.m.

The sky was beginning to lighten with the first rays of dawn. Patterson rubbed his hands together as he warmed up the plane. The thermometer at his house read eighteen degrees, and he wondered how Jane had survived the night. Was she indoors and warm or outdoors and freezing? Was she still alive? Experience told him she wasn't alive, and he feared all the kidnapping victims were dead. He hadn't heard any reports of missing people since Jane disappeared. This was both good and bad. He was glad the kidnappers hadn't taken anyone else. Still, he feared that once they knew the troopers and the FBI were looking for the Beaver and Blake Parker, the operation would cease, and they'd never be able to find the missing people and arrest those responsible for taking them.

"You guys buckled up?" Patterson looked at Wildlife Trooper Loren Stanley sitting beside him, and Stanley nodded. Patterson turned his head to the back seat, and Trooper Brandon Smith said, "Yes, sir," into the microphone on his headset. Trooper Mark Traner, seated next to Smith and behind Patterson, gave a thumbs-up to Patterson's inquiry. Traner was not a wildlife trooper like the other two, but Patterson wanted him along in case things got dicey. Patterson trusted Traner's common sense and ability in the field.

The sky was cloudless, and the winds were calm. Patterson couldn't ask for better flying weather, but he knew a low-pressure system with high winds was headed toward Kodiak. He wanted to return to base no later than early afternoon. He preferred to check a hunting camp in the late afternoon when the hunters would likely be returning for the day. This operation couldn't wait, though, and he hoped that by going early, he'd catch most of the hunters before they left camp for the morning.

He'd briefed the troopers on the purpose of this trip. They were to politely check licenses and tags, chat with the hunters, and keep their eyes and ears open. When they left, Patterson planned to circle the island several times, but he doubted they'd see much through the thick Sitka spruce forest.

When they reached the island's north end, Patterson glided to a smooth landing and pulled into a sheltered cove near the hunting lodge. The troopers jumped out and helped secure the plane to a tree on the beach.

Patterson was surprised that no one from the lodge came down to the shore to meet them when they pulled up to the beach. In a low voice, he said, "Have your weapons ready."

He led his troopers up the worn trail toward the lodge. He noted four surveillance cameras high in the spruce trees pointed down at the trail.

Traner said in a low voice, "They know we're coming."

Above the door, a sign read Artemis Shuyak Wilderness Lodge. Beneath the wording, someone had carved a symbol depicting a half circle pierced by an arrow. Patterson knocked on the door with his left hand, his right hand resting on the grip of his Glock 22. He'd unsnapped the holster, but he left the gun in it. Whether or not he removed the weapon would depend on the reception he and his men received.

No one came to the door for a minute or longer. Patterson had raised his fist to knock again when the door finally swung open. A beefy, middle-aged man with gray streaks running through his short, brown hair greeted Patterson with a smile.

"Officer," the man said. "I thought I heard a plane circling a while ago but didn't hear you land."

"I thought one of your many surveillance cameras might've alerted you to our presence," Patterson said.

The man made a dismissive gesture with his hand. "We don't monitor those during the day."

Patterson nodded, but he knew the man was lying.

"I'm the lodge manager," he said. "I'm Cage Marks."

Paterson introduced himself and his troopers, and Marks shook their hands. Still, he didn't budge from his stance in front of the open door.

"May we come in and check your hunters' licenses and tags?" Patterson asked.

"Sure," Marks said. He quickly looked behind him into the lodge and then stood aside for the men to enter.

"We only have four hunters right now," he said. "They're all deer hunters."

Marks led the troopers into a large, open space. A dining room or mess hall occupied the far end of the room. One man sat at a long table eating a stack of pancakes. The end of the room closest to the main door was a great room with comfortable-looking chairs and couches. Large windows provided views of the spruce forest.

Two men sat in the great room, conversing softly. A third man was busy rearranging the gear in his pack. Patterson found it curious that none of the men looked up when the troopers entered the lodge.

"Guys," Marks announced to his clients. "The troopers are here to check your licenses and tags."

The four hunters pulled the necessary paperwork from their pockets, and Patterson's men approached them and began to record the details. Patterson stayed with Marks.

"How's the hunting been?" Patterson asked Marks.

"Fair," he said. "We had a lot of winter kill last winter. It was hard on the population."

Patterson nodded. "That's what we've heard from around the island this year. How much longer do you plan to operate?"

"Another month," Marks said. "We'll wrap things up by December fifteenth and close the lodge for the year."

"Will you have a winter caretaker?"

Marks shook his head. "No, we'll just close it up tight."

"Have you had many hunters this fall?"

Marks nodded. "It's been a good first year. We've stayed busy."

"How many hunters can you take at a time?"

"We usually only take eight at once, but if it's a big group, we might sneak in another one or two."

"But you only have four now?" Patterson asked.

"Most of our groups are four to six hunters. We don't like to have more than two hunting groups in camp at one time."

"Do you have one group right now?"

"No," Marks said. "This is two groups of two." He laughed softly. "Those guys"—he pointed to the two men sitting in the great room—"are from Texas, and the other two come from Illinois. The two groups don't like each other much." He shrugged. "That's why we don't have more than two groups in camp at a time. Men can be jerks."

"Have they gotten their deer yet?" Patterson asked. He hoped Marks would say yes so he'd have a reason to look at the trophies and ensure they were properly tagged.

Marks shook his head. "No one's gotten anything yet."

"What day of the hunt is it?"

"Day four of six," Marks said.

"And no deer yet?"

Marks shook his head. "They're all holding out for nice trophies, but I imagine they'll lower their sights today."

Patterson nodded. "Hunters often have unrealistic expectations."

He noticed Traner, who'd checked the license of the man still sitting at the table eating breakfast; now he was slowly walking around the room looking at things. The other two troopers finished with their hunters and returned to stand by Patterson.

"Is there anything else I can do for you gentlemen today?" Marks asked.

Patterson knew he had no legal reason to ask to see the rest of the lodge. Once Traner rejoined the other troopers, Patterson thanked Marks for his time, and then he led his group out of the lodge.

As soon as the lodge door had shut behind them, Patterson walked around the side of the building and stared into the impenetrable forest.

Everything checked out with Marks and his hunters, but something seemed off here.

* * *

Once they were airborne, Patterson spoke through the microphone on his headset. "What did you guys think about the lodge?"

"The guy I checked seemed nice enough," Trooper Stanley said.

"It sure took Marks a long time to answer the door," Trooper Smith added.

"And then he stood blocking our entry until you finally asked him if we could come in and check licenses," Stanley added.

"They knew we were there when we landed," Traner stated. "I'm sure they heard the plane and saw us walking up the trail on all those surveillance cameras."

"Yes," Patterson said, "they didn't want us to enter the lodge until they'd made a quick sweep to hide anything they didn't want us to see."

"You know, we run into this all the time," Stanley said. "We enter a camp, and someone distracts us while the others make sure everything appears legal."

"Possibly what they were doing back there," Patterson said, "but I got a strange feeling about the place."

"I find it hard to believe that none of those hunters has shot a deer yet," Traner said. "The guy I talked to said no one had anything, and this is day four of a six-day hunt."

"My guy said the same thing," Smith said.

"I think they didn't want us to look at their deer," Traner said. "Something was going on there."

Patterson was glad he'd brought Traner with them. The trooper had good insights and a deductive mind.

He glided the Beaver to a smooth landing at Trident Basin. When he pulled up to the dock, he saw Sid pacing back and forth, apparently waiting for them to return.

The retired trooper walked to the end of the dock and helped tie the plane to the cleats. "What did you find?" he asked as soon as Patterson and the other troopers had stepped onto the dock.

Patterson shook his head. "We didn't see anything actionable, but something isn't right at that camp. I'm not saying it's where they took Jane and the others, but we got the feeling they're hiding something there."

"We need a warrant to search the island," Sid said as he walked with the troopers up the dock.

"You know as well as I do that we don't have probable cause for a warrant."

"Did you fly over the island?" Sid asked.

"Several times," Patterson said, "but we couldn't see much through the thick layer of spruce trees."

"No black plane parked along the shore?"

"Unfortunately, no," Patterson said, "but we did see a large warehouse, and I think a Beaver would fit in it."

They topped the ramp and stood next to Patterson's SUV. "What now?" Sid asked.

Patterson rubbed his head. "Now, I have to think of a way to get back to Shuyak Island with a warrant. I plan to talk to a judge and my superiors in Anchorage."

CHAPTER 46

Monday, November 10

8:15 p.m.

Rain pelted the porous covering over me, and it was beginning to fill the depression around me. I couldn't remain in my little hole in the ground any longer. My bladder was ready to explode, and my back was killing me. Despite the high-quality rain gear Millie had given me, I felt soaked to the bone. It took me several minutes to stand straight and get the feeling back in my legs. I put my hand inside my raincoat and was relieved that my wool sweater was still dry.

I felt better once I'd gone to the bathroom, but I knew I needed food and another water bottle.

Millie had mentioned food stations, but I had no idea where they were. I turned on my headlamp and pointed it at the ground as I made my way through the trees. I cinched my hood around my head and fought my way through the pelting rain. Twenty minutes later, I wondered if I was walking in a circle or headed in a particular direction.

Suddenly, I heard the sound of voices, and I ducked behind a tree. I considered finding another hiding spot, but one of the voices was female, and for some reason, the presence of another woman made me feel relatively safe. I crept toward the talking couple. A few minutes later, I saw two people standing beside a metal box. A dim red light illuminated them.

The pair looked young, and I guessed they were in their early twenties. They faced each other, the man stroking the woman's right shoulder. They were both dressed like me, but their clothes were dirtier.

I slowly walked toward them. The woman saw me first and held up her hand in greeting. "It's okay," she said. "We're friendly."

The man followed her gaze. "You're new here," he said. "What's your name?"

"Is this where I get food and water?" I asked.

"Yes." The woman opened the metal lid and pointed at the contents of the bin. "Take a paper sack and some water. You can leave your old water bottle here. When you're done with your sack, you can also drop it in the bin."

"You'll get sick of ham and cheese sandwiches," the man said.

"I don't know why they don't give us something different," the woman said.

"I don't think they're concerned about keeping us happy," the man said. "We're unlikely to leave a Yelp review."

"I'm Brooke," the woman said, "and this is Troy. Isn't the rain awful?" Brooke was a beautiful young woman with black hair and big, green eyes. Troy looked a few years older than Brooke and had short brown hair and deep-blue eyes.

"I'm Jane, I said. "This is my second night here. Were you guys kidnapped from Kodiak?"

They both shook their heads. "We were both kidnapped," Troy said, "but I was abducted in Anchorage, and Brooke was taken in Homer."

I stared at Brooke. "You disappeared in front of the Homer Bookstore. I read about you."

Brooke said nothing, but tears streamed from her green eyes, and she nodded.

"Do you understand what's going on here?" I asked.

"We're prey," Troy said. "These maniacs are hunting us like they would a wild animal."

I grabbed the edge of the food bin to steady myself and fought a wave of nausea. "Have they killed anyone?"

Brooke nodded solemnly and brushed the tears from her cheek. "The hunters shoot people all the time. Haven't you heard the shots and the screams?"

"I've heard shots," I said, "but I haven't heard anyone scream."

"You will," Brooke said.

Another woman emerged from the woods and shared hushed greetings with Troy and Brooke. She reached into the food bin and grabbed a paper sack and water bottle, dropping her empty bottle and sack in the bin.

"This is Janet," Brooke said.

"I'm Jane," I said to the newcomer.

Janet studied my jacket and then looked at Troy. "She must be special prey, too," she said.

"What do you mean?" I asked.

Brooke and Troy also looked at my jacket. "You're special like Janet," Brooke said. "You have an orange triangle on your jacket, and Janet has a purple one, while most of us have a white triangle. Someone, or a group of people, ordered you specially to hunt. They probably paid a lot of money to have you kidnapped. At least, that's what Icy says."

I looked down at the orange crest on my jacket and then at Janet's purple crest. Nothing made sense.

"Our crests are different colors so our hunters don't get confused, I guess," Janet said.

Suddenly, it hit me. "You are the senator's daughter, aren't you?"

Janet gave a slight nod. Troy and Brooke turned and stared at her. "A senator's daughter?" Troy asked.

Janet sighed. "Yes, my mother is a US senator. When I was kidnapped, I was crewing on a fishing boat on Kodiak."

"Do you think you're special prey because of your mom?" Brooke asked. "I mean, do you think someone who hates your mother is trying to kill you?"

"Maybe," Janet said. "My mother has enemies, but I didn't think anyone hated her this much."

Janet began to cry, and I put my arm around her shoulders. "Your mother is very worried about you, and the Alaska State Troopers and the FBI are looking for you. They're looking for all of us," I said.

"But will they know to look here?" Troy asked.

"Do you know where we are?" I asked.

They all shook their heads. "Icy says we're on an island," Brooke said.

"Who is Icy?" This was the second time Brooke had referred to someone named Icy.

"It's not her real name," she said. "She won't tell us her real name because she doesn't want to get close to any of us. She's not friendly, so Troy nicknamed her Icy."

"She's been here several weeks," Troy said. "I think she's seen too much."

I looked up at the towering trees. "If we're on a small island, then we must be toward the northern end of the Kodiak Archipelago. There are no spruce trees toward the southern end of the archipelago." I tried to think. "I guess this could be Afognak or Raspberry."

"Why do you think we're near Kodiak?" Troy asked.

"Because I watched men load drugged people onto a floatplane in Kodiak, and the pilot flew them somewhere. My friend, who's a pilot, guessed the floatplane pilot was delivering the people to a destination somewhere close to the town of Kodiak. Do any of you remember what happened to you after the kidnappers drugged you?"

"I woke up in the middle of the forest," Troy said.

"I remember someone helping me get dressed," Brooke said.

Janet shook her head. "The sound of a gunshot brought me around, and I was leaning against a tree trunk. I've been terrified ever since."

I opened the paper sack, unwrapped my sandwich, and took a bite. The taste of food made me want to vomit. I dropped the sandwich back in the sack.

"You have to eat to keep your strength up," Brooke said.

"I'll eat it later," I said. "Does anyone have any ideas about getting out of here?"

Troy and Brooke looked at each other. "I hiked to the main compound two nights ago," Troy said. "It's well protected with surveillance cameras and a guard." He shook his head. "It wouldn't be easy to breach, but we might be able to sneak around the large warehouse on the far side. I plan to go back and take a closer look at that area."

"What would we do once we got into the compound?" I asked.

Troy shrugged. "They have guns. We need to get our hands on some."

"They must also have satellite phones," Janet said. "We could call for help."

Troy's plan sounded very dangerous. Surveillance would most likely detect us, and the guards would shoot us. Still, I couldn't think of any other way to get out of here. It seemed insane to hide every day and sneak out for food at night. Sooner or later, the hunters would shoot all of us, or we'd die from exposure.

As if reading my mind, Janet said, "I was freezing last night. I don't know how much longer I can stand this." She wiped tears from her eyes. "I've been thinking I should just walk through the woods one of these days and get it over with."

Brooke put her arm around Janet's shoulders. "Don't say that. It's warmer tonight."

"The temperature might not be as cold, but the rain is freezing." She paused for a few moments. "If you plan to attack the compound, I'm with you," Janet said. "I'd rather die trying to escape than live like this much longer."

After a few more minutes of listening to the other three discuss their hopeless plan to attack the lodge, I told them good night and searched for another hiding spot. The rain had stopped by the time I found a deep hole by a tall spruce. I spent several minutes laying a bed of moss at the bottom; then I scavenged for fallen branches and spruce cones to cover me. I carefully covered my tracks and then hopped down into my new bed. Once I was hidden, I curled into a tight ball and cinched my hood tight. I wanted to stay as dry as possible if the rain started again. The ground was cold, and I knew it would sap what little energy I had. I pulled my sandwich from my sack and forced myself to eat it, then took a long drink of water and placed the bottle beside me.

Who would want to hunt me? I guessed I was special prey only because the pilot and two other men had seen me at Trident Basin. Perhaps the owner of the camp wanted to hunt and kill me himself.

CHAPTER 47

Tuesday, November 11

6:40 a.m.

Sid poured his fourth cup of strong coffee that morning. His stomach protested, and his hands shook. He hadn't slept well ever since Jane's disappearance, and he needed to do something to help find her. He understood the constraints Patterson faced. He'd sat in Patterson's chair only a few years earlier, and he knew the trooper had no probable cause to search the Shuyak camp. Not only would a search be illegal, but powerful people owned the lodge and leased most of the island. They had to be well connected to have convinced the state government to change the destination from a state park to a private lease. Patterson's hands were tied until he could obtain more evidence to suggest that something illegal was happening on the island. Sid planned to be the one to hand Patterson enough evidence to convince a judge to sign a search warrant.

How could he get to Shuyak without the people in the camp noticing his arrival? Shuyak was a small island, but the lodge was located on the island's northern end. Perhaps if he approached the island's southern end, he could sneak onto it without being detected. He considered taking his boat, but with violent fall storms approaching, he was afraid he wouldn't be able to find a safe anchorage. Maybe he could convince a pilot to drop him off on the island's south end. Sid looked at his watch. It was early, but he grabbed his phone and called Steve Duncan.

Steve answered on the second ring. He sounded awake and alert.

"Steve, it's Sid Beatty. Sorry to call you so early."

"No problem," Steve said. "I'm at KFS doing office work. I haven't been able to sleep." He chuckled. "Linda's getting tired of me, so she volunteered to bring me to the office early."

"I can't sleep, either," Sid said. "I can't imagine what Jane is going through, and I feel so helpless."

"I know," Steve said. "I feel responsible. I pulled her into this mess. She'd be okay if I hadn't asked for her opinion about the black Beaver."

"I have an idea," Sid said. "Sergeant Patterson needs more evidence before he can obtain a search warrant for Shuyak, and I want to go to the island and find that evidence."

"Wait a minute," Steve said. "Why Shuyak? Is that where the pilot took those people?"

"We don't know, but I believe it is. Did you hear about the land designation change?"

"Yes. I was shocked when I heard about that, and no one seems to know who owns the lodge."

"Sergeant Patterson flew over there yesterday, and while he didn't see anything overtly suspicious, he said he got a strange vibe. No one met the plane at the beach, and the manager stalled the troopers from entering the lodge. Patterson had a feeling they were trying to hide something."

"They could've just been hiding hunting violations," Steve said.

"You said the pilot flew north, and you didn't believe he had enough fuel to fly very far, right?" Sid said. "I think it's likely he flew to one of the islands in the archipelago, and Shuyak makes the most sense."

Steve was quiet for several moments; then he said, "It sounds dangerous, but if you want a lift to Shuyak, my head pilot Stan and I will fly you there. When do you want to leave? I don't think we can do it today with this weather. I doubt we'll be able to do any flights today."

"How about first thing tomorrow morning, then?" Sid asked. "This low-pressure system is supposed to clear out of here tonight."

"Where do you want to go on Shuyak?"

"The lodge is on the island's north side, in Shangin Bay," Sid said. "I want to land as far away from it as possible."

"There's a protected cove near Port William, on the south side," Steve said. "It's a fairly good spot to land."

"I don't know," Sid said. "The cannery might be occupied—possibly by people connected to the lodge."

Steve said nothing for several moments and then added, "Well, if it's fairly calm, I guess Stan could land at the southeast corner inside Big Fort Island in Fort Channel."

"Let's try Fort Channel first. If it's too windy to land there, we'll have to risk landing near the cannery."

"I'll put you on the books for nine a.m. tomorrow," Steve said.

Sid decided not to tell Patterson about his plan. This was one of those cases when it was better to ask for forgiveness than permission. He knew what he'd say if he were in Patterson's position. His plan was dangerous and possibly illegal. After all, he didn't have permission from the leaseholder to step foot on the island. Telling Patterson about his plan would put Patterson in a risky position.

He wondered if Agent Morgan would ignore the rules and come with him if he asked. He knew Nick and Jane were in a relationship. He'd thought it was casual, but Nick seemed distraught over Jane's abduction. Sid had more feelings for Jane than he should. He felt an electric spark every time she was around. There was just something about her. He thought she was beautiful in a nonconventional way, but it was her brain that attracted him most. He couldn't stop thinking about her, and he planned to do everything he could to find her and bring her home. He'd do it without Nick's help.

CHAPTER 48

Tuesday, November 11

9:30 a.m.

Nick rubbed his tired eyes while he listened to Patterson. They were sitting at trooper headquarters, seated around the table with Detective Horner. Patterson was bringing them up to date on the investigation from his angle.

"So, you didn't see anything suspicious, but something didn't seem right?" Horner asked.

"Exactly," Patterson said.

"I'd like to see the look on the judge's face when you present that evidence and ask for a warrant," she said.

Patterson nodded. "I know, I know. We need more."

"Don't think of this as you would for a burglary," Nick said. "You have numerous kidnapping cases here. Under these conditions, most judges wouldn't require much evidence to issue a warrant. But, unfortunately, you'll need more than a suspicious feeling."

"I've been trying to dig into the Shuyak Island leaseholders, but I'm getting nowhere," Patterson said. "The island is leased by a corporation called Artemis, Inc., but it's an offshore corporation, and I can't find anything about the board members. I spent all of yesterday afternoon on it."

"Who okayed the land designation change?" Nick asked. "Someone in the state government must have dealt with an actual person."

"I went all the way to the governor's office," Patterson said, "but I was told the deal is sealed, and it's none of my business."

"Let me try," Nick said.

Patterson shrugged and nodded.

"If I remember my Greek mythology," Horner said, "Artemis is the goddess of the hunt."

Patterson and Nick stared at her. "Good observation, Maureen," Nick said.

Patterson sat back in his chair. "Great observation," he said. "What does it mean?" He drew his phone from his pocket and googled "Artemis." He showed his phone to Horner and Nick. "This sign was over the front door of the lodge. It's a half circle with an arrow through it. Apparently, it's the symbol for the goddess Artemis."

"It's a hunting camp," Horner said. "I'm not sure this information helps us."

"No," Nick said, "but I find it interesting that it's the name of the corporation that leased the island. Does this corporation have other hunting lodges? If so, maybe we can learn more about them through their other holdings."

"Good idea," Patterson said. "I'll look into it."

"I can help you," Nick said. "This might be a long shot, but if we learn that Artemis has other hunting lodges, we should check with the local authorities near the lodges to see if they've had a rash of missing persons cases."

"At least the abductions here seem to have stopped," Horner said. "That's some good news."

"Maybe," Nick said, "but I fear if the kidnappers think we're getting close, they'll disappear."

Horner said, "I'll reconnect with the Anchorage and Homer police and bring them up to date. If we can get them on board, perhaps we can convince a judge to issue a search warrant for Shuyak."

* * *

Nick worked in the conference room while Patterson returned to his office. At noon, Patterson entered the conference room with sub sandwiches and a pot of coffee.

"Thanks," Nick said. "The food looks good, but I can't drink any more coffee. My hands are shaking as it is."

Patterson left and returned a minute later with two bottles of water. He placed them both in front of Nick.

"Have you gotten anywhere?" he asked.

Nick shook his head. "Your governor doesn't play well with the feds. He says state decisions are none of our business. I told him we had good reason to believe multiple crimes were occurring on the island, and we needed access to the names of the leaseholders." Nick shrugged. "He asked me for the evidence."

Patterson sighed. "I ended up in the same place with him."

"I'm used to dealing with politicians," Nick said, "so I tried to scare him. I told him this would land squarely in his lap if people died because he refused to help us."

"What did he say?"

"He hung up on me. How about you? Did you get anywhere this morning?"

"Artemis, Inc., owns a hunting lodge in Idaho and another in New Mexico. I suspect they have more, but I'm checking state by state, so it's slow going."

"Good news." Nick nodded. "Since I'm getting nowhere on my end, I'll help you check the different states, and then we can follow up by contacting local law enforcement in the areas of the lodges."

"Maureen called a few minutes ago," Patterson said. "The Anchorage detective, of course, wants us to fly up there for a meeting, but she told him we're not leaving Kodiak because the action is here."

"I don't see how they could help us at this point," Nick said, "but it's good to have them on board. We'll need them when we investigate Blake Parker and Alaska Wilderness Adventures."

"Maureen can't do anything else to help us right now. She got called out to investigate a murder. She says it'll take her the rest of the day to work the scene."

By the end of the day, the two had found five hunting camps in the United States owned or leased by Artemis, Inc. They were in Idaho, New Mexico, Nebraska, Arkansas, and Vermont.

The next step would be to contact local law enforcement near each lodge, but since it was already 5:30 p.m. Alaska time and much later in the rest of the country, they decided to wait until morning to begin calling sheriffs and police chiefs.

"I'll be here at six a.m.," Nick said.

Patterson nodded. "So will I."

CHAPTER 49

Tuesday, November 11

8:10 p.m.

Troy and Brooke stood by the food trough and quietly discussed their plans. On the one hand, Troy wanted to recruit a larger force, but on the other, he didn't want to feel responsible for the safety of any more people. He wished he could talk Brooke out of accompanying him, but she refused to be left behind again.

Suddenly, Janet appeared from out of the forest. They exchanged greetings, and Janet grabbed a food bag and began unwrapping the sandwich.

"Promise me you'll stay in the trees and be the lookout," Troy said to Brooke.

"What good would that do?" Brooke asked. "How would I let you know if I saw the guard headed in your direction? We don't exactly have radios."

Troy blew out a breath. She was right, of course. He wanted to protect her, but she was a grown woman. No matter how much he cared about her, he had to respect her decision to go with him to the lodge.

"What are you talking about?" Janet asked.

Troy and Brooke looked at each other for a few moments, and then Troy said, "We're planning to hike to the lodge tonight and see if we can get inside the perimeter by entering on the far side of the warehouse."

Janet looked from one to the other. "Just the two of you?"

"Yes," Troy said.

"I'll go with you," Janet said.

Troy folded his arms over his chest. "It'll be very dangerous. We could get shot by the guard."

"Everything here is dangerous," Janet said. "I'll try anything to get out of here. When are you leaving?"

"Now," Troy said.

"Okay." Janet grabbed a bottle of water and stuffed it into the pocket of her raincoat. "I'm ready."

The rain came in waves. It was heavy at times but tapered off to a drizzle, followed a few minutes later by another downpour. The wind had subsided to a stiff breeze. Troy welcomed the wind and rain for a change because it muffled their footsteps in the forest. He didn't know how many guards monitored the area near the lodge. Perhaps some of them were stationed farther out in the woods, watching for anyone approaching the perimeter of the compound. He shined his headlamp at the ground, and Brooke and Janet followed closely behind him, their headlamps turned off. The three remained silent as they proceeded toward the lodge.

As they neared the buildings, they followed a well-defined trail used by the hunters and ATV riders. Troy wondered if surveillance cameras were monitoring the trail. He looked up at the trees but didn't see any blinking lights. If they were there, the cameras must have been concealed. He didn't believe there were any cameras in the forest, probably to make the hunt seem "wilder" to the hunters. He thought about how ridiculous the idea of a "fair chase" hunt seemed when the prey was a human. If he found a loaded gun at the lodge, he'd kill as many of these monsters as he could.

Troy guessed it took them nearly two hours to reach the lodge. The rain had stopped, and the wind had decreased to a slight breeze. He stood with Brooke and Janet, staring at the large warehouse in the distance.

"Do you see any cameras?" he whispered.

"Not in the dark," Brooke said. Despite the sliver of the moon and the distant lights in the lodge's main building, it was difficult to see anything.

"Look for small blinking lights," Troy said.

"I don't see anything," Janet said, "but you can bet they're there."

"Let's wait until it gets later," Troy said. "I don't want to make our move until the hunters have gone to bed."

The trio receded into the forest and sat on the damp ground. They took turns hiking to a point where they could see the lights in the main building.

It seemed as if they'd been waiting for hours, and Troy wondered if the hunters left the lights in the lodge on all night. He leaned back against a tree trunk and dozed.

"The lodge is dark," Janet said, jolting him awake. "The lights are off."

Troy shook his head and wondered how he could fall asleep when he was under so much stress. He looked at Brooke, who also appeared as if she'd been sleeping. "Are you ready?"

Brooke nodded. "Let's get them," she said. Her words sounded confident, but her tone did not.

Troy walked to Brooke and put his arms around her. He pulled her close to him and whispered in her ear. "I love you," he said. "Please be careful."

Brooke looked up at him, her green eyes moist with tears. "I love you, too," she said. "I'll be okay, but you be careful, too."

Janet turned her back to them while they embraced.

"Okay," Troy said. "When we get close, I'll head toward the far side of the warehouse. You two wait in the woods and see what happens. If nothing happens in ten minutes, follow me. I'll wait for you."

"We don't have watches," Brooke said. "How will we know when it's been ten minutes?"

"Wait a while, then," Troy said. "Give the guards plenty of time to respond. I don't think they're patrolling this end of the compound, so if a camera detects me, it might take them a few minutes to get here. If no one responds, then it's safe for you two to follow me." Troy paused and looked from Brooke to Janet to make sure they were listening to him. "When you head for the warehouse, run one at a time, as fast as you can."

Brooke and Janet both nodded. Brooke's eyes were wide, and he noted her trembling arms as she hugged herself. In contrast, Janet stood with hands on hips, her eyes laser-focused.

"You run first, Brooke, and Janet will follow you," he said. He thought that if Brooke faltered, Janet would get her to safety.

"What do we do if one of us gets shot?" Janet whispered.

Troy pondered the question for several seconds and then shook his head. "If I get shot or apprehended, you guys carefully return to our hiding spots. There's no sense in proceeding if they catch me." He paused for several minutes. "If I make it across to the warehouse"—he could hear his voice waver—"I'll keep going if something happens to the two of you."

Janet nodded. "Sounds good," she said.

They walked as quietly as possible through the woods. Now that the storm had passed, Troy wished for pouring rain and heavy winds to disguise their approach, but no such luck.

When they reached the edge of the trees near the opening in front of the lodge, Troy waited and watched for any activity near the buildings. He saw no lights in the main lodge or the cabins. Someone had turned off the generator, but he felt certain the lodge ran on battery power during the night. In the morning, they'd turn on the generator to recharge the batteries. Right now, there was nothing to disguise the noise of him running across the opening.

Troy didn't look at Brooke or Janet. He feared his waning resolve would melt if he looked into Brooke's eyes again. He put his head down and raced across the opening, expecting to hear the crack of a rifle shot at any moment.

He reached the far side of the warehouse and stood with his back against the wall of the building. The pounding of his heart deafened him to any other sounds. *Hide*, he reminded himself. He twisted the knob on the side door to the warehouse and was surprised when the door opened. He slid through it and closed the door quietly.

Troy turned off his headlamp for several minutes and looked for the flashing lights of security cameras in the warehouse. When he detected none, he turned on his headlamp and swung the beam in an arc, illuminating the interior of the building. He was surprised to see a large, black floatplane occupying nearly the entire warehouse. The sight of the plane brought back a fuzzy memory of someone pushing him into the back seat of a similar plane. Maybe this was the plane the kidnappers had used. Hadn't the new woman, Jane, said something about reporting the plane's tail number to the authorities? Maybe the lodge owners had hidden the plane in this warehouse so the authorities couldn't find it.

He skirted the inside walls of the warehouse, looking for anything he could use as a weapon. He picked up a crowbar and stuffed a dull utility knife in his pocket, but he didn't see any guns. The warehouse had big front doors that swung open, as well as the small side door he'd used. Troy turned off his headlamp and waited near the plane's propeller, where he could keep an eye on both doors. He prayed that Brooke and Janet would make it safely to the warehouse.

Several minutes later, Troy heard a loud blast, followed by a woman's scream. He bolted to the side door. He knew the screaming woman was Brooke, and someone had shot her. He opened the door and heard a deep voice say, "I'll take care of her. You check the warehouse. There's another intruder here somewhere. If you see them, shoot to kill."

Troy closed the door and retreated to the far side of the plane. He saw only one place to hide, and he was sure to get caught if he hid there. Still, he had no other options. He climbed onto the plane's float and slid through the rear passenger door. He crawled over the back seat and huddled behind it. His body shook with fear and grief. Was Brooke dead? He'd heard nothing after her initial scream, but perhaps she was just injured. What would the guards do to her if she was still breathing? He knew the answer. They couldn't very well call the coast guard to come and transport her to a hospital. One way or another, Brooke was dead.

Troy didn't think he could hate the people in this lodge more than he already did, but his anger grew. He wanted to beat them all to death with the crowbar he held in his right hand.

The overhead lights in the warehouse clicked on, and Troy heard someone's footsteps. After a few minutes, a man opened the pilot's door of the plane. Troy hunched behind the rear seat. Next, the man walked around the plane and opened the door Troy had used to climb into it.

Instead of fear, Troy felt blinding rage. When the man crawled into the plane to check out the cargo area behind the seats, Troy gripped the crowbar in both hands, rose on his knees, and hit him as hard as he could on the head. He dropped into the row of seats without uttering a sound. The gun he'd been holding in his right hand skittered out of the plane and onto the warehouse floor.

Troy couldn't stop himself. He continued to pummel the man with the heavy bar until he was exhausted. Then he climbed over the seat and the man's battered body. He pushed open the door and slid out of the plane. He looked under it, searching the floor for the gun, but he didn't see it. After a few minutes, he knew he needed to give up on finding the gun and get out of the warehouse before the other guard came searching for his comrade.

Troy walked out the side door. He saw no sign of other guards, but he knew it would be pointless to continue on to the other buildings in the compound. The guards knew he was there and would eventually find and shoot him. He needed to retreat and return when he was more prepared. He continued out into the open space between the compound and the forest. He looked for Brooke's body, but they must have taken her away already. Troy turned and ran as fast as he could through the woods. When he couldn't run anymore, he stopped, fell to his knees, and vomited.

CHAPTER 50

Tuesday, November 11
9:03 p.m.

I had no idea what time it was, but I couldn't stay in this hole any longer. I stood slowly and stretched, waiting for the blood circulation to return to my hands and feet. My state of constant terror when I was first released into the woods had muted to apathy. I hoped Nick and Patterson were making progress on the case, but for some reason, I believed Sid would be the one to find me. I hoped I could survive until he finally got here.

I headed toward the food bin. I had a feeling it was late, and my feeling was confirmed when I opened the bin and saw five empty water bottles and only two sacks of food remaining. I opened the paper bag and unwrapped the sandwich. My appetite had improved, and I guessed I must have been adapting to this insane world.

I heard footsteps to my right and turned to see a woman approaching me. She pulled off her hood when she got close. The rain had momentarily stopped, so I pulled back my hood so she could get a better look at me.

"Hi," I said. "I'm Jane."

She held up her hands. "I don't want to know your name. It's best not to know anyone here."

The woman had short, black hair plastered to her head. Her dark-blue eyes studied me as she drew closer. She was slightly older than Troy, Brooke, and Janet, but I guessed she was a few years younger than me. I wondered if this was the woman they called Icy.

"Have you seen anyone else tonight?" she asked.

I shook my head. "No, but most of the food bags are gone. Have you seen anyone?"

She didn't answer my question, instead saying, "It's getting cold. I wonder what they'll do with us when they shut this place down for the winter?"

"I hope someone finds us before then," I said.

She shrugged. "They haven't found us yet."

"The troopers and the FBI know about the abductions," I said. "They're looking for us."

"Do you know where we are?" she asked. "The Alaska wilderness is endless. We'll probably just disappear like the thousands of others before us."

This woman was a downer, and I didn't need to be any more depressed than I already was. "I hope you're wrong," I said.

As I walked back toward my hiding place, I wondered again where we were. Steve didn't think the pilot had enough fuel to fly far, and we were in a Sitka spruce forest. I felt sure we were on one of the islands in the Kodiak Archipelago. I had to believe that between Nick, Patterson, and Sid, one or all of them would find us.

I sat next to the shallow hollow at the base of the large spruce tree. I was not yet ready to crawl into my hiding spot. I leaned against the trunk and ran my hand over the orange patch on my jacket. *Who ordered me as special prey?* I guessed it must have been the people in charge of this insane operation. The pilot and the kidnappers had caught me snooping around the dock at Trident Basin, and they wanted to get rid of me. *Who ordered Janet so they could hunt her? Is it one of her mother's enemies? Is it another senator or a powerful lobbyist?*

I touched the patch again. It felt hard. I thought about the probability of a hunter finding the prey he'd ordered within the ten-day or two-week timeframe of his hunt. *What happens if he never finds the person he's ordered to kill?*

I removed my jacket and turned on my headlamp to study the patch. I picked at the stitching that attached it to the jacket. Without scissors or a knife, it was a tedious process to rip out the stitches. I must have worked on it for an hour or more, but I found what I expected when I finally held the orange patch and turned it over.

I removed an electronic piece the size of a button from the small pocket on the back of the patch. I knew it must have been some sort of tracker. If the person who'd ordered me didn't find me during the duration of his hunt, he could resort to following the tracker to my hiding place and shoot me then.

I hiked for what felt like hours and threw the tracker into the woods. I had no idea where I was, and it took me the rest of the night to find the food bin. From there, I hiked back to my hiding spot and covered myself with moss and branches just as the sky was beginning to lighten. I needed to find Janet as soon as possible and warn her about the tracker in her patch.

CHAPTER 51

Wednesday, November 12

7:00 a.m.

Sid climbed up to the deck of his sailboat and groaned. It was a calm morning, but thick, fluffy snowflakes filled the sky, obscuring visibility to less than a hundred feet. They'd never be able to fly to Shuyak in this weather.

He waited until eight to call Steve. "It doesn't look good, does it?"

"Not until this stuff stops," Steve said. "Snow was not in the forecast, so I have no idea how long it will last."

"Okay," Sid said. "I'll wait to hear from you when it's a go."

Sid couldn't sit still and do nothing. He called Patterson.

"Patterson," the sergeant said after two rings.

"Dan, this is Sid. Have you learned any more about Shuyak?"

Patterson paused momentarily, probably wondering how much information to release to an ex-trooper. "Agent Morgan and I have not yet been able to determine who's behind the corporation leasing Shuyak, but we have learned that this corporation owns other hunting lodges around the country."

"Interesting," Sid said. "What's the name of the corporation?"

"Artemis, like the Greek goddess of the hunt and the wilderness."

Sid fired up his laptop and googled "Artemis."

After a long pause, Patterson said, "I want to run something by you, Sid. You remember the Robert Hansen case?"

"Sure, the serial killer up in Anchorage?"

"Do you remember how the police thought he flew his victims out into the wilderness and then told them to run while he hunted them like big game animals?"

Sid sat hard on the bench in the galley. "Do you think that's what these maniacs are doing?"

"What do you think?"

"I don't want to believe it, but it makes sense," Sid said. "Jane must be terrified—if she's still alive."

CHAPTER 52

Wednesday, November 12

8:25 a.m.

After Patterson disconnected with Sid, he stood and stretched. He and Nick had made progress this morning, but what they'd found was disturbing. Patterson had decided not to share their latest findings with Sid until they knew more. He didn't want Sid to do his own off-the-books investigation.

They were in the process of calling the small-town law enforcement departments closest to the Artemis lodges in Idaho, New Mexico, Nebraska, Arkansas, and Vermont.

According to the police chief in Green Valley, Vermont, six years earlier, they'd had four abductions from Green Valley and the surrounding area. Neither the missing people nor their remains had ever been found. The police chief said the abductions had stopped as quickly as they'd started. Patterson asked the chief if he'd suspected the owners of the Artemis hunting lodge in relation to the kidnappings. The question seemed to have surprised the chief, who said they'd never had any problems with the lodge, which brought money into the community.

Nick reported to Patterson after he talked to the sheriff in Halstead, New Mexico, and learned they'd had six kidnappings in the area two years earlier. When Nick asked the sheriff whether he'd ever suspected the hunting lodge could be involved in the abductions, he said he'd visited the lodge when investigating the disappearances, but he felt everything was in order there. He said he'd had few leads, and the cases for the victims remained open. "Let me know what you find out in Alaska," the sheriff said. "If you find evidence suggesting the Artemis people are responsible for your abductions, I'll look harder at the lodge here."

The police chief in Nebraska had a different response. Chief John Stubbs told Patterson, "You bet I suspected the lodge. A new hunting lodge opens, and our citizens start disappearing. You didn't have to be a genius to see a connection. I tried everything I could to learn more about what was going on there and who owned the place. We brought the manager into police headquarters and grilled him for seven hours, but we got nowhere, and then the abductions stopped."

Chief Stubbs told Patterson that seven people in the area had disappeared four years earlier: three males and four females. They were all in their twenties and were in good physical shape. "The community still hasn't recovered," he said.

Patterson asked Stubbs if the lodge was still open, and he said it had closed a year after the abductions stopped.

"I was happy to see it go under," Stubbs said. "It brought money into the community, but I didn't trust the folks who ran it, and I held my breath, expecting the abductions to begin again."

"If you suspected the lodge people for the abductions, did you have any ideas about what they were doing with the people they'd kidnapped?"

Stubbs paused so long that Patterson thought the call had ended. His gruff voice dropped to a whisper. "The lodge owned nearly ten thousand acres," he said. "I think their clients were hunting humans, but I can't prove it, and I've never voiced this thought to anyone until now."

Patterson felt sweat trickling down his back. The pain in his neck had moved into his head. "Did everything seem normal at the lodge the year after the abductions?"

"After that year, I believe it operated as a normal hunting lodge, at least as far as I could tell. They offered hunts for white-tailed deer, pheasants, and other birds."

Patterson thanked Stubbs and promised to keep him apprised of the investigation in Alaska. He sat back in his desk chair and felt nauseated. What kind of depraved human would get off on hunting humans? He wondered what such a hunt would cost.

He walked down the hall to the conference room to tell Nick what he'd learned from Chief Stubbs. Nick listened quietly while Patterson talked, but his face grew redder by the moment.

"We have to search this lodge," Nick said. "I wonder how many people have already died there?"

"I think they ran small operations at these other lodges," Patterson said, "and when they got away with it, they moved to Alaska and expanded."

"I just got off the phone with the police chief in Planes, Idaho," Nick said. "They had three abductions seven years ago. It was before the current chief was in office, and he said his predecessor never linked the abductions. He just thought it was a run of bad luck."

Patterson shook his head. "I don't know how you can chalk up a kidnapping to bad luck."

"The guy I talked to insinuated that the chief at the time wasn't the sharpest knife in the drawer."

"I guess not," Patterson said. "Is the Artemis lodge there still open?"

"It is," Nick said, "and apparently, they're very successful."

"I'll call the sheriff in Arkansas," Patterson said, "and then we can decide what to do next. We don't have enough for a warrant yet, but we're getting closer."

"I'll see if I can find any priors on the lodge manager, Cage Marks," Nick said.

Patterson returned to his office and placed the call to Petersville, Arkansas. After waiting a few minutes, the receptionist connected him with Sherriff Del Bussart. Patterson introduced himself and asked Bussart the question he'd asked the previous law enforcement officers. "Have you had a series of abductions in or near your town in recent years?"

"Kidnappings?" Bussart asked. "Why does a state trooper in Alaska want to know about kidnappings in Arkansas?"

Patterson sighed. This guy wasn't going to make it easy on him. "Because we've had a rash of kidnappings here, and I think they could be related to a newly opened Artemis lodge. I'm contacting every sheriff or police chief in a town near an Artemis lodge."

"Artemis? That's hogwash," Bussart said. "I know the people who run the lodge here. They've invited me over there several times to go duck hunting. I even got a nice deer there a couple of years ago. They're good people."

Bussart had such a thick southern accent that Patterson could barely understand him. He returned to his initial question. "Have you had any abductions there in recent years?"

"We had some here last year," Bussart admitted after a long pause.

"How many?" Patterson asked.

"Five," the sheriff said.

"Are they still missing?" Patterson prompted.

"They're open cases," Bussart said. "One of them was my nephew, Todd."

"I'm very sorry," Patterson said. "When did the Artemis lodge open there?"

"Four or five years ago. We've never had any trouble with them."

"What do you know about the owners of the lodge?" If Bussart was friends with the lodge manager, he might know something about the lodge owners.

"Don't know anything about them," Bussart said. "The manager, Buddy, told me a corporation owned the lodge. He said there were several owners."

"Who does Buddy report to?"

After a long pause, Bussart said, "Some guy he calls Mr. Holden."

"What is Buddy's last name?"

"Frank," Bussart said. "Look, this guy is my friend. I'm telling you he's a good guy, and he runs a by-the-book lodge. You're barking up the wrong tree."

"I understand how you feel," Patterson said. "Do you know Mr. Holden's first name?"

"No," the sheriff said. "I never had a reason to ask Buddy what his boss's first name is."

Patterson thanked Bussart for his time and asked the sheriff to keep their conversation confidential. Bussart grudgingly agreed. Patterson ended the call. He swallowed two Excedrin and returned to the conference room.

"Five people disappeared last year from Petersville, Arkansas," he told Nick. "The sheriff is buddies with the lodge manager, and he didn't believe the lodge people had anything to do with the kidnappings."

"Does he know anything about the owners?" Nick asked.

"He said the manager, Buddy Frank, reports to a guy he calls Mr. Holden. He didn't know Holden's first name."

"I'll search police records in Arkansas for Buddy Frank, but Buddy might be a nickname," Nick said.

"Did you find anything on Cage Marks?" Patterson asked.

Nick shook his head. "The guy doesn't exist, but I did find a rather extensive record on a man named Calvin Marks. He did ten years for an attempted bank robbery in Los Angeles and was released three years ago." Nick turned the computer monitor toward Patterson. "Is this the man you know as Cage Marks?"

Patterson studied the photo. "His hair is much shorter now, and he's put on a few pounds, but it's the same guy."

"He's been in and out of prison most of his life."

"The leaders at Artemis, Inc., must not let a little thing like a prison record stand in their way when hiring," Patterson said.

He took a seat at the table and pulled a small notebook and pen from his right-rear pants pocket. "Let's take a look at this. Vermont's abductions occurred six years ago, and the kidnappings in New Mexico happened how long ago?" He looked at Nick.

"Two years ago."

"Nebraska's abductions happened four years ago."

"Idaho's kidnappings were seven years ago," Nick said.

"And five people disappeared near the Artemis lodge in Arkansas last year," Patterson said. "That makes it one year for Arkansas, two for New Mexico, four for Nebraska, six for Vermont, and seven for Idaho. What happened three years ago and five years ago?"

"Maybe they took those years off," Nick suggested.

"Or we missed some lodges," Patterson said.

"I checked every state for Artemis land holdings or leases," Nick said, "but they could be operating outside the US. Let me make some calls to the State Department. I know people who can search outside the US better than we can."

"Did you find anything about Artemis on the internet?" Patterson asked.

Nick shook his head. "When I searched for 'Artemis,' all I could find were articles about the NASA moon launch or articles on Greek mythology."

"I'll call a judge and see if what we have is enough for a warrant to search the Artemis lodge and Shuyak Island, but I'm doubtful."

"I'll keep digging," Nick said.

Patterson's desk phone was ringing when he returned to his office. "Patterson," he said.

"Dan, it's Maureen. I'd like to get together with you this afternoon to review what you've learned about the Shuyak lodge, but first, I have a question. Does the name Jerry Burns mean anything to you?"

Patterson closed his eyes and searched his memory. He thought the name sounded familiar, but he couldn't place it. "I don't think so," he said. "Why?"

"He's my murder victim. Someone stabbed him to death in his hotel room."

CHAPTER 53

Wednesday, November 12

12:20 p.m.

Patterson and Nick decided to grab a quick lunch at Henry's for a change of atmosphere. As they walked out the door at trooper headquarters, Patterson groaned. At least five inches of snow had accumulated and continued to fall rapidly.

Nick helped clear the snow from his SUV, and then both men sat in the vehicle, waiting for it to warm up.

"I should have brought gloves," Nick said. "I didn't think it would be this cold and snowy here."

"It shouldn't be," Patterson growled. "I have an extra pair in my desk drawer you can use."

"I hope Jane is indoors and not out in this stuff."

Patterson didn't respond. He wondered if Jane was still alive and, if so, was someone hunting her in the wilderness of Shuyak Island?

Both men ordered hamburgers for lunch. While they waited for their food, Patterson delivered the bad news. "The judge said we don't have enough evidence for a warrant."

"Can you try another judge?" Nick asked.

Patterson shook his head. "He's our only guy."

"Did you tell him that we suspect they're holding people against their will on the island, and the people are in danger?"

Patterson watched Nick while he talked, noting his bloodshot gray eyes, red face, and tousled hair. He was taking Jane's abduction hard.

"I told him everything," Patterson said, "and he wavered a few moments before refusing. He said he needed just a little more evidence. If we can find anything, I think we'll be able to persuade him to sign the warrant."

After lunch, Patterson navigated the unplowed streets back to trooper headquarters. "We wouldn't be able to do much in this weather, anyway," he told Nick.

"Is the forecast better for tomorrow?"

Patterson shrugged. "Snow wasn't in our forecast for today, so who knows?"

* * *

At 2:00 p.m., Detective Horner rushed into the conference room. She removed her wool cap and snow-covered coat and dropped them in a chair. "Can you believe this weather? If they don't plow the streets, we won't be able to get home."

Horner sat across the table from Nick. "Sorry, I haven't been much help the past two days. Feeney didn't think I had enough to do, so he assigned me to a murder investigation."

"Are you getting anywhere on it?" Patterson asked.

"Not really," Horner said. "The victim is, or was, a banker in Anchorage. He's the head of the consortium that wants to reinvent Kodiak as a tourist mecca."

Patterson nodded. Now he remembered where he'd heard the name Jerry Burns. "Do you have any suspects?"

"Madeline Turner, another consortium member, was seen arguing with Burns in the bar of the Baranof a few hours before someone murdered him. We're looking for her, but she flew to Anchorage yesterday. We don't know what happened to her after the plane landed in Anchorage, but we'll find her."

"From what I've heard, this consortium is not very popular with most Kodiak merchants," Patterson said. "You could have a wide suspect pool."

"Have you found any evidence at the scene?" Nick asked.

Horner shook her head. "It was a brutal attack. The hotel room is a blood-splattered mess. We're still processing it. I was happy to have an excuse to get out of there for a while."

Patterson and Nick filled Horner in on everything they'd learned about Artemis and the various lodges around the country.

"It looks like an obvious pattern to me. I'm surprised Judge Cohen refused the warrant," she said.

"You know Cohen," Patterson said. "He's by the book. I think if we can find anything else, he'll cave."

"What about the mysterious Mr. Holden?" Horner asked.

"I haven't gotten anywhere with that name or with the name Buddy Frank, the Arkansas lodge manager," Nick said. "I suspect they're both aliases."

The three investigators stared at each other.

"I wonder if your murder has anything to do with the kidnappings and the lodge?" Patterson said.

Horner sat back in her chair and stared at Patterson. "Do you think this consortium is involved with Artemis?"

Patterson shrugged. "Maybe they *are* Artemis."

"I'll watch for that connection in my investigation," Horner said.

CHAPTER 54

Wednesday, November 12

7:12 p.m.

I'd spent a long, miserable day trying to survive in a crazy nightmare that only got worse by the minute. Snow poured from the sky all day, and I fought against being buried alive. I used a small branch to poke holes in the accumulating snow around my face, but I felt as if the sheer weight of it was crushing me. I didn't want to disturb the snow too much and reveal my hiding spot to any hunter who might happen upon me. Although my only view of the world was straight up through my little breathing hole, I knew from the rate of accumulation that visibility must be poor. I doubted anyone was hunting in these conditions. Still, I didn't want to test this hypothesis with my life. I stayed awake, maintained a breathing hole through the snow piled on top of me, tried to keep myself as warm as possible, and waited for nightfall.

When darkness finally came, I struggled to push my way through the snow and stand. I took a step and sank into over a foot of snow. I tamped down a small circle near my cave and jumped up and down, trying to restore circulation and warmth to my feet. At the same time, I wiggled my fingers in my gloves and wondered where I'd hide tonight. Any disturbed snow would signal a hiding spot to the hunters, and unless I returned to this spot, I'd never be able to find another natural depression under all the snow. I guessed I'd have to make a cave in the snow like a bear entering hibernation for the winter. Maybe I'd hike to the coast and find a hiding spot among the rocky cliffs. After I took a few steps through the deep snow, however, I knew any amount of hiking would exhaust me.

I post-holed through the deep drifts, taking one deliberate step after the next. At least it was calm. The heavy snow continued to fall, and while visibility was bad, it wasn't a blizzard.

I didn't see the red light above the food station until I was a few feet away from it. I opened the metal lid and removed a sack and a water bottle, then dropped my empty bottle and sack into the container. I counted eight food sacks still in the box. Perhaps one or two people had already visited the station, but I was one of the early ones tonight. I wondered if the snow had buried anyone. Hopefully, they'd awaken before they suffocated.

I looked in my sack. Besides the usual ham sandwich and apple, the kitchen staff, or whoever filled these bags, had included four chemical foot and hand warmers. Feeling suspicious, I massaged them to see if they contained any hidden GPS trackers, but they seemed to be clean and in their original packages. I'd never been so happy to see foot warmers, and I decided to wait to activate them until I'd found my hiding spot for the next day.

I ate my sandwich and apple and put the warmers in my pockets. I then dropped the empty sack in the food bin. I had no desire to dig into the snow for a while, so I decided to wait by the bin to see if anyone else would appear. I needed to tell Janet about the tracker in her patch.

I jumped up and down and vigorously rubbed my hands. It took all my willpower to wait until later to activate the warmers. Finally, I saw the form of someone approaching through the heavy snow.

Janet brushed the snow off her coat. "This is all we need, isn't it?"

I nodded. "Now we have to worry about getting shot, dying from hypothermia, or getting smothered by heavy snow."

Janet opened the bin and removed a sack. She opened it and said, "Well, at least they gave us hand warmers."

"They could stand to put a heat lamp by the food station," I said.

"Wouldn't that be nice?"

Janet seemed even more subdued than usual. She rolled down the top of her sack without eating anything and stuffed it in her pocket.

"What happened?" I finally asked.

"Brooke is dead." Her voice cracked when she spoke.

"What, when? I assumed the weather was too bad for anyone to hunt today."

Janet shook her head. "It happened last night."

"Someone was hunting in the dark?"

"No," Janet said. "Troy, Brooke, and I hiked to the lodge, and a guard shot her." Her words were only a whisper.

"Oh," I said. I couldn't believe they had gone through with their crazy plan. "How far were you from the lodge when she got shot?"

"We were there. Troy thought we might be able to access the compound by skirting around the warehouse on the far side of the complex." She took a deep breath and wiped at the tears on her face. "We waited until the lights went out in the lodge, and then Troy ran across the opening in front of the buildings and made it to the warehouse. We followed Troy's orders. He told us to wait several minutes to see if a guard detected his entry from a surveillance camera. Then, he told Brook to run across the opening next. I was supposed to wait a few minutes and then follow them. When no one appeared after several minutes, Brooke said she was going and took off across the clearing. She nearly made it, but then I heard a rifle blast."

Janet began to sob, and I put my arms around her.

"She dropped," Janet said, wiping her nose with the sleeve of her coat, "and didn't move. Two guards walked toward her. One of them kicked her and then kneeled and checked her pulse. He told the other guard to look for the first intruder and said he'd take care of Brooke."

Janet stopped talking and looked at the ground. I took a step back. "What happened to Troy? Did the guards find him?"

Janet shook her head. "When the guards went in separate directions, I turned and ran as fast as I could. They must have found him, though. There are cameras all over that compound. We were foolish for thinking we could infiltrate it and get their weapons."

I didn't know what to say next. A feeling of despair settled over me. How were we ever going to make it out of here alive?

As I thought about Troy and Brooke, I finally remembered something. "You need to take the patch off your jacket," I said.

"Why?" Janet looked down at her purple patch.

"There's a tracker in it."

She ran her hand over the patch. "Does everyone have a tracker?"

"I don't know, but I bet only the special-prey patches have them. If the person who ordered you doesn't find and kill you without any aids during the duration of his hunt, he can simply follow your tracker to where you're hiding and shoot you."

"How did you get yours off?" she asked.

"I picked at the stitches with my fingers. It wasn't easy." I walked toward her and studied her patch. "I'll help you get it off. Take off your coat."

We studied the patch with our headlamps and began picking at the threads. We were making progress when a form approached through the falling snow.

"Troy!" Janet ran toward him and threw her arms around him. "You're alive. How did you get away?"

Troy returned Janet's hug, but his face remained emotionless. "I got Brooke killed," he said. "At least you made it back here."

Janet stepped away from Troy. "You can't blame yourself for Brooke's death."

"It was my idea to go to the lodge." His voice was a monotone.

"Brooke was a grown woman. She and I chose to go with you. It was a big risk, but it beat waiting to get hunted down by someone."

"How did you get away?" I asked Troy.

"I overpowered the guard and ran," he said. "By then, I knew Brooke was dead, and I didn't care if they shot me."

"Did you get in the warehouse?" Janet asked.

"I got in through a side door," Troy said. "There's an airplane in there?" His statement sounded like a question.

"An airplane?" Janet asked.

"What kind of plane?" I asked at the same time.

Troy looked at me and shrugged. "I don't know much about planes," he said, "but it had floats."

I felt a flutter in my stomach. "Was it black?"

Troy nodded. "How did you know?"

"It sounds like the plane I saw ferrying people away from the dock in Kodiak. If so, it's the plane I found the tail number on and reported to the authorities."

Janet, Troy, and I stared at each other for a few moments. "They must be hiding it so the police can't find it," Troy said.

The spark of hope I still held for being rescued died. *How will Nick and Sergeant Patterson ever find us without the plane and the pilot? We need a good plan—better than the one Troy, Brooke, and Janet just tried— to take over this camp and rescue ourselves.*

"If we could get the plane to the water," Troy said, "maybe we could fly out of here and go for help."

"Do you know how to fly a plane?" Janet asked him.

Troy shook his head. "If it meant getting out of here, I'd give it a try."

I remembered my harrowing adventure when I was forced to land a floatplane alone. I had no wish to replay that incident. "If we can take over the lodge," I said, "I'm sure we can find radios and satellite phones to call for help."

"How do we take over the lodge?" Janet asked. "They'll be on their guard after last night."

"I have an idea," Troy said.

I stiffened. I wasn't sure I liked Troy's ideas.

"I'll let you know if it works," he said.

"Troy," Janet said, "don't try to do something on your own. It's too dangerous."

"I'm not involving anyone else this time," he said.

"How many people like us do you think there are here?" I asked. "I've only seen you guys and the woman you call Icy."

"There are several of these food stations in the woods," Troy said. "The others must use those."

"I hear people get shot all the time," Janet said. "If they aren't bringing any more people here, maybe there aren't very many of us left."

"We need to get a message to the others so we can all meet and make an escape plan," I said. "If we work as a group, we might succeed."

"Some of the troughs are several miles from here," Troy said, "but once the snow melts, I'll hike to them and leave a message."

"We could write a note and put it in the various food bins," Janet said.

Troy shook his head. "What if no one visits a particular trough?" he asked. "Then the people at the lodge would know our plan."

"I guess we can't do much until the snow melts some," I said.

Janet looked up at the sky. "If it ever stops snowing," she said.

"Where's your coat?" Troy asked Janet.

"Jane is helping me remove my patch," she said. "She pulled hers off her coat and found a tracker in it."

Troy touched the white patch on his coat. "I wonder if they all have trackers."

"I don't know," I said, "but it would be a good idea to take it off your coat and check it."

Janet and I went back to work on her jacket, and a few minutes later, we were able to rip the patch off the jacket. I pulled the electronic chip from the pocket on the back of the patch and showed it to Janet and Troy. Troy took the tracker from my hand and threw it into the forest.

"Do you want us to help you remove your patch?" Janet asked.

Troy shook his head. "I'll do it tonight when I return to my hiding spot."

We discussed where to hide in the deep snow. Janet said she planned to return to her usual spot and bury herself. "I hope when I'm done, it will look like something a deer or bear did."

I didn't point out the obvious, mainly because I couldn't think of anything better. If there were only human tracks leading to the disturbed snow, the hunters would easily find her.

"We should go now," Troy said. "If it keeps snowing like this, maybe the snow will cover our tracks."

I headed toward where I thought the coast was, but after several minutes of fighting through the deep snow, I gave up and buried myself at the base of a large spruce tree. I prayed for more snow and fought against the cloud of depression smothering me. For the first time, I doubted I'd survive this nightmare.

CHAPTER 55

Thursday, November 13

7:03 a.m.

Sid stood on the deck of his boat and looked at the blue sky. Nearly two feet of snow had fallen the previous day and night, but the storm had passed. He returned to the galley and called Steve Duncan.

"It looks good for today," Steve said. "But it will take us a couple of hours to get the snow and ice off the plane. Be down at Trident Basin at nine."

"Who's the pilot?" Sid asked.

"Stan will fly," Steve said, "but I'm coming along, too. I want to get a closer look at that lodge."

"Good," Sid said. "So, you'll drop me off today and pick me up in the morning?"

"Roger. Are you sure you want to do this? It sounds dangerous."

"I'll be okay. I want to find enough evidence so Sergeant Patterson has probable cause to convince a judge to sign a search warrant."

"I wish I could go with you," Steve said.

Sid arrived at the KFS office at 8:40 a.m., and five minutes later, Stan, the head pilot at KFS, told him the plane was ready. Stan knocked on the door to Steve's office. He entered the office and emerged a few minutes later, pushing Steve in a wheelchair. Due to the morning low tide, the ramp down to the dock was steep and slippery with the packed-down snow.

"Hang on," Stan told Steve. "This could be a wild ride."

Sid followed Stan and Steve down the ramp. He watched Stan turn the chair around and slowly back it down the steep incline with Steve's head pointed toward the top of the ramp. Steve gripped the arms of the wheelchair, and Sid breathed a sigh of relief when they reached the level dock without a mishap. Stan pushed the chair up close to the plane, and then he helped Steve out of the chair. Steve leaned heavily on Stan, but Sid was impressed by how much progress he'd made in his recovery. Stan helped Steve into the rear seat of the plane and then motioned for Sid to climb into the front-right seat.

Sid looked at Steve. "You can sit up here if you want," he said.

Steve shook his head. "It's too hard for me to crawl up there."

* * *

They were in luck. The winds were calm when they approached Shuyak, and Stan said he'd be able to land in Fort Channel on the southeast corner of the island. Sid hoped Stan could sneak in and out without anyone noticing. He and Stan had discussed the landing, and the pilot said he'd try to come in low and not circle before landing.

Stan smoothly landed the Beaver and pulled into a protected cove. Sid had no idea if anyone from the lodge had detected them. He hoped not, but he'd remain on guard. He strapped on his backpack and thanked Stan and Steve for the ride.

"I'll try to get here by ten a.m. tomorrow to pick you up," Stan said. "Do you want me to land in the same place?"

Sid nodded. "If anything changes, I'll send you a message on my inReach."

He watched the plane taxi and take off. He stood in knee-deep snow, unsure what to do next.

He struggled through the snow for the next hour. Sweat poured from his face, and he unzipped his parka to cool down his body. The snow rarely built up enough at sea level to need snowshoes while hiking in the winter on the islands in the Kodiak Archipelago, but Sid wished he'd thought to bring some with him for this trek. While there was less snow under the thick umbrella of trees, it had still accumulated to a foot or more. The worst part was that he couldn't see the dips and rises in the earth or the rocks, roots, and limbs buried under the snow. He had to make each step deliberate and careful. A broken or sprained ankle could be deadly in these conditions if he couldn't seek shelter.

He leaned against a tree trunk for a few minutes to cool down and slow his breathing. *I'm getting too old for this.* According to his Garmin, he was heading in the general direction of the hunting lodge. He didn't plan to contact the people at the lodge, but he wanted to get close enough to observe the activities around it.

After a short rest, Sid continued his arduous journey across the island. After forty-five minutes, he was about to take another rest break when he heard the unmistakable sound of a gunshot and the simultaneous scream of a man. The sounds weren't close, and at first, Sid thought he'd imagined them, but then he heard one more shot, followed by silence.

Sid knew what he'd heard. Someone had just shot and killed a man. He couldn't determine how far away the shots were, but he was close enough to hear the scream. *Is Patterson right? Are the hunters at the lodge hunting humans? Are there game cameras situated around the island? Do they know I'm here?*

Sid looked up at the trees but didn't see any cameras. The camouflaged game trail cameras were easy enough to hide, though. He decided it was too dangerous to continue hiking toward the lodge during the day. He assumed the hunting would stop once it got dark, and he could resume his trek then.

He dropped his pack at the base of a spruce tree and removed the emergency space blanket from the pack's top pocket. He unfolded the thin metallic blanket and wrapped it around himself, keeping the shiny surface toward his body so it couldn't be seen by someone looking through binoculars.

He dropped to the ground, sinking into the snow. He sat on the side of the tree away from the lodge and hoped no one would hunt this far from the camp or a trail. After a few minutes, his physical exertion had caught up with him, and he fell asleep.

CHAPTER 56

Thursday, November 13

12:30 p.m.

Patterson's desk phone rang, and he angrily swiped it out of its cradle. He and Nick had been trying everything they could to learn more about Artemis, Inc., but they had found nothing of interest.

"Patterson," he barked into the phone.

At first, the caller said nothing, and Patterson was about to hang up when Steve Duncan said, "I need to tell you something."

Patterson sat forward and hunched over his desk, waiting for Steve to say more. "Yes, Steve?" he finally prompted.

"He asked me not to tell you, but I'm concerned about him."

"Steve, what are you talking about?"

"Sid Beatty," Steve said. "One of my pilots and I dropped him off on Shuyak this morning?" he added tentatively.

"What?" Patterson shouted the word into the phone. As if he didn't have enough to worry about, now he had to rescue Sid along with everyone else.

"We're supposed to pick him up in the morning," Steve said. "I just wanted to let you know in case we have a problem."

Patterson exhaled a long breath. He knew he shouldn't yell at Steve for something Sid had done. "Do you know what Sid planned to do on Shuyak?"

"He wanted to collect enough evidence to give you probable cause to search the island."

"Let's hope he doesn't get himself killed in the process," Patterson said. He respected Sid. He was smart and had been a great trooper. Patterson trusted his opinion and insights, but Sid wasn't Superman, and this time, he'd gone too far. "How was he planning to hike in this deep snow?"

"I don't know," Steve said. "I saw him take a few steps, and it was a struggle for him. I don't think he had snowshoes with him. I hope he can make it back to the pickup spot in the morning."

Patterson had a sudden thought. *If he doesn't make it back in time to get picked up, we'll have a reason to search the island to look for him.*

After Patterson disconnected with Steve, his phone rang again.

"Dan, it's Maureen."

"Have you learned anything new?" Patterson asked.

"Unfortunately, no," Horner said. "I've been tied up with this murder case."

"Are you making any progress with it?"

"Not much. My prime suspect, Madeline Turner, had already returned to Anchorage at the time we think the murder occurred."

"Do you have any other suspects?"

"Not yet," Horner said. "How is your investigation going?"

"Not well," Patterson said. "We keep hitting dead ends." He considered telling her about Sid's impromptu trip to Shuyak but decided to wait to see what happened.

After hanging up, Patterson returned to the conference room, where Nick was working. He'd sent one of his young troopers out to buy sandwiches for Nick and him, and the food now sat untouched on the conference room table. Nick was finishing a call when Patterson entered the room. He sat at the head of the table and pulled one of the wrapped sandwiches toward him.

Nick put his phone on the table. "That was my contact in the State Department," he said. "She found an Artemis lodge in Argentina and another one in Kenya, but she didn't learn anything about missing people in those areas."

"Did she find out anything more about Artemis, Inc.?"

Nick shook his head. "Nothing."

While Patterson found the information about the foreign Artemis lodges interesting, it did nothing to further their case.

"I have something interesting," Patterson said and then told Nick about Sid's trip to Shuyak Island.

Nick nodded when Patterson finished. "He's put himself at great risk," Nick said, "but it was a smart move. If he learns anything about the situation there, we'll be able to get our warrant."

"And if he isn't at the pickup spot tomorrow morning, we'll have a reason to search the island to try to find him."

CHAPTER 57

Thursday, November 13

2:54 p.m.

Troy checked the sharpened edge of the utility knife. He'd used a rock to sharpen the blade and had worked at it all night. Once it was fairly sharp, he cut the white patch off his jacket and looked at the back. There was no tracker in the patch. Apparently, only the special prey warranted trackers.

Troy crawled into his hole and took a nap as the sky began to lighten.

When he awoke, he pushed the snow and brush off himself and stood. *Now it's showtime.*

Except for the other morning when he'd sprinted through the dawn while hunters shot at him, he hadn't seen daylight since he'd arrived on the island. Although it was muted by the trees and the low angle of the sun on the horizon in November, he felt a sense of freedom as he looked around without the aid of his headlamp.

He sat by a tree near the main trail, clutching his weapons. He held the small knife in his right hand and the heavy crowbar in his left. The lodge workers had packed down the trail, making it easier for the hunters to traverse, so he felt confident someone would walk past his hiding spot. He waited for over an hour, but then he heard human footsteps on the trail. Troy crouched and waited for the hunter to walk past him.

The man seemed oblivious to his surroundings as he hiked through the woods. Troy didn't know what the hunter was doing. Was he headed somewhere to get a better vantage point, or was he looking for disturbances in the snow?

The hunter's plans made no difference. As soon as he walked past the spot where Troy was crouched, Troy sprang. He jumped on the man and sank the knife into his neck.

The hunter struggled to pull his rifle from his shoulder, but Troy didn't give him the chance. He hit the man hard over the head with the crowbar and stabbed him again in the throat.

Troy quickly dragged the hunter off the trail and into the woods. He heard gurgling sounds coming from his throat, so he stabbed him a third time. He dragged the man far enough from the trail so that passing hunters wouldn't see him. Now, he had a cleanup job to do.

Scarlet blood stained the pure white snow from the point where Troy had first stabbed the man to where he'd left his body. Troy spent over an hour trying to cover the blood with snow. He managed to lighten the stain, but he didn't obliterate it. He returned to the body and took the hunter's pack and high-powered rifle. With this weapon, the next hunter would be easier to kill.

Troy moved down the trail closer to the lodge so that he could get the jump on the next hunter before he reached the bloodstained snow. He stayed there until dark, but no one hiked past his position. Troy knew this was not the only trail leading away from the compound, so if others were hunting today, they must have followed different trails or taken off into the deep snow to forge their own paths.

Troy hiked through the woods away from the trail until he came to the large tree where he and Brooke had hidden. He buried the rifle and the hunter's pack in the snow under the tree and then hiked to the food trough. He wasn't hungry, but he knew he needed to maintain his strength until he'd accomplished his mission and every last person at the hunting compound had paid for what they'd done to Brooke.

No one was at the food bin when he arrived, and he helped himself to two lunch sacks and a bottle of water. He ate a sandwich and an apple and stuffed the other sack in his pocket. He was about to leave when Jane appeared.

"How are you doing?" she asked. She pushed her hood away from her head and watched him.

Troy nodded. "I'm okay," he said.

"What's on your coat?" she asked. "It looks like blood."

He ran his hand over the stain. He wanted to tell Jane what he'd done, but he wasn't ready to include her or anyone else in his plan until he had more weapons. "It's just mud."

Jane stared at him for a moment and then nodded. She opened the lid to the food bin, dropped in her empty water bottle, and removed a sack and a full bottle of water. "At least the snow stopped," she said, "but it's cold. I hope they put more hand warmers in the sack." She looked inside and nodded. "Good," she said, holding up two packages of warmers. She again gently squeezed the packages to check for trackers but didn't find any.

"There are extra sacks here," Troy said. "You could take two and have extra warmers. Besides, we should all be eating more than one sandwich and one apple every day. I think they're trying to weaken us so we'll be easier to hunt."

Jane stuck the paper sack and the bottle of water in her pocket. "I'll never eat another ham sandwich again after I leave here."

Troy nodded. "Or an apple."

"Did you hear a plane this morning?" she asked.

Troy shook his head. "No. Was it low?"

"Maybe I was hearing things," Jane said, "but I thought it sounded low."

"It was probably going to the lodge."

Jane said nothing for several moments and then stared into Troy's eyes. "Before you go to the compound again, tell me, okay? I know you want revenge for Brooke, but she wouldn't want you to get killed."

Troy watched Jane and thought about what to say. "I have a plan," he said, "but I'm not ready yet. I'll let you know when I am."

Troy didn't give Jane time to respond. He turned and hiked back to the big spruce tree where he'd buried the rifle and pack. He wanted to check the pack to see what was in it. Perhaps it held other weapons or gear he could use. He could also probably find some snacks. He felt a jolt. *Is there a radio or satellite phone in the pack?* He could call for help or at least monitor the radio traffic between those at the lodge and the hunters in the field. Why hadn't he considered this before now?

Troy uncovered the pack as soon as he reached the tree. He dug into the snow at the base of the spruce until he reached the ground. He stashed the rifle in the hole and sat on solid ground, pulling the pack onto his lap. He opened the pack and began removing its contents. In the front pocket, he found a small first aid kit, an emergency space blanket, and two energy bars. He ate one of the bars and continued to the large main pocket. He pulled out a raincoat, a sack lunch, a large water bottle, and a pair of binoculars. He discovered more ammunition for the rifle and dropped it into his coat pocket.

He found the electronics in the side pockets. He switched on the Garmin and stared at the date and time. *November 13?* He'd been on this island for over a month. The time made more sense than the date. It was 8:20 p.m.

He couldn't think of a practical use for the Garmin. By now, he was oriented to his surroundings. He could find his way from his hiding spot to the food trough to the lodge. Where else did he need to go? He dropped it into the pack and pulled out a range finder used by hunters to determine the distance of a planned shot. He silently thanked his father for taking him hunting when he was young. He immediately dropped the range finder back into the main pocket of the pack with the Garmin. He wouldn't need a range finder. He planned to shoot his game up close and personal. In the other side pocket, he found a small radio. He switched it on and set it to the side.

Troy next removed a thin cell phone and powered it up. His pulse quickened for a moment, but he soon saw that he didn't have a signal. Perhaps the hunter was carrying the device because he wanted a camera to record his kills. Troy dropped the phone back into the pack and then froze. Could the people in the camp track the hunter through his phone or Garmin? Maybe there was some other GPS tracker in the pack.

In the bottom of the right pocket, Troy found a pocketknife. He dropped it into his coat pocket. He zipped up the pack. He knew he'd have to get rid of it in case it could be tracked. Was it safe to keep the radio? He decided the benefits outweighed the risks. He'd have an edge if he could monitor what was happening in the camp. He switched the radio off for now to conserve the battery.

Troy hefted the pack onto his back and hiked into the woods through the deep snow. He went in the opposite direction from the body. He hiked for over half an hour and then buried the pack in the snow. He followed his footprints back to his tree. He knew he should try to cover his tracks, but he didn't have the energy. If a hunter or a searcher found him, he'd shoot them with his new rifle.

When he arrived back at his tree, he spread the space blanket over the bare ground and sat on it. He opened the sack and unwrapped a roast beef sandwich. He then ripped the top off a bag of chips and feasted on something different from ham and cheese and an apple. He switched on the radio and listened.

Voices immediately burst from the small device, and Troy fumbled with it to turn down the volume. He held it to his ear and listened.

"Hunter seventeen, this is base. Do you copy? Do you need assistance?" a deep voice asked.

The radio remained silent for several moments, and then the voice repeated the two questions.

"Ray?" the deep voice asked. "Are you there?"

The one-sided transmissions continued. After several minutes, Troy switched off the radio and buried himself in the snow. Soon, a search team would be sent to look for the missing hunter, and while Troy would like to kill them all, he thought such a move seemed too risky. He wasn't sure how many men would be sent to search, but he knew they'd all be armed, and they probably had night optics, or at least searchlights. He'd remain hidden until morning and then plan his next attack. If he could score another rifle or two, he could give one to Jane and perhaps one to Janet. At least then, they'd have a fighting chance against the animals who were hunting them.

CHAPTER 58

Thursday, November 13
7:25 p.m.

Sid awoke with a start and looked at his watch. He'd slept for nearly three hours. It was already beginning to get dark. He stood and stomped his legs to regain circulation and warmth. He waited impatiently for total darkness. He assumed any other shots during the day would have awakened him, but he couldn't be sure. He thought about the young man whose scream he'd heard. He was almost certainly dead, and he wondered what the hunter did after the kill. He couldn't do much with the body besides taking photos, and even that would be risky. *What kind of sick monster hunts humans?*

He felt his anger and resolve grow as he stood and watched the forest darken. He wanted to march into the lodge and murder everyone there, but he knew he had to return to Kodiak with evidence for Patterson. Once Patterson had a warrant, the troopers and the FBI could storm the island, shut down the lodge, arrest the hunters and those operating this business, and rescue the victims, including Jane.

Was Jane still alive, or had a hunter tracked and killed her? Perhaps they hadn't brought Jane to Shuyak but had murdered her soon after taking her. Sid shook these thoughts from his head. He had to remain rational and focused. He had to believe Jane was still alive.

Sid pulled an energy bar from his pack, ate it, and took a long drink from his water bottle. He also removed his handgun and put it in the pocket of his parka. As the last remnants of daylight faded, he donned his headlamp and turned it on. He looked at his Garmin and decided that instead of hiking toward the lodge, he'd head parallel to it for a distance, hoping to encounter victims hiding in the woods. They had to eat sometimes, and perhaps the lodge provided meals for them once it got dark. He checked the Garmin to make sure he was still tracking his movements. At some point in the night, he'd have to reverse his steps to return to the pickup spot. The muscles in his legs burned, and he knew the trek back to the pickup point would take him much longer than his day hike had. Not only would he have to navigate the snow-packed forest in the dark, but he'd need to fight muscle fatigue.

He was beginning to think he was wasting time and energy. With every step, he risked the danger of spraining or breaking an ankle, and then what would happen to him? He knew he already had enough evidence for Patterson to get a warrant. He was a retired sergeant with the Alaska State Troopers. A judge would believe him when he said he'd heard someone shoot a man.

Sid focused on the ground as he post-holed through the deep snow. He cursed himself again for not bringing snowshoes with him. After every few steps, he stopped and looked around the woods but only saw trees. He was about to turn around and begin retracing his steps to the coast when he saw the soft glow of a red light a hundred yards away. He slowly moved toward it, and as he got closer, he made out the figure of a man silhouetted by the light. Sid cautiously approached.

The man appeared to be eating something. Was he a victim or a hunter? His hood was pulled over his head, and Sid couldn't make out his features. He guessed he was male due to his size but couldn't tell if he was young or old.

Sid unzipped the right-side pocket of his parka and put his hand on the butt of his gun. He announced his presence when he was a few feet away from the man.

"Hello," he said, "I mean you no harm."

The man dropped the paper sack he was holding and attempted to bolt into the woods. The deep snow slowed his pace.

"Wait," Sid said. "I need to talk to you. I can help you get off this island."

The man stopped and looked at Sid. "Are you going to shoot me?" he asked.

Sid pushed the gun back into his pocket and held his hands in the air. "No," he said. "I'm a retired Alaska State Trooper. I came to the island to find out what's going on here. I'm leaving in the morning, and you can come with me. With your help, we can get a warrant to search the island and free the hostages."

The man stared at Sid for several moments and then must have decided that the possibility of rescue was worth the risk Sid might pose. The man retraced his steps and stood beside the metal crate under the light.

"How did you get here?" the man asked.

"A plane dropped me off on the southeast shore, and I hiked inland," Sid said. He held out his hand. "My name is Sid Beatty."

"Tom Stroud," the man said, shaking Sid's hand.

"How long have you been here?" Sid asked.

Tom shrugged. "They took my watch from me, and I've lost track of the days." A strand of long, blond hair escaped his hood. His brown eyes looked bloodshot and tired.

"What's going on here?" Sid asked.

"These madmen are hunting us," Tom said. "We're prey animals."

Sid nodded. "That's what I thought."

"The pilot's supposed to return for me in the morning," Sid said. "Would you like to go with me?"

"I'd give anything to escape this nightmare," Tom said, "but what about the others?"

"If you return to Kodiak with me and tell a judge what's happening here, the troopers and the FBI can get a warrant to raid the island, shut down the lodge, and rescue the captives."

A tear trickled down Tom's cheek. "I can't believe I'm getting out of here."

"Are you strong enough to hike?" Sid asked. "It'll be a long, slow hike through this deep snow."

Tom nodded. "When do we leave?"

"Now."

CHAPTER 59

Friday, November 14

7:45 a.m.

The sound of an engine and voices awakened Troy. He made a larger hole in the snow above his face and squinted through the spruce branches. It was still dark. They couldn't be hunting.

The previous day's events returned in a rush, and he hugged the hunter's rifle to his body. The people running the lodge must have sent a search team to look for the missing man. Troy remembered the radio. He turned it on with the volume as low as possible and held it to his ear.

He soon ascertained that three ATVs and search groups were combing the woods along the main packed-down trails. As the sky lightened, Troy remained hidden, waiting for the activity to die down. He knew once the searchers found the hunter's body, they'd focus their efforts on this area of the woods. He needed to escape and hike to another part of the forest. He'd wait near one of the other trails for a hunter to pass by him.

Once they found the body, would the lodge manager warn the other hunters to stay in camp, or would the added element of danger entice some into the woods?

Troy listened and waited for his chance to make a run for it. Finally, at midmorning, he heard a shaky voice on the radio. "Bingo," the man said.

"Is he okay?" a deeper voice asked.

"Negative," the first man said.

A long pause followed, and then the second man said, "Where?"

"About five hundred feet east of trail two."

"Give me your exact coordinates," the second man said.

The first man provided detailed longitude and latitude coordinates.

"I'm on my way," the second man said.

Everyone at the camp must have followed the second man because Troy soon heard two other ATVs and the voices of several men. He knew this was his chance. He could move unnoticed while the lodge crew focused on the dead hunter.

Troy pushed the snow and branches off of him and slowly emerged from his hiding spot. He looked around the woods, but he saw no one. In the distance, he could hear the rumbling ATV engines and the din of voices. He slung the rifle strap over his shoulder, turned off the radio, and dropped it in his pocket.

He made a wide trail around the voices. After a cold night, the snow crunched under his boots, and he feared the men would hear him. The searchers could easily follow his tracks through the woods, but several tracks now crisscrossed the deep snow. They'd have no reason to believe his belonged to the man who'd killed the hunter. If someone had asked him six weeks earlier if he could kill another human, Troy would have said no. Now, however, he wanted to go on a murderous rampage and kill every last person in the hunting lodge. He didn't care if he spent the rest of his life in prison. They all needed to pay for killing Brooke.

The sound of the ATVs faded as he hiked, and finally, he heard nothing. He continued to plow through the snow until he came to another packed-down trail. Then he hid behind the biggest spruce tree he could find.

CHAPTER 60

Friday, November 14

10:10 a.m.

Sid couldn't remember when he'd felt this tired. The muscles in his legs burned and felt cramped from the exertion of the previous day and night. He considered himself in good shape for his age, but after hiking through the deep snow for several hours, he felt every minute of his sixty-seven years. By contrast, the previous night's four-hour hike to the coast seemed to have invigorated his young companion. While Sid sat on a rock waiting for the plane to arrive, Tom paced the shore. Sid had reminded Tom several times to be careful. They were exposed on the beach, and while they were a long distance from the lodge, there was no guarantee a hunter wouldn't see them and shoot.

Sid studied the sky and watched the approaching wall of snow. He removed his inReach from his pocket and checked for messages. At 8:00 a.m., Steve had sent a message saying they had snow showers moving through Kodiak, but they still planned to arrive at the pickup point on Shuyak around 10:00 a.m. Had the snow grown heavier and more persistent? Was the flight delayed? The inReach didn't indicate any new messages, so he dropped the device back in his pocket.

Tom sat on the beach next to Sid. "What time is it?" he asked.

"Ten twenty," Sid said.

"Are they delayed?" Tom had pushed back his hood, and clumps of blond hair fell around his face.

Sid pointed to the distant clouds. "I think they might be fighting snow," he said. "If they have to avoid snow showers, it'll take them longer to get here."

Tom drew his knees up to his chest and hugged his legs. He stared at the sky and said nothing.

Twenty minutes later, Sid finally heard an airplane engine.

"Is that them?" Tom asked, jumping to his feet.

"I don't know," Sid said, "but I think so."

A few minutes later, they saw the approaching white and teal Beaver. The plane dropped altitude as it approached the cove where they waited. It bumped over the waves and pulled up to the shore. Stan jumped off the float and walked the plane into the beach.

"The snow is getting heavy," he said. "I thought I was going to have to turn around."

Sid crawled into the front-right seat, and Tom climbed into the back and sat next to Steve. In an earlier message, Sid had told Steve he was bringing a young man back to town. As soon as Sid shut the passenger door, Stan turned the plane around, pushed it away from the beach, and jumped on the float. He wasted no time powering away from the shore and taking off. Sid could read the tension in Stan's body language. He knew the weather was marginal for flying and could see the pilot was in no mood for conversation.

"The weather is dicey," Steve said. "We should let Stan concentrate, but I have to know. Did you see any sign of Jane?"

Sid exhaled a long breath. "No. Nothing."

"What about you?" Steve asked Tom. "Did you see Jane?"

"No," Tom said. "Sid described her to me, but I never saw her."

They remained quiet for the next hour while Stan navigated through and around heavy snow squalls. As a pilot, Sid understood how risky it was to fly in this weather. When the snow got thick, he concentrated on the GPS and other instruments to ensure Stan didn't get disoriented and fly the plane into the water. Luckily, the entire flight was over the ocean, so they didn't have to worry about crashing into a mountain.

When the hazy silhouette of Kodiak came into view, Sid felt his muscles relax.

Stan said, "I think this is my last flight for the day."

"We'll shut things down until it clears," Steve said.

A moment later, Steve said, "Sid, I called Sergeant Patterson yesterday and told him where you were. I'm sorry, but I was really worried about you, and I wanted the troopers to be prepared to mount a search and rescue if you weren't at the pickup spot this morning."

"It's all right," Sid said. "He's the first person I plan to call when we land."

Sid didn't need to call Patterson because he was standing at the end of the dock waiting for the plane as Stan nosed the Beaver into its stall. Patterson seemed oblivious to the snow cascading around him and piling up on his coat. He helped secure the float lines to the cleats and waited for Sid to emerge from the plane.

"I won't waste my breath telling you that you shouldn't have gone to Shuyak alone," Patterson said. "I'm sure you know better."

Sid smiled. "I didn't get myself shot, anyway."

Patterson's focus left Sid when Tom Stroud climbed from the plane and jumped onto the dock.

Sid motioned to Tom. "I brought you some live evidence," he said to Patterson.

Sid made introductions, and Patterson and Tom shook hands.

"Your friend Fred reported you missing," Patterson said.

Tom attempted to talk, but he choked up, and tears ran down his face. He fought to regain his composure and said, "Man, I'm so happy to be off that island."

"Let's grab you some food and take you back to headquarters," Patterson said. "You, too, Sid. I want to get your reports written and to a judge as quickly as possible."

Sid looked at the sky. "You won't be able to fly to Shuyak until this stuff moves through. We barely made it back here."

Patterson nodded. "I know, but we're on our way the minute it lifts."

While they talked, Stan and two KFS employees helped Steve out of the plane and into a wheelchair on the dock. Stan and Steve then joined Sid, Patterson, and Tom.

Patterson looked from Stan to Steve. "Can we borrow Stan and another pilot and two of your planes when we fly back to Shuyak? We'll need firepower when we invade the camp."

Steve nodded. "I wish I could go with you, but I wouldn't be much help."

"You've already done enough," Patterson said. "Without you, we never would've broken this case."

CHAPTER 61

Friday, November 14

12:30 p.m.

Tom said he wanted a hamburger, so Patterson stopped at McDonald's on the way back to trooper headquarters. He gave Tom and Sid a few minutes alone in the conference room to eat their lunch, and he called Nick.

"Sid's back," he said. "He brought one of the kidnapping victims with him. We're in the conference room here if you want to join us."

"Jane?" Nick's voice shook when he said her name.

"I'm sorry," Patterson said. "We don't have any more information about her."

"I'm on my way," Nick said.

When Nick stepped into the conference room a few minutes later, Patterson wondered how he'd managed to get to trooper headquarters so quickly. He'd neglected to send Vena to pick him up at the hotel, so he must have taken a taxi.

Patterson introduced Nick and Tom. "Sid was just telling me the harrowing story about his hike across the island and hearing gunshots."

Nick took a seat at the far end of the table and nodded to Sid.

Sid explained how he and Thomas had met at the food bin.

"They put sack lunches out for you?" Nick asked.

Tom looked at him and nodded. "Every night it was the same thing: a ham and cheese sandwich, an apple, and a bottle of water. After the big snow, they put hand warmers in the sacks."

"How thoughtful," Patterson said, shaking his head.

Tom continued to tell Patterson and Nick about how he hid all day and then visited the food bins at night. He explained that there were several bins throughout the forest. "I saw other food bins," he said, "but I mostly got food from the one closest to my hiding spot. One woman told me I should sometimes go to the other bins so they couldn't pinpoint my position." Tom wiped his mouth with a napkin and took a drink of water. "I stayed where I was, though, because I rarely saw any other prey animals there, so I thought the hunting pressure would be lower in my section of the forest." Tom looked from Patterson to Nick. "I tried to think like a hunter," he said.

"They called you a 'prey animal'?" Nick's voice was low, but Patterson could sense the growing rage in the FBI agent.

"That's what the woman I met at the food bin called us," Tom said.

"What did this woman look like?" Patterson asked.

As Tom described her, Patterson thumbed through the missing person reports he'd collected. He shook his head. He looked at Nick. "She doesn't fit the description on any of my reports."

"She told me she'd been on the island for a long time," Tom said. "She wouldn't tell me her name because she said she didn't want to get close to anyone. She said she'd gotten to know too many people who'd died when the hunters shot them."

"Besides this woman, did you meet anyone else?" Nick asked.

"A few people," Tom said. "I met a girl named Charli and a guy named David."

"Charli," Patterson said. "That could be Charlotte Porter, the young woman who disappeared from the Alutiiq Museum. Can you describe her?"

Tom shrugged. "She was average height and had brown hair and brown eyes."

"It fits her description," Patterson said. "How long ago did you last see her?"

Tom blew out a breath. "Maybe a week ago?" he said.

"What about the other one—David?" Patterson asked.

"I only met him at the food bin once," Tom said, "and he didn't say much. He was terrified, and I could tell he was afraid to trust me."

"You only ever saw three other people at your food bin?" Nick asked.

"Yes," Tom said, "but I went to another food bin once and met two other people. I remember Brooke because she had beautiful green eyes. I think the guy's name was Troy. That's it, though. I tried to stay away from the main trails."

"Brooke could be the young woman who was kidnapped from Homer, and one of the Anchorage victims is named Troy," Patterson said.

"What about surveillance cameras?" Nick asked. "Did they have cameras in the woods or near the food bins?"

Tom shook his head. "I looked for them, but I never saw any."

Patterson and Nick questioned Tom and Sid for another hour, and then Patterson asked one of his troopers to take Tom and Sid home.

"I hope I still have an apartment," Tom said. "I haven't been there to pay my rent."

"Detective Horner with the Kodiak Police Department told me that your friend Fred made your last rent payment for you," Patterson said.

Tom nodded. "He's a good guy."

Sid looked exhausted, so Patterson shook the ex-trooper's hand and told him to go home and get some sleep.

As soon as Sid and Tom were gone, Patterson returned to his office and wrote up everything the pair had told him. He then called Detective Horner and filled her in on the recent events. She said she'd meet him at the courthouse. He disconnected, and then he and Nick headed out into the snow to find Judge Cohen.

Twenty minutes later, they returned to trooper headquarters with the warrant. Now, they just had to wait for the snow to stop.

CHAPTER 62

Friday, November 14

4:00 p.m.

The snow fell relentlessly all day. Troy periodically listened to his radio and heard the lodge employees talk about where they were searching for the hunter's killer. He heard them discussing trail cameras and knew they were mounting the small surveillance cameras near where they'd discovered the hunter's body. He'd stay away from that area of the woods. They must have realized the killer had taken the hunter's radio, but they continued to talk freely on it. Perhaps they didn't care if he heard them.

Finally, as it was beginning to get dark, Troy heard someone noisily stomping through the deep snow. He injected a shell into the chamber of the rifle and again silently thanked his father for taking him hunting when he was a kid. He wasn't much of a hunter now, but he knew how to handle a rifle, and this was the most important hunting trip of his life. He gripped the weapon and waited until the man got closer. Then, Troy stepped out onto the trail and shot the man in the center of his torso. The hunter fumbled for his rifle but then dropped to the ground. Troy approached him and then shot him again in the head. He hoped the rifle shots wouldn't give him away and that the employees at the camp would think another hunter had just bagged his prey. He grabbed the hunter under his arms and pulled him into the woods. He started covering the trail of blood, but the snow was quickly obliterating the crimson stain.

Troy took the hunter's rifle and unsnapped a large hunting knife from the man's belt. He then rummaged through the hunter's coat pockets until he found the radio. It would be good to have a second radio when the batteries died on the first one. He felt certain there weren't GPS trackers in the radios, or the searchers would have found him by now. He discovered extra ammunition in the hunter's pack and dropped it into his pocket.

He waited until dark and then circled the area where the lodge employees had mounted the trail cameras. He needed to avoid detection, but he wanted to return to the food trough where he thought he'd find Jane and Janet.

When he approached, Janet stood under the red light, eating her sandwich. She looked at him and then froze and backed away.

"It's okay," he said. He pulled back his hood. "It's me."

Janet continued to back away from him. "Where did you get the guns?" she asked.

"I took them," he said.

"How? Did you go back to the lodge?"

Troy shook his head. He wasn't sure if he should tell Janet what he'd done to get the weapons. Still, she needed to know about the extra trail cameras and the searchers in the woods. They'd stopped their search for the day, but they'd be back at it in the morning.

Jane then stepped into the clearing and stared at Troy. He placed the two rifles on the ground so he'd look less threatening.

"Where did those come from?" she asked.

"I killed one hunter yesterday and another today," Troy said. "I have their rifles and radios."

"How did you do it?" Janet asked.

Troy explained how he'd stolen the utility knife from the warehouse when he, Brooke, and Janet had gone to the lodge. "I sharpened it the best I could," he said. "It wasn't much of a weapon, but I was determined to make it work. I jumped a hunter when he passed me on the trail." Troy left out the part about beating the man with the crowbar. Janet and Jane didn't need to know everything.

"They searched for and found the hunter this morning, and they're looking for his killer," Troy said. "They mounted trail cameras around the area where they found the body. Try to avoid the area to the east of here." Troy pointed in that direction, although the forest looked the same in all directions.

"I heard the commotion in the woods today," Jane said. "Now it makes sense."

"What about the second rifle?" Janet asked. "How did you get that one?"

"I shot a second hunter late this afternoon," Troy said. "I can try to get more rifles tomorrow, but I suspect that when a second hunter doesn't return tonight, they'll shut down the hunt until they find the killer."

Jane nodded. "They'll probably also try to flush us out of hiding and kill us. With the heavy snow and now this, they might shut down the camp for the winter."

Icy suddenly appeared from out of the woods. She'd obviously been listening to the conversation for a while because she said, "You'd better take extra food tonight because it won't be safe to approach a food bin by tomorrow evening."

"Why?" Janet asked.

"Think about it," Icy said. "They have us conditioned to believe we're safe once it gets dark, and they've trained us to gather at the food bins. All they have to do is round us up here and shoot us."

Jane nodded. "They were content to leave us alone at night when they had all the power, but now that Troy's made the woods more dangerous for them, their game won't be as much fun to play, and they'll end it."

"How do we tell the others?" Janet asked. "Is there any way to get the message to them?"

They stared at each other. "Besides those rifles," Icy asked, "what other weapons do you have?"

Troy unsnapped the sheath on his belt and removed the six-inch hunting knife he'd taken from the second hunter. He then showed them the much smaller pocketknife he'd found on the first guy. "I also have two of their radios," he said.

"We don't have any choice," Icy said. "We have to act now, or soon, we will all die."

"I'm ready to attack the lodge tonight," Troy said, "but I haven't been able to come up with a good plan."

"Why don't we wait until morning?" Jane asked. "Darkness gives us cover, but it also limits our visibility. We can't see where the guards or the surveillance cameras are."

"It's also very quiet at night," Janet said. "If they're looking for the second missing hunter in the morning, we might be able to sneak into the lodge undetected while they're distracted."

Icy nodded. "Let's get into position tonight. In the morning, we can monitor the radio and watch the camp. When some of the people leave to search for the missing hunter, we can make our move, take over the camp, and call for help."

"It sounds like a good plan to me," Jane said. "I'll take one of the rifles."

"Do you know how to shoot it?" Icy asked.

"Oh yes," Jane said. "I've had practice."

CHAPTER 63

Friday, November 14

8:10 p.m.

Nick sat at a table by the window in the bar at the Baranof Inn. He watched the fluffy snowflakes drift past the window toward the ground. Patterson had said the snow was supposed to end sometime in the middle of the night. He also told Nick that he'd have his plane cleaned off, warmed up, and ready to go by dawn. He told Nick to be at Trident Basin by 7:30 a.m.

Steve said he'd make sure that two of the KFS planes were ready to depart at the same time. Nick, Patterson, and four troopers would ride in Patterson's plane. Maureen Horner and four KPD officers would go in the second plane, and the third would carry a mixture of KPD officers and troopers. The group had met for three hours earlier in the day to plan their assault. Patterson would land his plane in the cove in front of the lodge. The third plane would also land there, but the second plane with Horner and her officers would land on the other side of the island and await further instructions. If all went well, the pilot of the second plane would follow the other two planes and land near the lodge, but Patterson said he didn't want to put all his eggs in one basket. If the people at the lodge managed to ambush the first two planeloads of troopers and officers, he wanted Horner free to mount an attack from a different angle. Horner said she planned to give Patterson and his group thirty minutes, and if she hadn't heard from him by then, she and her officers would begin the long trek across the island and approach the lodge from the other direction.

251

Nick pushed his half-eaten hamburger to the side and sipped his scotch. He liked Patterson's plan, but it was risky. His biggest fear was that some of the victims would get caught in the crossfire if things turned ugly. If Jane was still alive, he knew she'd be planning some way to escape, and her visibility would make her vulnerable. Still, he couldn't think of a safe way to approach the lodge. If the people in the compound were hunting humans, they'd probably do almost anything to hide their dirty secrets. The troopers and police had to mount a sudden and forceful attack.

Nick paid the dinner tab and headed back to his room. He knew he wouldn't sleep.

CHAPTER 64

Friday, November 14

10:15 p.m.

Before leaving the circle of light near the food bin, I checked the rifle Troy had handed me to ensure there was no shell in the chamber. I saw Troy do the same thing with his rifle. Troy gave me extra shells for my rifle, and I dropped them in my pocket. I slung the rifle strap over my shoulder and tried to ignore my burning stomach. I knew there was a good chance I'd be dead in twelve hours, and I was not feeling particularly brave. I willed myself to "do" and not "think."

Troy led our ragged little group through the deep snow. Flakes continued accumulating, and it was well over my knees in the deepest spots. Icy followed behind Troy, and Janet trailed behind her. Since I had the second rifle, I brought up the rear. Troy painstakingly stomped his feet into the snow with each step, and Janet, Icy, and I tried to follow in his footsteps. We each lost our footing and fell several times as we tried to navigate the snow and the uneven ground. While the snow cushioned our falls, standing again was no easy feat, and we soon became exhausted and forced to slow our pace.

Troy followed a circuitous route around the area where he suspected the surveillance cameras were located. He also avoided the main trail. While walking on the packed-down trail would have been much easier, he believed those in the camp were monitoring the few trails leading from the lodge into the forest. I agreed with him. The guards probably thought any possible attackers would have to approach the lodge on one of the trails due to the deep snow in the ungroomed portion of the woods.

We took several rest breaks and spoke quietly. Icy made it her job to monitor the trees for mounted trail cameras, but I wondered about the effectiveness of a trail camera in the heavy snow. Despite, or perhaps due to, the difficulty of our strenuous trek, I believed these were the perfect conditions to approach the compound, and I thought we'd arrive undetected.

My legs burned, and I didn't think I could go much farther. I had no sense of the time, but I knew we'd been hiking for hours. Suddenly, Troy stopped, and Janet, who'd been watching her feet, bumped into his back.

Troy turned to look at us. "This is it," he whispered. "The lodge is in front of us."

Icy and I move alongside Troy and Janet. Through the falling snow, I could barely make out the soft glow of the lights at the lodge. Icy led us a few steps back into the woods, and we found places to sit at the bases of two huge spruce trees. Less snow had accumulated near the trunks of the trees. I sat, pulled my knees up to my chest, and managed to fall asleep within minutes. Exhaustion had overwhelmed my muscles and my brain, and my body demanded time to recharge.

I don't know how long I slept, but I awoke to Janet gently shaking my arm. She lowered her mouth to my right ear. "There's activity at the lodge. It's nearly daylight. The searchers must be preparing to head out to look for the second missing hunter."

CHAPTER 65

Saturday, November 15

6:03 a.m.

Nick had already downed three cups of coffee and couldn't wait any longer. He called a taxi for a ride to Trident Basin and the floatplane dock.

As he'd predicted, he hadn't slept at all the previous night. He could think of nothing but Jane. How was she faring in this deep snow? From what Sid and Tom had reported, Nick knew she was probably in the woods trying to stay hidden and warm—if she was still alive. He shook his head. It did him no good to think the worst, but from his training and experience as an FBI profiler, he knew the odds were against Jane.

When he arrived at Trident Basin, he saw Patterson hard at work cleaning the snow off the trooper plane. Nick hurried down the ramp to lend a hand.

Patterson acknowledged Nick with a smile. "I knew you'd get here early."

"I thought you could use some help with this," Nick said. He glanced over at the dock used by the charter floatplane companies and saw Stan and another pilot cleaning off two of the KFS planes.

"Thank God the snow finally stopped," Patterson said. "It's supposed to be in the midforties today, so the streets will be a mess when all of this starts to melt."

"It'll be easier for the Shuyak victims if some of the snow melts, though," Nick said.

"I plan to rescue all of them today."

Nick nodded. "It might be tough to convince them to come out of hiding."

"I'm bringing a bullhorn," Patterson said. "I hope to announce our presence and convince them the threat is over, and we'll give them a ride back to town."

"How will we know when we have everyone?"

Patterson stopped pushing the snow off the wings and stared at Nick. "I don't know," he said at last. "We'll have to question everyone we rescue and ask them if they think we've missed anyone. Then, once we shut down the lodge, we'll need to return in a few days to see if anyone else comes forward."

Nick nodded. "I don't know what else we can do."

The troopers and police officers began arriving at Trident Basin a few minutes later. Detective Horner joined the two men on the dock.

Nick smiled at Horner. "Are you ready for this?"

Detective Horner had her long hair in a ponytail and wore a blue wool cap pulled down over her ears.

"I'm getting used to dangerous assignments with you," she said.

"Just don't get shot this time."

"I don't plan to," she said. She looked at Patterson. He'd started the plane and was standing on the float. "I'll wait for your call before we approach the lodge."

"Roger," Patterson said.

Nick climbed into the front-right seat of the plane and nodded to troopers Mark Traner, Sara Byram, Peter Boyle, and Brad Simpton as they climbed into the rear of the aircraft. He knew and respected all four troopers from previous assignments in Kodiak. Patterson had assembled his A team for the frontline assault on the lodge. The four troopers wore their game faces and looked ready for action.

"We'll lead the way," Patterson said. "The second plane of troopers and police will follow us, and Maureen and her officers will bring up the rear." He looked behind him at his troopers. "Are you ready?"

The troopers responded in unison. "Yes, sir!"

"Good," Patterson said. "I'll let the plane warm up, and we'll wait for it to get a little lighter."

CHAPTER 66

Saturday, November 15

7:04 a.m.

I was sure everyone could hear my heart thumping in my chest. I stuffed my gloves in my coat pockets and gripped the rifle. My hands shook so much that I doubted I could hit anything I aimed at.

Troy looked at me. "Since we have the rifles," he said, "we should go first." He looked from Janet to Icy. "Stay right behind us," he said. "Let's move fast and get to the warehouse before they can see us."

The snow had stopped, but it was still dark, and I could see little of the compound except for the glow from the interior lights and the pinpricks of lights from the flashlights and headlamps of those moving in the dark in front of the main building. Two four-wheelers choked to life, and a third one soon followed.

"I bet they wished they had snowmachines," Janet whispered.

"They probably weren't expecting snow this early and thought they'd be shut down for the winter before snow began accumulating," I whispered back to her.

"We should wait until the searchers leave the compound," Icy said. "They'll probably send most of the guards in the search party."

Troy nodded in agreement. "As soon as they take off, we go. We don't want to give them time to regroup and begin to again carefully monitor the perimeter of the compound."

I took a deep breath and let it out slowly. I closed my eyes and willed my fear into resolve.

Troy reached over and put a hand on my back. "Are you okay?" he asked.

I forced a smile and nodded. "I'll be fine," I said.

A few minutes later, the engine revved on one of the ATVs, and it sped away from the lodge down a trail, fighting its way through the deep snow. When the second ATV took off, Troy motioned for us to go.

Troy raced across the clearing, and I followed on his heels. No one stopped or shot at us, but I saw several mounted surveillance cameras and knew we had to move fast. Someone in the compound would soon detect our presence, and we'd lose the element of surprise.

Troy stopped when we reached the side of the warehouse and looked behind him. He nodded at each of us. "Ready?"

I nodded and tried not to think about what would happen next. The sky was beginning to lighten, and the lights in the compound provided us with enough visibility to see where we were going. We planned to sneak past the outlying guest cabins and head straight to the main building in the compound.

The first guest cabin was dark, but lights showed through the windows of the second cabin. Just as we were about to walk past it, the door burst open, and a man emerged. We froze, and Troy lifted his rifle, preparing to shoot if necessary. The man didn't glance in our direction, instead hurrying toward the main lodge. I exhaled, and we continued our march.

Someone had shoveled the main walkways, but they were illuminated, so we stayed in the shadows and fought our way through the deeper snow, pushing through it as quietly as we could.

I heard shouts from somewhere in the compound and feared someone had looked at the surveillance camera footage and detected our presence. A moment later, another ATV engine growled and sped into the woods.

"We're okay, I think," Troy whispered.

When we reached the side door of the main building, Troy looked at us again. "Once we're inside, we need to rush toward the main gathering room of the lodge. I think that's where we'll find most of the hunters and staff. From watching the lodge the other night, I know the dining room and great room are on the far side of the building. I'm not sure, but I think it should be a straight shot down the hall to those rooms."

Troy ratcheted a shell into the chamber of the rifle, and I followed suit. I held the gun with the barrel pointed toward the sky. Troy quietly pulled open the door and looked into the building. He stepped inside, and I followed him.

I recognized the wood-planked walls and hardwood floors of the building. This must've been where I was before Millie pushed me out the door and told me to run.

Troy lifted his rifle to his shoulder and rushed down the hall as quietly as possible. He looked as if he knew what he was doing, but I expected someone to open fire on us at any moment. I kept my rifle pointed at the ceiling so I wouldn't trip and accidentally shoot Troy. I felt Janet's breath on the back of my neck.

Troy didn't even pause before bursting into the dining room. He moved to the side, and I put the rifle to my shoulder, ready to shoot. It was challenging to focus on the gun and also look around the large room to take in the scene.

I heard curses and raised voices. "Everyone put your hands up and come into the dining room," Troy said.

No one moved. "Now," Troy yelled, "or I will start shooting."

I felt my adrenaline surge as I moved next to Troy. "Do what he says!"

"Hands in the air," Troy said.

The three men in the other room slowly moved into the dining room and joined the two men sitting at the table. They all held their hands in the air.

"You guard them, Jane, while we look for others," Troy said.

I moved closer to the men sitting at the table and pointed my rifle at them. Troy, Icy, and Janet began opening doors and searching for people. I watched the men carefully, making sure none of them dropped a hand to reach for a weapon. I hoped Troy and his rifle returned soon.

Icy soon shepherded four women wearing aprons into the dining hall. She clutched the hunting knife in her right hand, and the women held their hands in the air. I recognized Millie as the third woman in the group. She seemed scared as she entered the room.

Icy looked at me. "We need something to tie them up with," she said. She turned back to the women. "Are there any ropes here?" she asked.

The women remained silent, so I swung my rifle barrel toward them. "Answer her," I said.

One of the women nodded, and Icy grabbed her arm. "Show me," she said, "and walk slowly."

I wondered what Icy would do if she encountered armed guards or hunters. The hunting knife would provide little protection against a high-powered rifle.

"You'll never get out of here," a heavyset man told me. He appeared to be in his sixties, with a big belly, large jowls, and very little hair on his head. He looked familiar to me. I'd seen him somewhere before, but where?

"Shut up," I said.

"I'm telling you: you don't stand a chance."

"I said to shut up." I pointed the rifle at his head.

"You don't have what it takes to shoot a human," he said.

I considered firing a shot to scare him, but I didn't want to alert others in the compound to our presence. "I've killed before," I said. "I'd have no problem shooting you. Especially after all you've put us through."

"Shut up, Martin," the man sitting next to the talkative man said. "You'll get us all killed."

Troy and Janet returned a moment later. "We didn't find anyone else in this building," Troy said. "I'm going out to the guard shack."

Icy returned to the dining room with her captive and a large coil of rope.

"Let's tie these guys up first, and then I'll go with you to the guard house."

Icy used her knife to cut the rope into pieces, and she and Janet began with the men, tying their hands and feet. The fat guy stomped his feet, making it impossible for Janet to secure them. Troy approached him and pointed the rifle barrel at his head.

"Hold still, or I will shoot you," he said, his voice steady and calm. The man complied.

Next, we tied the hands of the female lodge workers. Millie cried when Janet cinched the rope around her hands.

Icy walked from the dining room into the adjacent great room. From where I stood, I could see the room's floor-to-ceiling windows and comfortable chairs and couches. She returned a minute later with two hunting rifles.

"Look what I found," she said. She handed one of the rifles to Janet.

Janet looked at the weapon as if it were a snake. "I don't know how to use this," she said.

"I'll show you," Icy told her.

"Good," Troy said. He looked at me. "Let's go to the guard shack."

We walked out the front door of the lodge and examined the paths leading away from the main building of the compound. One led down to the beach, but it hadn't been shoveled since the recent snow, and only a single set of deep footprints marred its perfect surface. Other than the footprints, I could only tell it was a path because of the hand railing beside it. The second path led around the side of the lodge toward the woods. Workers had cleared most of the snow from this path.

"This way," Troy said, quickly walking down the groomed path.

"Do you think we'll find guards?" I whispered. "If they're monitoring surveillance camera footage, they'll know we're here by now."

"I can't believe they'd leave this place unguarded while they search for the missing hunter," Troy said. "The people we captured are hunters and lodge workers. Where are the guards?"

I understood what he was saying. Something wasn't right. It had all been too easy. We'd marched into the lodge and captured everyone there. No one resisted.

We approached a small cabin at the edge of the clearing between the compound and the forest. "I think this is the guard shack," Troy said.

Large windows dominated three of the four walls of the shack. The door and two smaller windows faced the forest. Troy and I dropped to our knees and crawled through the deep snow under the windows. Every time I moved my hands and knees, the rifle, slung over my shoulder, slapped me in the head. Troy seemed to struggle less than I did with the deep snow and heavy hunting rifle, and before long, he was several feet in front of me. When he reached the far edge of the building, he stopped and waited for me. When I caught up with him, he crawled around the corner and approached the door. Without waiting for me, he stood, readied his rifle, and opened the door.

When I didn't hear any gunshots or shouts, I followed him to the door and into the cabin. The interior of the small building looked much like what I'd expected. Five monitors covered a wall above a computer and desk. Four monitors showed images of various areas outside the compound, and the fifth displayed revolving images from cameras both at the compound and in the woods.

"Where are they?" Troy asked as he studied the monitors.

I shrugged. "They must all be in the woods looking for the missing hunter."

My eyes drifted from the monitors to the desk. A satellite phone lay next to the computer and keyboard. I grabbed it, pushed the power button, and stepped out of the guard shack. I studied the screen until it had a signal, then punched in FBI Agent Nick Morgan's phone number, surprised and grateful that I actually remembered it.

CHAPTER 67

Saturday, November 15

7:40 a.m.

Nick sat in the passenger seat of the Beaver, impatiently staring through the window while Patterson turned lazy circles in Trident Basin. He knew Patterson was not only warming up the plane on this cold morning but also waiting for daylight. Nick studied the sky. The heavy clouds were beginning to dissipate, and he saw a pink horizon to the east.

"Everybody buckled in?" Patterson asked. "I think we're good to go."

Nick's phone buzzed in his coat pocket. He reached inside his coat, unzipped the pocket, and retrieved the device. He nearly ignored it since it was an unknown number, but his internal voice told him he should accept the call.

"Morgan," he said. Patterson glanced at him and then began taxiing for takeoff.

"Nick?" a familiar voice said.

"Jane?"

Patterson pulled back on the throttle and aborted the takeoff. He slowly taxied toward shore.

"Are you okay?" Nick asked. A moment later, he said, "Do you know where you are?"

Nick listened intently for several seconds and then said, "We think you're on Shuyak Island. We're on our way there now. Hang on."

He disconnected and looked at Patterson. "Jane and some of the other captives managed to get some hunting rifles and take over the main lodge. Jane found a sat phone in the guard shack."

"This might be easier than I thought," Patterson said. "Before we head out and lose cell coverage, would you call Maureen and pass along the news?"

Nick nodded. "I'll call someone in both planes and let them know what's happening."

While Nick talked on the phone, Patterson taxied. The plane lifted into the air, and Nick returned his phone to his jacket pocket. The knot in his stomach loosened, but he knew dropping his guard would be a mistake. The situation at the hunting lodge was fluid, and it could change in the forty-five minutes it would take them to fly to Shuyak. He wished he could stay in touch with Jane, but they'd fly out of cell phone range soon. He knew Patterson carried a satellite phone on the plane, but Jane needed to focus on the situation at the compound. The fewer distractions she had, the better.

Nick sat back in the airplane seat and tried to relax and ready himself for what could be a battle. He patted his chest to reassure himself that he hadn't forgotten his bulletproof vest or the gun nestled in his shoulder holster.

CHAPTER 68

Saturday, November 15

7:51 a.m.

Troy and I watched the monitors on the wall in the guard shack. No one appeared in the images from the cameras mounted near the lodge, but I saw an ATV on the fifth monitor—the one displaying rotating images from the cameras in the woods. While the cameras mounted near the lodge recorded videos, those in the forest showed only still pictures. The shot of the ATV showed three men behind the vehicle pushing it out of the deep snow while the man at the wheel presumably gunned the engine.

Troy laughed. "They need snowmachines. Maybe they'll all get stuck out there."

I'd already relayed my conversation with Nick to Troy, so we both knew help was coming. I felt almost giddy with excitement, knowing Nick, Patterson, and other law enforcement personnel were on their way to rescue us. I might actually survive this place. I thought about returning to my home and stepping into a warm shower. While my mind roamed, I dropped my guard.

A rifle barrel poked into my back. "I thought I might find you here," a deep voice said.

I stood straight and held up my hands. Troy reacted in the opposite manner. He grabbed his rifle and swung it toward the man holding me hostage. A sharp crack sounded from near the door of the shack, and Troy crumpled to the floor.

I screamed.

"Shut up," the man poking the rifle barrel in my back said. "You're nothing but trouble, Jane."

I swung my head around to look at him. What I saw took my breath away.

CHAPTER 69

Saturday, November 15

7:59 a.m.

"Jane, Jane, what am I going to do with you? You're always sticking your nose where it doesn't belong." He pushed the rifle barrel into my back again and told me to walk up the trail back to the lodge. Two other men followed behind us.

I grappled to make sense of everything that had just happened. Troy, the leader of our little rebel squad, was dead. I'd seen his open, sightless eyes. He'd been so brave to attack the hunters to get their rifles and then lead us to the lodge. But he was right to believe we hadn't detained everyone in the lodge's dining room. Had they been watching us and waiting for their moment to trap us?

I tried to push my grief over Troy's death to the back of my mind. I'd end up like him if I didn't use my brain to find a way out of this mess. Would Nick and Patterson arrive before these animals murdered me? I feared the investigators would let down their guard since I'd told them we'd tied up the people in the lodge. The guards at the lodge would likely shoot the troopers and police the minute they stepped ashore. Nick and Patterson would be better off if I'd never called them.

I wiped furiously at the tears on my cheeks as we approached the door to the lodge.

"Open it," he said.

I turned the knob, dreading what I'd see inside. *Are Janet and Icy still holding rifles on their nine captives, or are they dead?*

I walked down the short hall and turned into the dining area of the large room. I was both relieved and depressed by what I saw. Icy and

Janet sat at the table, their hands and feet tied, their mouths gagged. I searched their faces as I walked toward them. Janet looked terrified, and Icy appeared furious. I saw no sign of our recent captives.

I headed toward Janet and Icy, expecting the men to restrain me and seat me next to my two cohorts. My captor jabbed the rifle into my back. "Keep walking down the hall."

With a backward glance at Janet and Icy, I complied. We walked halfway down the hall until he told me to stop and open a door on the left side of the narrow corridor. I stepped inside, and he flipped on a light switch. We were in a small office with a desk, chair, computer, filing cabinet, and a small dark-brown futon pushed against one wall. No art or photos decorated the small office.

He told me to sit on the futon, and then he sat in the desk chair and rolled it toward me.

Until now, I'd considered Corban Pratt handsome or even gorgeous. Why had I never noticed his flat, dead eyes? His eyes seemed darker now than they had when I'd enjoyed easy banter while dining with him. I'd thought the man a bit self-obsessed, but I'd never considered him evil.

"This lodge is yours?" I hated that my voice shook.

"Not all mine," Pratt said. "I'm one of many shareholders."

"You hunt humans?"

He smiled and shrugged. "Humans are the ultimate prey animals. They aren't very self-sufficient, but their brains put them on the same level as the hunter, and you must outwit them. You're my special prey, and I admit, you're a worthy opponent. I'm not about to let this little act by you and your friends ruin my hunt."

"What do you mean?"

"I'm sending you back out into the woods." He studied me. "I see you found the tracker on your jacket. I have to hand it to you, Jane. You're smart."

I wanted to tell him that the FBI and troopers were onto him and would be here soon, but if he didn't know they were coming, I wouldn't give him advance notice.

A knock sounded on the office door. Pratt opened it. He spoke quietly to someone and then glanced back at me. He stepped out into the hall but left the door open. I looked around the room. *What can I use as a weapon?* I didn't see a gun or a knife. The desk lamp looked flimsy, but maybe I could find something in the desk drawers. Unfortunately, Pratt kept glancing back into the room at me. After a few moments, he shut the door and returned to the chair where he'd been sitting earlier.

"Who did you call on the satellite phone?"

My stomach dropped.

"The guards have the number, and a camera outside the guard shack captured your end of the conversation. The man I just spoke to attempted to call the number, but he was sent to a generic mailbox with no personal greeting." He rolled the chair closer to me. "I need to know who you called, Jane."

"A friend," I said.

He smiled and shook his head. "I think you know I need more than that."

"What does it matter?" I asked. "I have no idea where I am. I couldn't very well call for help."

Pratt studied me for several moments. "Good point," he said. "We're planning to shut down the lodge this week, and then there will be nothing here to find."

"What about the captives?" I asked.

"The prey animals?" Corban Pratt shrugged. "We'll have to terminate them. It would be inhumane to leave them here to fend for themselves, don't you think? They'd die slow, painful deaths from exposure or hunger. We'll begin extinguishing them tonight."

"'Extinguishing them'? These are human beings," I said. "They're young humans with their entire lives ahead of them."

Pratt shrugged again. "I plan to continue hunting you for a few more days. One hunter and one prey animal. It should be an even match, and I won't need your tracker." He smiled. "If you won't tell me who you called on our satellite phone, then I suggest you run out into the woods and find a place to hide from me. Until now, except for the trackers on the special prey, we have enforced the rules of fair chase. We haven't allowed game cameras in the woods and do not hunt when it's dark. Hunters also can't use aircraft to look for their prey. Those rules all end now. I'll employ any method at my disposal to hunt you down and shoot you. I'm also cutting out the free meals and little perks like hand warmers. You'll have to forage for your food like a wild animal."

"What if I refuse to go back into the woods?" I asked.

Pratt smiled. "Then I'll have to kill you here, just as I plan to kill your two friends in the dining room. I'm giving you a chance, Jane. I suggest you take it."

Pratt led me down the long hall to the door that Troy, Icy, Janet, and I had entered when we arrived at the lodge. He held it open and looked down at me. "I'll count to ten, and then I'll start shooting."

I stared at him and wondered how many people he'd killed.

"One," he said.

I turned and ran around the side of the lodge. I ran fast over the tramped-down snow between the compound and the woods, but as soon as I stepped into the deep snow in the forest, my pace slowed.

Crack! A bullet splintered a tree in front of me. I headed back toward the main trail. I knew I'd die if I stayed on the trail long, but I had to put some distance between me and Pratt, and I could move much faster on the partially groomed trail. I heard two more shots, but they were well behind me. I stayed on the path until I heard the engine of an ATV heading in my direction. Then, I departed the trail and fought my way into the thick forest.

CHAPTER 70

Saturday, November 15

8:17 a.m.

"We're approaching Shuyak," Patterson said. "We don't have much wind, so I think I can land straight in at the lodge."

Nick nodded. "It would be better if you don't have to circle and warn them of our approach."

He knew that Patterson had already discussed a straight-in approach with the pilot of the third plane. He'd follow Patterson and land a few minutes behind him.

Nick again patted the Glock 22 in his shoulder holster. Once ashore, he'd draw the gun and have it ready for action. He peered out the front window of the plane and watched the island grow larger as they approached. If circumstances were different, he knew he'd enjoy the beauty of the scene—thousands of Christmas trees frosted with white. Now, however, the deep snow and dense forest would only make rescuing captives and locating their captors more difficult. Still, Jane should be easy to find. He expected to see her in the lodge's main building, holding a rifle on some of those responsible for this nightmare.

The plane dropped altitude, and Patterson glided to a smooth landing in a small cove before taxiing up to the shore. The troopers in the rear of the plane jumped out and tied the Beaver to a tree.

"Is the tide coming or going?" Nick asked.

"It will be high in two hours. The plane should be fine here. Still, I want to leave at least one trooper on the beach to guard the planes. It would be embarrassing if one of the perpetrators escaped in the trooper plane."

Nick wondered why no one had met them on the beach. If Jane and some of the other captives were in charge of the compound, where were they? He had a bad feeling about this. He and Patterson exchanged glances, and he could see the sergeant also had doubts.

"Let's wait for those in the second plane," Patterson told his troopers and Nick. "I'll assign someone in that group to watch the planes, and the rest of us will head up to the lodge."

Nick knew Patterson wanted his A team with him, and he'd leave a less experienced trooper to guard the planes. He hoped the other aircraft would land soon because he felt like a target standing on the shore.

CHAPTER 71

Saturday, November 15

8:27 a.m.

I stopped plowing through the deep snow and bent over with my hands on my knees, trying to catch my breath. In the distance, I heard the revving engine of an ATV. I guessed the machine was stuck in the deep snow. I heard raised voices but couldn't make out the words.

I fought back panic. I needed to think. Pratt had his hands full back at the lodge. I doubted he was pursuing me now. Plus, why would he? He wanted a challenge. He could have quickly overtaken and killed me if he'd chased me when I ran from the compound. He was stronger and in better shape than I was. He could fight his way through the snow with more ease. I felt certain he'd give me time to cover some distance, and then he'd look for me. Unless the authorities somehow stopped him, he'd find and kill me. I couldn't simply hide and hope for the best. I needed to do something.

I retraced my steps and headed toward the sound of the revving engine. I struggled with each step as I post-holed through the snow. Pain seared the muscles of my legs, and I fell several times. The engine noise and voices continued, and I relentlessly pushed toward them.

After what seemed like hours but was probably only twenty minutes, I realized I could make out some of the words being spoken and yelled. Then the engine stopped, and I could hear more of the discussion.

"It's not going anywhere until the snow melts," one man said. "It's stuck."

A round of curses followed.

"What should we do, then?" another man asked.

"I have something!" The shout came from the woods. "I have a body."

I saw the ATV through the trees. The four men standing by the vehicle turned and walked through the trees toward the man who'd shouted about finding a body.

This was my chance. Moving as fast as I could, I headed toward the ATV. In the distance, I heard someone making a radio call. When I was only twenty feet from the vehicle, one of the men walked out of the forest toward it. I hid behind a tree and held my breath. After a few moments, I hazarded a glance toward the ATV. The man had apparently returned to the vehicle for his backpack. He was now retreating into the forest with a green pack on his back.

I continued toward the vehicle. If the men returned before I got there, they'd kill me, or at least, they'd capture me and take me back to the lodge. I focused on the ATV and struggled through the snow toward it.

When I neared the four-wheeler, I stepped onto the packed-down trail. The vehicle had turned off the trail, accidentally or on purpose, and that's when it got stuck in the snow. I reached the ATV after taking only ten steps off the trail in the deep snow. When I got there, I found what I wanted. Three rifles in soft gun cases lay in the cart behind the vehicle. I grabbed the top one and hoped the men wouldn't immediately notice it was missing. I followed my footsteps back to the trail, scooping snow into the deep holes I'd made to disguise them. The men would see my tracks if they looked closely at the ground.

I peered up at the snow-covered spruce trees. Had a game trail camera recorded my actions? Were cameras following my every move? Would Nick and Patterson reach the compound and detain Pratt before he started hunting me?

CHAPTER 72

Saturday, November 15

8:36 a.m.

When the next plane taxied to the beach, Nick watched as three troopers and two Kodiak city police officers jumped from the floats into the shallow water. Patterson motioned for them to hurry to shore, and while the pilot secured the plane, Patterson briefed the officers on the situation and the plan for approaching the lodge.

Nick stood to the side as Patterson pointed at one of his troopers. "Stay with the pilot and guard the planes." He looked at the rest of the officers. "Do you see the cameras? They know we're here. This is an extremely dangerous situation." He pointed at a Kodiak police officer and a trooper from the plane that had just arrived. "Brad, I want you two to remain at the rear of the building, with your backs against the wall. I don't see any cameras pointed in that direction. If you hear shots fired, call Detective Horner and tell her we need more backup. Make sure she knows it's urgent."

The officer nodded. "Yes, sir."

Patterson looked around the circle of faces gathered around him. "The rest of you, stay behind me and Agent Morgan."

Nick maintained his game face but could feel the sweat on his forehead. His job rarely called for him to draw his weapon. He usually stayed behind the scenes and offered advice. He only put his life in danger when he came to Kodiak, where Sergeant Patterson seemed to have no qualms about inserting him front and center in a takedown.

"Are you ready?" Patterson asked the group. Heads nodded. "Have your weapons accessible, but only use them as a last resort."

Nick wondered how much evidence those in the building had destroyed while he, Patterson, and the others stood on the beach getting organized. He nodded to Patterson. He was ready to go.

Boots crunched over barnacles as they walked up the beach to the trail leading to the lodge. Nick unzipped his coat and unsnapped his holster. He removed the Glock and held it at his side. He saw that Patterson had unsnapped the holster on his hip. His right hand curled around the grip of his weapon.

Patterson knocked on the door of the lodge and then stepped back. A few seconds later, a large, middle-aged man with graying hair opened the door and stood with his arms crossed over his chest. He didn't look much like the photo Nick had seen, but he knew this was Cage Marks, the manager of the lodge.

"What can I do for you today, Sergeant?" Marks asked.

Patterson withdrew the paperwork from the pocket of his jacket. "I have a search warrant for the buildings and the grounds."

Marks took a step back. "Why?" he asked. He seemed genuinely surprised.

"I'd like you and everyone at the lodge to gather in the great room while we conduct our search."

Marks stood aside while Patterson, Nick, and the six officers filed into the lodge.

CHAPTER 73

Saturday, November 15

8:53 a.m.

Sara Byram was the last trooper in the group. As the others followed Patterson into the lodge, she paused, her back against the wall of the building. Every one of her senses told her something was terribly wrong with this situation. She felt certain they were walking into a trap. She believed alarm bells were also ringing in Patterson's head, but what choice did he have? He had to go inside the building to search it.

She decided she'd hang back for a few minutes and listen. She knew others might perceive this move as cowardice or a failure to follow instructions, but she believed Patterson would approve of her decision. He wanted his troopers to follow his orders, but he also stressed that they should think for themselves.

After a matter of seconds, she heard someone yell, "Drop your weapons. You're surrounded." The voice didn't belong to either Patterson or Morgan.

Byram keyed the microphone attached to her bulletproof vest. "Brad, we have a situation," she said. "We need backup. Now! Get up here, and call Detective Horner and tell her to get here as fast as she can."

"Roger," Simpton said.

Trooper Sara Byram's body trembled, from her toes to her chattering teeth. She took a deep breath and exhaled. She needed to think. What should she do if the people at the lodge had surrounded Patterson and the others? If she, Simpton, and the other two officers marched into the lodge, they'd probably be outgunned and would also end up hostages or even dead. She'd heard no shots yet, but she feared those in the lodge planned to kill the police and troopers and escape the island. She hoped Simpton would have an idea.

A few seconds later, Trooper Brad Simpton, Trooper Eddie Valdera, and Officer Warren Bates quietly approached her.

"Something seemed wrong," she whispered to Simpton, "so I held back a minute and heard someone yell, 'You're surrounded. Drop your weapons.'"

"Are you sure it wasn't one of our guys you heard?" Simpton asked.

Byram shook her head. "No, it wasn't Patterson or Morgan. I've never heard the voice before. It was deep and sharp."

"What should we do?" Simpton asked. "Should we wait for Horner and the others?"

"I don't think we can afford to wait. Besides, they'll hear the plane coming and be on alert. I hope they think they have all the law enforcement officers surrounded. Maybe we can take them by surprise."

Simpton nodded. "I'm ready," he said. "Do you want me to take the lead, or do you want to approach first?"

"I'll go first," Sara said. "Stay a few steps behind me. I'll try to sneak into the building and see if I can assess the situation."

Sara slowed her breathing. She knew panic would overtake her if she allowed it. She relied on her training and instincts as she placed her hand on the doorknob and slowly pushed the door open. She heard voices and knew that unless someone was guarding the entrance, the men in the next room wouldn't hear her enter. She had no idea whether they could see her, however. Patterson had briefly described the layout of the area of the lodge he'd seen on his previous visit. She remembered him saying the door entered into a short hall and a mudroom. Then, the interior opened into a large sitting room or great room straight ahead and to the right and a mess hall to the left. If everyone was gathered in the great room, they might have a view of the entryway.

Sara pushed the door open a few inches and peeked inside. To her relief, the hall light was off, and no windows illuminated the area. She turned to the three officers behind her and held up her hand, signaling them to stay where they were. She stepped into the mudroom before quietly closing the door behind her to shut out the daylight. She tiptoed forward in her heavy boots.

She couldn't see the great room until she'd taken several steps. The closer she came to the indoor lights, the more vulnerable she felt. If some of the suspects were in the mess hall area of the room, they'd soon see her. She took one more step and peered around the corner toward the couches and large windows. What she saw paralyzed her for a moment.

She began to backtrack slowly. She wanted to turn and flee, but she knew she couldn't. She had to get back outdoors, huddle with Simpton and the other two officers, and make a plan. They had no time. They couldn't afford to wait for Horner and the others. The lives of Patterson, Morgan, and the other troopers and police officers in the room depended on them doing the right thing, and fast. But what was the right thing?

CHAPTER 74

Saturday, November 15

9:04 a.m.

I headed back toward the lodge. I considered taking the main trail but decided against it. I could probably reach the lodge in ten or fifteen minutes on the trail, but it was too risky. I stayed in the woods and pushed my pace as fast as possible.

Before long, I heard an ATV heading toward the lodge. In the distance, I could hear another engine. *Has someone called the searchers back to the compound? Do they know Nick and Patterson are approaching the lodge, and are the security guards planning to ambush the law enforcement personnel?* I hadn't heard a plane land, but the revving ATV engine would have covered the sound of an approaching airplane.

I pushed my exhausted legs to move faster through the deep snow, but I knew that at this pace, I'd never make it to the lodge in time to help the two men. I feared they were walking into an ambush, and I had to warn them.

I struggled back to the main path and loped toward the lodge. I knew I was fully exposed to the cameras lining the path, but I hoped everyone was too busy to pay attention to the video feeds. When I heard the sound of an ATV behind me, I leaped off the trail into the deep snow. I hid behind a tree while the vehicle sped past me.

I struggled back to the trail and pushed toward the compound. I focused on the trail so I wouldn't stumble or fall back into the deep snow. I couldn't afford to injure myself now. I tried not to think about what to do when I reached the lodge. I had no idea what the situation was there, and I prayed that Nick and Patterson had things under control and had detained everyone. Still, if they'd been ambushed or were about to be ambushed, I had to do something to help them.

Suddenly, the forest opened into a clearing, and the lodge stood before me. I hurried toward the door Pratt had opened for me earlier— the same door Troy, Icy, and I had entered when we'd first reached the lodge. A vision of Troy's lifeless body floated through my mind, and I rejected it. I needed to focus on the present and not the past. I opened the door, expecting someone to grab me, but no one was there. I crept into the hall. It was empty. I stayed against the left wall of the corridor and tiptoed toward the dining hall.

I heard raised voices as I drew nearer to the large open space. After a few more steps, I heard the words they were speaking.

"We can't kill these lawmen," a man with a southern accent said. "Are you insane, man? Let's tie them up. Between their planes and Blake's Beaver, we can get out of here. I'm a pilot. I've never flown a Beaver, but I'm sure I can figure it out."

"No," another voice said. "They've seen our faces. We have to kill them and then set the place on fire to cover any forensic evidence. Then, we can escape."

"We can't kill Alaska State Troopers and an FBI agent," the first man said. "Every law enforcement agency in the country will come after us."

"They won't know who we are," Corban Pratt said. "If we get rid of everything here, they'll never trace us. I've made certain to conceal the identities of every guest and worker at the lodge."

The first man barked out a laugh. "Nothing is one hundred percent secure," he said. "It's just a matter of time before they find us. When I get off this God-forsaken island, I'm flying first class to a country lacking an extradition policy with the United States. Maybe I'll move to Vietnam or maybe even Qatar."

"That's fine for you," another voice said, "but I don't want to leave my family. I vote we kill the police officers. Then we'll have more time to cover our tracks and get out of here."

Several men began to speak at once, and I knew I had to do something, but what?

CHAPTER 75

Saturday, November 15

9:10 a.m.

Troopers Sara Byram, Brad Simpton, and Eddie Valdera and Officer Warren Bates waited in the darkened hallway, watching the drama unfold in front of them. Sara and Simpton stood beside each other and in front of the other two officers. She wanted Simpton's input about how they should approach this situation. If they waited too long to enter the room, the perpetrators could shoot Patterson and the others, but if they barged in without a plan, they could easily become four more hostages. More men had arrived through side doors as they'd stood there, and now, at least a dozen men held guns pointed at Agent Morgan, Sergeant Patterson, and the officers. How could they overtake so many men with rifles? If they got into a firefight with the armed men, the officers would likely get shot in the crossfire. The troopers and police officers were kneeling with their hands and ankles zip-tied. They were helpless and surrounded by the perpetrators.

Simpton whispered in her ear, "I think the one in the dark flannel shirt is in charge. I can rush in, put a gun to his head, and tell him to order the others to drop their weapons. The rest of you can follow behind me with your guns drawn."

She didn't love the plan. She believed the most likely scenario would be that someone would shoot Simpton as soon as he left the shadows of the entryway.

"Are you with me?" Simpton asked.

She locked eyes with her fellow trooper and gave one sharp nod. She then turned and whispered the plan to Valdera and Bates. Valdera nodded, and Bates gave a thumbs-up.

Simpton held up his hand. He held up one finger, then two, then three. He paused a beat and then rushed toward the man with the dark-blond wavy hair wearing the blue flannel shirt. The man was locked in a tense discussion with some of the other men, and he didn't even react to Simpton until the trooper had pushed the barrel of his Glock to the back of the man's head and told him to drop the weapon. At that exact moment, Sara, Valdera, and Bates emerged from the entryway, their guns drawn. They fanned out around the room, pointing their weapons at the men who held guns on the troopers, police officers, and Agent Morgan. As they rushed in, all three officers yelled for the men to drop their weapons.

The blond-haired man dropped his rifle on the floor. The other twelve armed men stared at the newcomers but did nothing.

Sara knew the bad guys outnumbered Simpton, Bates, Valdera, and her. The only thing they could do was to buy time until Horner and her officers arrived.

CHAPTER 76

Saturday, November 15

9:18 a.m.

Patterson saw his chance while their captors debated whether to kill them or leave them incapacitated. He predicted they'd decide to shoot all of them and torch the building, and he wanted no part of that plan. The guards had made a mistake by zip-tying their hands behind them instead of in front of them. Although it wasn't easy, he could reach the pocketknife he still had in his rear pocket. Mistake number two—the guards had been in such a hurry to restrain the officers that they hadn't frisked them for knives.

While the man with the rifle pointed at Patterson was arguing with the others, Patterson removed the knife and gripped it firmly in his left hand so he wouldn't drop it. With the fingers of his right hand, he fought with the blade until he opened it. Then he began sawing at the zip tie. He glanced down the row of officers and saw Traner and Boyle also sawing at their restraints.

Once Patterson had his hands free, he nodded to Nick to scoot closer to him. With an eye on their captors, Patterson waited until he had his chance. When Simpton raced into the room, he knew it was now or never. He cut through Nick's hand ties and then quickly sawed through the ties binding his ankles. He handed the knife to Nick and lunged for one of the handguns on the coffee table a few feet in front of them. Mistake number three the captors had made was to leave the guns within easy reach of the officers if they somehow managed to free themselves.

Patterson felt sure that the man who'd been pointing the rifle at him was a hunter and not a guard or employee of the lodge, although of course that made him no less dangerous. He seemed confused by the commotion in the room. Instead of focusing on Patterson, his head swung from Byram to Valdera to Bates to Simpton. When none of the other captors dropped their weapons, he held on to his, but he wasn't watching Patterson.

Patterson grabbed his Glock from the table and, in four quick steps, moved behind his captor and held his gun to the man's head. "Drop it," he said.

The man let the rifle fall to the floor and held up his hands.

In a similar manner, Nick and Traner forced the men guarding them to drop their weapons while Boyle began cutting the restraints from the other officers.

Suddenly, one of the captors grabbed a young Kodiak police officer, whose name Patterson didn't know. Instead of holding a rifle, this man held a handgun to the officer's head. The officer, who was barely more than a kid, looked terrified.

"Drop your weapons, or he dies!" the man yelled.

CHAPTER 77

Saturday, November 15

9:27 a.m.

I stood frozen as the events unfolded in front of me. I wasn't sure what to do but thought it was best to stay in the shadows as long as possible. I watched the reactions of the guards and other men from the lodge when the four officers rushed into the room. Corban Pratt immediately dropped his rifle when the trooper held the gun to his head, and at first, I thought the others were also going to drop their weapons. When they didn't, I thought about rushing the room from the other direction.

Then I saw Patterson lunge for his gun, and soon, Nick and several other officers began grabbing their own weapons. I thought the law enforcement guys had things under control until one of the hunters grabbed a young police officer and held a gun to his head.

Pratt and the trooper guarding him stood to the side of the action. When the hunter took the young officer hostage, he turned toward the armed officers at the other end of the room. At that moment, the hunter had his back to Pratt and the trooper holding a gun on him.

The trooper didn't hesitate. He let go of Pratt and charged the man holding a gun at the young officer's head.

Once Pratt was free, I watched him remove something from his pocket and begin quickly backing toward the dining area.

I rushed up behind him and stuck the rifle barrel in his back. "Where do you think you're going?"

Pratt stopped and then turned toward me. "We have three minutes to get out of here, or we're all going to die. I'll save your life if you let me go."

"You're bluffing," I said.

He held out his hand to show me. In it, I saw a small, black device that looked like a key fob. "I just started the timer," he said. "The entire compound is rigged with explosives. They'll ignite in"—he looked at his watch—"a little over two minutes."

I didn't know whether to believe him, but I couldn't take the chance. I let Pratt go and raced toward the commotion in the great room. While I'd been talking to Pratt, another group of Kodiak police officers had arrived, and it seemed as if everyone was talking at once as the officers rounded up the men from the lodge.

"Hey!" I yelled as I approached the group, but my shout was lost in the din of voices. I tried again, but no one seemed to hear me.

I wanted to run for the door and save myself, but I couldn't leave Nick, Patterson, and the other troopers and officers in the building to die. I did the only thing I could think of. I lifted the rifle butt to my shoulder and fired into the ceiling. The kick of the weapon knocked me to the floor.

I scrambled to my feet and was pleased to see everyone staring at me. "Get out of the building!" I yelled. "It's rigged with explosives, and they'll detonate in about a minute."

Everyone stared at me. "Run!" I screamed, and then I ran.

When I reached the front door, I encountered a traffic jam of bodies pushing through the small opening. As soon as I fought through the crowd, I headed for the beach and scrambled over the rocky shore as fast as I could. The slippery, rounded shale rocks slowed my pace, but at least the tidal movements had removed the snow from the beach.

I don't know how far I traveled before a loud explosion shook the earth and blasted me forward and down into the rocks. I didn't lose consciousness, but I couldn't hear anything, and I could only make out the blurry shapes of others on the ground.

CHAPTER 78

Saturday, November 15
9:48 a.m.

I rolled into a sitting position and touched my face. It felt wet, and when I pulled my hand away and looked at it, blood ran from my fingers. Another careful examination revealed a deep cut on my forehead and more abrasions on my nose and cheeks. *Head wounds bleed a lot. As long as you can stand up and move, you're okay.* At the moment, I'd ignore any possible internal injuries.

I struggled to my feet and immediately vomited. I bent over with my hands on my knees and tried to regain my equilibrium. While a nonexistent siren blared in my ears, the world around me was muted. Through my foggy vision, I saw others attempting to stand or lying still on the beach.

I pulled a glove from my coat pocket and blotted the blood running down my face; then I stood straight and took a tentative step. Slowly, I walked toward the chaos near the lodge. The closer I got to the compound, the worse the carnage. The bloody face of either a lodge worker or a hunter stared up sightlessly at the sky, and from the mangled, bent form of a Kodiak police officer, I knew he must be dead.

I neared a man whose mouth was open wide in a scream, but I couldn't hear him. I passed the young, auburn-haired trooper who'd stormed the lodge. She cradled her arm, and blood ran from one ear. She looked around her and seemed in shock.

I didn't stop but took one shaky step after the next toward the burning building where the great room and dining room had been. Someone touched my arm, and I looked up into the blue eyes of Sergeant Dan Patterson. He had a deep cut on his forehead, where he'd probably face-planted onto a rock covered with barnacles. He stared into my eyes, and his mouth moved. He was speaking to me, but I couldn't hear anything he said.

I touched my ears and shook my head. He nodded and then made the same gesture. He apparently couldn't hear anything, either. He made the "okay" signal with his hand, and I nodded. I didn't feel okay, but I was in much better shape than others I'd passed. I returned the signal to him, and he nodded.

"Nick?" I asked. I tried to enunciate the word carefully so he could read my lips.

Patterson shrugged and made a palms-up gesture.

I saw something out of the corner of my eye and turned to see a black Beaver take off from the water and head away from the island. Patterson also saw the departing plane, and I watched him close his eyes for several seconds.

It took me a moment to understand Patterson's evident frustration, but then I realized what had just happened. Corban Pratt and the pilot of the black Beaver had escaped the island.

I eventually found FBI Special Agent Nick Morgan lying in the snow in the woods about one hundred yards from the lodge. Blood stained the snow around him, and I thought he was dead. He lay motionless with his left leg bent away from his body at an unnatural angle. I walked toward him and noted other bodies dotting the snow in the forest. I sat beside Nick. I knew I shouldn't move him. He likely had spinal damage, but I couldn't leave him in the snow. I sat beside him and slowly lifted his head into my lap.

My fingers trembled as I placed them on his neck. I began to cry when I felt the drumbeat of a pulse.

CHAPTER 79

Saturday, November 15

4:00 p.m.

I sat on the beach for several hours, watching helicopters and planes come and go to the island. I cried and thought about Troy and beautiful young Brooke. *How many people have died on this island in the past few months?* I cried for Nick and myself. I couldn't afford to cry when my life had been in danger, but now the tears seemed endless.

My hearing and vision slowly began to return, and I watched the activity around me. I admired Sergeant Patterson. He was dazed and injured from the blast, but he directed the activities and tried to control the chaos on the beach.

One of the Kodiak Flight Services Beavers had sustained severe damage and wouldn't fly again without a significant makeover. The second KFS Beaver and the trooper plane looked better but were still too damaged to fly. I watched Patterson make several calls on his satellite phone during the day, and I assumed he was calling for more planes and assistance. Since most of the law enforcement personnel from Kodiak were either injured or worse, I knew he must have been calling the coast guard in Kodiak and law enforcement in Anchorage for help.

Patterson corralled the troopers and police officers who weren't too badly injured, and they began a triage, assessing victims who needed immediate evacuation, those who could wait for later flights, and those who were beyond rescue. I fit into the second group.

I'd sat with Nick until coast guard medics lifted him onto a litter and rushed him to the beach and a waiting helicopter. The coast guard and every charter plane in Kodiak seemed to be helping to shuttle the injured to town.

Once Nick was gone, I returned to the beach and sat on the rocks. My head throbbed, but I was slowly regaining my equilibrium. Finally, as darkness approached, it was my turn. Patterson helped me into the coast guard chopper and then pushed the auburn-haired trooper in after me.

"Can you hear yet?" she asked me.

I nodded. "How about you?"

"Some," she said. "I wanted to stay and help, but Sergeant Patterson said this might be the last flight of the day, and he insisted I go back to town to get medical care." She looked at her right arm resting in her lap. "It's broken, so I need a cast. My name is Sara, by the way."

"I'm Jane."

"I know who you are. We've been looking for you for a while."

"How many died?" I asked, afraid to hear her answer.

Tears sprang from Sara's eyes. "I don't know," she said. "A few, and there were also some serious injuries."

I nodded and sank back in my seat.

Somehow, I fell asleep on the flight back to Kodiak. When I awoke, the helicopter was touching down at the coast guard base. Sid Beatty had somehow talked his way onto the base and stood on the tarmac. As soon as I climbed out of the chopper, I ran to his open arms, and he held me while I cried.

CHAPTER 80

Sunday, November 16

11:00 a.m.

When I got out of the shower, I heard rapid knocking on my front door. I pulled on a robe and hurried to answer it.

My friend Dana Baynes rushed through the door and hugged me. "Thank God you're okay," she said, tears streaming down her cheeks. "I've been trying to call you, but you don't answer."

"I don't have a phone," I said. "They took it from me, and I'm sure it's been blown to bits. I guess I'll have to buy a new one."

"I'm so sorry, Jane." Dana stood back and looked at me. "Did I interrupt your shower?"

"No. It's my third one since I got home last night. I don't think I'll ever feel clean again."

"Have you watched the news?" Dana asked. "The Artemis lodge is all they're talking about. Janet Friland's mother came to Kodiak to meet her."

"What about Charlotte?" I asked. "Have you heard anything?"

Dana nodded. "I talked to Mandy, and she said Charlotte is home and doing well. She wants to go back to work as soon as possible."

"That's good news."

"Also," Dana said, "I found out what Carter Brown was up to, and Parsons is one angry man right now."

I had to fight through the fuzz in my brain to remember who Carter Brown and Parsons were.

Dana tilted her head and squinted her eyes at me. "You look a little out of it, Jane. Do you know who I'm talking about? Charles Parsons is my boss, the Refuge manager, and Carter Brown was the guy sent here to be the assistant manager of the Refuge?"

"Right," I said. "My brain isn't working. What about Carter Brown?"

"He was sent to Kodiak from Washington, DC, as an undercover operative."

"What? That sounds like something out of a spy novel. What was he investigating?"

"The consortium contacted the feds in DC to inquire about possible changes to the Kodiak National Wildlife Refuge. When the Secretary of the Interior heard about it and then learned about the land use designation change on Shuyak and the opening of the Artemis lodge there, he started wondering what was going on in our little corner of the world, so he sent Brown on a mission. Carter Brown is an investigator with the Department of the Interior."

"They didn't tell Parsons who Brown was and what he was doing?" I asked.

Dana shook her head. "They thought Parsons might be involved with the consortium."

"What did Brown have to say about it?"

Dana shrugged. "Nothing. He was here one minute and gone the next. I pity the man or woman who takes his place. Parsons will never trust another assistant manager."

"It sounds like a mess," I said.

Dana reached over and squeezed my arm. "You look exhausted. I want to hear about everything that happened on Shuyak," she said, "but you need a few days of peace and quiet first."

"Thank you, Dana. I promise I'll tell you all about it soon."

Dana hugged me again and told me to call her if I needed anything.

As soon as she left, I got dressed. I'd called the hospital already, but they wouldn't tell me anything about Nick's condition.

I turned on the TV and switched the channel to CNN. Wolf Blitzer was discussing the situation on Shuyak with a panel of experts. I only had to watch for a few minutes before they showed Senator

Laura Ames hugging her daughter, Janet Friland, outside Providence Hospital in Kodiak. Then, a still photo of Florida senator Martin Cale filled the screen.

"Senator Cale was arrested along with two other hunters at the lodge," Blitzer said. "Although it's still unconfirmed, we've heard from a reliable source that Cale was hunting Ms. Friland." The screen showed the footage of Cale consoling Ames on the Senate floor after her daughter's disappearance. "If this is true," Blitzer continued, "it's almost too horrific to imagine. How do we make sense of it, Dr. Jameson?"

The image switched to the interviewee. The text under his name identified him as a psychologist and former FBI agent.

I turned off the TV and fell back on the couch. No wonder I'd recognized the bloated, obnoxious hunter at the lodge. I'd seen his photo on TV. I wasn't ready to deal with what had happened to me and the others on Shuyak Island. I needed a few days to think about nothing, but first, I wanted to check on Nick.

CHAPTER 81

Sunday, November 16

1:10 p.m.

For a change, I wasn't the one in the hospital bed. I knocked softly on the closed door and slowly opened it. Nick looked up at me, and I could tell he'd been sleeping. He looked slightly better than a day earlier, but his face was still pale. His eyes were more red than blue, and his black hair sprang from his head in disarray, adding years to his age.

I'd learned that, in addition to his broken leg, he'd suffered a fractured rib and a traumatic brain injury. Amazingly, his spinal column seemed intact.

I kissed him on the cheek and sat in the chair beside his bed. "How are you doing?" I asked.

"Not great, I guess. The doctors here think I'm bleeding internally. I'm not losing much blood, but enough to concern them."

I frowned and placed my hand on his arm. "What are they going to do about it?"

"They were planning to ship me to Anchorage, but the Bureau is sending a medevac jet to fly me to Seattle."

"When?" I asked.

"The jet should be here in two hours."

"I'll fly down to Seattle, too," I said.

Nick took my hand and pulled it to him. "I don't think that's a great idea, Jane," he said.

"Oh." His comment stung, and I didn't know what to say.

"My ex-wife somehow heard about what happened and is flying to Seattle. I don't know why, but she says she wants to make sure I get the best care possible."

"Oh," I said again. I had no other words.

"Believe me, I'm not getting back together with her. I just don't want you to have to deal with her."

I nodded. I wasn't sure I believed him.

"She won't stay long, and I'd love to have you fly down when she returns to Virginia."

"Right," I said. "Have you talked to Patterson? What's happening on Shuyak?"

Nick stared at me for several seconds. I knew he was trying to guess my thoughts, but I didn't want to discuss him and his ex-wife. "I talked to Dan this morning," he said. "He was on his way back to Shuyak. He said a barge delivered four snowmachines to the island early this morning, and FBI agents are scouring the island for any victims who might still be hiding."

"How many have they found?"

"Eight so far, counting you, Janet Friland, and Candice Frack."

I'd learned the previous day that Icy's real name was Candice Frack.

"What are the names of the others?" I asked.

Nick reached for his notebook on the table next to his bed. "You probably already know that we found Charlotte Porter," he said.

I nodded. "Dana says she's doing okay and ready to return to work."

"The shock could be delayed," Nick said. "She should talk to a therapist."

I nodded. "Who else did they find?"

Nick looked at his list. "They found John Shriver. He's from Chiniak. Cindy Gardner—she was kidnapped from the Safeway parking lot, Austin Green from Anchorage, and Sylvia Conners, who's also from Anchorage." He paused for a moment. "Wait a minute," he said. "I forgot about Tom Stroud, the guy Sid rescued."

"Sid?" I asked.

"You didn't know? Sid is the true hero in this case. He went to Shuyak alone to get enough evidence for a judge to issue us a search warrant for the compound. While he was there, he met Tom Stroud, one of the captives, and brought him back to Kodiak."

"He didn't tell me that," I said.

"You'd better watch out for that old guy." Nick smiled at me. "He is quite fond of you."

"We're just friends," I said.

"I think he feels differently," Nick said. "He risked his life for you."

"How are the other troopers and policemen doing?" I changed the subject. I didn't want to discuss Sid Beatty with Nick.

"As you probably already know, two policemen and one trooper died during the explosion. One other trooper is still in critical condition, and Dan told me this morning that four of his troopers and three Kodiak police officers remain in the hospital."

I shook my head. "What about Stan and the other KFS pilot? I saw the coast guard medics treating them."

"Stan had a broken arm and a traumatic brain injury," Nick said. "I don't know what injuries the other pilot had, but Patterson said they've both been released from the hospital."

"What about the lodge employees and the hunters? I haven't heard any news about them."

"Two hunters were hiding in their cabins and died in the explosion. Three more were taken into custody. The FBI and troopers are still sorting out how many guards, guides, kitchen workers, and housekeepers died. I doubt they'll ever know the full count. There's not much left of those who were still in the lodge when the explosion occurred."

"What about Millie?" I asked.

"Millie? Did she work at the lodge?"

I nodded.

He shook his head. "I don't know about her. The troopers did arrest Cage Marks, the manager of the lodge."

"Have they found the men who kidnapped the people in Kodiak?"

"No," Nick said, "and we haven't found the kidnappers in the other towns, assuming they were different people. Unless we find Blake Parker, and he talks, we'll never find them, but I imagine the prosecutors will offer him a lesser sentence if he gives them some names."

"Parker and Corban Pratt are still missing?" I asked, feeling a rush of anger just thinking about the man.

Nick nodded. "Blake Parker put his plane in the water sometime after we entered the lodge. The warehouse wasn't wired with explosives, and I guess the Beaver was far enough from the blast to escape any major damage. Parker and Pratt flew away in the confusion during the minutes following the explosion."

"And no one's seen the plane since? They had to land somewhere."

"They did," Nick said. "Patterson said a pilot spotted the plane this morning. It was abandoned at Hidden Lake on the Kenai Peninsula. Apparently, someone picked them up and took them somewhere. Patterson has issued the usual BOLOs to the Canadian border agents, TSA, and the Alaska Marine Highway System. They'll show up somewhere."

"What about the owners of the lodge? Do you know any more about them?"

Nick let out a long breath. "Artemis, Inc. Brighter minds than mine at the FBI are attempting to learn the names of the humans behind the corporation and how many hunting lodges they own across the world. One of the hunters arrested at the lodge is a US senator from Florida. Another owns a multibillion-dollar real estate business. We'd love to get our hands on a client list to learn what other perverted power brokers are involved in Artemis."

"These warped people are powerful and rich. They want what they consider the ultimate hunt," I said. "Money is not an issue. They'll pay whatever it takes to hunt humans."

"I wonder how much they paid for their hunts?"

I shrugged. "I'm sure it costs more to order a specific human to hunt. Corban Pratt ordered me."

"Jane," Nick said. He stroked my hand. "You've been through a horrible ordeal. You should talk to a therapist. Believe me, it helps."

I smiled. "I'll think about it."

Silence filled the room for several minutes. The ticking of the IV sounded loud in the void.

"What do you think will happen to Shuyak Island and the politicians who leased it to Artemis?" I eventually asked.

"The blame game has already started," Nick said. "I'm certain someone other than your governor will end up as the fall guy."

"Do you know what they did with the people they killed?" I asked. "Have Sergeant Patterson and his team found any human remains?"

Nick shook his head. "Everything was blown to pieces. I doubt the police could find evidence of human remains, even if there were any to find. I think they disposed of the bodies immediately. They probably burned them or dumped them in the ocean."

The door to Nick's room opened, and a young nurse entered. "Agent Morgan," she said. "We need to get you ready for your flight."

I pulled my hand from Nick's grasp, stood, and backed toward the door. "Good luck," I said. "Call me and let me know how you're doing."

"Jane, wait," Nick said.

I turned and walked out of his room.

CHAPTER 82

Monday, November 17

8:03 a.m.

Geoff Baker stood in the lobby of the marine center when I walked through the door. He rushed toward me and gave me a bear hug. Then he held my shoulders and looked me over. "Man, Doc," he said. "I thought you were gone."

I smiled into his blazing blue eyes. "Me too," I said.

"I want to hear everything."

"Okay, but not now. I have to prepare for my nine o'clock class."

"About that . . . ," Geoff said. "I taught the class while you were gone, so you'll have to undo some damage. I'll bring you my notes so you'll know what we did."

I smiled and thought I was going to start crying. "Thank you," I said.

"The genetics class is another matter. Peter couldn't find anyone qualified to teach that class."

"Good," I said. "At least I know I'm still needed here."

My high school students didn't want to talk about biology. They wanted to know about me and what had happened on Shuyak Island. Rumors and speculation had roared like a tsunami through the residents of Kodiak. I appeased my students by offering a scaled-down version of my experiences. But how do you soften the reality of humans hunting humans? By the end of the class, I felt exhausted. I returned to my office and sat staring out the window.

I barely noticed the knock on my door. I thought it must've been Geoff, and I didn't think I had the strength to talk more about my horrific experiences on Shuyak.

"Come in," I said.

Peter Wayman opened the door. He held a bouquet of flowers in his hand. He looked as if he was afraid I might hit him, and I must admit, I wanted to. Until then, I hadn't realized how mad I was at my boss for forcing me to date Corban Pratt so the center could get more grant money from Tamron Oil.

He handed me the bouquet, and I waited to hear what he'd say.

"I'm sorry, Jane," he said. "I feel terrible about what happened to you. Pratt seemed like a good guy to me."

"He wasn't," I said. My words sounded harsher than I'd intended. In truth, Pratt had seemed like a good guy to me, too. He was self-obsessed, but he was always nice to me.

"Detective Horner with the Kodiak police interviewed me yesterday to find out my connection with Pratt," Peter said. "She told me that they have evidence connecting him to the murder of Jerry Burns in his hotel room at the Baranof Inn."

I was surprised. I hadn't heard about Jerry, and I hadn't thought about the consortium since my kidnapping. When Jerry had called me and asked me out to dinner, he'd said he wanted to talk to me. Was he trying to find a way to warn me about Pratt? Perhaps he'd figured out what was happening at the Artemis lodge and had confronted Pratt. I knew Pratt would kill to protect his nasty little secret and the identities of the hunters at the lodge.

"What's happening with the consortium?" I asked.

Peter shrugged. "I don't know." He paused for several seconds. "Please accept my apology for my role in this mess."

I forced a smile. After all, this was my boss. "I don't blame you, Peter, but I'm out of the fundraising business."

CHAPTER 83

Saturday, November 22

6:58 p.m.

Steve and Linda were already seated at the table in Henry's restaurant when I arrived. I saw no sign of the wheelchair, but Steve didn't attempt to stand when I approached the table. I reached down and gave him a quick hug.

Linda stood, put her arms around me, and held me for several seconds. "I'm so glad you're okay," she said. "I feel as if we were responsible for dragging you into this mess, and you were nearly killed."

I squeezed her arm. "No," I said. "Steve's observations of the plane landing at Trident Basin after dark broke this case wide open, and he—with your support—saved many lives. I'm glad you called me. As usual, my reckless behavior got me in trouble."

The waiter arrived with a glass of white wine for Linda and a cup of coffee for Steve. I ordered a glass of merlot.

Steve pointed at the coffee. "I'm sticking with nonalcoholic beverages tonight. My balance is bad enough as it is."

"Did you walk into the restaurant on your own?" I asked.

"With Linda's help," he said. "I have a walker and a cane, but I hate to use them."

"He's very stubborn," Linda said.

"I'm so happy you're getting better," I said. "I can see a huge improvement from a few weeks ago."

"I'm determined to fully recover and get back to flying in a few months."

I nodded but wondered how long it would take him to regain his motor skills to the point where he could pass the medical exam for his pilot's license. But if anyone could do it, I believed he could.

"What's going on with the investigation?" Linda asked. "We haven't heard much."

I shrugged. "I don't know. I've been keeping my head down and trying to get caught up at work."

"How is Agent Morgan?" Steve asked. "I heard he was whisked away to Seattle for medical treatment."

"I think he's doing better," I said. I didn't tell them I was basing my statement on the fact that he'd tried to call me eight times in the past three days, and I'd let the calls go to voicemail. He'd left messages to say he would be discharged from the hospital soon, and his ex-wife had already returned to Virginia. In the last message, he'd asked me if I would fly to Seattle so we could talk. I didn't respond. I had nothing left to say to FBI Special Agent Nick Morgan.

Linda, Steve, and I ate hamburgers and chatted. As far as we knew, Corban Pratt and Blake Parker were still missing. With the lodge blown to pieces, it would be impossible to track down everyone involved in the operation, unless they could get someone to talk. It was likely that if they ever caught Pratt, he'd receive a reduced sentence for telling the authorities everything he knew about the operation and those involved. They'd have to catch him first, however, and I believed Pratt had somehow slipped out of the country.

When the waiter brought the bill, Linda grabbed it and refused to let me pay for my dinner.

"The least we can do is buy you a hamburger and a glass of wine," Steve said.

I walked out of the restaurant with Steve and Linda. His steps were slow and clumsy, and he leaned on his wife, but he was improving.

"I'll call you in a week or two to go jogging with me," I said.

"Give me three weeks," he said and smiled.

Afterword

The Kodiak Archipelago stretches 177 miles from the uninhabited Barren Islands at the northern end to Chirikof Island and the Semidi Islands in the south. Kodiak is the largest and most populated island in the group. Shuyak Island is in the northern part of the archipelago and lies south of the Barren Islands and north of Afognak Island.

Shuyak Island State Park encompasses most of the island, and yes, unlike my fictional account, the state park still exists. Shuyak is unique to the archipelago because only one species of tree grows there: a beautiful virgin Sitka spruce forest covers the island. The island also has miles of rugged coastline, beaches, and protected waterways. It supports many species of sea birds, Sitka black-tailed deer, and Kodiak brown bears. If you want a rugged Alaska adventure, Shuyak Island State Park is a great place to visit.

If you visit Kodiak (and I hope you do), be sure to check out the Alutiiq Museum. The stated mission of the museum is to "preserve and share the heritage and living culture of the Alutiiq people." To learn more about the Kodiak Archipelago, its people, and its wildlife, I also recommend the Kodiak History Museum and the Refuge Visitor Center.

Dr. Jan Whitefield inspired a critical component of the plot of this book. A few years ago, I had Guillain–Barré syndrome. I was not completely paralyzed like Steve Duncan was in this book, and Steve's paralysis manifested much more rapidly than mine. Still, I landed in the hospital for several days and have never fully recovered. When I was in the hospital, my friend Jan Whitefield visited me and said, "I bet one of your characters will have this syndrome in a future book." I couldn't wait to prove him right.

The characters in this book originated from my imagination. I have not consciously based my fictional characters on living beings.

Thank you, Evan and Lois Swensen, for your guidance and assistance at Publication Consultants. From the cover artwork to the interior design, the folks at Publication Consultants create beautiful books.

I cannot thank Bill Siever enough. Bill has now edited four of my books. He polishes my grammar and punctuation and carefully looks for inconsistencies and holes in the plot. He takes a great deal of time to help me become a better author. You have no idea how much I appreciate you, Bill.

Thank you to my husband, Mike Munsey. In addition to patiently listening to me talk nonstop about my books, he's my logistics, weapons, and aircraft expert. On the rare occasions when Mike can't answer one of my questions—such as how to hide the tail number on an airplane—I ask one of the floatplane pilots when they land at our lodge to shuttle guests back and forth to Kodiak. They usually squint at one of my strange questions and say, "Why? Is this going in one of your books?"

I have written five previous novels: *Big Game, Murder Over Kodiak, The Fisherman's Daughter, Karluk Bones*, and *Massacre at Bear Creek Lodge*. I've also written two nonfiction books: *Kodiak Island Wildlife* and *Murder and Mystery in the Last Frontier*. My books are available at amazon.com, barnesandnoble.com, authormasterminds.com, publicationconsultants.com, and other online booksellers.

Please check out my website at robinbarefield.com. While you're there, you can sign up for my monthly newsletter about true-crime stories in Alaska. If you prefer to listen to your true-crime stories, check out my podcast, *Murder and Mystery in the Last Frontier*.

www.ingramcontent.com/pod-product-compliance
Lightning Source LLC
Chambersburg PA
CBHW071856020726
47502CB00003B/776